HIGH CONQUEST

ALYSON McLAYNE

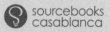

sourcebooks
casablanca

Published by Sourcebooks Casablanca, an imprint of Sourcebooks,
Inc.
P.O. Box 4410, Naperville, Illinois 60567-4410
(630) 961-3900
Fax: (630) 961-2168
sourcebooks.com

Printed and bound in Canada.
MBP 10 9 8 7 6 5 4 3 2 1

For Trina—my Isla of forty years. I know you've got my back. Love you for another forty.

One

FISTFULS OF HAIR FELL TO THE BED LIKE STREAMS of molten iron. The growing pile, more orange than gold, resembled a dragon's nest, and gleamed seductively in the firelight. Amber sighed at the sight. If only it were a real dragon's nest and a beast could rise and smite all her enemies. One very much in particular.

She almost smiled at the fanciful thought as she chopped off her hair. Almost. In truth, her plan was an act of desperation with little chance of success. By all that was holy, she'd need a miracle to get away this time.

Grabbing another handful, she raised the knife and sawed off an even bigger chunk. The remaining strands sprang up to curl around her neck and ears, a light, airy feeling at odds with the heaviness in her heart.

Laird Machar Murray would come after her, of that she had no doubt. If he found her, no amount of false hexes or curses or threats from the devil would deter him from destroying her this time.

Her lost hair would grow back. Her lost spirit and soul could not.

The heavy wooden door rattled as a key entered the lock from the outside. It pushed open. Amber spun around to face the intruder, her heart in her throat and the knife pointed outward. Niall, the old steward, shuffled in, his worn plaid sagging below his belt. She huffed in relief and went back to cutting off her hair.

"You scared the life out of me, aye?"

"You should be scared, lass. I doona know how you've lasted this long with Laird Murray breathing down your neck. He'll turn the keep upside down to find you."

"I couldnae leave with Erin so sick, now could I? Her mother and father would ne'er recover if she died. And Ian needed me to speak for him or he would've ended up in the dungeon for who knows how long."

"You'll ne'er recover if the laird gets a hold of you—although you wouldnae end up in the dungeon. Nay, he'd lock you in his bedchamber first. And no doubt Father Odhran would consider it a just punishment for all the help you've given the women."

"He's a wee ablach, that one. The devil take him."

"The devil take them both."

Her knife cut through the last chunk of her hair and she held it in her hand, staring at it. The strands twisted and curled in long, silken waves, a last gift from her mother. Her father had loved her hair. Her grandmother had brushed it every night, singing the songs of the Highlands that Amber had so loved. Sorrow welled within her at the loss, and she squeezed her eyes shut to push it away.

Bah! Her hair had caused her nothing but trouble. How many times had she wished herself plain when some irritating man came knocking at her door, asking for her hand? Too many to count.

She tossed the curls down on the linen quilt, glad to be rid of them. She had no time for self-pity.

"Did you bring the lads' clothes?" she asked. "And the band?"

"Aye." He pulled some material from under his plaid.

Amber reached for the silver brooch that held her arisaid in place over her left breast, and released it. Niall squawked as her dress fell off, and he quickly turned around. "Lord have mercy, lass, I'm an old man. My heart willna survive looking upon the pride of Clan MacPherson in such a way."

"Is that what they call me?" She tucked up her linen shift and shook out the tautly woven cloth Niall had tossed on the bed. "I thought 'twas 'witch' and 'temptress.' Sometimes 'evildoer,' depending on who did the talking."

"Doona be daft. Only Laird Murray and his plague of rats say such things. The MacPhersons know the sacrifices you've made, the danger you've courted for us. We couldnae be more thankful."

Amber didn't speak—couldn't speak—as his words washed over her. Her throat tightened and she had to blink back tears. Instead, she looked down and secured the end of the cloth over her breasts, trying to squash down the overripe mounds that had done naught but get in the way since they'd started jutting out from her chest when she was fourteen.

"Aye, neither could I," she said finally, her voice sounding thick. "I'll miss you all." She lifted the end of the band trailing on the floor and held it out to Niall. "Here, hold this tight now while I wrap it."

Niall grabbed it, eyes lowered, and held the cloth taut with surprising strength as she turned herself into it and knotted the band in place, flattening enough of her bust that the rest could still be concealed beneath the loose shirt. Her breath came short, her ribs compressed, but it was a strain she could bear. The bulk of the boy's plaid should hide the slight tuck at her waist and roundness of her bottom. Her legs were long and strong, and if she muddied them they should pass for a lad's. Her face too—although nothing could disguise the startling color of her eyes. Those were an inheritance from her beloved grandmother, and had led to much trouble for her as well as for Amber.

Men envied uncommon things, beautiful things, and would go to great lengths to acquire them. Luckily, the MacPhersons were good people, and Amber's grandmother an excellent healer. She'd taught Amber everything she'd known before she died, and Amber's place with the MacPhersons had been secure. They'd cherished her and she them.

Not so Laird Machar Murray. Nay, the conniving laird would as soon burn or drown her for a witch—as their good-for-naught priest wanted. After Murray tired of raping her.

Amber pulled the lad's shirt over her head and tried to belt the plaid in place by herself. In the end, Niall had to show her how it should be done—a complicated ritual of pleating and tucking and twisting the material.

When she had finally mastered it on her own, Niall moved to a chest against the wall in the corner, and on his signal, Amber shoved the heavy piece of furniture to the side so he could crouch down and count the stones.

"This is it," he said, pushing against the block while Amber waited impatiently beside him. Finally, a space appeared that was barely big enough for her to squeeze through. She grabbed a candle from the table and lit it in the fire before passing it through the dark hole in the wall. A dank passageway appeared ahead of her, just big enough for her to stand, and a narrow stairwell descended at the end.

"Are you sure it goes all the way down?" she asked. "When was it last used? Is it safe?"

"I doona know, lass, but anywhere is safer than here with Machar Murray."

She nodded reluctantly, laid down the candle beside her, and pulled Niall into a tight hug. "I'll miss you, you old badger. You've been a staunch friend to me, and to my grandmother before that. Our family wouldnae have survived this long without you."

Niall squeezed her even tighter before pushing her away. "Go on with you, then. And doona even think of coming back. Go find a life for yourself away from the hell of this one. Marry a good man and have plenty of fine children." He let go and lifted a bag from his shoulder. "Some food and coin until you find your new home."

After she took it, he picked up the candle and handed it to her. "When you get to the end, the bottom stone should push out. I've already loosened it from the other side. The ground is muddy. Use some dirt to darken your bare skin, especially your face. There's no hiding you're a woman without that, even with your hair shorn."

Amber nodded as he talked, trying to quell the panic that had tied her stomach into knots.

"Once you're out of the keep, go to the east wall by the tanning hut. Look for a cart missing a wheel, with a rope attached. Throw the rope over the wall, then climb up the hay bales to the top. I've tethered a horse on the other side."

Amber squeezed his arm, afraid to speak lest she start crying again, afraid to even look at him. He moved over, and she wedged herself through the hole. Once on the other side, she couldn't resist and glanced back over her shoulder to see Niall's face, wet with tears, one last time.

"Be safe," he said, shoving the stone back in place and leaving her with only her candle for company.

⁂

Lachlan MacKay, laird of Clan MacKay, lay on his belly in the scrub, staring at the pockmarked and tumbling-down walls of the once-grand MacPherson castle. He'd counted fourteen places his men could breach the fortress, carefully noting the poorly planned circuits the guards walked on the perimeter, the easy footholds to get over the wall, the young, inexperienced men at the gate. There was even a horse grazing alongside the wall that anyone could use to hide behind.

Surely the crafty MacPherson laird, Machar Murray, would never be so careless, so lax in his defenses? It had taken Lachlan five years to identify and find

Murray after he'd murdered Lachlan's older brother and tried to murder Lachlan himself—in order to take over Clan MacKay. Murray had covered his tracks well, hiding behind silenced accomplices, false names, and convoluted trails.

So why would his home be so poorly protected? It would take Lachlan less than an hour to conquer the castle as it was. It didn't make sense.

He turned to his foster brother, Callum MacLean, laird of Clan MacLean, who lay beside him on the slight rise. He watched the castle as well, his perceptive green eyes bright against the dirt he'd used to muddy his face and neck. He'd even smeared some of it into his short, dark hair.

"Do you think it's a trap?" Lachlan asked, voice barely above a whisper.

"Maybe. I canna believe anyone would be so careless. But if it were a trap, there would only be one easy way in, two at the most. Not fifteen."

"Fifteen? I only saw fourteen."

"Aye. You always had trouble counting past ten."

Lachlan snorted and resisted punching his foster brother in the shoulder. Callum would have expected it, of course, and most likely jumped out of arm's reach, if they hadn't been intent on staying hidden.

There were five of them that had been taught how to fight—how to lead—by the great Gregor MacLeod. Gregor had bonded the lads, all now lairds of their own clans, into a tight, cohesive unit, even if they did still like to provoke one another as often as they could.

'Twas a time-honored tradition, and both men were good at it.

"I doona need to count past ten; I'm not the one who left my betrothed behind tossing daggers and running wild in her castle. How many months has it been since you last saw Maggie? Almost forty? You can bet she'll be counting every one of them. She may use those daggers on you when you finally decide to claim her. If she'll still have you."

"She'll have me," Callum grunted.

Satisfied, Lachlan went back to studying the castle, looking for the way in he'd missed. If Callum said another existed, then it did. His foster brother was an excellent strategist, with a sharp mind and eyes that saw everything. Except, of course, the identity of the traitor in his own clan—the reason he'd left Maggie behind for so long. He was afraid to bring her home with him while his father's murderer was still loose.

"Ah, there it is," Lachlan said, finally seeing the entrance. "The ditch they've dug under the wall. We can widen it, get at least one man through at a time."

Callum nodded. "The ground's still wet from last night's rain. It should dig out easily and quietly." He scanned from one end of the castle to the other. They'd been scouting all day and had already looked at the fortress from every angle. "Will you split the attack?"

"Aye. Four fronts: the gate to the north, over the top of the east and west walls just south of the keep, and through the ditch at the far end." His jaw clenched; a surge of rage he'd been trying to contain pushed up from his belly. The emotion had been riding him hard the past fortnight—ever since he'd received confirmation that Machar Murray, laird of Clan MacPherson, was his brother's killer. "I doona want to leave that bastard any way out. I'm going to gut him slowly for what he did to Donald."

Lachlan would never forget the look of delight on his brother's face that terrible day. He'd held up the fish he'd just caught in the loch, bragging that his catch, like everything else about him, was bigger than Lachlan's. Lachlan had been laughing too. Then an arrow had pierced Donald's chest from behind. He'd toppled to his knees in the boat. The delight. The laughter. Turning to pain and horror.

It had shredded Lachlan, but he hadn't gone to help Donald as the archer expected. 'Twas a killing shot, and no good would have come of it. Instead, he'd dived into the water and swam as long and hard as he could, arrows hitting the water above him, some of them nicking and piercing his skin. When he surfaced and made it to the trees unseen, he returned to the castle, heartbroken and enraged, only to find Donald's wife missing. After a thorough search, they found her at a secluded cottage, murdered along with one of her guards and her maid. She'd been killed in an intimate setting, a love nest, and Lachlan had determined she'd made a cuckold of Donald, most likely with the murderer, who had cleaned up his tracks after Lachlan survived the assassination attempt.

The very next day, Lachlan had assumed the unwanted mantle of Laird MacKay and begun his search for his brother's murderer and would-be usurper.

Drumming his fingers on the ground, Lachlan tried to tamp down the memories and uncharacteristic burst of emotion, tried to think without the haze of fury that wanted to overwhelm him. He was so close to Machar

Murray. "If it isna a trap, then what's he thinking? Doesn't he intend to keep the castle? The land?"

"I doona think so. 'Tis said he took the castle right after he murdered your brother. Maybe it was a fallback position for him."

"He'll fall back, all right. Under my sword. And anyone else in the clan who aided him."

Callum laid a hand on his arm. "You're too hot, Lachlan. Look at them. They're not warriors—not even the guards. And Murray is a snake. He would have attacked the leaders in the clan from the dark, not a full-frontal assault. The MacPhersons may not even know he killed their old laird. I canna believe they supported him in the attack." He shook his head. "I wish we had more information."

"As do I, but I willna wait one more hour, Callum. The best way to kill a snake is to cut off its head before it strikes."

"Aye, and you'd win for sure, but there'd be too many losses. Too many innocents caught between our forces and Murray's. Gregor charged us to bring peace to the Highlands, not forge a bloody massacre."

Lachlan knew it was true but still he didn't want to hear it. When he'd received word that his brother's killer had been found, he'd wanted to charge right in, sword swinging, arrows flying. Callum had been the voice of reason, nattering at his side, pulling on the reins as best he could. Lachlan had even tried to leave without him, but Callum had anticipated that move too. Bloody bastard.

Lachlan smashed his fist on the ground, wanted to spit in disgust. "Why haven't the clan killed him themselves?

The few reports we have say he's not loved by the MacPhersons. What kind of people let a monster live?"

"What would you have them do? Should the cook have poisoned his food? The maid he's tupping slit his throat, or the groom put a stone in his mount's hoof? Most people doona have it in them to murder a man in cold blood."

"The guards, then."

"Look. At. Them," he said again. "They're not properly trained. Murray most likely killed all the seasoned warriors. We want to go in as soft as we can. Give the MacPhersons a chance to lay down their arms. We want them on our side. Besides, 'tis said their healer is a miracle worker. You know how upset Gregor will be if she's harmed or turned against us."

"Bah. She should have poisoned the demon the first chance she got."

The light had waned considerably since they'd started scouting, and the shadows were almost full upon them. Movement atop the east wall caught Lachlan's attention, and he strained to make out what it was. "Did you see that?" he asked.

Callum squinted. "Someone's climbing over. A man by the looks of it. Maybe a lad."

Whoever it was attempted to descend the outer wall using the rope but lost their grip and fell, landing in a heap at the bottom. The horse lifted its head and moved toward him, revealing a bridle attached around its neck.

"An escape, then. The horse wasn't just grazing, it was placed there deliberately." After rising, the man limped toward the horse, led it to a rock that had fallen from the wall, and used the stone to mount. "Must be just a boy if he doesn't have the strength to pull himself up."

Lachlan cursed as horse and rider turned in their direction. "Hell and damnation, he's heading right for us."

Callum glanced over his shoulder and looked at the tree line. They'd crawled forward on their bellies as close as possible to get a better look at Murray's defenses. "We'll ne'er make it back in time. We'll have to wait, and pray the lad turns."

"And if he doesn't?"

"I doona know, but we canna let him spot us and sound the alarm."

"Aye. Watch the castle and see if the patrol notices him escaping while I get in position." Lachlan edged forward until he lay in a small dip beside the trail and spread his dusty plaid over his body.

Callum also moved lower, his gaze searching for the perimeter guard. "Even if they doona see him, they'll be sure to see the rope he used."

"We'll have to move fast. I'll bring down the rider. You grab his horse and head for the trees."

Lachlan studied the lad as he approached, rumpled and filthy with jagged, amber-colored hair that hung just past his chin. The horse kept slowing, a lazy, old nag, despite the lad trying to increase its speed with soft kicks to its belly and slap of the reins on its sides. The boy wasn't much of a rider and the horse knew it, taking full advantage. If Lachlan were on its back, the nag would be running full tilt.

Waiting until the animal was almost past him, he jumped and dragged the lad from the horse, one hand clamped over his mouth, the other arm wrapped around his torso.

The lad screamed into Lachlan's palm, more a high-pitched whine, and struggled to get away. Lachlan slammed him into the ground facedown and lay on top of him, hoping the guards hadn't been looking in their direction. Ahead of him, Callum had pulled the horse down the rise and headed swiftly toward the trees.

The first thing Lachlan noticed was how determined his captive was, keeping up the fight when it was obvious he was defeated. The second thing he noticed was how soft he was.

The notion jolted him. Christ Almighty, where in hell had that come from? He hesitated, then rolled the lad beneath him to see a mud-covered face, hair sticking out in all directions and blood smeared below his nose. When he lifted his gaze to Lachlan's, darkly lashed, violet-colored eyes stared up at him. Lachlan sucked in an audible breath at the sight—just as the boy bit down on Lachlan's hand and smashed their foreheads together.

Lachlan cursed under his breath but didn't let go, and they rolled to the bottom of the hill. He made sure he landed on top, his weight bearing down on the boy. Another time, Lachlan would have admired his determination, his resilience. Now it was just damned annoying.

'Twas obvious he was young and untrained in formal fighting, but he knew enough to go for Lachlan's weak spots: eyes, hair, nose, fingers, and groin. And when he pinched the nerve on the inside of Lachlan's elbow, Lachlan barely contained his bellow.

Flipping him over, Lachlan jammed his knee into the small of the lad's back and pressed sharply on the vein below his ear, just long enough for him to weaken, before wedging a gag in his mouth and tying his hands together over his belly.

He roused seconds later as Lachlan finished.

"You're done, lad," Lachlan whispered in his ear. "You put up a good fight, but you'll ne'er get out of those knots. We're going to crawl to the tree line or I'll drive a stake into the ground and leave you tied to it for the wild animals to eat. Do you understand?"

The lad nodded, fear and panic in his eyes as he looked at his captor, and for the first time, Lachlan felt bad for assaulting him. "I didn't intend to hurt you, but you were riding right toward us and we canna be seen yet." He tried to pat the boy's hair in a reassuring manner and couldn't help but notice how soft it was. When he realized he'd gone from patting his hair to running his fingers through it, he stopped, heat rising up his neck. "It looked like you were trying to escape the castle. Is that right?"

On the boy's hesitant nod, he continued. "I'll get you to safety and away from whoe'er is chasing you, but not till my forces have gone in undetected. That's if you haven't compromised our attack already. Now crawl for the tree line, keep your head and arse low, and make no sound!"

❧

Amber used her knees to dig into the ground and push forward toward the trees, trying not to lift her bottom into the air. Every time she did, the large man with the muddied-up face would cover it with his big hand and shove it back down.

To "help" her, he'd grabbed her plaid between her shoulders and hauled her along beside him.

"Christ Almighty, lad," he said as he squashed her bottom down yet again, "get your knees to the side, dig in with your elbows, and push with your feet. Have you ne'er crawled across the fields hunting game before? The quail and pheasants would see your arse waving in the air and be long gone before you could e'er shoot them. You wouldnae bring home any supper for your mother."

He'd said all that in an exasperated whisper, and Amber grunted around her gag, her furrowed brow and angry eyes telling him exactly what she thought of him. Maybe if she'd been able to use her hands to help propel her body forward she wouldn't have to lift her backside, but her wrists were still tied together.

Earlier, when the candle had blown out halfway along the hidden stairway in the keep, she'd known it would be a difficult escape. But she'd managed to make it to the end by feel alone and push the stone out of her way. The cart had been easy to find, and she'd made it to the top of the wall, only to fall as she climbed down the other side, twisting her ankle—another reason she was having a hard time crawling right now.

Still, that was naught compared to being dragged from her horse by the big, demented ape who'd loomed up from nowhere and practically killed her. When he'd pressed the side of her neck and almost knocked her out, she'd thought surely she was about to die. Only to rouse trussed up like a pig.

The worst part of it was that she thought he was enjoying himself. Aye, he'd liked fighting with her, dragging her about like a sack of oats.

Ignorant oaf.

His light-brown hair was pulled back in a leather tie, and his dark-blue eyes had laugh lines at the corners. She'd looked at his plaid, noting the blue-and-green weave, maybe from the dye of the blaeberry and heather, and tried to narrow down the region in which those plants grew abundantly.

He was neither a Murray, with their predominantly red plaid from the dye of the tormentil, nor a MacPherson, with their more colorful red, yellow, and blue plaid, with the added yellow dye from the bog myrtle. Perhaps he was a MacKenzie or a MacLeod—their plaids were both mostly blue and green, although why they'd be here, she had no idea.

When they finally reached the tree line, she sighed with relief. Her knees and ankle were sore beyond belief, her face scratched and bruised from being dragged through the brush, and there was dirt in her teeth. A few feet in, the man hauled her up and pulled her farther into the trees. A moment later, she saw three horses—two big, braw stallions and her smaller nag—held by a second man. He was as tall as her captor, both of them broad-shouldered, but this one slightly leaner and with a different plaid.

"Did he give you any trouble?" the second man asked.

"Aye, he almost took out my eye and near paralyzed my arm. Gregor would love to get ahold of him. I had to almost knock him out to get the ties on him."

To Amber's surprise, her assailant smiled as he spoke of her transgressions and looked almost...proud.

The second man stepped close and studied her face and eyes. She recognized his expression. She'd worn it many times when examining a sick child—concern. He was worried the pressure on her neck might have done permanent damage. She would have told him she was all right—just weakened—but she still had the gag in her mouth.

"He's not hurt, Callum," the first man said. She waited to hear his name too, hoping Callum would respond and say it, but her captor kept talking. "I squeezed just long enough to weaken him."

"Aye," Callum agreed. "His gaze is clear and bright. And would you look at the color of his eyes— not quite blue, yet not quite purple either. The lasses will be after you in droves soon, lad. Once you get the muck off your face. You doona smell poorly, so you mustn't have been held for long. Is it the laird who's after you?"

She hesitated, then nodded. 'Twas obvious they meant her no harm, other than what had already been done. But who was this Gregor and what would he want of her?

"Can we untie him?" Callum asked.

"Nay, not until we reach camp. He's a right scrapper. He'll make a break for it as soon as he can and head straight back to the MacPhersons now he knows we're attacking, won't you, lad?"

Amber was annoyed at his insight and tried not to let it show, but she obviously failed when he grunted and nodded.

"As I thought. All right, up with you, then." He grabbed her waist, lifted her as if she weighed no more than a bairn, and placed her on the huge brown stallion with a black mane and tail. The beast barely moved, it was so well trained.

He pulled himself up behind her and urged the horse forward. Muscled and sinewy arms closed around her, and Amber found herself holding her breath. Her heart raced and her stomach fluttered as if a handful of butterflies were trapped inside.

And not out of fear. Nay, the strange thing was she felt safe with him, safer than she had in a long time—which made no sense as she was trussed-up, gagged, and his prisoner. He'd pulled her from her horse, almost knocked her out, dragged her through the brush, yet she felt no worry for herself, just for her clan.

If he meant to rape or kill her, he could have done so any time after entering the woods. Instead, he and this Callum had been almost gentle, even concerned for her welfare. She could trust him long enough to find out what he was planning to do next.

And why were they attacking the castle anyway? Did they want it for themselves, or were they warring with Machar Murray? She didn't think the MacPhersons had a grudge against anyone other than Murray, who wasn't really their laird. Naught could be proven, but she knew he'd murdered their old laird and his cousin, along with several of the experienced men of the clan. Including her father.

Somehow Murray had just taken over—living in the castle, giving orders, controlling the people. The only person he'd been afraid of was her grandmother, whom he thought a witch—a lie she'd encouraged, making good use of her knowledge of herbs, her irascible manner, and strange, vivid eyes. Amber's eyes.

When she died, Amber had kept up the ruse, knowing Laird Murray would come for her if he thought her in any way vulnerable.

She sighed in frustration. There was naught she could do right now to escape, and the men were taking her farther away from the village and castle. If she could just get the MacPhersons out, she'd be more than happy to leave Murray and his band of thieves— for that's what they really were—to be killed. The world would be a better place without Machar Murray in it. Father Odhran, the wee shite, too.

But there was no way she'd reach them in time.

The man gave her a squeeze. "We're not looking to harm any but those who did us harm, lad. We'll leave the village in peace, unless they hide Machar Murray from us."

Which left the castle…and all the MacPhersons guarding it. And Niall—*oh, dear God, Niall*. Plus all the cooks, maids, stable hands, and the housekeeper. All of them innocent of any wrongdoing.

She knew it was futile, but she struggled again in earnest. The man cursed and squeezed her tight to his body, so she slammed her head backward. He'd anticipated her move this time, and she bashed into his hard chin. Lights burst behind her closed eyelids as pain thrummed in her head. His arm wrapped along her middle, his hand just above her elbow, and his fingers found the same nerve she'd pinched on him earlier. He pressed down on it—enough to get her attention but not enough to really hurt.

"Cease, lad. If you move, I'll jab my thumb in— and you know what that feels like because you did it to me first. We're almost there. When we arrive, I'll take out the gag. You can yell and scream all you want. No one will hear you there."

They cantered quickly along the river now, and Amber knew exactly where they were headed—the waterfall. Aye, her screams would go unnoticed once they were in its vicinity, close to the roar of the raging rapids and the splash of the water as it plummeted over the cliff.

A whistle sounded above them, and she glanced up to see a man in a pine tree, wearing a similar plaid as her captor. She scanned the other trees and saw more men, some wearing the same colors as Callum.

Whoever these men were, their forces had joined together against Machar Murray.

The roar of the falls started softly but picked up volume as they approached, the river beside them running fast and deep. The waterfall came into view as they rounded a large outcropping, the sound now loud enough she'd have to yell to be heard.

She knew the area well, had spent much time here as a lass, exploring the caves behind the falls and swimming in some of the calm pools created by the rocks. That's not to say the river and falls weren't dangerous— they were. It seemed almost every few years some poor child fell in and died. A few she had managed to save.

The horse picked up speed as it anticipated its dinner, jostling her and causing her captor's thumb to dig in. When Amber jumped and yelped against the gag, he pulled his hand away. "Och, lad, I'm sorry. 'Twas an accident." He pressed his palm against the stallion's neck and commanded, "Easy, Saint."

She glared at the man, shooting him full of imaginary daggers. Accident or not, the jab had hurt like hell. And she saw the way his eyes danced as he looked at her.

"I'm not laughing at your pain," he said. "'Tis just you look so fierce—you are fierce—despite how wee you are. You're determined, aye, but small. If you like, I'll ask Gregor MacLeod to take you in. He'll treat you fairly and teach you how to be a good man and a strong warrior. You couldnae choose a better laird."

Gregor MacLeod? She knew that name. Everyone in the Highlands knew that name. His clan was large and prosperous and had several unbreakable alliances. She'd heard he'd fostered the sons of his enemies and raised them as his own sons. They were men now, and lairds of their own clans. 'Twas said they fought for all good people in the Highlands.

Could her attacker belong to one of those clans?

Horses and a few wagons were scattered about the clearings on either side of the waterfall. Some men cooked over low fires, others fletched arrows, still others practiced their fighting skills, using their hands and bodies as weapons. Other weapons were strapped to hips and down backs or leaned against rocks within close reach—swords, axes, stout poles. Even a huge hammer.

A fighting force of considerable size and skill by the looks of it—and well-armed. It would be a massacre against the untrained MacPherson men, and she felt bile rising in her stomach, burning away that momentary sense of safety. The people she loved, had cared for most of her life, were about to be annihilated.

A man strode toward them as they approached the waterfall. His old, puckered battle scars gave him a fearsome look, which only frightened her more. He gripped the horse's bridle.

"Laird MacKay, your cousin's here."

The name startled her, and she glanced back at her captor. He was a laird? Laird MacKay? She knew that name too, one of Gregor MacLeod's foster sons for sure. He didn't look like a laird, with his dirty, scratched, and bruised face, dried blood under one eye, and a tear in his plaid. With a jolt, she realized she had done that, fighting with him when he'd pulled her from her horse. He even had twigs and leaves in his tangled hair, which had come loose from his leather tie to hang in messy waves almost to his shoulders. 'Twas longer than her own locks, now, and for the first time, she felt ashamed that her hair was a sawed-off mess.

"Airril?" he questioned. "What's he doing here? Last I heard, he was in Inverness."

The man hesitated. "Not Airril. Adaira."

Laird MacKay stiffened and his face turned thunderous. "Adaira? How in God's name did she get here?"

"She hid in the food cart, Laird, under the canvas. We found her about an hour ago. She ran and we trapped her up a tree. She's not going anywhere."

"Good. She can stay there for now."

The laird dismounted, and Amber squeaked as she tumbled off after him. He caught her, keeping a firm grip on her arm as he marched them toward the waterfall. Callum fell in on her other side, the warrior next to Laird MacKay.

"Prepare the men, Hamish," MacKay said. "We'll attack in four groups—one at the gate to the north, two over the castle walls on the east and west side, and a smaller force from the back under a ditch. We'll have to widen it so two men can crawl through at a time. We leave immediately."

"Aye, Laird." The warrior turned away and whistled sharply. Men dropped what they were doing, grabbed their weapons, and scrambled to meet with Hamish in the clearing. More warriors streamed out of the woods.

Callum leaned around her to speak to the laird. "Adaira's stubborn, Lachlan. Doona start by yelling at her or she'll dig her heels in."

"She canna dig her heels in; she's in a tree. And I'm going to leave her there."

"Nay, you're not. And doona threaten her with consequences you canna keep, because she'll just push you to them."

"So what should I say to her, then?"

"I doona know. She's ten. Use your imagination. But whate'er you do, follow through."

"I'll do what Gregor did. He kept the five of us in line."

"You canna."

"Why e'er not?"

"She's a lass!"

Amber scoffed behind her gag and rolled her eyes at the same time as Lachlan shot Callum an incredulous look. "Is that what you intend to tell Maggie when she's tossing her knives at you for leaving her unwed for so long? 'Put the daggers down, Wife. You're a lass.' Nay, I'll make Adaira do what Gregor did to us—muck out the stalls, clean the chamber pots, and launder the clothes in the freezing loch during winter. After she's run around the castle ten times. That'll get her attention."

Callum harrumphed, then said, "Maggie's not my wife…yet."

Amber stared at her captor. At Lachlan. She liked the name—Lachlan MacKay. It suited him somehow, even though she'd known him for less than an hour and had yet to speak to him with anything other than her eyes and body. Nay, he'd done all the talking as he'd dragged her along.

Idiot man.

They were about to walk through the waterfall to the caves behind, when she realized her face might be washed clean. She panicked, trying to back up. Both men gripped her arms and dragged her through the torrent of water. She ducked her head, hoping her hair would keep the deluge from her face. It soaked the back of her head instead, down her temples and neck. She gasped as the cold water struck her skin.

When she was through, she couldn't help but stare at Lachlan in the flickering light from a torch that was mounted on the cave wall. He must have lifted his face up as he passed under to clean it, and the water streaked in muddy rivulets down his lean cheeks. She glanced at Callum to see that he had done the same.

They were both such braw men. Lachlan in particular appealed to her with his strong, scruff-covered jaw and his finely shaped lips, the lower one slightly fuller than the top one, his nose straight other than a small bump in the middle where it had obviously been broken. And she liked his eyes too.

Aye. She liked his eyes. Thickly lashed and dark blue—and staring hard at her face.

"How old are you, lad?" he asked in a low tone, a muscle ticking in his jaw.

Every hair on the back of her neck stood up. She felt something cold on her cheek and jumped as Callum's knife sliced through her gag. Lachlan pulled it out and she coughed. When she looked back at him, he still hadn't looked away.

"Um…fourteen," she lied, her tongue thick and her mouth dry.

"And your name?"

She brought to mind one of the boys she knew and tried to slouch in the same manner as him. "Ian."

"Are you a MacPherson, then?"

"Aye." She glanced around nervously then back at Lachlan. His face looked carved in stone.

"What did Machar Murray want of you, lad? Did he touch you?"

Her eyebrows shot up as his meaning and harsh demeanor sank in. He was worried the laird had forced her into unwanted carnal acts.

"Nay. I…um…stole from him. A loaf of bread. My sister was hungry." A true story on the real Ian's part. That had led to Amber pleading for his life at the castle, which in turn had led to Amber having to run for her life tonight.

"And that's all? How did you escape?"

"I had help. The steward, Niall, got me out. Many good people work at the castle, Laird MacKay, including the guards. They had no part in Machar Murray's treachery. They doona deserve to die at the hands of your warriors."

"And my men doona deserve to die either. If the MacPhersons fight back, they'll be disabled, possibly killed. What would you have me do? Let my brother's murderer live?"

"Nay, he's killed many of my clan too, including my father. But the MacPhersons need help, not more death and destruction."

"As do we all, but I canna promise you more than I already have."

"Then find another way!"

"Nay, that's impossible now. The guards will be on the alert, looking for you. Even if they haven't realized you've gone, they'll stumble o'er your rope sooner or later. We strike now and hope they havenae realized we're coming, which means you'll stay here until the castle is taken."

He led her toward a second, smaller cave at the back of the cavern and passed her to another guard. "Keep him tied up, and doona underestimate him. He'll run straight back to the MacPhersons and sound the alarm."

"You canna leave me here!" she yelled. But he'd already turned away and headed toward the waterfall. "Come back, Lachlan, I need to tend to my people!" He ducked under the waterfall, Callum ahead of him.

Panic rose and took over her body. Her clan was in trouble and she wasn't there to help. She ran after the men, but the guard held her back and tugged her farther into the cave, kicking and screaming.

"Lachlan MacKay! Come back!"

Two

LACHLAN COULD JUST SEE THE TIPS OF HIS COUSIN'S shoes hanging from one of the branches near the top of the big pine tree. "Adaira, climb down right now." His voice was rough with frustration, and Callum laid a warning hand on his arm.

"Nay." She sounded small and scared.

Taking a deep breath, he tried to find a nugget of calm within his anger. He had neither the time nor the patience to reassure her that everything would be all right, but if it got her down safely and quickly, he would try to be more reasonable.

"If you doona come down, lass, I'll come up and get you. And if I have to come up and get you, I'll send you back to live with your mother and her husband at the farm for four months. I am your laird, and I willna abide anyone living under my roof who treats the people who care for her with such disrespect. Did you think about how worried everyone at the castle would be? How your mother would feel? Do you understand that a warrior has been sent back to the castle to report that you are here, and I am now one man short? These are the consequences of your actions. So, you can now be brave and choose to come down on your own and continue living at the castle, knowing you will be assigned tasks you willna like for the next three months as penalty, or you can make me come up and get you. The choice is yours—just like it was your choice to climb into the food wagon. You have ten seconds to decide. One, two, three, four, five, six, sev—"

"I'm coming, I'm coming. Stop counting."

Lachlan suppressed a grin. Aye, she hated the counting. A technique one of his clanswomen with six of her own bairns had taught him. He looked at the moon rising in the sky, and his anger welled again. The battle plan had been drawn, the warriors waited on their horses, weapons at the ready, yet here he stood at the base of a tree coaxing down a ten-year-old lass when he should be riding to avenge his brother.

"Faster!" he yelled, and regretted it when her foot slipped in her haste and she almost fell. A minute later, she stood before him, wispy blond curls that she hated sticking out from her head, soft cheeks wet with tears, though she'd made not a sound as they formed, and thickly lashed green eyes that always met his no matter what she'd done. She was small for her age, but made up for it in personality and grit.

Her mother had no idea what to do with her; she'd sent Adaira to Lachlan after she'd married again. Adaira's older brother Airril was in Inverness, and Adaira had refused to show any respect to either her mother or stepfather.

Lachlan crouched in front of her, quelling his impatience. "I am pleased you chose to stay with me at the castle, lass. Now you will wait for me here and write a letter to your mother, your stepfather, your tutor, and everyone else at Clan MacKay who may be worried about you. I will read the letters before they are sent off, and if I doona feel you properly understand the gravity of your behavior, you will start again. Are we in agreement?"

"Aye, Lachlan."

"Nay, Adaira. In this matter, I am your laird, not your cousin. You will address me as such."

"Aye, Laird MacKay."

"Good. Now you will hug me as your cousin, and promise me ne'er to do anything so foolish again."

Adaira threw herself in his arms, tears breaking free, and he held her tight as she sobbed. "Are you hungry, lass?" he asked after a minute when she'd calmed down. She shook her head. Of course not, she'd been hiding in the food wagon. "Thirsty, then?"

"Aye."

He pushed her to arm's length. "Go have something to drink and get started on your letters. I have to leave now. 'Tis important to all of us that we get justice for Donald. I'll be back in a day or two. When I return, we'll ride home together, aye?"

She nodded, and her eyes rounded. "Are you going to stab the bloody MacPherson in his black heart? You should twist the sword in again and again, then run over him with your horse. Then you should give him to a pack of wild dogs, so they can eat him."

This is what he got for allowing her to watch his men train. "First of all, he's not a MacPherson. His name is Machar Murray. And second of all, when did you become so bloodthirsty? I doona like you thinking such grisly things."

"I canna help what I think, Lachlan. My thoughts just come and go. Sometimes I think they're bad thoughts, like when I wanted to pour the ink pot in tutor Gwynn's drink, and sometimes I think they're really good thoughts, like when I decided to climb into the food wagon and follow you here."

Lachlan grunted and rose to his feet. "Well, doona think either of those again. Now, off you go. Sleep in the cave behind the waterfall. My extra blanket is there to keep you warm, and you will find pen and paper in my bag for your letters. You will listen to Earc, and above all else, you willna talk to the lad who is my prisoner."

"Is that who you brought to the camp earlier? The one who's yelling? I saw it all from the tree."

"Aye. He's a MacPherson lad who stumbled upon us, and we had to bring him back so he wouldnae tell anyone. He's worried for his clan, but we canna let him go, lest he warn the guards we're coming."

"So he's a spy, then?" She looked far too intrigued for his liking.

"Nay. I told you, he's a child just like you, who loves his clan and is worried for them." He handed her over to one of the men. "Go now. And Adaira, whate'er you do, doona follow us—and doona talk to the lad."

She nodded solemnly and walked off with the guard. Lachlan watched her go until she reached the waterfall and ducked behind it, then he mounted his horse. Callum was already mounted and waiting. Like

Lachlan, half his face was painted blue for the coming battle, an homage to his Pictish ancestors. All the foster brothers wore the blue during battle—a tradition started when they were just lads living with Gregor. His eyes were cold and hard yet burned with ferocity, giving him a frighteningly grim visage.

A reflection of Lachlan's own face.

"Was that imaginative enough for you?" he asked his foster brother.

"Aye, you did well. But you know she'll go straight to your prisoner now and talk his ear off."

"'Tis what I wanted. He needs something to keep him occupied and his mind off the attack. And Adaira will be fascinated by him."

"What lass wouldnae be, with those eyes? I doona think I've e'er seen a bonnier lad."

"Nay, me neither. 'Tis why I worried when I saw him in the light with some of the dirt washed off. We doona know if Murray is the type to abuse children."

"The boy seems well enough, just angry."

"As I would be. You were right, Callum. We need to go in soft and encourage the MacPhersons to lay down their arms. I'll give the order. I doona want to look the lad in the eye tomorrow and know I havenae done everything possible to save his clan."

❧

Amber watched the young lass peek around the rock wall at her. All she could see was one eye, some dark-blond curls sticking out from her head, and the bottom of her skirt. Amber had stopped yelling about a half hour ago, her voice hoarse and throat raw, and had slumped onto the damp cavern floor—tied by the guard to a ring embedded in the rock and left there with only a single candle to see by.

When she'd finally accepted the futility of her situation, the tears had streamed down her face. Why hadn't she told Lachlan her true identity? Explained her situation? He might have let her come with them. Instead, she'd hidden behind her disguise until it was too late, and now her people were in harm's way.

Unless this girl could free her. Which meant Amber would have to win her over. She bit her lip, trying to be patient. She couldn't afford to scare her off.

"I thought you were a lad," the girl finally said in a whisper.

Amber's eyes widened in surprise. None of the men had recognized her for a lass, yet this girl hadn't been fooled. "Nay, I'm a woman. My name's Amber. Come closer, lass, so I can see you. 'Tis Adaira, right?" she croaked.

Adaira's whole head poked around the corner. "How did you know that?"

"Lachlan told me…before he left and the lad escaped."

The MacKay lass stepped fully into the light, eyes round, mouth open. "How did he escape? Did he tie you up and take your dress? Is he pretending to be a woman so he can sneak back and help the MacPhersons? They killed my cousin, you know."

"Not the MacPhersons, lass. 'Twas Machar Murray who killed him and many others, including my father."

The girl's head jerked up, her breath catching audibly in her throat. "My father was killed too."

Och, poor lass. Amber still felt the devastation of

her father's death, who'd been a commander of the old Laird's warriors, and she knew Adaira must as well. But…Amber could use that pain to bind them together.

'Twas a deplorable act, but necessary to help her people.

"I'm so sorry. How long ago was that?" she asked.

"Two years. A horse kicked him in the head. My mother married someone else last spring. He's all right, I suppose, but he doesn't toss me in the air like my da used to, or chase me around the yard. Now I live in the castle with Lachlan and the other foster brothers when they visit."

"That sounds most agreeable, but I wager you miss your da."

Adaira shrugged and dropped her eyes, but not before Amber saw the tremor in the girl's lip.

"I miss my father," Amber continued. "He used to tickle me all over and sometimes let me ride on his back like a pony."

The girl's eyes lit up. "Aye, my da used to do that too. And sometimes he'd rear up and I'd have to hold on tight or I'd fall off." She squinted and stepped closer, gaze trained on Amber's head. "What happened to your hair? It's shorter even than mine, and sticking out all o'er the place. Did the lad cut it off? Did he tie it to his head, so he'd look more like a lass? Lachlan said he was a spy."

Amber nodded wisely and leaned forward. "I think he is, Adaira. Free me, so I can tell your cousin the lad's escaped before something awful happens."

"Like what?"

"Like Machar Murray getting away, or Lachlan and

his men being ambushed. You wouldnae want to lose him too, would you?"

A panicked expression crossed the girl's face and guilt punched Amber hard in the gut. Her stomach turned at the idea of using the wee lass, but lives were at stake. MacPherson lives.

She would make it up to Adaira when she could.

The girl squatted beside her and stared at the rope binding Amber's wrists to the metal ring. "These look like the knots Lachlan taught me. I practiced until my fingers bled."

She sounded proud of her accomplishment and Amber repressed a smile. "Aye, the lad said Lachlan had tied him up. He must have remembered what to do. Can you undo them?"

"Maybe, but 'twould be faster if I cut them off."

"You have a knife?" Amber tried to keep the excitement out of her voice.

"I always have a knife."

As happy as Amber was that the wee lass could cut the rope, it worried her the girl might hurt herself. If Amber had the opportunity when this was over, and she wasn't thrown in the dungeon, she'd speak to Lachlan about it.

"Will you cut the cords for me, then? Please, Adaira?"

"Aye." The girl moved the candle closer, reached into the folds of her dress, and brought out a small knife, like one she might have used at dinner. She placed it on the hemp at Amber's wrists, who scooted back as far as she could, hope trembling through her.

"You're shivering."

"I'm just cold. And excited, of course, to tell Lachlan about the lad."

"Can I come with you?" Adaira asked.

"Nay, I'm sorry, lass. It's too dangerous. Please hurry."

Adaira sighed and began to saw through the cord. "That's what Lachlan said, but I doona think he understands how much I practice with my weapon—just like his warriors."

"I daresay, for I'm sure he wouldnae like it if you got hurt."

"I did get hurt once. Well, twice, but I ne'er made those mistakes again. 'Tis good to know how to defend yourself."

"I agree. My father taught me how to fight with my hands and body in case I was e'er attacked. I can teach you what to do when this is all over, if you like."

Adaira's eyes lit up. "I'd like that verra much!"

It took longer than Amber expected to cut through her restraints—the hemp was tough and the knife dull—and the lass didn't have much strength. Finally, the rope gave way.

"There!"

Amber rubbed her wrists to ease the blood flow, and wrapped her arms around her young savior. "Thank you, Adaira. You're a brave lass." She pushed away and rose to her feet "Can you tell me how many guards are outside?"

"Just one. Earc. He watches me often at the castle." Adaira tossed the knife in the air and caught it. "Are you sure I canna come with you? I fight with the men all the time."

"'Tis different to wrestle with your laird's warriors than to fight his enemy."

"But I want to battle the MacPhersons too."

"I'm not going to battle the MacPhersons, love. I'm a healer. I'm going to help anyone who's hurt."

A stunned expression crossed Adaira's face. Amber moved away from her to a small pool of water that had collected in a corner of the cave. She crouched down and splashed water on her skin to wash away the mud and dirt. If she could surprise the guard, she should be able to incapacitate him long enough for her to get away.

Adaira followed, hands on her hips. "You canna help the MacPhersons!"

"I can, and I will. I'll help the MacKays too. I would even help Machar Murray just so I could see him hang afterward." Amber wet her hair and dragged her fingers through it to try and smooth out the strands as best she could.

Adaira nodded, looking serious. "I'd like to see that too. Lachlan says 'tis our duty to seek justice for Donald."

"As long as it's justice and not vengeance."

"What's the difference?"

She sighed and shook her head. "Sometimes, I doona know." Finishing with her hair, she looked at Adaira. "Does that look better?"

"Nay. Parts of it are longer than others. Do you want a brush? Lachlan has one in his bag."

"A brush will help, but it canna fix the length. I did a…that is, the lad did a terrible job cutting it."

When Adaira ran out of the small cavern to get Lachlan's brush, Amber tugged open her plaid and shirt to loosen the band around her breasts. It had helped surprisingly well. She was pulling it free when Adaira came back.

"Why'd you do that?" she asked, handing her the brush, so she could help unwind the material from Amber's body.

Amber tucked the brush between her knees. "'Tis easier to ride a horse, especially if you're going fast."

"Then why take it off? You'll have to ride back to the castle."

"Well, um, my breasts have been bound too long and are starting to hurt. Doesn't your mother e'er bind her breasts when she's working?"

The material finally pulled free and Amber's breasts released to push against her linen shirt, still damp and cold from the water. Adaira's eyes widened. "Nay, I doona think so. But my mother doesn't have breasts as big as those."

"They're not that big." Amber couldn't help feeling a wee bit miffed.

"Aye, they are. I hope mine are wee like my ma's."

Amber brushed her hair and had just finished tucking it behind her ears and adjusting her shirt and plaid, when she heard Earc yell, "Adaira! Lass, are you in there?"

"Aye! I'm in here with—"

Amber clamped her hand over Adaira's mouth. "Shhh. Let me surprise him. Stay here." The last was an order and she stared directly at Adaira until the young girl nodded.

With one last adjustment to her plaid so it fell to her ankles like a woman's skirt, Amber dropped the brush in her pocket and left the small chamber. She tried to put a sway in her walk like she'd seen many other women in her clan do, but she just felt awkward. With her luck, she'd either fall or twist her other ankle.

The bigger cavern was lit by a torch, and Adaira clearly saw Earc, the guard who had tied her up earlier, near the waterfall entrance, searching through his sporran for something. He was large, even larger than Lachlan, but she'd noticed he moved slowly and with a limp. She'd also noticed how strong he was.

So...catch him by surprise and move quickly out of his way.

She was halfway toward him when he looked up with a smile on his bushy face. He was missing a few teeth and wore his red hair tied into several braids. His mouth dropped open when he saw her and he stared at her like a man besotted, not saying anything as he looked her over.

She smiled slowly, in what she thought was a seductive manner, and tried again for that sway of her hips.

"Lord have mercy," he said under his breath, his gaze on her face, then her breasts, then back to her face, as if he couldn't decide where to look.

"Earc. Laird MacKay has a message for you," she said softly.

He allowed her to get close, looking down at her cleavage as she rose on her toes to whisper in his ear. When she was in position, she slammed her knee sharply into his groin and pressed down hard with both thumbs on the nerves above his elbows. He toppled over with a painful squeal at odds with his size and maleness, and rolled onto his side, knees and arms tucked into his body.

She jumped back and raced around him to the path leading out from behind the waterfall. A gasp sounded behind her, and she turned to see Adaira standing at the entrance to the smaller cavern, eyes wide, hands covering her mouth in shock and fear.

Amber hesitated for just a second. "I'm sorry, lass. 'Twill all be all right. I promise." She ducked beneath the water and ran for the only horse still tethered to one of the wagons.

Three

LACHLAN SQUEEZED UNDER THE MACPHERSONS' CUR-
tain wall through the ditch he and his men had spent
the last fifteen minutes quietly digging out. His heart
beat steadily in his ears like a drum that marched him
into battle. One of his warriors crawled beside him,
their shoulders rubbing, their breath loud in the con-
fined space of the tunnel.

No sounds of battle had erupted yet, so he assumed
the other forces—one at the gate and two over the
walls on opposite sides—hadn't been spotted. Or if
they had, no one had been able to give the alarm. The
plan had been to proceed with stealth for as long as
possible, converging on the keep in the center of the
bailey and incapacitating as many MacPhersons as they
could before the real fighting erupted.

After five years, Lachlan was finally on his way to
kill the man who'd murdered his brother and tried to
murder him—putting the lives of several hundred men
at risk—yet all he could think about was the lad with
the violet eyes and soft, amber-colored hair he'd left
tied up back in the cave.

Something niggled at him, and he couldn't figure out what. The lad had somehow gotten under his skin. But how? And why?

Arriving on the other side of the ditch, he raised his head from the hole to see several of his men crouched in the shadows—along with an unconscious MacPherson who'd been bound and gagged. The moon was covered with clouds, and the night was lit with only a few torches. He could hear men on the stone walkway above.

The MacKay warrior beside him exited at the same time he did, and they crawled silently to the shadows.

Once there, Lachlan scanned the wall and saw three men on top. They could shoot them with arrows, but that might kill them, and what if one of them was the lad's family? Or if the men cried out when they fell and alerted Machar Murray? No, the MacKays needed to go up and bring the men down.

Quietly.

A hay wagon missing a wheel leaned against the stone wall, a rope pooled on the ground beside it. From Lachlan's calculations, 'twas the same place the lad had crawled over earlier in his bid for freedom. Someone must have either pulled the rope back down from below or kicked it over the top from above.

He signaled Hamish, his second-in-command, to meet him at the cart, then he darted between the shadows and crawled up the hay bales. Three men stood talking and laughing on the curtain wall while another sat propped against the crumbling battlements. Only one of the watch occasionally glanced over the trees and scrubby field below, but he never looked down to where the remainder of Lachlan's force crouched in the shadows.

Crawling back down, Lachlan met up with Hamish, who waited for him beneath the wagon.

"There's another guard on top. I'll need three men," Lachlan whispered.

"You'll want a distraction, then?"

"Aye. A quiet one."

Hamish rubbed his hands together and smiled. "'Tis time for a wee song." He returned to the other warriors, three of whom joined Lachlan at the wagon, before he disappeared from sight. The men quietly helped Lachlan pile up more hay bales as they waited, high enough so they could jump to the top of the wall together.

From the opposite direction along the walkway came the sound of a bawdy tune, softly sung, the singer a wee bit worse for drink. Lachlan shared a quick smile with his men.

When the guards looked away from them to see who was singing, Lachlan quietly sprang forward, his men beside him. They'd had their knives secured in their mouths during the climb to keep their hands free—but not longer. The farthest Macpherson was Lachlan's target—a big man with a bushy beard and a hearty laugh. For the first time, he was glad his options were limited—just in case the lad knew this man.

Lachlan dragged him down, one hand over his mouth, the other holding a knife against his throat. "Not a sound, or I swear I'll cut through your neck to your spine. Do you understand?" The man barely nodded, just enough so Lachlan knew he agreed. "I'm Lachlan MacKay. I've no quarrel with the MacPhersons unless they get between me and Machar Murray. When he's dead, you can go home to your family and help choose a better leader for your clan. One who willna hurt a lad for stealing bread to feed his sister."

The man relaxed, and Lachlan easily gagged and bound him with the other men who had capitulated. "Someone will come back for you when we're done."

After slipping back down the wall, they spread out. The group made their way toward the castle's interior, incapacitating several more MacPhersons along the way. He'd been hoping to get to the keep before sounds of their invasion erupted, but they were just coming up on the stable when shouts of alarm and clashing swords broke through the quiet night.

Lachlan cursed. "Pick up the pace," he ordered.

They moved quickly through the stables, opening up the horse stalls just in case a fire erupted. 'Twas something Gregor, who had a love of horses, had taught Lachlan and his foster brothers long ago.

In a back room, they found the stable master snoring noisily in his bed. He woke with a start as he was hauled from his covers wearing only his linen shift. Two frightened groomsmen crouched in an empty pen, and the MacKays dragged all three outside before tying them to the wooden corral post.

Lachlan raised his voice to be heard above the growing din. "I'm Lachlan MacKay, laird of Clan MacKay. If you see any of your people, warrior or not, spread the word that we do not want them harmed. We're here for Machar Murray only. If they lay down their arms, they willna be hurt."

The stable master stretched out his fingers to Lachlan.

"I'm Osgar, the stable master. Please, doona let them burn the keep. There's a woman and a young lad in there who need help. They may be in the dungeon."

"You speak of Ian?"

"Aye, and Amber. The laird may have her in his bedchamber. She couldnae hold her tongue and made him verra angry."

"Ian is safe. He made it o'er the wall earlier. I promise to look for the woman. Where is the laird's bedchamber?"

"On the third floor facing west toward the mountains."

Lachlan gripped the man's hand. "I'll do what I can."

They took off at a steady run toward the keep, which loomed four stories high in the distance. Clearing the area as best they could from the south end of the bailey, they were more focused now on getting to the battle and trapping Machar Murray within the keep. Still, it slowed things down when they had to fight without seriously injuring anyone. But the lad had been right. The MacPhersons laid down their arms once it became clear the attack was on their laird, not the clan in general.

In the bailey, groups of men fought in tight clusters, while many others kneeled in submission. Torches had been lit, and long shadows danced over the stone walls of the kitchens and barracks and stretched across the open, grassy area.

Lachlan saw an old man holding a ring of keys hobble up the stairs to the front entrance of the keep. The steward, most likely. What had Ian called him?

"Niall MacPherson! Hold right there!" Lachlan shouted.

The steward stopped and looked around. He met Lachlan's gaze as Lachlan marched toward him, ready to do damage, his sword clenched tight in his fist. The old man jumped with alarm and hurried through the door, which banged shut behind him.

"I want a perimeter around the keep," Lachlan yelled to Hamish as he ran to catch up to Niall, taking the stairs two at a time.

"Lachlan!"

He turned to see his foster brother racing toward him, and though he chafed to get inside, he waited at the door, glad to see Callum was unhurt.

"The west side is taken," Callum said, gripping Lachlan's arm in greeting. "We had little resistance and none were wounded. The men hold the quadrant."

"Aye, 'twas the same from the south. The steward just ran in here. He'll have information on Murray. The laird is probably inside."

"Do not rush in. Wait while I arrange for more men. We need to be cautious—sweep through the keep, so we doona miss anything."

"He's getting away!"

"Maybe, but you canna go alone. 'Tis too dangerous. And he could easily slip past you."

Lachlan gritted his teeth, trying to rein in his temper even though he knew Callum was right. He was still too damn hot and making mistakes. Emotion had no place on the battlefield. "Get on, then, you old woman. I promise to wait."

Callum dashed back down the stairs to the bailey and rounded up several warriors—a mix of MacKays and MacLeans. Once they were at his back, Lachlan yanked open the heavy, wooden door, surprised it hadn't been barred from the inside. Men went in with their shields raised, followed by archers in case MacPherson archers had been set in place to repel an invasion from above—as Lachlan and Callum would have done.

They moved with care into a large hall, lit only by a dwindling fire in a hearth at the far end—and no guards. Stairs to the upper levels rose against the wall opposite the door. At the top, a balcony circled the hall, an ideal perch for archers, with murder holes cut into the stones that looked out onto the bailey—but it was also empty.

"We need candles," Lachlan yelled. "I want every corner of the keep lit!"

Several men ran to build up the fire, while others brought candles and placed them in the sconces on the wall. Minutes later, the hall blazed with light. Clean rushes covered the floor, and four worn, but well-cared-for chairs surrounded the hearth.

It was obvious somebody still saw to the keep, even though no thought had gone into its defenses.

"Search behind the tables," Lachlan said, pointing to the pile of tables and chairs that had been stacked in a corner.

"Clear," one of his warriors said a moment later.

Lachlan turned to Hamish, who stood beside him. "Hold this room. No one goes in or out without permission. I want two men at the door, three on the balcony, and two more at the top of the stairs while we search this level. Also, send men to search the storerooms below, and keep an eye out for a dungeon of some kind. There may be a woman or other prisoners inside. And reinforce our perimeter. We'll not be losing Murray again!"

"Aye, Laird," Hamish said, then assigned the men their positions and headed outside. Darach, Callum, and several others moved away from the hearth to the dark hallway on the opposite end of the great room. A closed door was set in the corner on the same wall as the stairs—the steward's or housekeeper's room, most likely.

Lachlan pointed to two of his men. "Guard the passageway while we check the room."

The men did as asked, and Callum tried the door. "'Tis barred from the inside."

Lachlan leaned close to the wood. He rapped it with his knuckles. "Niall MacPherson. 'Tis Lachlan MacKay, laird of Clan MacKay. We mean the MacPhersons no harm. Our fight is with Laird Machar Murray. I have a young lad back at my camp by the name of Ian who asked me to see to your well-being."

He strained to hear a response over the sounds of the ongoing conflict outside. A thump sounded inside, followed by a scraping noise. Maybe a chair being dragged across the floor? "Ian is in the dungeon," a frail voice finally said.

"Nay, he escaped. He said you helped him to get out. Please, Steward, we need your help to find Machar Murray without hurting any more MacPhersons."

"The lad, what color is his hair? And his eyes?"

"His hair is the color of amber, and his eyes a most unusual blue."

"Nay, not blue," said Callum. "They're almost purple. Like a violet."

"Who's that?" the voice shouted.

"I'm Callum MacLean, laird of Clan MacLean, raised by the great Gregor MacLeod, who has charged us with bringing peace to the Highlands. We mean no harm to any innocents."

"Please, Niall," Lachlan asked again. "Open the door."

A moment passed. Lachlan let out a relieved sigh as the bar lifted and the door swung inward.

A stooped old man with tufts of curly gray hair on his head and a disheveled plaid stood before him, his cheeks damp from tears. "What took you so long, man? I've been writing to Gregor MacLeod for years."

❧

Amber gripped the old nag's mane as the mare, who had resisted leaving the castle earlier, now ran full tilt toward it despite the clangs, crashes, and shouts of warfare coming from inside. Most likely the determined pony was deaf and unaware of the danger it ran toward, thinking only to get a meal and warm stall to sleep in.

The portcullis was up and the gates wide open when she reached the curtain wall. Torches lit the night—she'd never seen so many in use before, not even when the old laird was alive. People hurried out of the entrance, mostly women and children.

None who might be Murray's men, she realized.

Amber jumped down from her pony, trying not to put weight on her sore ankle, but she stumbled as she landed. Pain shot through her foot and stole her breath. She leaned against the stone wall for just a moment, trying to will away the tenderness and work up the courage to take another step.

A lad with hair as black as night ran past her. "Ian!" She just managed to snag his plaid before he was out of reach. "You're free! Are you all right, lad?"

He spun around, his face dirty and his eyes wide with fright. His expression brightened when he recognized her, and he wrapped skinny arms around her. She squeezed back just as tight.

"Amber, I thought for sure you were dead. Laird Murray was so angry when you called him a thieving toad. They threw me in the dungeon, but then the fighting broke out. Men I didn't recognize let me out."

"'Tis the MacKays and the MacLeans. They're after Machar Murray and his dogs. If they catch him, he'll be hanged. He killed Laird MacKay's brother."

"Verily?"

"Aye. Ian, it's over. We can take back the castle and the clan. Live without fear that we'll be dragged from our beds at night. You and Breanna willna have to go hungry anymore. You can come and live with me, if you like, or we'll find a place for both of you at the castle."

He hugged her tight again, his body trembling. "Does that mean we'll have a new laird? One who'll take care of the clan?"

Amber's breath stopped as she thought about Lachlan. "I hope so."

She heard a scream of pain from inside the castle and pushed Ian away. "Run as fast as you can to my cottage and bring back my satchel—the one with my bandages and herbs in it. I'll need it to help the wounded."

"What about Breanna?"

"She's safe. Doona worry about your sister. I

stashed her with Nell before I came to speak for you at the castle earlier. Go now—and be careful!"

Ian ran down the path and disappeared into the night.

Pulling her plaid up over her butchered hair, Amber stepped lightly onto her sore foot and limped past the curtain wall. She'd gone barely ten paces and could see MacPherson men huddled together on the ground, when a young warrior in a MacKay plaid stepped in front of her. He held his sword loosely at his side, but she could tell he was alert.

"No one's allowed in, lass." His stance was firm but non-threatening.

"I'm a healer. I just want to tend the wounded— MacPhersons and MacKays. I doona support Machar Murray."

"Aye, 'tis good to hear, but I have my orders."

She stepped closer and pulled her cloak back while keeping the ends of her hair covered. His eyes widened, and she hoped it would be enough to sway him. "But Lachlan—Laird MacKay—asked me to come. Callum too. Surely you wouldnae want anyone to die because I couldnae help them in time."

He had to clear his throat before speaking. "Nay, lass. You canna enter. I'm sorry."

She laid her hand on his arm. "Please. I'd be most grateful. Perhaps even enough for a kiss afterward." Aye, she'd kiss him, covered in blood and worse, and smelling of death. She'd treated several serious injuries before and knew she wouldn't look bonnie by the time she was done. The thought almost made her smile—if she weren't talking about grievous injuries.

A slight tremor ran through his muscles, but still

he didn't move. Curse Lachlan MacKay and his finely trained men. She considered a physical assault, but even if she made it into the bailey, the other guards would soon take her down.

"Malcolm, let her pass. I'll speak to her."

"Aye, Hamish."

The guard she'd been talking to stepped aside, and she recognized the grizzled warrior behind him from Lachlan's camp—the one who'd told Lachlan that Adaira was in the tree. She quickly pulled up her plaid lest he recognize her too.

He was older than the rest, with hardened eyes and a lifetime of battle scars. Her feminine wiles wouldn't work on him, she was sure.

"What's your name, lass?"

"Amber MacPherson. I'm the clan healer. Please, I'll help your men as well as mine if you let me in."

"Aye, you will. This way." He clamped his hand around her upper arm and led her toward the keep. She had to practically run to keep up, hopping a wee bit to lessen the weight on her foot.

"You're hurt?" he asked, coming to an abrupt halt.

"Just a sprain. I'll be all right."

He kneeled in front of her and lifted her injured foot. "May I?"

"Um…aye."

She couldn't help being suspicious, and frowned as she watched him unlace her shoe then squeeze and roll her ankle. She bit her lip to stop from crying out.

"'Tis sprained," he said.

Annoyance made her tart. "Really? I had no idea."

His lips quirked, then he rummaged in his sporran

and brought out a length of narrow linen. Before she could protest, he'd wrapped her ankle up tight and laced her shoe.

He stood and pulled her along again. She didn't hobble quite so badly this time—he'd done a good job. Almost as good as she would have done.

"We'll bring you a crutch too," he said.

"Thank you, but I need supplies—blankets, bandages, old sheets we can cut into strips, needle and thread and some sharp knives. Sticks I can use to set bones if I have to. And I'll need help. Can you assign me some men?"

"Doona worry, lass. There aren't as many wounded as you're imagining, and none dead that I know of. The battle's winding down as we speak. 'Tis not that bad."

"By the looks of you, Hamish, you've seen many battles. Most hard won, I'm sure. What you consider bad isn't necessarily what I consider bad, so just bring me the supplies and set me up in the great hall to care for them."

He grunted, and she thought she detected a wee smile. "Anything else you want while I'm at it?"

"Aye, you need to let in a lad named Ian when he comes. I sent him for my satchel. I have herbs in there that can help with the healing."

He looked sideways at her, his eyes sweeping over her from head to toe. "My mother was a healer. She always gave me foxglove when I had a toothache. She'd mash up the petals in my tea."

Amber snorted. "She didn't love you much, then, did she?"

"And why is that?"

"Because you'd be verra sick, possibly dead, if she gave you that."

He nodded, and this time his smile was a wee bit wicked. "'Tis true. Have you actually met Laird MacKay and Laird MacLean then?"

She hesitated for just a second. "Of course."

"Ah, 'tis a story there, I can tell. One I canna wait to hear. Maybe I'll even put it into song."

He hummed a few bars, and she knew he was laughing at her. She'd just opened her mouth to rebuke him when she noticed the area they were walking past was not lit up like the rest of the bailey.

"Surely now's not the time to save on torches," she said.

He looked at her quizzically, then his eyes opened wide, and he shoved her to the ground behind a crate full of firewood. An arrow flew past her, then a second arrow embedded in Hamish's forearm, and his sword went flying. He darted behind another crate.

"Stay down, lass!" he yelled just as two more arrows crashed into the crate she hid behind, threatening to topple it over.

"MacKays! MacLeans!" Hamish roared, then let out a sharp whistle. "Archer at the barracks! Hold the perimeter! Hold the perimeter!" He whistled again.

Another arrow hit her crate and broke it apart, sending the firewood down on top of her. She wrapped her arms around her head and curled into a ball, feeling the thud of three more impacts. One arrow poked through just a hand's span from her face, the head sharp and shiny, and sent panic racing through her.

This was how her father had died. An arrow to the face during a "hunting" accident a week before Laird MacPherson died in his sleep—and Machar Murray took over the clan.

She would not die in the same manner.

She would run.

⤝⤜

Lachlan closed his eyes and inhaled slowly through his nose, trying to control the mix of anguish and frustration that pushed up from his gut and threatened to send him into a killing rage. He stood with Callùm, the steward Niall, and two other warriors in the lit passageway by the laird's bedchamber.

'Twas the last room in the castle to be searched.

He had little hope Machar Murray was inside. Why would he be? The door was locked from the outside; the person on the other side of this door was a prisoner. The woman the stable master mentioned to him earlier, most likely. Probably crouched behind the bed and frightened to come out.

Amber, he'd called her. Another victim of Murray's greed and depravity.

The battle outside had quieted, the MacPhersons defeated other than a few pockets of resistance—and no sign of Murray or his three friends, commonly referred to as "the laird's dogs."

To have come this far and lose the blackheart after all these years of searching, maybe never to be found again—it sat like a burning, lead ball in his stomach. He clenched his jaw so tight he feared it might break, yearning to batter the door down with his bare hands.

Instead, he stood by as Niall fumbled his key ring with shaky fingers, peering at each key in turn with squinting eyes, before finally trying to push one in the hole.

Callum laid a hand on Niall's shoulder and said, "Thank you. You've done enough. If the laird is trapped inside, he may be dangerous. We'll let you know when you can enter."

He nodded and stepped back. Callum easily turned the key and pushed the door open.

No sound came from inside the darkened bedchamber.

Still, they moved forward cautiously, weapons raised, eyes sharp. The fire had burned down to embers. They quickly put more wood in the hearth and lit the candles that were on either side of the bed and resting in sconces on the walls. A chair covered in beautiful blue silk with a matching footstool sat in front of the fire, and a shiny silver pitcher with a basin sat beside the bed. On the wall hung a remarkable painting of a laird receiving fealty from his clan.

'Twas obviously the richest room in the keep, and one Machar Murray kept for himself.

Lachlan moved toward the bed, high and well sprung with a draped canopy over the top. The quilt matched the chair other than a pool of orange-gold silk in a pile on top. No, not silk. He reached down and picked up a handful of the long, curling strands that lay on the bed.

Hair.

An astonishing color that gleamed in the firelight, the strands were as long as his arm and twisted in big, springy curls. And the feel. He couldn't get over how soft it was.

A sense memory came to him. The same silky softness running through his fingers, the same luminescent color, but not in long ropes like this. No, the other had been shorter, jaggedly cut, on a dirty face with startling violet eyes. He found himself holding his breath as his brain sought to make the connection. Then it hit him.

The lad.

He spotted a woman's dress on the floor and picked it up in his other hand.

"Christ Almighty."

Callum glanced over from where he'd been peering out the window into the black night. "What is it?"

Lachlan showed him the handful of hair, a fine tremor running beneath his skin, his heart feeling like it might burst from his chest.

Callum frowned as he came over, looking at the fiery tresses. "The lad?"

"Aye, the 'lad.'"

The one he couldn't stop thinking about, with the bonnie face and soft body despite how wee he was. The lad who'd been so yielding beneath him, pliant— until he'd bitten Lachlan's hand and smashed their foreheads together.

The lad whose arse had fit so snugly between his thighs on his horse and in his palm as they'd crawled across the field.

He looked at his palm. Felt his hand tingle, and an answering tingle in his groin that turned into a surge.

She'd felt soft. *She'd* bitten his hand and smashed

their foreheads together. *She'd* fit snugly between his thighs, her arse pressed up against him, his arms around her waist.

"Nay." Lachlan raised the hair to his face. Smelled it…so sweet, like lavender. "The lass."

He pinned his gaze on Niall, who hovered in the door, wringing his hands. "'Tis Amber. You cut her hair, dressed her like a boy. Did you get her out in time?"

By the way his face darkened, Lachlan knew Niall understood his meaning—did Amber escape before Murray raped her?

"Barely. If you hadn't come when you did, he would have gone after her. He's…obsessed. Amber held him off for a long time. She pretended to be a witch, as did her grandmother before her. Laird Murray is superstitious."

"I doona understand. The lass is the lad's sister?" Callum asked.

"Nay. The lad, with the bonnie face and bright blue eyes, is the lass."

Callum's brow lifted as understanding struck. "Of course. How could we not have seen it? That face, those eyes. And they're more purple than blue."

"Violet," Niall said. "Same as her grandmother's in her day." He sounded wistful.

"Aye, violet," Callum said as Lachlan nodded his agreement.

He glanced around the room, looking for signs of another exit. "How'd you get her out?"

Niall dropped his gaze to his key ring, fiddled with it. "Och, surely I doona understand what you mean?"

Callum strode toward a sturdy wooden chest with a

shell inlay that sat against the wall by the inner corner. "'Twould be here, most likely."

"Aye. It would bring her out right by the hay wagon." Lachlan had just taken a step toward the chest when he heard a sharp whistle followed by, "Archer at the barracks! Hold the perimeter! Hold the perimeter!"

His heart raced again as hope filled his breast. Who else would be fighting them now? Not the MacPhersons. And a bow was Machar Murray's preferred weapon. "'Tis him!" he said, and strode purposefully to the door.

Callum followed, shouting orders to the men. "Find the passageway and block it off at both ends. Then search for others."

Lachlan ran along the corridor and down both flights of stairs. He was almost in the great room when he realized he still carried Amber's hair clenched in one fist, and her dress in the other. He hesitated. He should drop the hair, let it disappear amongst the rushes, but his hand closed tighter, everything within him rejecting the idea. Instead, he opened his sporran and stuffed the hair inside.

As he exited the keep and started down the stairs to the bailey, he held on to the dress too. He'd give it to one of his men to return to Amber at the waterfall. He wanted her to know he *knew* she was a woman. That he *saw* her.

He was almost at the bottom when he glanced up and stopped short.

Aye, he saw her all right. Running across the bailey, her plaid hiked up to her knees, her hood back, looking like the devil was after her when she should be tied up and under guard at his camp.

How in the name of all that was holy had she escaped?

A few weapons lay on the ground and spots of blood stained the grass, but considering how crowded the bailey had been not long ago, now it was surprisingly clear. The MacPherson prisoners were tied up together in the barracks, and his men were all either guarding them or on patrol around the castle and keep. Whoever had been in the bailey had most likely run to Hamish's aid—as Lachlan should be doing now.

Instead, he stepped off the last stair and moved to intercept Amber. No one chased her, so he assumed she'd been allowed in, and mindless panic showed on her cleaned-up face. Maybe the archer had frightened her?

She looked up at the last minute and barely avoided barreling into him. He found himself disappointed, and realized he wanted to feel her against him again, especially now that he knew she was a woman— possibly the loveliest he'd ever seen, even with wood chips in her hair and the cut strands sticking out all over the place.

Her cheeks were flushed and her violet eyes bright, her lips full and rosy. She panted through her mouth as she caught her breath, and he could see a sliver of pink tongue between her teeth. He wanted to move closer and capture it with his own.

His eyes dropped lower to her heaving chest, and the blood drummed hard in his temples. God's truth, she wasn't built like a boy in the slightest. Her plaid had fallen back and her breasts pressed against the damp white linen shirt. They were high and lush with pebbled nipples he wanted to roll between his fingers. Better yet, on his tongue.

No wonder she felt soft. He couldn't believe he'd been fooled.

She pulled the plaid back up around her shoulders, and when he raised his head to meet her gaze she turned even pinker from embarrassment. Still, she lifted her chin just a notch and crossed her arms over her chest.

"Laird," she said, sounding prim and condemning all at once.

"Lass," he responded, irritated by her frigid tone. She was a fighter and her spirit was hotter than Hades. He'd seen it. Felt it.

They continued to stare at each other, neither willing to give quarter. He heard Callum snort with amusement from somewhere behind him, and his annoyance heightened.

Then he remembered her dress—and her cut hair tucked into his sporran. Raising a sardonic brow, he fished out her shorn locks and let them drift away in the wind before holding out her dress. "Your arisaid."

Her eyes widened slightly before she took it. After a moment, she reached in her pocket and held something out to him. "Your brush."

When he saw the brush from his pack, the dam broke. He scowled at her. "You went through my bloody things, you lied, you stole from me, God knows what you did to poor Earc."

She scowled right back and placed her hands on her hips. "I didn't steal anything from you. Adaira gave it to me after *she* went through your things, and I'm giving it back, you idiotic, interfering—"

"I'm interfering? You almost brought all of Machar Murray's forces down on us and ruined a finely planned attack. And you better not have hurt my cousin, or so help me—"

"I would ne'er hurt your cousin, although how you could just leave her there barely protected is beyond me. Your guard was too lost staring at my bosom to notice anything was wrong, and Adaira was only too happy to cut through my bonds. What if I'd been a threat?"

"You are a threat! You almost broke my nose and paralyzed my arm."

"You pulled me from my horse and choked me. Then you tied my hands and dragged me through the rocks and bush like a bag of oats. You enjoyed it!"

"Nay, I was too worried I'd get an arrow in my back because you couldnae stop waving your arse in the air!"

"I had a gag in my mouth. I could hardly tell you I'd ne'er crawled like that before, now could I?"

"You wouldnae have told me anyway. You're an imposter and a trickster."

"You're the one who invaded our castle. Threatened my clan."

"Liberated your clan."

"Took us over. Which means you are now responsible for us."

"What?"

"You chased away our old laird, so now you have to be our new one."

"Your old laird threw a lad in the dungeon for

stealing bread and locked you in his bedchamber to use for carnal pleasure."

"I didn't say he was a good laird, but he killed all of the men who could have replaced him, so now Clan MacPherson belongs to you. *We* belong to you. If you refuse to help us, we'll be scooped up by the next monster who comes along. What would Gregor MacLeod say if he knew you planned to leave?"

"He'd say: Run, Lachlan! Fast as you can! The clan's all right, but the lass is as daft as a bat!"

"We need help!"

"Then go petition a laird for protection."

"I'm petitioning you."

"Nay, you're not. Petitioning implies asking. You're telling!"

She stamped her foot in frustration, then almost crumpled to the ground as she cried out in pain. Lachlan darted forward and caught her before she fell.

"'Tis nothing. A sprain," she said, trying to push out of his arms. The feel of them around her brought back the secure feeling she had when she'd ridden with him on his horse to the waterfall. A feeling she now knew was false. He had no intention of making sure she and the rest of the MacPhersons were safe.

"How did you manage to run across the bailey like hellhounds were nipping at your heels with a sprained ankle?"

"I doona know. I was scared. Arrows were flying past my head. Are you going to question everything I do?"

"Aye, most likely."

"Well, if you're not staying, I doona have to answer. You're not my laird."

He grunted, swept her into his arms, and sat her on the steps leading up to the keep. "Stay off it until it heals."

"I doona have to do what you say, either."

"Well, I doona have to be a bloody healer to know that if it hurts, you should stay off it."

She was about to say she was a healer and could make her own assessment, when a horse with a big, redheaded rider galloped into the bailey. The rider carried a child in his arms, her head and arm red with blood.

As he drew closer she recognized Earc, Adaira's minder, and her breath stopped. *Dear God. No!*

"Adaira!" Lachlan yelled, disbelief and horror in his voice. He ran toward Earc. "What happened?" Amber hurried after him.

"Men came to the waterfall. Three of them." Earc slowed and handed Adaira down to Lachlan. "I fought them off, but then I slipped on the rocks and fell into the river. I saw Adaira charge them with a knife as I was swept downstream. I got to her as soon as I could—she'd been stabbed and left for dead."

Lachlan fell to his knees, Adaira in his arms. "Oh, Christ, no! Not Adaira!"

Amber crouched beside him and felt for the girl's pulse, faint but still there. "Take her into the keep. We'll set up the wounded in the great hall."

"We need a healer! I know you have a good one. Get her now!"

"I am the healer, Lachlan MacKay. And I am good. Now take her into the keep and lay her on one of the tables. I promise to heal her as long as you promise to lead my clan until we can safely lead ourselves."

Four

LACHLAN SAT IN THE GREAT HALL ON ONE OF THE chairs he'd pulled up beside Adaira's makeshift bed, holding her hand and cursing himself for the hundredth time that he hadn't sent her home straight away when he had the chance.

She'd been on the table for over two hours while Amber worked on the stab wound to her lower abdomen—washing and stitching and smearing her with herbs and salves. Amber's arisaid was covered in his cousin's blood by the time she finished. The biggest worry now, she said, was infection. Though the girl had also lost a concerning amount of blood.

She'd moved on to treat other injuries after Adaira—MacPhersons, MacKays, and MacLeans. He'd watched as she'd limped around, checking and dressing head wounds, stitching cuts, setting bones, wrapping sprains, treating burns, and even realigning a shoulder that had popped out of joint. Ian had brought her satchel long ago, and she'd sent him back out to her cottage at first light, along with a guard, to pick more herbs from her garden.

Niall and the housekeeper, Finola, had been on hand to help wherever they could, mostly cleaning up after Amber and replenishing her supplies. And a young lass named Mary, who'd made eyes at Ian, had come up from the village to assist Amber.

Everyone was exhausted, but none had worked harder than Amber or had the added burden of a sprained ankle. She'd grimaced in pain several times, causing him to grind his teeth with frustration. None could do the work she did, but it bothered him that she tended to everyone but herself.

Earc lay on the bed next to Adaira's. He'd been battered and bruised after his fight and subsequent near-drowning, and he'd swallowed much water. Amber had treated him and kept him close for observation. Instead of being angry at her for assaulting him in the cave, Earc's puppy-dog gaze followed her around the great hall as she worked. As did the eyes of many other men from all three clans.

That bothered him too.

He couldn't fathom the sway she held over the men. Aye, she was lovely, but she was covered in blood and gore, her hair was sawed off, she shouted out orders to everyone, she was too busy to give a whit about her patients' feelings, and when an injury turned out to be more serious than she thought, she even cursed like one of his men. He couldn't remember how many times he'd heard "God's blood!" explode from her mouth.

His eyes went back to following her—just like the other men—except his gaze was filled with annoyance. When would she be done? Where would she sleep? Why wouldn't she eat the food he'd brought her?

He'd just caught Niall's eye and signaled him over when the outer door opened with a squeak. Callum and Hamish entered and wound their way toward him between the beds.

News on Murray, then, and by the looks on their faces, not good.

He was about to stand and tell them he'd meet them outside, when Amber pinned him with a stern gaze. She jerked her head toward the door, indicating for him to leave. Even though it had been his plan to go all along, his spine stiffened, and he found himself wanting to do the exact opposite of whatever she wanted. The woman had no idea how to ask for anything, she just gave orders.

He rose slowly, staring back at her, his own face stern, until she huffed and spun away. Well, that was something. At least she'd turned away first.

Rolling his eyes at his childish behavior, he gave Adaira's arm one final squeeze before intercepting Niall, who was rushing toward him.

"Has Amber eaten anything?" he asked the steward. Idiot question. He knew she hadn't; he'd been watching her. "Maybe put the food on a slice of bread and feed her a bite while she works."

The steward's mouth dropped open. "I doona think she'll take it. When she's hungry—famished—she'll eat. Not before then."

"She needs to take care of herself too."

"Aye, but she won't. Not before she knows everyone is safe. 'Twas the same with her grandmother."

"And did you tell her to choose one of the bedchambers upstairs? I had the fires lit."

"Laird McKay, she willna leave the wounded."

Lachlan rubbed his hand over his eyes. God's truth, he was tired. He could only imagine how exhausted she was. "Make her a bed down here, then, and tell her if she doesn't at least sit on it and put her foot up, I'll...I'll..." he tried to think of something the healer back home had an aversion to. "I'll release my hounds into the sick room."

"It willna work. Amber likes dogs." He looked at Lachlan curiously. "I didn't realize you brought dogs with you."

"I didn't. What will work then?"

Niall shrugged his shoulders. "Naught. I'll make a bed nearby, and if she's tired enough and feels she isna needed at the moment, she will rest."

Lachlan sighed. "Aye. Go do it then."

The steward nodded and headed to the stairs. Lachlan looked one last time at Amber's back as she leaned over a patient, her shaggy hair, still home to several wood chips, irritating him as much as her limp—for what both things represented—and strode toward the door. It would do him good to get some air.

The morning sun was bright in his eyes after the dim light of the keep, and he raised a hand to shield them as he made his way down to the bailey. He glanced around, amazed to see it looked like naught had happened here last night. It was a miracle he and his men had taken over the castle with such little damage—to it and to the men. No deaths, and Amber said everyone, including Adaira, would heal.

That wasn't to say the castle was safe. Nay, the walls were crumbling and the portcullis was rusted, not to mention the poor training of the guards. He had much work to do to get Castle MacPherson repaired, more safety measures in place, and its warriors properly trained, if people were to be protected in the future. Until then, he was beholden to the irritating, redheaded witch inside, who gave too much of herself and expected too little in return—unless it was her demand that he be their laird.

"What did you find?" he asked as he joined Callum and Hamish in the bailey, the ground only somewhat chewed up from the fighting.

"Machar Murray is gone," Callum said.

Lachlan closed his eyes briefly. "As I suspected." The bile rose in his throat, but he swallowed it down. They would begin their search again. This time, they had a name and a place to start.

The rat had nowhere to hide.

"We couldnae find any more escape routes in the keep, but there were three dug in recent years from other places—two from the barracks and one from the chapel. Both lead outside the perimeter wall."

"Have you spoken to the MacPhersons? Did anyone else know?"

"Nay, I doona think so. Not at the barracks, anyway. Murray dug the tunnel under a chamber his personal guard used—the three we think attacked Hamish and Adaira. Everyone called them the laird's dogs. No one was allowed into the chamber but them. Come have a look."

They strode across the open area toward a long, low building on the far side of the bailey. "What of the chapel?" Lachlan asked. "You think the priest was in on Murray's escape?"

"I wouldnae be surprised. 'Tis said he ran out in fright last night rather than tend to his people." Callum couldn't stand hypocrisy.

"Being a coward doesn't make one guilty, Brother."

"Aye, just unworthy of judging others, which the MacPhersons said he did with great enthusiasm."

Lachlan had known many brave priests in his day, but he'd also known the opposite. Like all men, they were fallible. Wearing the cloth no more made you a worthy leader than wearing the laird's mantle.

As they neared the barracks, he noticed several broken wooden crates, a few arrows still stuck in the pile of firewood that had tumbled out. The wood chips on the ground looked like those he'd seen in Amber's hair. "What happened here?"

Hamish tugged on the ends of his beard. "Murray, we think. An ambush once the fighting was o'er. 'Tis a good thing your lass noticed the torches were out, or she'd be dead. Me too, most likely."

Dead? Lachlan stopped in his tracks and stared at Hamish, who'd also come to a stop. The blood began to pound in his veins. "You speak of Amber?"

"Aye. The arrows were intended for her. I barely had time to push her behind the crate before we were attacked."

Lachlan backtracked to the knocked-over crates of firewood, feeling like he'd swallowed a handful of gravel. That's why she'd had wood chips in her hair, and why she'd been running in a panic through the bailey last night.

Machar Murray had just tried to murder her.

The pulse thrummed in his temples, and he found

himself wanting to wrap his fingers around the rat's neck—and not only for his brother this time, but for Amber as well.

He pinched the bridge of his nose and tried to get past the rising anger, focus on the facts. "Someone— possibly Machar Murray—stayed behind, risked capture and certain death in order to kill her?"

Callum reached down and pulled out an arrow to give to Lachlan. It was newly made, with a distinctive knot in the twine and warp to the shaft. The feathers were from a raven, and the metal still shiny in places. "'Twas Murray, all right," Callum said. "That's his arrow. I heard he makes them himself, doesn't let anyone else use them. And Niall did say he was obsessed with Amber. She held him off for five years. He must think she arranged the attack."

Callum had a look in his eye that Lachlan recognized—he was plotting—and every one of Lachlan's muscles tensed in anticipation: he just knew this plot somehow involved Amber.

Sometimes his foster brother was too good at strategizing.

Still, he had to listen. "Go on."

"He'll harbor that hatred. That obsession. He wouldnae like his 'possession' defying him…unless, of course, she was involved somehow with his escape."

Lachlan's hand had clenched into a fist at the suggestion, and he had to force himself to relax it. "I doona think that's the case."

"Aye, but when Murray's plot to take o'er the MacKays failed, he killed your brother's wife so she couldnae identify him."

"I said 'tis not the case. He and Amber were not involved, and she did not help him."

"Most likely, but he may still return for her. Either to kill or abduct her. He willna be able to let her go."

Lachlan let out a tense breath and rubbed his palm over his jaw. "So…you want to use her as bait."

"'Tis a possibility worth considering."

He nodded, but his stomach had tied into knots. His forced calm deserted him at the thought of the danger it would put her in—danger she'd courted for so long already. Snapping the arrow in half, he tossed it to the ground and resumed his trek to the barracks. "She ne'er should have stayed with the clan when she was in such peril. She should have left long ago. 'Tis a miracle he didn't try to kill her sooner."

"Aye. But she's stubborn. And dedicated. 'Twould be difficult for her to leave."

"Bah, difficult or not, she should have done it to save her life. And her clan should have made her go. They asked too much of her. They still do."

They reached the barracks, and Lachlan paused with his hand on the door. "He'll come back for her, have no doubt. I want four guards on her at all times until he's caught."

"She willna take well to that," Callum said. "Put the guards on her, but let them know she canna suspect their true purpose. They can pretend to be among the 'besotted.'"

Hamish grunted in amusement. "I doona think they'll have to pretend. Half the men have already gone in for treatment just to see her, and for injuries they wouldnae have bothered with before."

Lachlan rounded on his second-in-command, the heat of his anger turning to deadly calm. "I will beat the next man bloody who does that—whether he's a MacKay, MacLean, or MacPherson. She's already worked to the bone. She hasn't slept or eaten, and her own injury goes untreated."

"Nay, I'll beat the MacLeans," Callum said.

Hamish's amusement faded, and he squeezed the back of his neck with his palm. "Aye, you're right, of course. I ne'er thought of that. I shall tell them."

"You do that. And tell them to leave her alone, while you're at it. If she doesn't smile back or gesture them over, she doesn't want their attention."

"Aye, Laird."

They entered the barracks, and Lachlan was surprised to see the MacPhersons laughing and joking with his and Callum's men. They were still under guard, and the warriors took their task seriously, but the MacPhersons didn't seem to mind.

A cheer went up when they saw Lachlan and Callum. "Laird MacKay! Laird MacLean!" several of the MacPhersons shouted. Some of them had imbibed too much, despite the midmorning hour, and an air of celebration permeated the room.

One of the men started singing—a song of victory—and Lachlan's anger slowly dissipated beneath the hope and good cheer that filled the room. Aye, these were decent people, as Amber had said, and he had no doubt they loved and appreciated her very much.

In the absence of a laird or clergy who cared for them, they'd turned to their healer. She had become their leader in the face of Machar Murray's treachery, and she would likely no more abandon her clan—despite the dangers to herself—than he would abandon his. He sighed, caught Callum's smiling gaze, and accepted the mug of ale someone handed to him. He even sang a few bars of the song.

'Twas one of his favorites, and he'd sung it many times after a battle.

"Laird MacKay!"

He looked up and saw the big man he'd taken down on the wall last night—the one with the bushy beard and hearty laugh. Aye, his laugh was still hearty, and Lachlan couldn't help smiling.

He nodded at the MacPherson. "Are you all right, then? I didn't hurt you?"

The big man laughed and pounded his stomach. "It takes more than a scrawny whelp of a man like yourself to hurt ol' Tavis."

"More like too much ale and an errant chicken bone!" someone else shouted.

Everyone laughed, including Tavis. When he caught his breath, he turned his shining face to Lachlan. "'Tis said you are to be our new laird."

The room quieted. Every MacPherson stared at him, hope on their faces as they waited for his answer.

Lachlan stared back at them. They were good-hearted men who'd been ground into the earth far too long. How could he step on them once again?

"Aye, I suppose I am. If I doona, I'm sure Amber will come after me, and I wouldnae want to risk her grim countenance."

The men all laughed again, even more excited now. One of them shouted out, "Our Amber's an angel!"

Another yelled, "She's our Queen of Elfame!"

"Nay, she's none of that," Tavis said. "She's the pride of Clan MacPherson."

✦

"What are you doing?" Amber shouted up at Niall as he struggled to carry bedding down the flight of stairs to the great hall. She signaled for Mary to take over bandaging the shoulder of the MacKay warrior she was working on, then limped across the room to give Niall a much needed hand.

"I'm setting up a bed for you down here. On orders from our new laird."

She stopped in her tracks, her arms full of the pillows and quilts Niall had given her. "You're what?"

"Aye, he wants you to sleep and eat. He's concerned you're working too hard, so I'm to build you a bed down here and hand feed you as you tend the wounded."

Amber's jaw dropped open in shock. "Feed me? Has he lost his mind?"

"Aye, he must have if he thinks he can make you do anything you doona want to do."

She scowled at him. "Since when has he become our laird?"

"Since you blackmailed him and he complied."

"I did no such thing."

"Aye, you did. You said you wouldnae help Adaira unless he became our laird, which we both know is a lie."

"Nay, I said I would help Adaira, and he should bloody well help us too!" That was what she'd said, wasn't it?

"Well, either way, we now have a new laird."

"Since when? Adaira isna even healed yet."

"Since he told the lads in the barracks 'twas so." Niall pushed two benches together against the wall and laid several quilts and a pillow over them. "Do you think he'll want us to change our name?"

"What are you talking about? You're full of nonsense this morning."

"Well, if he willna become a MacPherson, we'll have to become MacKays, aye?"

Amber handed off her last pillow and placed her hands on her hips. 'Twas no wee matter to change a clan's name.

"O'er my dead body!"

"Doona fash, Amber. He's a decent man. More than decent. I'm sure he wouldnae ask such a thing of us. Especially if you were nice to him."

"Nice to him?"

"Aye."

"How nice?"

"Well, it wouldnae hurt you to smile at him once in a while, now would it? He isna like the other men here. I'm sure he knows many fine women and willna have his head turned by a simple smile."

Many fine women.

The words echoed in Amber's head as she imagined Lachlan surrounded by well-groomed women wearing expensive silks and fine woolen arisaids, their hair brushed and styled, their hands and nails clean.

She looked down at her own hands. Blood was caked in the lines at her wrists and under her fingernails, despite washing them regularly last night and this morning. And not one nail was smooth. Aye, they were broken and jagged, like her hair. She had tried to smooth them out as she didn't want to scratch her patients, but she hadn't done so in a uniform shape, that's for sure.

Not that she cared. Besides, Lachlan was responsible for half of her nails breaking when he'd dragged her across the scrubby field, and she'd be happy to tell him that if he dared to comment.

Niall waved a hand at her arisaid as he continued. "Of course, he may turn his head because of the blood, dirt, and God knows what else on your clothes. Not to mention the state of your hair."

Amber almost raised her hands to smooth her jagged tresses. She caught herself halfway and slammed her arms back down to her sides. "If he doesn't like the way I look—or smell, for that matter—he can leave."

"Or you can take a moment for yourself to wash up and have a sleep."

She narrowed her eyes at him. "Niall MacPherson, are you trying to manipulate me?"

"I would ne'er do such a thing, because it would ne'er work."

She scoffed, then picked up the last quilt, which sat on a nearby chair, and handed it to him. As he laid it on the bed, she couldn't help but think how comfortable the wee nest looked. Aye, she was tired, and her ankle felt like it had been pounded by the MacPherson blacksmith on the forge—with double hammers.

He patted the pile of blankets. "If you sit, lass, I'll be able to sit too, and my bones do ache. You can rest your foot in my lap, and I'll look at your ankle."

"So, 'tis blackmail, then, is it?"

"Aye, I've learned from the best."

Amber looked back at her patients, thinking on the state of each one before deciding everything was under control. She lifted herself onto the makeshift bed.

"Lie back," Niall instructed as he sat on the end.

She did with a groan, her eyes closing as her head hit the pillow, her feet lifting. Niall grasped her sore foot gently and worked to loosen the laces on the boots Hamish had cinched tight. When Niall slipped the first one off, she pressed her forearm across her eyes and bit her lip to stop from crying out.

God's blood, that hurt.

His fingers loosened the ribbon at her knee then pulled down her sock and unwrapped the binding. Amber peeked out from beneath her arm when he clucked with concern. Her entire ankle and foot were swollen, despite having been strapped up, and it had darkened to an ugly, black bruise.

"What can I do for it?" Niall asked.

The concern in his voice almost brought tears to her eyes. Aye, she was tired.

"I've checked it. 'Tis not broken, just a sprain."

"A bad one, by the looks of it. Can you stay off it?"

She laughed, unable to help herself. "Nay, I canna stay off it." Then she sighed and closed her eyes again, her body all but melting into the bedding. "I promise to use the cane more, and I'll have a wee rest right now. That'll help. Have Mary bind it for me while I close my eyes, then lace my boot back up—tight. If I have time later on, I'll go down to the loch and dip my foot in for a few minutes. The cold water will take down some of the swelling."

"You willna have time, of course, so I'll bring water in a bowl from the well."

"Aye. Thank you, Niall."

"Nay, thank you, Amber. You came back to help us after we couldnae help you."

She reached out with her hand and squeezed his. "You did help. You got me out of the castle and defied Laird Murray to do so. We all did the best that we could under terrible circumstances."

"And now he's gone. Maybe not dead, but gone for good from our lives. God sent us a miracle when he sent us Lachlan MacKay."

"I'm not sure Lachlan would think of it that way. Callum either. They may have saved us, but our 'miracle' came at a terrible price to Clan MacKay. He is much aggrieved, though he may not show it."

She thought back to the emotion she'd heard in his voice when he spoke of his brother Donald, and of Machar Murray. Aye, he hated Machar as strongly as he'd loved his brother.

"Have you thought on what I said to you before you went into the tunnel?"

She cracked open an eye to look at him, trying to get her sluggish mind working again. "What would that be?"

"About taking time for your own life now. Finding a good man, a decent man, and having a house full of bairns. You have a lot to give, Amber MacPherson, even though you pretend to be so fierce at times."

"I am fierce. I would ne'er have survived if I wasn't."

"Aye, but you're also a mother bear, and you should be filling your den with cubs who tumble all o'er you."

Amber closed her eyes again. She loved children, but the last thing on her mind these past five years had been finding a husband and having a family. How could she, when she'd been so busy protecting her clan and herself from Machar Murray? She didn't dream of kissing a handsome laird; she had nightmares of being raped by one.

And her nightmare had almost become a reality. If not for Lachlan and his men, she would most likely be dead or back in the brutal embrace of her former laird.

Still, she knew Niall well. Knew that he had a plan lurking in the back of his mind.

"And this decent man you mentioned wouldnae be Lachlan MacKay, now, would he?" she asked.

"Aye, he's decent and strong enough to protect you and those you love. Would it be so wrong to try and catch the eye of a laird? Especially one as loyal, braw, and caring as him? He ordered me to feed you and make you a bed."

"And that's a good trait?"

"Aye, Amber. The man willna use you. He cares for your well-being and asks for naught in return."

"Give him time. He'll be wanting a kiss at least— once I wash and change my arisaid, anyway."

"And what's the matter with that? 'Tis hard for you to imagine, after defending yourself from Murray, but being intimate with a person you love is one of the most beautiful and pleasurable acts God gave us. You may find yourself wanting to kiss him back—and more."

Amber's eyes popped open, and she stared at Niall for a moment in shock before clapping her hands over her ears. "Och! I canna believe you said that. God's blood, I may have to pour hot wax in my ears to burn out the words! Niall MacPherson, you canna talk to me about tupping!"

"Aye, well, you canna curse in such a manner or say 'tupping'! I have long ago poured hot wax into my ears to keep your curses out."

Amber tried to hold it in, but she burst out laughing. Niall joined her and they couldn't stop for nigh on several minutes. 'Twas a good release after all they'd been through.

When the laughter subsided, she sighed—long and deep. Then she yawned. She tried to say something else, something about Lachlan MacKay and his love of fine women, tried to say that the state of her clothes, her hair, was not Niall's concern. But the black hole of exhaustion dragged her under like a demon dragging a sinner to hell, and she slept.

Five

AMBER SURFACED SLOWLY, STILL LOST AMIDST A DREAM of fine silks and linens. The sounds around her were muted, the lights and colors blurry. She drifted in a sea of contentment that lulled her under again and again. This time, when she crested the cocooned warmth, she managed to open her heavy eyelids.

A man sat at the end of her bed, but he didn't frighten her, didn't make her feel like she had to protect herself. Nay, he made her feel safe. She stared at his profile—his head leaning against the stone wall, his eyes closed, his chest rising and falling evenly. She blinked, losing focus, and had to drag herself back from the depths again so she could continue her perusal.

Her foot rested on his lap like it had with Niall; the snug pressure around her ankle would be a bandage, her sock pulled up to cover it. Her shoe wasn't tied yet, and she wriggled her toes. His hand closed gently over them, stroked them.

Aye, that felt right too.

She drifted back under then opened her eyes a third time to gaze at his face—a strong jaw darkened with several days' worth of stubble, his lips relaxed, the lower one soft and rounded, the top one slightly firmer, the small bump in his nose a testament to his willingness to fight.

His eyelashes fanned out against his cheeks, hiding the gaze she wanted to see. She must have made a noise, a small sound of enquiry, for he turned his head and looked at her. They locked eyes. She stared to her heart's content, drowning in the dark-blue color, fascinated by the laugh lines that fanned out from the corners. He'd pushed his hair behind his ears, and it framed the strong planes of his face.

When she saw his lips move, heard a whispered sound, she wanted to answer, wanted to say his name—Lachlan—but she couldn't move her tongue to push the word past her teeth.

Her lids weighed down, and she gave in with a sigh, drifting under, hoping he'd still be there when she woke up. She wanted to touch him this time. Scratch her fingers through the rough growth on his face. Wanted to sit up and press her lips to the temptation of his.

Wanted a kiss.

Surely, she must be dreaming.

Moments later, or what felt like moments, she surfaced again to the sounds of yelling. Groaning, she opened gritty, heavy eyes. She must have slept several hours more, going by the slant of the shadows through the high, narrow windows and quality of the light.

The end of her bed was empty and her shoe tied tightly over her ankle. Her brow furrowed. Lachlan had been sitting there, holding her foot. Or had she dreamed that? The MacKay laird must have better things to do than watch her sleep. But she felt the weight of his hand holding her toes and the depth of his eyes as he gazed at her.

Aye, she must have dreamed it. All that nonsense talk from Niall about taking a husband, Lachlan MacKay in particular.

A screeching voice dragged her attention across the room, and she pushed herself up, dropping her feet to the floor. She winced as her foot nudged the bench. Her body ached, and her stomach felt like it gnawed on itself in hunger.

She recognized the man yelling by the long, tan-colored tunic he wore belted at the waist. A scowl creased her face. Rising from the bed, she intended to march over there, but the pain in her foot was even worse than before. All she could do was hobble.

"Get out! Get out!" he yelled, his back to Amber, his black hair clipped short. When the priest waved his arms and darted forward, she saw her friend Isla, heavily pregnant and looking distressed, retreating to the door, her hands pressed into the small of her back.

"Isla, wait!" she called out.

Relief flooded Isla's face as she saw Amber over Father Odhran's shoulder. He spun around, hatred darkening his countenance. He made the sign of the cross at the sight of her, and Amber's hackles rose. God's blood, she knew it was wrong to detest a priest, but this man was the worst of his kind—condemning and bigoted. And according to almost everyone, he'd been the first to run last night when the attack on the castle began.

"If you're not here to provide comfort to the wounded, Father, leave."

"Nay, I shall protect them from you, witch. Be gone from our laird's castle."

He actually made a flicking motion at her, as if to cast her out. She almost laughed, but she was too tired and sore and worried about Isla, who hovered in the background looking harassed and scared, her face pinched in discomfort.

"Which laird would that be? Your friend Machar Murray, who's been forced out and will be hanged if he e'er shows his face here again? Or Laird MacKay, whose cousin and clansmen I've been healing all last night and this morning? Murray's reign is over, Father, and I doona think Laird MacKay will be as willing to condemn good folk as you are."

"He will condemn you when I tell him you're a witch. Look at you, covered in the blood of your sacrifices, dressed to tempt a man, your hair chopped off and surely used in some spell—maybe given to the devil as payment."

Amber's eyes widened in disbelief. Did he really believe what he was saying? And how could anyone interpret her current state of disarray as *tempting*? "'Tis the blood of the wounded, you wee ablach. And I cut off my hair to escape Machar Murray. Surely even you would consider it a grievous act to—"

"There is no more grievous act than what you do to this woman." The priest swung around to point a condemning finger at Isla, who shrank back against one of the empty beds. "'Tis Eve's sin she pays for with every contraction in her belly, every tear in her womb. God condemned all women with the pain of childbirth. 'Tis the work of the devil to take that pain away with your potions and witch's hands."

He must be referring to the massage she performed on the pregnant women. She made a sound in the back of her throat—one of anger and disgust. She'd heard Father Odhran preach this shite before, knew that he visited the clan women to try to scare them away from coming to her for help, but thank the Lord he'd been seen as an outsider, brought on after Machar Murray had taken over, and they didn't listen.

She searched around for something to shoo him off, to force him out of the keep, and spotted her cane. Nay, that might hurt him if things got out of control. Instead, she picked up a thin twig from the floor. She was about to wave it at him when he continued speaking: "And 'tis not for you to say what a man can or canna do. 'Tis God's will for you to submit to men in all ways, to grow bairns in your belly and suffer in their passage. Eve gave Adam the apple. You will all pay for that sin!"

Eyes hot, chest and jaw tight with anger, she dropped the twig. Amber limped toward her cane, feeling as if steam must be pouring from her ears.

She'd just laid her hand on the weapon, for that's what it had become, when the door squeaked open. Lachlan strode in, gaze falling first on the women before focusing on the priest. He stopped to whisper a few words to Isla and help her onto the bed before continuing forward.

Father Odhran turned around slowly and shrank before Lachlan. It's not that the MacKay laird threatened him—or anyone—but he exuded such force and command, with an underlying edge of danger, no one would dare cross him.

Amber found herself unable to speak under the weight of his presence, and she could do naught but stare at him, noticing the way his hair, the color of a young doe, had fallen across his forehead, and his shoulders filled out his linen shirt—not to mention the wee muscle that twitched in his jaw, belying his calm.

"Father Odhran, I am Lachlan MacKay, laird of Clan MacKay and Clan MacPherson. 'Tis good to have a man of God tending to the spiritual needs of the wounded and helping such a fine healer as Amber, but I would speak to you outside about Machar Murray. I'm sure you wouldnae want to disturb anyone here."

She let out a squawk at that, and Lachlan lifted his gaze to hers, eyes narrow and direct. Then he looked down her arm, at her closed fist gripping the cane. "I'm glad you're using the cane for support, Amber. I wouldnae want you to do any further damage to your ankle—or anything else. 'Twould make me happy if you ate something while I speak to the priest. 'Tis time to take care of yourself for a change."

She was about to say, "I'm not hungry," but just the mention of food caused her stomach to growl angrily.

The priest gasped and crossed himself again. "'Tis the demon inside her, Laird, wanting to get out. No one is safe as long as she's here!"

"'Tis an empty stomach, Father, wanting to be filled. Amber has been too busy tending the wounded to eat." He took the priest's arm, not forcefully, but with the expectation of obedience, and led him to the exit. "Come now, before you wake my cousin."

When the door closed with a soft thud behind them, Isla let out a heartfelt sigh. "Oh, Amber, did you see him? I swear if I weren't already with bairn and in love with Alban, I'd be mooning over him like all the other young lasses in the bailey." She struggled to get off the bed, and Amber hobbled to help her. "I canna believe Laird Murray is gone and Lachlan MacKay has taken o'er," Isla continued as she clapped her hands together. "Can you imagine? I've heard stories of Gregor MacLeod's foster sons, and now one of them is here. Callum too, I'm told, although I havenae seen him."

"Aye, he's here, although he's betrothed to a lass who likes to throw daggers, so our lasses need not waste their time mooning over him."

"Daggers! She sounds like you."

Amber huffed. "I doona throw daggers! I stitch people up from thrown daggers."

"The daggers you throw are with your eyes and mouth—and such bonnie eyes and mouth too—'tis why all the lads love you and our priest does not. But look at your poor hair. What happened to it?"

"Machar Murray, that's what happened."

Isla reached up and ran her fingers through the uneven tresses, eyes assessing. "Did he cut it off?"

"Nay, I did. Niall got me out of the castle, but I had to dress up like a lad. I rode straight into the MacKay ambush. The laird didn't know I was a lass till after."

Isla stared at her, eyes wide, mouth open as if to catch flies, then she burst out laughing.

Amber couldn't help smiling back. "'Twas not a laughing matter at the time, I assure you."

"Aye, I'm sure, 'tis just...you are the last of us to be mistaken for a lad, now, aren't you? Doona we all wish we were as well-endowed as you and had as lovely a face. And you not caring a whit about it." She played with Amber's hair again, lifting parts, arranging it around her face. Isla had an eye for style. "What did you use to cut it? An axe?"

"Not as bad as that, but almost. 'Twas my own fault, though. I was in a rush."

Isla rested her hands on Amber's shoulders and squeezed. "Aye, and frightened, no doubt."

She nodded and had to swallow to loosen her suddenly tight throat. "He locked me in his bedchamber while he spoke to his dogs, but Niall had a key. He took a great risk."

Isla pulled her into a tight hug. "He loves you. We all do. I doona know what I would have done if you hadn't been here for my pregnancy. What any of us would have done, if not for you."

"Och, you're speaking nonsense now. You would have been all right. All of you. Speaking of the bairn, how are you? I saw you holding your back?"

"Aye, 'tis a wee bit sore, but not that bad. I was checking on you, mostly. I would have come sooner, but Alban wouldnae allow it."

"And he was right. A battlefield is no place for a pregnant woman."

Isla gave her a sly grin. "Truth be told, I like it when he becomes all commanding."

Amber laughed—an unexpected burst from deep in her chest. "Aye, I imagine you do." Alban was short, shorter than his wife, and not one to throw his weight around, although no one would call him weak. Isla was lucky to have him and the bairn she would soon bring into this world—with Amber's help, no matter what Father Odhran said.

An unwelcome pang of envy filled her heart, and her eyes widened in surprise. She'd ne'er wanted bairns before, ne'er even thought of them or of finding a lad to marry despite how many had come knocking. She'd always considered men's interest in her to be more of a nuisance than a boon.

But now…now something else beat at her chest. Put there by Niall's words, no doubt.

Not that there was anyone in the clan she wanted to marry. Still…her eyes drifted past Isla's shoulder to the door through which Lachlan and Father Odhran had disappeared. That funny feeling in her chest grew, and she shook her head in exasperation.

'Twas hunger, naught else.

"I need to eat. I swear my stomach will turn inside out, it's so empty." On cue, her belly let out another loud growl. She turned and looked around the room, spotting some food by her bed. How had she missed it?

Using her cane, she hurried over as fast as she could, her mouth salivating when she saw the oats and berries with milk, the dried meat and a glass of mead. "Doona watch me eat, Isla. It willna be a bonnie sight." She scooped up the oats first and lifted spoonful after spoonful into her mouth, almost desperate. The milk helped wash it down. She finished the meat and mead at a more leisurely pace.

Isla had wandered to the door and cracked it open to peek outside. "The laird's talking to Father Odhran, and the father doesn't look happy. Nay, he's waving his arms about and pointing back this way."

"What's Lachlan doing?" Amber asked.

"He's standing still, arms over his chest, looking…well, not stern, exactly, and not forbidding, but…implacable."

"*Implacable*, that's a good word."

"Aye. 'Tis one I use to describe my Alban, sometimes. Stubborn, yes, but also implacable." She squealed softly. "Oh, that must be Callum! He's there now too, and also braw! What did they feed those lads at Clan MacLeod? Although Callum's not stoic at all. Nay, he's frowning at Father Odhran…and he just looked at Lachlan and rolled his eyes. I like him."

"Me too." She finished her food and went to check on her patients. Five were still there, Adaira being the worst of them, so she crossed to the sleeping lass first. The girl was lucky not to have been wounded more seriously than she was. The sword had gone in clean, nothing but a nick to her bowels, and that not a puncture.

Amber had worked hard to sew up the damage both inside her body and out before dousing the wound with a salve to help the healing. The lass would have only clear broth and healing herbs to eat for a while, but as long as the injury didn't become infected, she should heal.

After washing her hands, she pulled back the dressing and eyed the cut. 'Twas slightly red and swollen, but not overly so. And it wasn't hot to the touch.

She applied more salve, redressed it, then moved to another patient, who'd broken his leg when he fell off the wall. Amber had set the bone, something she'd done numerous times over the years, and secured it tight, so the bone would knit back together in a straight line.

"How are you, John?" she asked, pressing her hand to his forehead.

"Tired. I canna keep my eyes open."

"Aye, that's to be expected. Your body is working hard to heal, and the herbs I gave you will make you sleepy. I'll reduce the amount as the days go by."

"Thank you, lass."

She tucked the blanket around him again then moved on to her next patient, and the next. Finally, she was on the last one, Earc, who'd banged his head and inhaled water when he'd fallen into the river defending Adaira from the laird's dogs.

"How do your lungs feel?" she asked him, pressing her ear to his chest to listen to him breathe.

"A wee bit heavy, but not too bad."

She saw the puppy dog look in his eyes when she straightened, and she frowned at him, so there'd be no misinterpretation. "Doona get any ideas, Earc. Ask any MacPherson lad around, and they'll tell you I am not interested in being anyone's dearling."

"Aye," he said, "you'll be wanting a better man than me." But the look in his eyes didn't go away.

Amber sighed, grabbed a candle and held it in front of his pupils to see how they reacted to the light. Normal.

"If you doona have any more headaches or dizziness, you can leave in the morning. But if you find yourself vomiting, unable to wake easily, or feverish, come back and see me."

"Aye, lass, for sure I will."

She'd just replaced the candle in its holder when Isla called out from the door. "They're coming back!"

Amber jumped, suddenly self-conscious, and found herself tucking the jagged ends of her hair behind her ears.

"Why doona you treat yourself to a bath now, lass," Niall called down to her from the top of the stairs. "There's one ready in the upstairs room, along with a fresh arisaid and shift that used to belong to Laird MacPherson's mother. I'll have the laundress wash your dirty one—just put it outside the door in the hall. And doona worry about anything down here. Mary will be back to watch o'er your patients."

She hesitated then hurried for the stairs before the men entered the keep. It wasn't running away if she really did want to bathe. Not that she cared if Lachlan saw her like this—or Callum, for that matter.

At the top, she gave Niall a quick hug. "When is Finola returning? You shouldnae be up and down these steps so much."

"She was here earlier when you slept. She's helping Cook organize the supplies, so we have enough to feed everyone."

"The MacKays brought their own supplies. I saw the wagons full at their camp. Adaira hid in one of them to get here."

"Aye, but they'll be here longer now until we know for sure Murray is caught. We doona want him sneaking back in."

Her stomach clenched, and she thought back on the arrow whizzing past her head last night. "Nay, we doona. Do you think—"

The outside door squeaked open, causing Amber to jump into motion, her previous worry forgotten. The lairds entered the keep below as she limped down the narrow passageway and out of sight of the great hall. Candles in sconces lined the stone walls, as well as faded and worn hangings intended to keep out the cold on a winter's night.

Uncertain which chamber Niall intended her to use, she tried several rooms, most of them cold, until she saw one halfway down the passageway with a roaring fire, fresh sheets and quilts on the bed, and a jug on the side table.

A standing wood screen inlaid with colorful shells was set up on the far side of the bed, and Amber peeked around the corner to see a tub filled with steaming water. A bar of soap pressed with rose petals and a large, soft-looking bath linen and facecloth lay on a table beside it.

Amber dipped her hand into the water and groaned. 'Twas the perfect temperature. God bless Niall. She quickly stripped out of her clothes and put them in a pile outside the door as he'd asked, then shut it but didn't lock it in case he or Finola wanted to get in.

Limping back to the tub, her cane left on the bed, she carefully eased herself into the water, keeping her sore foot elevated on the rim. She sank backward with a sigh, blissfully relaxed against the wooden sides worn smooth from years of use.

The water covered her to the tops of her shoulders, and her breasts bobbed to the surface. Wetting the soap and facecloth, she washed off all the sweat, blood, and dirt she'd accumulated over the last two difficult days. She tipped her head back and rinsed her hair too, amazed at how it felt in the water now that it was short. Lathering up the soap in her hands, she scrubbed them into her hair several times to get out the grime.

When she saw a few wood chips and a twig floating in the water, she laughed—although, really 'twas no laughing matter. The wood chips had lodged in her hair after the arrow had hit the barrel she'd hidden behind last night, and the twigs could have been from either her fall from the wall or her horse. Or being dragged through the scrub brush. Aye, that was probably it. All thanks to Lachlan MacKay.

No wonder Father Odhran had disparaged her appearance. She scooped out the offending debris and dropped it on the table to throw in the fire later.

Settling back again, she closed her eyes and let herself drift. The clan's worries certainly weren't over—at least not until Machar Murray was caught and justice served—but certainly everyone felt safer now that Lachlan had declared himself laird of Clan MacPherson. People had hope again, and brighter futures. Something none of them—certainly not Amber—had thought about for a while.

Her hands rested on her breasts, and she gently squeezed the mounds. Maybe a bairn would suckle there one day. Her fingers drifted lower, over the sensitive skin surrounding her nipples, which had hardened into pointed nubs.

Or a man.

She leaned her head back, eyes closed, and imagined Lachlan, his hair loose around his face, his eyes hot on hers. The water lapped at his bare shoulders as he sat in the tub across from her, the muscles in his chest heavy and defined, covered in a sprinkling of dark hair.

She strummed her thumbs over her nipples as he watched her, rubbing back and forth, then circling the tips and squeezing them just hard enough to make her breath whoosh from her lungs.

Leaning forward, he lowered his head, his breath a tease on her wet skin. Digging her hands into his hair, she held on as his hot and needy mouth closed over a breast and sucked. First one, then the other, rolling her nipples across his tongue. His hand slid down her body and between her spread legs to rub over and inside her swollen folds with heavy, rhythmic strokes. Up and down... up and down as he continued to nuzzle her breasts.

She thrust her hips to meet his fingers, and water splashed over the edge of the tub. The sound brought her back to the present to find the chamber empty and quiet except for her own stifled moans and the crackling of the fire. She sighed. She might be a virgin, but she was no stranger to self-pleasure.

Unfortunately, now wasn't the time. Poor Niall or Finola could walk in on her at any moment, and if Niall keeled over from the shock of finding her stroking her own body, she'd never forgive herself.

A wry smile tilted her lips as frustration mixed with embarrassment simmered through her. She'd never felt so good so quickly before. Or lost herself in that kind of fantasy—a man watching her, touching her.

No, not just a man. Her laird, which somehow made it hotter, caused a renewal of the pulsing in her thighs, a heaviness in her core that begged for release.

Her hands slid down her body and she hugged

herself, squeezing with all her might to relieve the ache. The emptiness.

And tried not to think about Lachlan MacKay as she lay wet and wanting in the tub.

≈∂

Lachlan climbed the stairs with heavy legs and gritty eyes, barely able to contain a yawn. He'd been awake now for what seemed like days. He'd only stolen small amounts of sleep in the week leading up to the attack, and had none last night. He'd managed to rest for a short time while Amber slept in the great hall, taking Niall's place at the end of her makeshift bed in order to keep her foot raised, but he hadn't actually drifted off. He'd been too attuned to her, listening for her breath or any wee sigh, aware of any movement.

Which he found…confusing.

He'd just met the lass, so why did he feel this way? She was bonnie, aye, but he'd known many bonnie lasses in his day. Although none quite as lovely as she. Which said a lot, considering he had yet to see her face clean—or even showing a smile.

God forbid she did that, or he may end up like all the other besotted men in her clan—and now his and Callum's—following her around like puppies.

But this feeling, this urge, wasn't about lust, although he certainly felt that—had felt it even when he'd thought her a lad, which had confounded him to no end and would set him up for much teasing if his foster brothers ever found out. Nay, the urge that confused him was the need to protect her. To care for her.

And not in the general sense that he cared for others. This was something very specifically Amber.

Maybe the need existed because he'd fought with her, hurt her when he had to restrain her. Or maybe because she'd been in danger for so long and still was, if the arrow attack last night was any indication. Or because he'd seen how she took care of everyone else and had no one to take care of her.

Machar Murray may have been the MacPherson's laird, but she was their leader.

She was also unusual in that most of the unmarried young lasses he knew tried to catch his eye—either by enticing him or being agreeable. Amber, on the other hand, did neither. She argued with him, ordered him and everyone else about, and often cursed up a storm. She had no agenda other than doing what was best for her clan—and if that meant blackmailing him, she'd do that too.

What would it feel like to be on the receiving end of such care and loyalty from a woman?

His mother had never provided it. She'd been distant at best, manipulative and controlling at worst. And he had no sisters, aunts, or grandmothers to provide it. No close female friends other than Darach's wife, Caitlin.

Women had always been on the periphery.

Until he couldn't stop thinking about a disagreeable, redheaded witch.

As he walked down the hall toward the chamber Niall had assigned him, he wondered about Amber. She'd taken this same path not long ago. Was she in the bath now in her own room, or had she fallen straight into bed? No matter how tired he was, his cock rose beneath his plaid at the picture in his mind—her naked and wet in the water, hair slicked back, skin glowing.

His toe caught on a pile of clothes on the floor outside his door as he entered his chamber, and he nudged them out of the way. Left there by Niall, no doubt, perhaps for the laundress.

The room was warm and welcoming, a fire crackling in the hearth and a jug that likely held mead on the stand beside the bed. An upright screen that presumably hid a tub full of water stood on the opposite side of a bed covered in soft-looking quilts and pillows.

He walked to the bed, sat down, and pulled off his boots, letting them fall to the floor with a *thunk*. Leaning back, he closed his eyes just as his fingers touched something smooth and hard in the folds of the quilt. His eyes opened and he looked over.

His body reacted before his mind could put the pieces together—his heart racing, his fatigue dissipating, even more blood engorging his already stiff cock. Wrapping his hand around a wooden rod, he pulled out Amber's cane. He stared at it, then slowly looked to the door, remembering the dirty clothes on the floor outside his chamber.

The breath left his lungs in a whoosh just as water splashed from behind the screen and he heard a soft yawn.

He rose from the bed and found himself rooted to the spot as sounds of someone getting out of the tub reached him. He should leave. Now. But he couldn't make his feet move, and he couldn't work up enough moisture in his mouth to speak.

Footsteps padded across the floor before Amber—her skin glistening with moisture, wet hair hanging past her chin in curls, sleepy eyes glowing at him from her flushed face—stepped into view from behind the screen. She held the towel before her, partially concealing her naked body as she rubbed her hair dry. One breast, full and high with a rosy tip and pert nipple, swayed enticingly as her arms moved. One long, muscled leg stretched down from a narrow hip and tucked-in waist.

When her gaze fell on him, she stopped, eyes wide and disbelieving, jaw falling open, and he knew she hadn't tried to trick him. To seduce him as had happened with other women before.

He raised his hands, palms up. "Doona scream, Amber. You're in my chamber. I'm not here for anything."

Six

LACHLAN GRITTED HIS TEETH AND TRIED TO KEEP HIS eyes on Amber's face as she wrapped the towel around herself and stepped back with a squeak, her cheeks blushing a fiery red. "What?"

"I said this is my chamber. I didn't follow you."

Her mouth opened and closed until finally she said, "Niall sent me here."

"Well, he didn't mean in here. This is my room. I left my saddlebags right over there."

She looked in the direction he pointed. A dusty pack lay in the corner where he'd dropped it a few hours ago when he'd come up for a quick wash. He saw the comprehension dawn on her face, and she swallowed.

"I'm sorry. I looked through the rooms and this was the first one I found with a fire going and a…" She waved her arm in the direction of the screen and the tub behind as if she couldn't say the word. "I didn't see your bag."

"Several rooms were prepared, including one for you." Lachlan shifted his feet, conscious that his cock stuck straight out beneath his kilt, hard as an anvil. She couldn't miss it.

When her eyes flitted down then quickly back up again, she pulled the bath linen around her more securely.

"God's blood," he swore softly and rubbed his hand over his forehead.

"I'll leave," she said as she stepped toward the door.

"You canna. I'll leave." He headed to the exit then darted back to the bed, and she let out a wee squeak. "I forgot my boots." He grabbed them, and at the door, he hesitated, his back to her, his hand on the bar that he'd slid across when he came in. "Why didn't you lock it?" he asked.

She cleared her throat. "I thought Finola or Niall might need to come in. I would have heard you but I...fell asleep."

He noted her pause and wondered about it. He'd heard her yawn and didn't for a second doubt she'd done just that, but why had she paused? Embarrassed, maybe.

"Amber?"

"Aye." She sounded wary. She should be.

He didn't know what made him say it, the wee devil in him, he supposed, or the built-up annoyance at all the orders she'd slung about earlier. Maybe the way she'd blackmailed him to lead her clan.

Or perhaps it was simply hope.

"Next time you show me your breasts, dearling, I'd like to see both of them, not just one."

He darted out of the room before she could say anything and closed the door behind him. With a one-sided grin, he leaned back against it, listening for her response. Something hit the door from the inside, and his grin widened. His saddlebags, no doubt.

He bent down to tie his boots then straightened with a shake of his head and stared into space. He'd just seen Amber naked—and clean. Even if she hadn't been smiling.

Good lord, she was beautiful. Round and lean all at once. He wandered toward the stairs, no longer sleepy in the slightest as the images of her walking toward him played in his mind. He came to a halt when he glanced at his protruding kilt and realized he couldn't go down in such a state.

He'd just turned around and headed back down the passageway, intent on going to the laird's solar, when he saw the door to his chamber open ahead of him, then silence.

After a moment, Amber whispered, "Lachlan." The urgency in her tone had him hurrying forward. "Lachlan," she whispered again, louder this time.

"I'm here. What is it?"

She ducked back into the room and spoke through the crack. "I doona have any clothes."

"What?"

"You have to find them. Niall said he would put a clean arisaid on the bed for me and I was to place my dirty one outside the door. 'Tis gone, and the clean one isna here, obviously."

Lachlan looked to the floor where he'd seen the pile of dirty clothes only minutes before. "'Twas here when I entered. I saw it."

"Well, that doesn't help me now, does it? Someone obviously picked it up after you intruded."

"I did not intrude. I came into my chamber to find you had intruded."

"Argue with me all you like, but if you doona find my clothes before someone finds me in here, naked as the day I was born, you'll be saddled with a verra unhappy bride."

Her words washed through him, and he suddenly found his straining cock retreating back to the safety of his body. Talk of a bride was the surest way to keep that part of him pliant.

"Aye, I thought you'd understand," she said, reading the alarm on his face.

"Where would it be?" he asked.

"In one of the other chambers."

"All right. Lock the door and doona open it for anyone but me."

"Of course not! Do you think I'm addled?"

When the door shut and he heard the bar slide across, he hurried down the hall, checking each chamber in turn. The second one had a bath waiting and fire lit but no arisaid on the bed. He spotted Callum's saddlebags in the corner, and went back into the hall to keep looking.

Finally, at the end of the passageway, he found another room with a fire, a tub full of water, and an arisaid and clean shift on the bed. After snatching up the clothes, he turned around and hurried back to his bedchamber. Before he reached it, however, Callum and Niall appeared at the top of the stairs.

He darted into an empty room across from Callum's. His foster brother heard him, of course, and slowed, his hand on his sword. He raised a brow when he caught sight of Lachlan, who signed with his fingers what he wanted Callum to do.

"Will you show me the room, please?" Callum asked Niall. "I couldnae find a mug for the mead that was there. Maybe it fell down somewhere?"

"Oh, aye. I'd be happy to look for it, Laird MacLean."

Niall preceded Callum into the room. Callum paused and shot Lachlan an enquiring look. Lachlan shook his head and stepped back into the hallway, not thinking to hide the arisaid he carried.

Callum saw it and his brows shot upward. "Amber?" he mouthed, barely even a whisper.

Lachlan tucked the incriminating dress under his plaid and frowned at his foster brother, refusing to answer. He hurried down the hallway to his chamber, followed by Callum's chuckle.

Before alerting Amber he was back, he turned to see Callum had shut the door to his room. Good lad.

"Amber, open up," he whispered as he knocked.

The door cracked open, and she peered at him. "God's blood, it took you long enough."

She widened the door just far enough so her bare arm could reach through. Her skin shone fair and clear in the candlelight, her arm lightly muscled with a sprinkling of orange-gold hair over it.

The sight was enough to send his pulse pounding again, and his cock thickened. When he passed over the arisaid, their fingers touched, lingered for just a moment. A spark flew between them, and he felt it all the way up his arm and into his groin.

From the way her eyes jumped to his, he'd wager she felt it too. Then she pulled back her hand with the dress and clean shift in it and shut the door. When he heard the bar slide across, he let out a long, slow, painful breath and rested his forehead on the wood. He stayed there for what seemed like hours, but was most likely a minute at most.

Steps sounded in the distance, coming up the stairs from the great hall, and he started. He heard a woman's voice singing breathlessly and knew it was the housekeeper, Finola. By all that was holy, he'd be trapped in matrimony for sure if Amber was found in his room. And if any saw him standing at the door, with it locked from the inside, they'd know someone, most likely a woman, was in there.

As long as they didn't see him, they'd assume he had locked it and didn't want to be disturbed. He darted down the hall in the opposite direction toward Callum's room, but just before he got there, Callum's door opened. Niall emerged, looking down at his key ring as he spoke.

"I doona know how the mug got down there, Laird MacLean. Maybe the wind caught it just right and blew it behind the chair?"

"Aye, maybe," Callum said, looking over Niall's head and catching Lachlan's eyes, which he was sure were wide with panic.

Lachlan skidded to a halt and retreated back the way he'd come. Nowhere to hide. The ruse was up unless he could get Amber to let him in. "Open up—now!" he whispered.

"Laird MacKay. There you are!" Niall said cheerfully as he hustled toward him. Callum followed, his face filled with anticipation, aware he watched a disaster in the making. "I didn't hear you come up. Let me come in and check the bath water. It must be cold by now."

"Nay, 'tis not necessary," he said, his hand pushing on the barred door. "I'll not have a bath now, anyway. You can change the water later." He yawned loudly, and Callum snorted in amusement. "'Tis time for a wee nap. I'm going in now. Alone. I'll let you know when I need anything." He hoped Amber would catch on and let him into his room, elsewise he'd look like a fool, standing in the hall after saying that. A married fool.

"Well, I'll come in and turn down the covers for you, then. 'Twill be my pleasure for all you've done for us."

"Nay! I can manage on my own."

The door suddenly gave way beneath his hand, and he stumbled into his room. Niall hurried forward, and Lachlan blocked the way just in time, his heart pounding like he was facing off with a deadly opponent on the battlefield. He shut the door so only his head poked out.

"But, Laird. I should check the room for…"

"For what?" Lachlan asked, beginning to suspect something. Perhaps Niall had been vague with Amber about which room was hers on purpose. "I assure you naught is amiss." Then he shut and barred the door from the inside.

Amber stood beside him, her hands clenched together over her stomach, her chest rising and falling with rapid breaths, her cheeks flushed—a doe trapped by approaching hounds. She'd dressed hurriedly by the looks of it, her pleats uneven and the dress sitting awkwardly on her shoulders.

He raised a finger to his lips as he listened through the door.

Niall knocked, tried the handle. "Laird MacKay! Laird MacKay!"

"He's exhausted, Niall," Callum said. "I'm sure he's quite capable of readying his own bed. Making it too, and lying in it."

The last was said for his own ears, no doubt.

As footsteps receded down the hall, he heard Callum ask, "Will you take my arm, Niall. The stairs can be difficult, and you've been up and down them numerous times today."

Lachlan's breath left him in a loud exhale, and he rested his forehead on the door. Callum would take Niall down to the great hall, keep him occupied until either Lachlan or Amber reappeared.

He swiveled his head to gaze at Amber, who leaned her shoulder against the door next to him. Their eyes met, hers still looking a wee bit wild.

"My heart is racing like I've run from here to Inverness," he said. "Or just beaten an opponent who had a great, bloody axe."

"Mine too. He's determined."

"And wily too. He knew you were in here. I think he set you up."

"Aye. Tricky bastard."

"Not tricky enough."

A wee smile cracked her face. She tried to hold it back, but it broke through, and they both burst out laughing—in relief, but also at the absurdity of it, at what had almost happened. How he, a grown man and laird, a warrior and defender of good people, had been running from chamber to chamber trying to outwit a decrepit, interfering old man. And how she, a healer and leader of her people, had skulked behind a closed door like an errant child.

They laughed in waves, inciting each other, their sides heaving and breath gasping. Legs threatening to drop them to the ground, they leaned beside each other against the door.

Finally, they sighed, the tension dissipated, the humor settled.

Their eyes met, and she smiled, her face clean and luminous, so beautiful his heart hurt—even though her hair had dried into different lengths all around her shoulders and face. And he knew he must be looking back at her like all the other men in her life. Like an adoring puppy, as he'd once feared.

But she didn't look away or scowl at him like she did all the other men. Nay, when he raised his hand to cup her cheek, soft like the feathers in his pillow, she rested her head in his palm, her lips parting slightly, her own hand rising to his chest. And when he angled his body to hers, she turned to him as well, her chin rising, her eyelids drooping to half-mast. And when he lowered his head, breathed into her mouth, she breathed in unison with him.

His lips pressed hers gently, reverently, not a question, but an exploration, and she leaned into his body. Those breasts he wanted to suckle, cushioned his chest. His other hand trailed up her arm and around her waist, coming to rest on her rib cage. Her back arched, an opening up of her spine, and she welcomed him in with a sigh.

The kiss deepened as their tongues tasted each other, rubbing leisurely and learning the feel of each other, the shape of their mouths. Their lips sucked playfully while teeth nibbled.

His tongue delved even deeper inside the warm cavern of her mouth as she grasped her other hand around his nape, her fingers tangling in his hair, tugging the strands, which only incited him more.

A surge of blood, hot and heavy, filled his groin, and he pushed her back against the door, his knee sliding between hers. She moaned into his mouth, wrapped her leg around his, and pulled him even closer into the juncture of her thighs. Her arms hugged him in a stranglehold and the kiss grew carnal—tongues and hips thrusting and rubbing, hands squeezing.

When he slipped one palm down the small of her back to knead the soft, round bow of her arse, and curved around her breast from the underside, she pulled her mouth from his, panting, and tilted her head back. He took every advantage and kissed, heavy and wet across her cheek before closing his lips around her earlobe and sucking it onto his mouth.

She mewled as she bucked against him, a high-pitched sound that shot straight to his stones, tightening them to hard hammers against his body. She was close to release.

Christ Almighty, they both were.

He pulled his head away and stared down at her flushed face—her eyes closed, her lips parted as the breath blasted through her teeth in ragged gasps. His hand on her breast had pulled her arisaid to the side, and most of her soft flesh was exposed—high, pink, round. He swept his thumb across her areola to uncover her nipple, and his mouth watered as he stared at it.

He wanted it on his tongue, the hard nub red and tight. He wanted his tongue on her other nub too. Nuzzle it. Lick it.

He could pull her skirt up now and she'd let him, he was sure of it. He could push his fingers, his cock, into her wet center, and she'd explode all over him, her breasts bouncing, her screams of release matching his guttural groans as he pumped into her against the door.

He'd never felt this needy before, this desperate for a woman—even when he'd been young.

He looked at the bed. He could lay her down, kiss and lick his way down her body, push his tongue inside her. He wanted to taste her so badly, to feel her opening pulse on his lips.

But that other part of him, the part he couldn't ignore, was yelling at him to slow down, to pull them both back from the edge. They'd burned up too hot, too fast for any rational thought to intervene, and she'd have naught but regrets afterward.

She might never forgive him for her own wanton feelings. May never allow it to happen again. And he knew one time would never be enough. He wanted more. Much more.

She had a different attitude toward men than most young women, and she knew herbs to stop his seed from taking root. Maybe she would want to be with him on a regular basis.

He'd never had a leman in his own clan before, but

once things were safe for the MacPhersons, he would set up a strong leader here and only visit on occasion. Visit her. She hadn't grown up with him, he didn't know her father or mother, so it wouldn't be the same as taking a leman in the MacKay clan.

And marriage, for him, was out of the question. Maybe he'd been scarred by his mother, but he never wanted to take a wife. He would pass the lairdship to a MacKay warrior he'd trained and trusted. Someone who could continue in his footsteps when the time came.

He shifted her dress back in place and raised his hands to cup her head, rested their foreheads together as he took a deep breath. She protested at first, rubbing against him, but he moved his aching body back just enough so they weren't pressed so tightly together.

"Amber, breathe with me, sweetling. We need to... calm ourselves." His voice sounded strangled and his heart still thundered in his chest. "Believe me, I want to continue, but we canna. Not yet. 'Tis verra tempting, lass, but I doona want you angry at me afterward."

She stilled, and he knew he'd finally gotten though the haze of desire that likely clouded her mind the way it did his. She lifted her hands and pushed him back a step until his arms dropped. Keeping her head down, she stepped to the side and straightened her clothes.

Lachlan almost groaned at the loss of her warmth. Her heat. Had he made a mistake? Aye, by the set of her shoulders, most likely. An uneasiness settled in his stomach. But if he wanted her for his leman, even for a short time, he had to play the long game—which he knew how to do. He'd hunted Machar Murray for five years, and he'd keep going until he caught him.

Amber MacPherson wouldn't be nearly as hard to catch.

"'Tis for both our sakes. It doesn't mean I didn't want to continue. I wanted naught more than to join with you, to feel your heat, believe me, but we can hold off till later."

Her hands stopped moving and clenched over her stomach. "I give you my thanks, Laird MacKay. I doona know what came o'er me."

She sounded stilted and stiff. And calling him Laird MacKay? He'd never heard her use his title before and didn't like it. Well, she'd used it once, maybe, when she pretended to be a lad. "It's Lachlan, Amber, not Laird MacKay." He raised a hand to her cheek, wanting to reestablish their intimacy, but she turned her head away. "And doona thank me. Next time we just need to go slower. Be prepared... I'm sure you have herbs or something for...well...bairns."

A low sound vibrated up her throat that almost sounded like a growl, and he drew his brows together. "Amber?" he prompted her.

She flattened her hands and smoothed them down her dress as if rubbing out any wrinkles. When her head raised, her eyes were ice. "Aye, I have herbs, but trust me, Laird MacKay, we willna be using them, and there willna be a next time."

Seven

LACHLAN STOOD WITH HIS ARMS CROSSED OVER HIS chest, frowning at the bumbling ineptitude of the MacPherson guards. One week had passed since the attack, and while he'd made good strides on repairing the wall and the portcullis, and seeing to different safety measures around the keep—setting up vigilant patrols, blocking off the secret escape routes, and burning the scrub from around the castle, so no one could hide in it—he'd made little progress with the MacPherson warriors.

And none with Amber.

God's truth, what did the woman want? He'd done everything he could think of to get back in her good graces—just like all the other men—right down to bringing her flowers. Except she went through the other men's bouquets and kept any part that had medicinal qualities, discarding the rest. His bouquet she'd tossed out in its entirety.

He should have tupped her when he had the chance, good and hard. Left her screaming her release and wanting more. Or been gentle and drawn out the loving, so when she finally released, it was like naught she'd ever experienced, and she'd want more.

But, nay. He'd stopped.

Idiot.

"You're making them nervous with your scowls," Callum said from beside him. "They did much better this morning when you weren't here to intimidate them."

He grunted, about the most vocal he'd been in the last week. Unless he'd been trying to talk to Amber, that was. Then his words had come tripping over his tongue as he tried to corner her, tried to reason with her.

Callum sighed, an exasperated sound that Lachlan was sure had been accompanied by an eye roll. He refused to look over to find out.

"Quit mooning o'er some lass and help rebuild your new clan. The warriors deserve your support and full attention."

"I'm watching them," he said.

"Nay, you're not. You're thinking about the next thing you can do to get Amber's attention. You have to let her go, Lachlan. You tried and you failed. Besides, you should be thinking about ways to use her as bait for Murray, not how to get under her skirts."

"You doona understand. I was this close." He held out his thumb and index finger a wee bit apart, then felt guilty for having admitted even that to Callum, which again made no sense—the brothers had always talked to each other about their lovers.

But nothing about his feelings for Amber made sense.

He blew out a frustrated breath. "I chose to take the high road. I thought she would thank me for stopping and want to continue with me later when it was safe.

She thanked me, all right, and she's barely spoken two words to me since. Even when I question her about Adaira's recovery, all she'll give are minimal answers, even if she's been teasing Adaira just minutes before."

"You sound like you're in love with her."

Lachlan rounded on him, shock lifting his brow. "Nay! 'Tis naught like that. I just…"

"You just want to be with her all the time, make love to her all the time. You said Darach was the same when he met Caitlin. If it's not love, then it's obsession—like Machar Murray."

The heat of anger rose on his chest. "Doona compare me to Machar Murray."

"Then doona act like him. Catch the bastard so the MacPhersons and Amber are safe, then let's go home. Use Amber as bait." He tapped his finger on his upper lip, thinking. "If you were Machar Murray—"

Lachlan growled, and Callum waylaid him with a raised hand.

"Just pretend. Murray stayed here for Amber, knowing the risk. He tried to kill her, aye, but hate and love are two sides of the same coin—"

"I am not in love wi—"

"Good. Then this should be easy for you. What one thing would bother you more than anything about Amber? Something she could do—if you were in love with her. Which you're not, of course."

He knew what it was immediately, but he didn't want to say it. When Callum raised his brow, Lachlan grumbled, "Take another lover."

"Aye, and if that lover is you—the man Murray hates more than any other—he would try to kill both of you. Or maybe just kill you and abduct Amber, so he could hurt her afterward. Or abduct both of you so he could hurt her in front of you before killing—"

"Stop! I understand your meaning."

It was a good plan, but he was torn. How could he knowingly put Amber in that kind of danger? And how could he not, when 'twas the best plan they had to capture or kill Murray, leaving everyone else safe? And getting justice for his brother, of course.

And if he spent his nights with her, alone with her, he'd have her right where he wanted. An intimate setting in close proximity to a bed. He could talk to her, reason with her.

Seduce her.

"It couldnae be at the castle. He'd need access to us in order to try anything," Lachlan said.

"Aye. We could find an isolated place, let it slip— maybe through Father Odhran—that it's your wee love nest."

"Doona use those words with her when you suggest it."

"Me? Why canna you tell her? You're her laird."

He scowled again. Not liking the reminder that Amber refused to call him Lachlan anymore. "She'll take it better coming from you, but I'll be there." He rubbed his hand over his neck and blew out a worried breath. "I doona want any others with us in the cottage, but we'll need watchers."

"Aye."

He drummed his fingers on his sword's pommel. "Callum, we're putting her life at risk. If he captures her, he'll—"

"I know what he'll do, Lachlan, and worse. We willna let that happen. We'll protect her."

Lachlan turned back to the MacPherson men, saw them sneaking worried glances at him, and knew what Callum had said about his demeanor was true. He'd brought down their morale, and they'd had enough of that with Machar Murray.

He forced a smile and reassuring nod. Many of the men returned the smile, their shoulders straightening, their grips tightening on their weapons. They renewed their training with vigor. Aye, he'd make warriors out of them yet.

"Let's walk the wall then visit the barracks," he said to Callum. If these men were feeling down because of his sour face and attitude, he'd bet the others were too.

He made sure to slap several guards on the back and say encouraging words as he and Callum made their way to the main gate. They inspected the new portcullis, declared the work excellent, then walked up the stairs to the walkway on top of the curtain wall. Repairs were underway on much of the stonework, and it was already significantly improved.

The gate faced north toward the village on the shores of the loch, a distant mountain range to the west. Lachlan and Callum had hidden in the brush to the east over a week ago, and to the south was more forest.

They'd made their way about a third of the way around the wall, stopping to talk to the guards and craftsmen they passed, when Lachlan spotted someone walking away from the castle to the northwest. Although he couldn't be sure because of the distance, it looked like a woman with short, orangey-gold hair.

He squinted. Surely it wasn't Amber? His stomach tightened and he swore. If it was her, where the hell were her guards?

Callum leaned on the wall beside him and peered out. "Is that Amber?"

"Exactly what I was wondering."

A warrior next to them followed their gazes. "Aye, 'tis her." He pointed toward the tree line in the distance. "Her cottage is over there. You can just see the thatched roof."

"She doesn't live in the village?" Lachlan's voice had risen, and his heart began to race.

"Nay, her family has been on their farm for as long as I can remember. I think her grandfather built it for her grandmother when they first married. 'Twas even more isolated then."

The pulse pounded in Lachlan's temple now, and he clenched his jaw to keep from yelling. "Would Machar Murray know this?"

The man looked nervously between the two lairds, sensing the tension even through their outward calm. "Aye, everyone does."

Lachlan leaned out over the parapet to look at the outside wall. It was too far a drop to make without injury or death, and all the wee crevices he could have used as handholds to climb down had been filled in.

"I need rope," he said, barely able to get the words past his tight jaw.

"You're not going that way," Callum said. "You'll be exposed. And horses will be quicker."

He was right, but Lachlan didn't want Amber out of his sight for even a second. He turned to the guard.

"Where are the nearest stairs?" He couldn't stop himself from yelling this time, fear for Amber a lead ball in his gut.

"Just around that corner." The man pointed to where the wall curved around an outpost.

Lachlan and Callum took off at a run toward it. Lachlan whistled sharply as he hit the stairs, alerting his men to be prepared and have his horse ready.

God's blood! She could be heading straight to her death. Where the hell were her guards?

"What's the matter?" the warrior called after them. "Is Amber in danger? Is Machar Murray still out there?"

Aye. And maybe waiting for her in her cottage.

❧

Amber pushed open the door to her home. The worn wood, warm from the summer sun, felt familiar against her hands, the squeak of the hinges just right to her ears, and the smell, a cacophony of scents from her herb and vegetable gardens inside and outside the cottage, just like her grandmother. She stepped over the threshold and looked around with a smile.

'Twas good to be home, especially as she thought for a while that she'd never see it again.

Ian and his younger sister, Breanna, had checked on the place and tended the gardens and animals while she'd been at the castle, so it didn't smell stale, and the herbs weren't overgrown. They'd done a good job with everything.

She would have come back sooner, but Earc had ended up sicker than she'd anticipated and needed round-the-clock care, as did Adaira, who had developed an infection in her wound, which wasn't unexpected but still worrisome.

The lass was awake now and talking up a storm, still trying to decide whether to forgive Amber for tricking her.

The worst had been trying to avoid Lachlan, who kept wanting to talk to her about…about… Gah! She didn't even know what to call it. A kiss, aye, but so much more than that. Until him, her experience of kisses—of any kind of physical intimacy—had always been her trying to avoid it. Sometimes with force.

Her carnal pleasure had only ever come from her own fingers—which some might call a sin, but she called the perfect way to fall asleep after a stressful day.

Not that she'd wanted to fall asleep since their… kiss. She spent all day trying not to think about Lachlan, only to spend all night dreaming about him, leaving her wet and wanting—and she refused to touch herself while thinking about him again. Which left her a mass of repressed urges.

To make it worse, she felt his eyes on her wherever she went, reminding her of what they'd done. Not that she felt they'd done anything sinful, as Father Odhran would say, but the notion that Lachlan wanted to tup her and not marry her had hurt. Which was confusing, because the last thing she wanted was to get married.

Still, she didn't like that he considered her good enough to tup on a regular basis, using her knowledge of herbs to avoid having bairns, but not good enough to marry.

Idiot man.

Nay, laird. He was her laird, and she'd best remember that...idiot laird.

She moved across the freshly swept, hard-packed dirt floor toward the shutters latched over the kitchen window, and opened them wide. Bright, midmorning sunlight poured in over her potted herbs on the sill as well as the counters and cupboards stacked full of pottery, medicinal tools, and ingredients. In the center of the kitchen sat a large table with several high-backed chairs around it. Her favorite had been her father's chair and her grandfather's before that. A cushion her mother had made still sat on the seat, worn from use but patched and restuffed on a regular basis.

A hearth took up one wall, and several pots hung above it: one for cooking food, a few others for brewing her medicinal teas and broths.

Three comfortable chairs sat around the hearth, not used as much since her father and then her grandmother died, although she often had visitors in the evening—friends as well as those in need of healing. Sometimes they stayed over, and she had a bed in a nook off the kitchen for them that had been hers when she was a child.

She slept there some nights, instead of the bigger bed in the corner, when she was feeling particularly scared or lonely. And she'd been scared often since her father had been killed. Scared even more when her grandmother had died, but she'd lifted her chin and continued in her grandmother's fashion, pretending to be a witch to keep Murray away from her. But she'd known it was only a matter of time, and if he were to come for her, she'd feared it would be at night.

But then Lachlan came. And Callum and the rest of the MacKays and MacLeans. And she knew she'd survive, even if Lachlan drove her a wee bit daft.

She sighed and moved past the foot of the bed, her grandmother's colorful quilt laying on top. She pushed open the shutters on another window, and a black, feathered missile darted through the window at her face. She shrieked and threw her arms up around her head as it cawed at her. It beat its wings before flying across the room to settle on the back of her father's chair.

"God's blood, Lucy!" she yelled at the crow. "You almost took my eyes out."

She glowered at her pet crow, his wing a wee bit droopy despite her best efforts to fix it two years ago when he'd fallen out of his nest. He'd stayed with her after that, following her about as best he could on the farm, but unable to make the longer trips when she had to go farther afield—like up to the castle.

She'd been worried sick about him, and the goats, Belle and Beele, when she had to run from Murray— even though she knew one of her friends would take care of them.

All three animals were named after demons from the stories her grandmother used to tell her. Not because she was a witch, as the priest accused, but because it secretly amused her. How better to send a rude message to Father Odhran after he'd accused her of keeping the baby crow and a pair of baby goats as her familiars. Crows and goats, he said, were the devil's helpers.

So, she'd named her pets Lucy, Belle, and Beele— shortened versions of the demons' names the priest accused her of consorting with. She'd told no one, of course, of the private joke, not even Isla or Ian.

She felt her face for any scratches from Lucy's talons as she walked across the room and held out her arm for him. He hopped onto it, cawing loudly several times as if to reprimand her for staying away so long.

"Oh, I know, I know. I canna tell you how sorry I am that you were so inconvenienced. The outrage of having to find your own food and shelter like a regular bird is beyond what any normal crow should have to endure."

She unbarred and pushed open her back door, which led to the path through the trees to her garden. The sunlight dappled through the leaves, and the air still held a slight crispness from early morning.

Her favorite time of day.

She closed her eyes and breathed deeply as she walked, taking in the scent of her wildflowers along the side of the cottage. But the scent changed as she neared the garden, became stronger and mixed. She realized something was wrong just before she heard the distressed bleat from the goats up ahead.

As Amber broke into a run, Lucy squawked and lifted into the air. He flapped ahead of her and landed on a tree. Horror lodged in her throat as she reached the end of the path and saw her beloved plants—both for eating and medicine—had been trampled beneath someone's feet, ripped up by malevolent hands.

She scanned about for Belle and Beele, fearing the worst. A moment later, she found Belle tied up tight to a tree, her eyes wild as she struggled to free herself. From behind the goats' shed, Amber heard thrashing and more bleating, and she ran around it to find Beele trapped beneath the wheelbarrow she used to transport dirt and plants. Lucy hopped along behind her, cawing as he went from tree branch, to fence, to shed.

"Oh, Beele. I'm here, sweetling," she cried out as she struggled to push the heavy barrow off the goat and set it back on its wheels. Beele sprung up as soon as he was free, shaking his head and bleating, before lowering his head and racing toward Belle. Amber raced after him.

"Beele, wait! I'll help her."

When she reached the goats, Belle was tangled even tighter against the tree, and Beele had lowered his head, ready to ram anything in defense of his sister—including Amber, who grabbed his horns and held on, trying to soothe him.

It didn't work, so she let go and just tried to avoid his head butts as she used her knife to saw through the rope and free Belle. Finally, the wee female loosed her head, but not before Amber was rammed several times by Beele.

"God's truth," she said, rubbing her thigh where Beele had pounded into her. "Serves me right for naming you after a demon."

She looked around at the mess of her garden and nearly broke down, her heart hurting and stomach sick. Who would do such a thing? Not only to her medicinal plants and food, but to the goats as well? 'Twas likely someone had been trying to tie up Belle, and Beele had attacked them.

But to what purpose? And when? Ian had been here yesterday afternoon and had said naught was amiss.

She kneeled in the dirt to look at her plants. The damage to the stalks was recent, and the smashed vegetables were still moist. This had happened just before she arrived. She rose and peered around her, suddenly uneasy. Whoever did it could still be out there. Watching her.

Was someone trying to take revenge? Could it have been Murray? Surely he wouldn't have stayed on MacPherson land, knowing what Lachlan would do to him if he were caught. 'Twas a sure way to die.

A loud, crashing noise sounded behind the goats' shed, and Lucy cawed and flew to the top. Amber raced around it to see Father Odhran sprawled at the base of a large pine tree. Her first instinct was to help him, even though she knew him to be an awful and undeserving man, but then she saw the state of his shoes and the bottom of his robe—stained with the berries and plants he'd stomped on, and the dirt beneath his fingernails. Her chest constricted so tight it felt like she might stop breathing.

"You did this!" she yelled at him, striding forward through the underbrush, fists clenched.

"Get away from me, witch!" He scrambled back until he cowered against the tree trunk.

"How could you? All those plants killed. All that food and medicine wasted. And what were you trying to do with Belle and Beele?"

"Demons, both of them! I heard you." He made the sign of the cross.

She avoided his flailing feet and grabbed the bottom his robe, yanking it so he rolled over and got a face full of dirt. "You killed living plants. God's plants. Put on this earth to feed and help people. You're the demon. Destroying His creation!"

"You pervert His will giving potions to the women, taking away their pain at childbirth. And you fornicate with that demon goat."

She reeled back. "What?" If she hadn't been so shocked by what he'd suggested, so disgusted, she would have burst out laughing. "You loathsome, foul creature. Nay, not even a creature, for even the lowliest worm brings life to the soil. All you do is hate and destroy, just like the demons you rail against." She picked up dirt and debris from the ground and hurled it at him. He cried out and tried to crawl behind the tree on his hands and knees, but she stepped on the end of his robe and leaned over him. "I bring bairns, God's bairns, into the world, and no matter how much I ease the pain for their mothers, it still hurts them, believe me. Not every child has as small a mind as you. You must have slipped through your mother like a wee shite, for that's exactly what you are."

She picked up another handful of dirt and smeared it into his hair. Then she planted her foot in his backside and pushed. "Get off of my land! And doona e'er speak to me again. If you see me, you run the other way, or I'll drag you to the nearest well and throw you in."

Her breath continued to saw through her lungs as he disappeared on hands and knees into the forest. Closing her eyes, she counted to ten, trying to find calm amidst all the destruction and chaos. Her beloved garden—ruined. All the food and medicine lost. And what had he intended for Belle and Beele?

She trembled again just thinking about it, and then she realized that the ground shook as well—shook beneath her feet, the vibrations rising up her legs. Thundering hooves assaulted her ears moments later, and she ran back through her garden and toward her cottage. Belle and Beele followed at her heels, and Lucy flew from branch to branch in the trees above.

"Amber!" she heard Lachlan yell.

"I'm here!" she responded, and was almost knocked over as he barreled around the corner, his big hands catching her shoulders just in time to keep her upright. The warmth and strength of them made her feel safe, and she wanted to lean all the way into him.

Callum and several other warriors fanned out around them, weapons drawn, eyes vigilant.

"What's going on?" she asked. "Is it Adaira? Or Earc?"

"Nay, they're fine. Are you all right?" When she nodded, he looked around, frowning at the sight of her garden. "What happened?"

Her chest and throat tightened, and she tried to hold it back, but a sob pushed up from her belly. "Father Odhran did this. Thank God I arrived in time, or he would have hurt the goats too. He had Belle tied up so tight to the tree she could barely breathe, and he'd trapped Beele beneath a wheelbarrow. He would have killed them, I know it. You should have heard the things he said to me!"

He pulled her against his chest, and she went willingly, her head tucking beneath his chin, her eyes closing. She realized she was shaking, her breath coming in sharp gasps, and he wrapped his plaid around her shoulders.

"Let's get her inside," he said to Callum. "And find that donkey of a priest."

Callum whistled then signaled with his hands as the warriors moved out. "Amber, where did you last see him and when?" he asked.

She lifted her head. "Behind the goats' shed. He crawled into the bushes just before you arrived."

"Crawled?" Lachlan asked.

"Aye, after my foot connected with his backside."

He squeezed her shoulders and turned her to the back door of the cottage, but she dug her heels in and looked behind him. "My goats! Belle, Beele, come now, dearlings!" They bleated and pushed past her and Lachlan, running to the cottage door. She whistled for Lucy, and he swooped low past their heads then perched on the windowsill, cocking his head and cawing as he watched them.

"Any other animals?" Lachlan asked. "A cow perhaps? Or a herd of sheep?"

"Nay, just an ass," she said, eyeing him.

He snorted as he walked her to the door, his big body shielding her, supporting her. "You should meet Caitlin MacKenzie, Darach's wife. The two of you would have much to talk about."

"Oh? Does her domineering husband try to boss her around too?"

A silence fell, and she regretted her words instantly. How could she have spoken so inanely?

"Aye, he does. But I'm not your husband, Amber."

She felt the heat rush up her cheeks. "I know that. 'Twas just a…twist of words. I didn't mean anything by it."

He grunted, his arm tightening around her as she tried to pull away. He didn't let go until they'd crossed the threshold and he'd placed her in her favorite chair in front of the hearth. Lucy flew across the room with a caw to land on the back of her chair, while the goats found their pillows on the floor by her feet. They both still panted and bleated anxiously before releasing huge sighs and flopping onto their sides.

Lachlan stepped over them and said, "Should I bring Saint in too? Let him have a wee rest on your bed?"

"Nay. Your jealous old nag is not welcome. He jolted me around on purpose after you made off with me."

"He did not. He was just hungry. I didn't want him full before the battle."

She scoffed. "'Twas more than that. He didn't want me up there with you. How did he get his name anyway? He's certainly no saint."

Lachlan smiled, looking almost sheepish, and she raised her brows. "My foster brothers and Gregor named him. Gregor thought it would be good fortune to name him after a saint, but they couldnae agree on which one. So…he became just Saint."

"Let me guess. They were trying to choose between the saints of thieves and scoundrels and the saint of lost causes?"

He laughed softly, and she knew by the amused look on his face it was true.

"Something like that."

He grabbed some kindling from a bin on the hearth and set about to build a fire. The smaller wood lit easily, and he added logs until it roared in welcome. She hadn't realized she was cold until she found herself leaning toward the flames.

"'Tis the shock," he said as he placed the kettle

above the flames. "I'll make some tea. Do you have any valerian root?"

"Aye, on the counter, second canister from the left. How do you know about valerian root?"

"Our cook used to make it for my mother when I was a boy. To calm her nerves, she said."

"Oh? Was she anxious?"

Lachlan made a derisive sound as he pulled down some cups and placed them on a tray. "Only when she wanted to be."

"I doona understand."

"Neither did anyone else...except me. My father and brother—both good men—tried to please her or fix things for her, but I knew she ne'er wanted them fixed. She had things exactly as she liked, and if they weren't to her preference, she manipulated and schemed until she got them that way. But it doesn't matter anymore. She's gone now."

"Ah...I'm sorry." Amber knew people like that, and they were a trial. It didn't matter what you did to try to make them happy, they would find something else wrong.

"Doona be sorry she died. I wasn't. Be sorry I didn't have a different mother." He pulled out the valerian root then looked through the rest of her canisters, lifting some to smell the contents. "My father and brother made up for her lack, though. I was much loved by both. And then by Gregor and the lads. 'Twas a happy childhood despite her best efforts."

She pulled her feet up onto her chair and wrapped her arms around her knees. "I didn't have a mother either. She died giving birth to me. 'Tis why I am so adamant to help the clanswomen with their births, despite what Father Odhran says. My father and grandmother raised me, and they loved me well, but I felt the loss of my mother even though I ne'er knew her."

"I ne'er felt the loss of mine, but I suppose I wondered from time to time what it would be like to have a real mother. Mostly when I saw my friends with theirs." He picked up the valerian root and pulled a small pot toward him.

"Doona put in more than a pinch," she said, watching with interest as he mixed up the tea, adding rosehip and chamomile as well. She liked seeing him in her kitchen and marveled at the supple strength of his hands. He had held her so firmly when he'd kissed her, but also stroked so softly over her breasts. She lowered her lashes and let her gaze wander up the corded muscles in his forearms and over the bulge of his upper arms and shoulders. The massiveness of his chest enthralled her, and she placed a hand on her cheek, remembering how she'd rested it there just minutes ago.

Her heart rate increased all over again, and she turned to look at the fire.

"You just have to ask, Amber," he said, his voice gruff.

She knew exactly what he meant—ask for his touch, his lips on her body. Her fingers itched to squeeze her suddenly aching breasts, to relieve the growing pressure between her thighs, but she clenched them together and ignored her urges. And why not? She'd had plenty of practice at ignoring them this past week.

He brought the tray over with three cups and

poured the herbs in the kettle before sitting in the chair beside hers. He must expect Callum to join them.

"Why are you here, Lachlan? Did you know Father Odhran was here? That he'd destroyed my garden?"

"Nay, not until we arrived. What did he say to you, Amber?"

She pressed her lips together, not wanting to foul the air again with such disgusting lies.

He leaned closer, his gaze firm upon her. "I'm laird of this clan. He has desecrated your property, threatened your person, and meddled in your livelihood. You willna starve; we will provide for you if you have need, but he has done you serious harm. I need to respond to this. He canna be allowed to harass any member of *my* clan. Matters with the church can sometimes be tricky, but I have the backing of several important lairds, including Gregor MacLeod, who has a love of healers." He leaned forward and squeezed her hand. "Amber, I will protect you. We can petition the Church to have him replaced."

She squeezed his hand back. "What if the Church decides I am a witch too, and comes to investigate? My grandmother played a dangerous game in order to protect me and the clan from Laird Murray. When she died, I continued it. Witchcraft was the only thing he feared."

"Does the clan believe you're a witch?"

"I doona think so, but if they're questioned, they'll have to say what they've heard. I've thrown many garbled words and threats at Murray, pretending they were hexes. I've threatened to shrink his manhood to the size of a rat's, plague it with boils, make all of his teeth fall out, and tie his bowels in a knot. I was most creative. If the situation hadn't been so serious, so life and death, 'twould have been amusing."

"'Tis ne'er amusing to have to lie to survive. What did the priest say to you today? Did you see him in the garden?"

"Nay, he fell out of a tree near where he'd trapped Beele. He must have climbed up when he heard me coming. The plants had been recently torn up, and he had the juice and pulp from the fruits and vegetables on his robe and the dirt under his nails."

"And when you spoke to him?"

She sighed, knowing he would press until she told him what he'd said. "He called me a witch."

"And?"

"He said I perverted God's will when I helped the women ease the pain of childbirth. But I doona always give them herbs! And sometimes when I do, there's naught in the tea but what we're having now. Just enough to calm them a wee bit, or make them think they've been dosed. Often, all they need is for me to rub their backs or help them into a better position for pushing. And if the bairn is turned the wrong way, I can push on the stomach from the outside to prod it into position. But the priest should like that because it can be painful for the mother."

When she finished, he continued to stare at her, finally raising one brow. "Amber, what else did he say to you? I know you're holding back."

She made a scoffing sound she'd learned as a wee lass at her father's knee. "How on earth can you know that?"

"Because I see it in your eyes. Tell me...please."

She dropped her gaze, even though she had naught to feel ashamed about. 'Twas the bloody priest who should be ashamed, not her. She lifted her chin and met his eyes. "He said the goats were demons and that...and that I fornicated with the male goat, Beele."

She watched, fascinated, as a thundercloud grew in Lachlan's eyes. His face tightened all over, and a muscle ticked wildly in his clenched jaw.

"He said what?!" he bellowed.

"Calm down, Lachlan." The words came from over Amber's shoulder, and she turned to see Callum standing in the doorway. "I know he's a disgusting, dangerous toad, but we need him to get to Machar Murray."

Eight

LACHLAN WATCHED FROM HIS CHAIR BESIDE AMBER AS Callum crouched in front of the hearth, petting the goats and trying to explain to her why they needed Father Odhran.

"Murray dug a tunnel from the chapel that went under the curtain wall," Callum said. "'Tis unlikely he did so without the priest's knowledge. They may still be in contact. We can use that alliance to plant information we want Murray to act on."

She sat spine-stiff in her chair, hands clasped around the cup of tea in her lap, eyes frosty as she listened.

The same look she'd worn every time she was in Lachlan's presence this past week.

Aye, he'd had a wee reprieve the last half hour or so when she'd been upset. She'd leaned on him, talked to him, looked at him with heat in her eyes once again, and he'd been hard-pressed not to kiss her. But now her walls were back up, and she'd firmly closed the door against both of them.

"Why on earth would Machar Murray stay around

here, knowing what you'd do to him if he were caught?" she asked.

"To get to you. To get to Lachlan." Callum spoke with his hands, and Belle softly butted him to get him to keep scratching her. "He's vain, cruel, filled with his own self-importance, and he thinks he's better than everyone else, smarter than everyone else. It will eat at him that Lachlan defeated his plans not once, but twice—the second time chasing him from what he thought was a secure position and locking him out. He feels entitled to Clan MacPherson, and he is obsessed with you. The fact that you kept him at bay for so long, using his superstitions against him—which he now knows was a ruse—will infuriate him. You got the best of him. He canna let that rest. He needs to dominate you, to crush you." He caught her gaze and held it. "If he can, he'll try to take you alive so he can abuse you before killing you."

Fear flashed in Amber's eyes before she hardened them again, but he saw the quick rise and fall of her chest, the wee tremble in her bottom lip.

Lachlan glared at Callum for being so harsh, even though he knew why his foster brother had done so. He wanted to scare Amber with the facts, so she'd agree to help. And she should be scared—of Murray and that bloody priest. Father Odhran may be a fool, but he was dangerous, and he wanted her dead as well.

He removed her cup, placed it on a small table between them, and held her hands tight as she tried to pull away.

"We're not going to let that happen, Amber."

"How can you stop it?" she asked. "According to Callum, you'll be dead."

"Because we're smarter than him. We're going to set a trap for him. Draw him out. He will pay for what he's done."

"The same way he's paid for your brother's death?"

"Aye. He may not be dead yet, but he will be. He's desperate now as well as everything else. Unlike before, we know who he is, and he doesn't want to leave. He'll stay within a day's ride, if not closer, I'd wager my life on it. He still thinks he can win. And that means killing both of us."

"And by killing me, you mean raping me and doing every other horrible thing he can think of, then killing me."

A muscle twitched in his jaw, getting worse the longer they talked about this. "Aye."

She blew out a shaky breath, and the fear returned to her eyes. This time her voice trembled. "I thought it was over. I thought we were all safe."

Callum moved closer and put a hand on her knee. A friendly, commiserating hand, but still Lachlan frowned, wanting to knock it off.

"We have a plan, and it involves you. Do you want to hear it?" he asked.

Amber pulled one hand from Lachlan's grasp and brushed Callum's hand from her knee. "You take liberties, Laird MacLean, to include me in a plan I haven't agreed to." She emphasized "Laird MacLean."

Lachlan couldn't help grinning. Neither could Callum. He straightened and stepped back to the hearth. "Aye, I do take liberties, especially as it's dangerous and will tarnish your reputation."

She threw her hand in the air, and her crow

squawked, then flew to the table. The goats sat up. "Are you daft?" she asked Callum. "Why would I want to take part in any plan that risked me and ruined me?"

Lachlan gently pulled on one of her shorn, jagged curls, which she had yet to trim. She turned to him, and their gazes locked. "Because your clan is in danger and needs your help. And you always help your people, no matter the risk to yourself."

She stared back at him, then her shoulders drooped and she sighed. "We need something stronger than tea."

She collected their cups and carried them into the kitchen, dumping the remainder of the tea out the open window. Then she crouched down, reached into the cupboard behind some clay pots, and brought out a jug.

"Wine?" Callum asked.

She made a scoffing sound. "Nay, whisky. My grandmother's recipe, passed down through her family for generations. It'll clean the fuzz off your teeth for weeks."

After rinsing the mugs out with water from a pail, she poured in three generous slugs of *uisge beatha* and set them on the table, then sat down. The men joined her, and the crow took the fourth seat, across from Lachlan. 'Twas unnerving looking into those black eyes.

"How on earth did you get a crow for a pet?" he asked.

"He fell from his nest and broke his wing. I nursed him back to health, although he still canna fly long distances."

Lachlan shook his head. "You really must meet Caitlin. The two of you will be fast friends."

"Does she have a bird too?"

"That I doona know, but when I first met her, she had Darach and the rest of us, all trained warriors, running around thinking we were under attack, when a wee bird had just fallen from its nest."

"She sounds like a woman of great compassion."

"Aye, she is," he said, and Callum nodded in agreement.

Amber lifted her cup into the air, and they followed suit. "To catching Machar Murray before I am killed, raped, or ruined."

"Amber—"

"Doona Amber me, Lachlan MacKay, just drink your damned whisky and tell me your plan."

He sighed then raised the mug again, and all three of them swallowed the whisky in one gulp. The fiery drink burned all the way down before it hit his stomach. He coughed, his eyes watering, and he sucked in great lungfuls of air, as did Callum and Amber.

"I see now why they call whisky the breath of life," he said, wheezing. "You gasp for air once you've swallowed it, like the first time you breathe when you enter this world—after you've had your arse slapped."

Amber dropped her hand to the table with a bang, still holding her cup, and laughed. 'Twas infectious, and Lachlan found himself joining in. Callum too, despite the terrible toast she'd given.

She pulled their cups toward her and poured another round.

"One more, I think, then tell me your plan. I'll be more likely to say aye if the whisky runs through my veins."

❧

Amber looked out the window from her perch at the counter in her kitchen and rubbed the back of her hand over her brow to stop the sweat from trickling into her eyes. She'd spent all day in her torn-up garden and kitchen, salvaging and preserving as many of the herbs, fruits, and vegetables as she could. Now the sun was setting, and she still had plenty to do.

Lachlan, Callum, and several others had helped as much as they could after she'd been told the "plan," but they'd been busy putting things in motion to catch Murray. Working in the garden, kitchen, and the surrounding forests had given them a reason to stay at her cottage all day, while surreptitiously locating the best places to hide additional men—in case Murray was nearby and watching them.

The plan was simple. Pretend that she and Lachlan were lovers in her isolated cottage and wait for Murray to attack. Callum had assured her she'd be safe. They'd have the best guards secretly watching the cottage while Lachlan waited inside with her.

Naught to worry about, other than her clan believing she was tupping their laird without the benefit of marriage. Or that Murray might slip past everyone like the tricky fox he was and kidnap or kill her. Or, and probably worst of all, being locked up in an intimate setting with Lachlan all night long—without giving in to her urge to touch him.

God's blood! How was she going to do that?

The lairds had left before supper, leaving men behind, hidden in the forest around her cottage. After the sun set, Lachlan would ride back with a few elite guards and spend the night with her. Every morning, just before dawn, he would return to the castle. The guards would be sworn to secrecy, but rumors would get out anyway. She had strict instructions that when Lachlan returned, she was to come to the door, stand in the light, and behave in an intimate fashion with him.

She didn't know exactly what that would entail, but Callum had said it could be as simple as a kiss on the cheek. She blew out a breath as she poured vinegar over some cucumbers and sealed the container. It may be simple for him, but he wasn't filled with the need to press his lips to Lachlan's, feel the slide of their tongues against each other again.

Or so she assumed.

She laughed at the idea of Callum pining away for Lachlan. Then she sighed and muttered to herself, "Quit worrying, Amber. You said 'aye,' exactly as they knew you would. So just make the best of it. Put Lachlan to work. That'll keep you both busy."

She stored the cucumbers in the cupboard then looked over her cottage. Every surface was covered in the rescued plants, waiting to be dried, cooked, or preserved. The fire burned hot to help with the drying, and she'd tied her hair back from her face with a ribbon because it was warm, despite the windows being open. She was certain her hair looked funny, probably sticking out in a jagged mess, but all the better to keep Lachlan at bay.

Still, she didn't want to feel soiled when he was here and not be able to wash herself, so she filled her kettle and set it over the fire to heat. She ate while she waited for the water to boil, then closed the shutters against the dusk and barred the cottage doors. After pouring water from the kettle into a pot of cool water until it was the right temperature, she stripped off her clothes, dipped her cloth, and washed in front of the fire.

The knocking at her door startled her, and she jumped, her heart racing. God's blood, she wasn't expecting him so soon. She dropped her cloth and grabbed her drying towel, wrapping it around herself, her hands shaking.

"I need a minute," she yelled, then ran to her trunk and pulled out a clean shift and arisaid. She dressed quickly, using the cloth to wipe her feet before putting on socks and shoes. She brushed her fingers through her hair as she walked to the door, then gave up and tucked it back under the ribbon.

Taking a deep breath, she tried to slow her frantic pulse, to no avail. She put a frown on her face to cover her excitement before changing it to a smile. She was supposed to be greeting her lover. How would that look if Murray watched from the woods?

She unbarred the door and opened it. "I was going to say you're early but…"

The night was almost black, and when the firelight from inside her cottage spilled out far enough to illuminate her visitor, she froze. "Niall."

His eyebrows rose. "But what?"

She opened and closed her mouth, then said, "But…I meant to say you're late. I expected to see your nosy face here much earlier." She cocked her hip and raised her chin, daring him to contradict her.

He scoffed, the same noise she'd used earlier when talking to Callum and Lachlan, and pushed past her over the threshold. He carried a sturdy bag on his shoulder, filled with something heavy.

"For the love of God, Niall. Did you carry that all the way from the castle?" She helped take it off his shoulder and laid it on the kitchen chair. It clunked noisily. "What's in here? Did you steal Lachlan MacKay's gold?"

"Pots to help with the preserving. I thought you may need more. And I would have come sooner, but Laird MacKay"—he emphasized Lachlan's formal title—"had me going over all of Machar Murray's letters and belongings in his room and in the solar, hoping to piece together what he's been up to the last five years. And maybe get some idea where he's gone."

She knew where he'd gone, or hadn't gone, according to Lachlan, but she didn't tell Niall that. The last thing she wanted was for him to fret.

But he surprised her by adding, "I worry Murray didn't go far enough, especially with you back here at your cottage—alone. What if he ne'er left, Amber? He's dangerous, that one. Maybe even deranged in his estimation of himself and about what he thinks is his. He's sure to want to do you harm. Canna you come back to the castle and stay until we know for sure he's been caught?"

She stared at him, confounded for the second time since he'd arrived. "Niall, thank you for your concern, but I'm safe here. I've been alone in this cottage since my grandmother died, and it's safer now than it's e'er been." She didn't like lying to Niall, but she couldn't tell him the truth. Lachlan and Callum had set her up as bait, and the sooner she got the steward out of her cottage the better—for a number of reasons. The most important being that she didn't want Niall to find Lachlan here.

"And thank you for the pots," she continued. "I plan to work through the night to get the preserving done, so 'tis best if you head back to the castle now."

His face grew mulish, and he sat himself down on one of the chairs. "Nay. I'll stay to help and sleep in your extra bed. No one will object to an old man spending the night."

Aye, but would they object to a young, virile man who was in the sights of all the young lasses, and happened to be her laird? The answer to that was obvious, and she sighed.

"Nay. You already work too hard. And I want to be alone. The encounter with Father Odhran this morning upset me. I need time to myself."

Another knock sounded at the door, and Amber cringed inside.

Niall shot up, his eyes wide. "Are you expecting anyone?"

"Nay…" She dithered with a cabbage on the table and the knock came again, followed by Lachlan's voice, saying "Amber?"

"Is that Laird MacKay?" Niall asked.

"I doona know. Wait here." She rushed to the door before he got there and opened it to see Lachlan, as expected, looking so big and brawny. Before he could speak, she said, "Laird MacKay, what are you doing here? Niall, you're right. 'Tis our laird."

Lachlan's eyes widened in understanding just before she stepped outside, closed the door behind her, and darted up to kiss his cheek—as Callum had asked. But Lachlan turned his head toward her just as she did, and their lips brushed.

So soft. Everything within her stopped for an instant, her breath, her heart, before speeding back to life. He grunted and leaned into her, putting his hand on the door behind her.

Unfortunately, Niall must have opened it at the same time, and Lachlan tumbled past her, just catching himself before he knocked the steward over.

"Laird MacKay," Niall squawked, frowning from him to Amber then back to him.

"Forgive me, Niall," Lachlan said, the color elevated in his cheeks. "I had just leaned my hand on the door to open it when you pulled inward."

"Why was it shut?" Niall asked.

"A big wasp flew by my head and tried to get in." Amber said, pleased at her quick response.

The steward looked out suspiciously and shut the door behind them. "A nasty creature, if e'er there was one. Reminds me of Machar Murray. They take what they want, hurting others, and think they can get away with it." He placed his hands on his hips and furrowed his brow. "Why are you here, Laird? Have you come to tell Amber she should stay at the castle? 'Tis not safe for her here. Machar Murray could still be out there. He dwelled o'er much on her."

If she hadn't been watching and waiting for Lachlan's response, she wouldn't have noticed his slight hesitation, he was that good. As it was, he looked at her, concerned, and said, "You can stay at the castle for as long as you like, Amber, you're always welcome, but I understand why you'd want to come home after what happened to your garden. We'll keep an eye on Father Odhran from now on to make sure he's no longer a bother. As for Machar Murray, I doona think you have to worry. We've tracked him out of MacPherson territory. It looks like he's heading to Inverness, most likely to catch a ship to France. There's nowhere in Scotland for him to hide."

"He's a tricky one, Laird. Make sure he doesn't circle around and come back."

"I'm committed to seeing him hang for what he did to my brother, Niall. I'll ne'er stop chasing him till he's dead."

A crafty look entered Niall's eye. "If you aren't here to warn Amber, then why are you here? 'Tis not proper for you to be alone with an unwed lass. I doona know how they do things at Clan MacKay, but at Clan MacPherson, if a man wants to be alone with a woman, he must marry her first."

Aye, here it goes, her reputation thrown out the door like slop for the pigs. She supposed 'twas no worse to be thought a *besom* than to be thought a witch. She was about to answer Niall, when Lachlan said, "But I'm not alone. You're here. I brought pots for Amber, just as you did."

He opened the door, reached outside, and carried in a bag about the same size as Niall's. When he opened it, Amber saw numerous pots she could use for preserving fruit and vegetables. Probably more than she needed, but she could always return the unused ones later.

'Twas a sweet thing for Lachlan to do—bringing

the pots and saving her reputation, even though it was at odds with their plan—and her throat tightened at the gesture.

Well, no need to spoil the ruse now. Taking the bag, she laid out the pots. "Since you're both here and intent on being so helpful, let's get to work."

She smiled at the surprised looks on their faces. "Have either of you e'er peeled an onion? 'Tis an experience you'll ne'er forget."

Nine

LACHLAN SAT IN HIS SOLAR—AYE, *his* SOLAR, FOR IT had come to feel like his the last few weeks, the MacPherson clan too—at the large desk covered in sheets of parchment, quills, ink, and scattered sand, and wrote a letter to his foster father, Gregor MacLeod. The floor was stone, and the hangings on the wall that depicted the castle's busy life faded. An open window let in the day's warmth and light as well as the cheerful sounds from the bailey below.

He needed Gregor's help, and not just on strategy. Nay, he needed something else, something harder to define, and it…unsettled him. He suspected it had to do with Amber.

Worry for her well-being, perhaps. Certainly, that had taken precedence over the outrage and need for vengeance he'd felt the last five years since his brother's death.

He should be out there with his and Callum's men beating the bushes to force Murray out of hiding, riding him down. Instead, he spent his days near Amber in the castle and rode to her cottage every evening, hoping this would finally be the night he could be alone with her. So far, he'd spent time with Niall, Finola, the children—Ian, Mary, and Breanna—Tavis, Osgar, and several other MacPhersons, which had been good to get to know key members of the clan but not so good to seduce Amber.

Although she was not the kind of woman who could be tempted. She'd either want to be with him, or she wouldn't.

Lachlan was hoping she would choose him.

After a few hours visiting at the cottage each night, he would return to the castle with his guards, filled with worry for her safety even though his men surrounded her home. He wanted to turn around, but he knew Murray might be watching, and Lachlan had to trust his men to keep her safe.

All he could do was make himself a better target.

As for the chaperones, he had no doubt Niall was the one responsible for that, although Lachlan couldn't understand why. Not after the steward had tried to catch him and Amber in a compromising position the first day he was here. Maybe the old fox had had a change of heart?

Or maybe he had bigger plans?

Leaning back in his chair, Lachlan raked his fingers through his hair and considered not going that night. It wasn't that he didn't enjoy himself—he did—it was only that the frustration of being close to Amber and not being able to touch her was killing him. Even when they were arguing, which they often did, he wanted to be near her.

He couldn't ever remember being this drawn to

a woman. This...enthralled, despite how much she annoyed him.

He'd had lovers in other clans, of course, lots of them. They were almost all older women with grown children and husbands who had died years before. They enjoyed his company and the boon of being leman to a laird, but never once had they loved him. Or needed him.

Or he, them.

Yet weeks ago, the morning after he'd taken the castle, he'd sat at Amber's feet in the great hall as she slept. When she'd woken that first time, stared at him sleepily, he'd felt like he was drowning. And it wasn't the unusual color of her eyes or beauty of her face still flecked with dried blood that held him captive, it was the way she had looked at him—soft, vulnerable. At that moment, in that brief period of time between sleep and wakefulness, the woman who surrendered to no one, had surrendered to him.

She'd needed him. And something in him had needed her back.

A knock sounded at the door, and he sat forward again as Callum walked in.

"I saw Niall talking to Isla," his foster brother said. "It looks like she'll be your chaperone tonight."

"Aye, I saw it too. From the window." He picked up his quill and tapped it on the parchment, the ink having dried long ago. "I was thinking, maybe I wouldnae go tonight."

Callum raised his brows as he turned a worn, wooden chair toward the desk and sat down. "Why e'er not?"

"'Tis just…what good is it doing? I'm not spending the night, so Murray hasn't attacked."

"You doona know that's true. Stay the course, Lachlan. 'Tis working. Possibly even better than we expected. Everyone thinks you're courting Amber. Murray will have had wind of it. You courting her, winning her, will be worse to him than if you just bedded her."

"Why?"

"Because it shows you care for her, and since she keeps inviting you in, she must care for you too. He'll want to crush that. And if he thinks you love her, he'll be more inclined to want to take her away from you."

A shiver ran up Lachlan's spine. He wasn't sure if it was because Callum had mentioned Murray taking Amber away from him or the notion that he might be falling in love with her. Nay, it couldn't be that. He had no desire to marry. Ever.

He frowned. "Sometimes, Callum, I think you're talking out your arse."

"Well, you can kiss said arse later when Murray is in your hands. Come now. All you have to do is ask yourself—how would you feel?"

"What do you mean?"

"Think about Amber taking a lover… Now think about her being in love with him."

Lachlan released a long, pent-up breath. His stomach had twisted in that way that left him feeling anxious and unsettled. Feelings he wasn't used to. "You may be right."

Callum reached forward and picked up one of the sealed letters from the desk, this one addressed to their foster brother Darach MacKenzie. "So, you've asked him to come?"

"Aye. Gregor and the rest of the lads too. And I asked Darach to bring the MacKenzie priest, Father Lundie. He's a good man. He can advise us on what to do with Father Odhran."

Another knock sounded, and Lachlan called out, "Come in."

The door pushed open, and Hamish entered, his grizzled face smiling at them in greeting. "Is this a good time?" he asked.

Lachlan nodded at his second-in-command. "What news?"

Hamish shut the door and stepped forward. "Still no sign of Murray. The MacPhersons are working with us to make sure we doona miss any caves or other natural hiding places, but so far, we've seen naught of him. We need more men, maybe some dogs. We could have crossed his path several times already if he's on the move."

"I've sent letters to Gregor and the lads, asking them to bring their men. I'll ask Darach to bring his dogs too. I thought we may have had Murray by now. Callum's plan with Amber was promising."

"It still is," Callum objected. "He'll move against her soon. I'd lay gold on it."

Lachlan fisted his hand on the table. "Then we'll stay alert. He's waiting for us to lose focus, most likely. We have to catch him before he hurts Amber more than he already has."

"Aye," both men agreed.

"What of Father Odhran?" Lachlan asked.

"We're watching him," Hamish said. "He's been shunned by the clan e'er since he tore up Amber's garden. And there was some discussion amongst the warriors about what he'd intended to do to her goats, especially the wee female he'd tied so tight to the tree. The men became quite lewd. Word will get out what was said, and it will add to his humiliation, isolating him further. He'll contact Murray in a few days if he hasn't done so already."

Lachlan grunted. He had no sympathy for Father Odhran—the priest had brought all this trouble on himself. He could have helped Amber and the MacPhersons against Machar Murray. Instead, he'd destroyed the letters Niall had written to Gregor MacLeod asking for help, he'd persecuted Amber and any pregnant woman who'd come to her in need, and he'd let Murray dig an escape route from the chapel under the castle walls.

Most importantly, he'd accused Amber of unnatural relations with the male goat. For that alone, as far as Lachlan was concerned, he deserved to go to hell.

"What other information would you have us leak to him?" Hamish asked.

"Let him know we've asked Gregor and our foster brothers to come," Callum said, "and that we're bringing in specially trained dogs to sniff out Murray. That'll put a fire under the rat."

Lachlan nodded, "And also…" He stopped as his heart began to race. Both men looked at him when he didn't continue. He had to slow his breath and clear his throat before he could speak normally. "Also… Callum thinks it will work to our benefit if Murray believes I intend to marry Amber. Arrange it so he hears those whispers as well as the others."

"Aye." Hamish returned to the door, then he hesitated, his fingers wrapped around the handle. He turned back, looking almost sheepish. "I've been asked by several of our men, Callum's too—and some MacPhersons—what your intentions are toward the lass? They want to pursue her, many saying they're in love with her, but they doona want to encroach if you've laid a claim."

Lachlan scowled. "First of all, I canna claim her like she's a horse or a cow. Amber will decide what she wants and no one else. Second of all, they canna be in love with her if they doona know her, and believe me, she hasn't let any of them close enough to know her." Then it struck him, and he felt his stomach drop as he turned to Callum. "Has she?"

"Nay, only you."

He nodded, suddenly pleased. Which really only proved he was an idiot, because he had no desire to claim anyone. Both he and Amber knew their "courtship" was a ruse.

"So what shall I tell them, then?" Hamish asked, his brow furrowed in confusion. "They can still pursue her, even though we want everyone to think Laird MacKay is courting her?"

Callum shook his head. "I think you should say anyone can pursue her, but they willna have any luck because she's fallen in love with Lachlan, and the two of them intend to formalize it verra soon."

"Formalize?" Lachlan's pleasure from before faded, and he found himself feeling yoked. "Doona you think that's going too far?"

"Aye, maybe. Hamish, instead, let it be known that when you asked Laird MacKay, he got verra testy at the idea of other men pursuing Amber, even though he said he had no claim on her." He pointed to Lachlan's face. "Try to mimic that expression when you tell them. And then say it's a risky move on their part."

Lachlan could see the glint of laughter in Callum's eyes and knew he was being deliberately provoked. 'Twas working.

He'd just opened his mouth to deny his irritable mood when another knock sounded on the door. He gritted his teeth. "Come in."

Earc poked his head through the opening, an expectant look on his face. He nodded at them. "Lairds, Hamish."

Lachlan took a deep, calming breath. "Is something wrong, Earc?"

"Nay, not wrong, exactly."

"What then?"

Earc looked at Hamish. "Did you ask him yet? About Amber."

"What about Amber?" But that puppy dog look had entered Earc's eyes, and Lachlan already knew. The heat in his body rose as his blood began to boil.

Earc continued. "'Tis just that I'm in love with her, and I want to know if—"

"Out! All of you, out!" Lachlan yelled. "Our meeting is over."

Earc jumped, and Hamish quickly pushed him through the door, shutting it tightly behind them. Callum fell forward in his chair, laughing. Lachlan watched him for a minute, knowing his other foster brothers would hear about this the moment they arrived. He picked up his quill, twirled it in annoyance, then tossed it at Callum. He caught it one-handed, still laughing.

Lachlan picked up his bottle of ink to toss next, then thought better of it and set it back down. "Let me know when you're done."

Callum wiped his hand across his eyes. "Done," but then he laughed some more. Finally, he sighed and said, "I'm done…for now. I doona think I've e'er seen you so undone since we came here, and not because of Machar Murray. 'Tis our bright, redheaded witch who's unsettled you."

Lachlan rubbed his palm over his stomach. There was that word again: unsettled. "I doona like you calling her that."

"A faery, then, for she's certainly cast a spell o'er you. If it's any consolation, I think she feels the same way. Which is a conundrum, because she's perhaps even less likely to marry than you are."

His gaze jumped to Callum's. "Why do you think she doesn't want to marry?"

"What are we now, a bunch of old women sitting around talking about other people's feelings?"

"Well, you certainly claim to know everything else."

"I can think like an obsessed man, but I canna know what is in a woman's heart. I doona think even they know. Best you ask Amber yourself. Why doona you wait until Isla and her husband leave tonight, then go back and see her. Or show up a wee bit early."

He grunted, then stretched out his hand toward Callum. "Give me my quill back. I have to add to my letter to Darach, ask him to bring the dogs."

Callum rose and handed it over. "Aye, you do that. I'm going to check on the men hidden around Amber's place. I have a feeling Murray will strike tonight."

His words left Lachlan cold. Once he'd finished his letter, he walked to the window and looked out over the bailey toward the loch and the sprawling village beside it. The air was warm from the summer sun, and it slowly leeched the chill from his bones as he watched the clouds drift across the sky.

Some might say he was brooding, but Lachlan preferred to think of it as solving a problem. Even though he wasn't sure what the problem was, precisely, or how to fix it.

When he heard Amber's name called from below, he looked down and saw her crossing the grass toward the keep, her healing bag in her hands, her orange-gold hair shining brightly in the sunshine.

He still had guards on her to keep her safe, but he'd ordered them to stay back when she was in the castle. When she left, she'd allowed them to ride with her, but only after much persuasion on his part. It would force Murray to attack at their one weak spot—her cottage—where ideally, Lachlan and his men would be waiting.

Two warriors who were not part of her guard dogged her heels, and Earc hurried from the keep to meet her. She kept going. Lachlan couldn't see her face, but he imagined she must find it annoying.

He certainly did. And more.

That familiar pressure grew in his chest, and he whistled sharply. The men looked up. A second whistle accompanied by a hand gesture indicated that they should scatter. All three of them stopped, then went in different directions while Amber continued up the steps and into the keep.

He listened for her steps, hoping she would come see him, but after a while he blew out a breath and returned to his desk. Maybe he would go see her early tonight, as Callum had suggested. A wee bit of alone time might do them some good. Or they'd end up fighting like they often did.

Either way, it would finally be just them.

Ten

AMBER CROSSED THE GREAT HALL, THE RUSHES SOFT beneath her shoes and the air still crisp due to the stone walls that kept in the cold. All signs of her makeshift hospital had been cleared away, and bright sunlight streamed through the high windows. Warriors had gathered in small groups for the noon meal, the tables and benches beginning to fill the space. The fire burned low in the hearth with cooking pots and kettles hanging over it—used to warm food and water from the separate kitchen.

She approached the stairs to the keep's second level, absently lifting a hand in greeting to those who called out to her. She breathed in through her nose and out through her mouth in an attempt to calm her racing heart. A moment ago, all she'd felt was annoyance as the men tagged along at her heels, trying to talk to her. She hadn't wanted to be rude to them; she never wanted that, but God's blood, the constant clamoring for her attention was enough to rile a saint. Especially as the men seemed to consider it a badge of honor when she rejected them—usually with a flat out "nay."

Then the whistle had come from above and the

men had scattered. She hadn't looked up; she'd known who it was. Now her blood whooshed through her veins like she'd imbibed too much ale.

A part of her wanted to go see Lachlan—whether to thank him for his help or tell him to refrain from meddling in her affairs, she hadn't decided yet. But just the thought of being alone with him had filled her body with the urge to rub against his.

So she tiptoed up the stairs and down the hall toward Adaira's room, as quiet as a mouse, not trusting herself.

What would it be like to be completely alone with him after all those nights of being in his company, surrounded by her friends and neighbors? Especially in a room as small as his solar.

They'd spent half their time together in the evenings arguing and baiting each other, even if their chaperones were unaware of it. It might be as subtle as a raised brow or tiny smirk or a more obvious eye roll. They shared a silent language that could say more between them than a whole night with someone else.

When she reached Adaira's door, she breathed a sigh of relief that she hadn't succumbed to her urges and gone to Lachlan's solar. After a brief knock, she pushed inside the chamber that was across from Callum's. The lassie lay on her back, the forest-green quilts pulled up beneath her arms. Ian sat in a worn, matching chair beside the bed with a book in his lap.

Adaira frowned at her. Amber frowned back, then stuck out her tongue. When Ian laughed, Adaira transferred her frown to him. For a lass of ten, she looked terribly fierce.

"What?" Ian asked her.

"If you're going to be friends with her, you canna be friends with me."

"That's just daft," he said as Amber settled onto the quilts beside Adaira. "Amber's our healer, and she takes care of Breanna and me."

"I thought you lived at the castle."

"We do now. The laird says it's safer. But when our ma died last year, we stayed in our cottage. Amber spent time with us making sure we were all right, especially Breanna. We couldnae live with her because of Machar Murray, aye?"

"Well, she's a liar," Adaira said, crossing her arms over her chest. "She pretended to be a lad and—"

"I ne'er told you I was a lad," Amber said patiently, letting Adaira get her list of complaints off her chest before she examined her—as she did every time Amber came to see her.

"Well, you told Lachlan you were a lad."

"Aye, and he's forgiven me."

"And you kneed Earc in his private regions."

"He's forgiven her too," Ian said, rolling his eyes. "And now he's mooning o'er her like some lass in a love ballad."

"Ian," she reprimanded him, and he shrugged, not at all sorry. "It's time for me to examine Adaira now. You can come back later."

Adaira jutted out her chin. "I want him to stay."

"Nay, lass. I canna." Ian rose and placed the book on the bedside table. "I have to collect Breanna from the miller's. One of their cats had kittens. We'll come by later. Maybe with a kit or two if they can leave their mother."

"All right, then. Doona forget."

"I willna." He patted Adaira's head and kissed Amber's cheek before leaving.

Amber moved closer. "Adaira, I'm sorry I deceived you. 'Twas a life-or-death situation, and I needed you to free me."

"You could have asked. I would have helped."

"Aye, perhaps. Or maybe you would have called Earc, and he would have restrained me. I needed to be here to help during the battle, do you understand? I was at my wits' end, and I couldnae risk it." She brushed a hand over the lass's forehead. "But then you came along and saved me. Saved us all."

Adaira scowled, but Amber saw her chin wobble. The lass was hurt by her actions, not angry, although anger was what she showed. She'd trusted Amber, connected with her, only to have that thrown back in her face.

"I understand you feel betrayed, and you have every right to be mad. I did betray you. But maybe, now that you're feeling a wee bit better, you can forgive me too, and we can move on to other things."

Adaira pressed her lips together as if trying to hold back her question, before blurting out, "What kind of things?"

"Well, you asked me to teach you how to protect yourself lest you were e'er attacked, how to use your hands and body as a weapon. Remember?"

Adaira's eyes grew round. "Aye. You said your father taught you."

"He did. And now I can teach you, if you like. But slowly at first. You're still healing."

The lass struggled to prop herself up, but Amber stopped her. "Nay, I want to look at your belly first." She pulled the pillows out from behind Adaira, laying her flat on the bed and uncovering her wound.

"You looked at it yesterday," the lass protested.

"Aye, and I'll look at it again tomorrow."

The cut was healing well. The wound had closed both inside and out, and the infection had abated. Rising, she poured some water into a bowl from the kettle by the fire and dipped in a clean cloth. After squeezing out the excess, she gently cleaned Adaira's belly, put on a salve, and rebandaged it.

"Tell me if it hurts," she said as she prodded in a circle around the injury.

"'Tis healed," Adaira said, then pushed her shift down and pulled herself up.

"Aye, it looks good." Amber put the pillows behind her back again and laid the quilt over her legs.

"Tell me now how you beat Earc. He's so much bigger than you, yet he couldnae walk for several minutes after you rode away. If I had known how to do that when we were attacked by those men, maybe they wouldnae have gotten away."

"'Tis doubtful, lass. You were surrounded by three trained warriors. The skill I'm going to teach you is for one-on-one situations, so you can escape like I did with Earc. Do you understand?"

"Aye, but if you'd had a sword, you could have cut off Earc's head. He was rolling around on the ground, moaning. You could have grabbed his dagger and ended him."

Amber repressed an exasperated sigh. "Adaira, I

didn't want to kill Earc, and you doona always win. Remember, I tried to get away from Lachlan too, but he just ended up tying my hands together."

"Well, of course it didn't work on my cousin. He's our laird!"

Her lips tightened in annoyance. "If he hadn't been expecting a fight, I might have bested him. He pulled me off my horse, so he surprised me. Part of what works with this technique is the attack is often unexpected, and it happens when you're in close quarters. So you have to wait until their guard is down."

Her eyes lit up. "You trick them."

"Aye, I suppose so."

"I like the sound of that!"

"Adaira, 'tis not something you use unless someone is trying to hurt you or control you. If you did what I'm going to show you on, say, Ian, he could be damaged for life."

"I would ne'er hurt Ian. He's my friend."

"That's good, but there may be others that you doona like, and you may be tempted to hurt them if they're riling you. But you must ne'er inflict violence on a person if it can be avoided."

"Is that why you ne'er hurt Machar Murray? I heard some of the men say he'd been after you."

Her stomach tightened. "'Tis more complicated than that. I used my wits to stay free of him, and then when that failed, I ran. Only to be caught by Lachlan."

"Why didn't you fight him?"

"Because Murray's a smart, strong, wicked man, and I didn't want to provoke him if I could avoid it. Chances are he would have defeated me, just like

Lachlan did, and then he would have been even angrier. It's a last resort, Adaira, do you hear me?"

"Aye, can you show me now?"

Amber nodded and put her healing bag aside. "You willna learn everything at once, and later on you'll have to practice, but start thinking about the points on our bodies that really hurt when you hit them—like our noses, the tops of our feet, and our ears—and other spots that are really hard and will hurt someone else if we hit *with* them—like our elbows, the heels of our hands, and our heads. So when we're in close to someone and they're trying to harm us, we can fight back using our minds to choose where and when to hit, as well as our bodies."

"So if I were to use my elbow to hit your nose, that would really hurt?"

"Aye, it might even break it."

"But you didn't do that to Earc?"

"Nay. I caught Earc with his guard down and pressed my thumbs here." She stretched out Adaira's arm and found the nerve ending above the elbow that hurt so much. "You tell me when you feel this." She pressed softly.

"Now! It sort of tingles."

"In a bad way?"

"Aye."

"So I pressed hard enough on Earc that his arm was rendered useless."

"And then you kneed him in the privates. I saw that."

"I did. And I'm sorry I had to."

"But you got away. And you made it back here in time to help everyone."

"Aye. Including you and Earc."

Adaira stared at her for a moment then looked down and plucked at the quilts with her fingers. Finally, she let out a deep sigh and said, "All right. I'll forgive you."

❧

"Amber MacPherson you wait right there!"

Amber turned and scowled at Isla as the pregnant woman waddled down the passageway toward her. Her friend got bigger every day, and that glowing, energized state she'd had two months ago had turned into uncomfortable exhaustion. "Or what? You're going to chase me down? Bump me with your belly?"

"Nay, I'll tell our laird and make him chase you down. And if that doesn't work, I'll tell my husband you were mean to me, and you willna like what he does to you then."

"I wasn't mean to you."

"Aye, you were. You made fun of my belly." Suddenly she leaned against the stone wall and made a pained face.

Amber rushed over. "What is it?"

Isla grabbed her sleeve and held tight. "My way of getting you to come here. You're right, I canna chase you, but I can hold on for as long as it takes." She straightened from the wall, her brown eyes determined. "I spoke to Niall and he said you were free for a while."

She blew a short, dismissive sound through her lips. "What does Niall know?"

"Everything. You canna fart without him knowing."

Amber laughed. "Having trouble, are we?"

"Aye, the romance in my marriage died the moment Alban got me with bairn."

"Tell that to your husband. He worships every inch of you—belly most of all."

When Isla simply nodded, Amber laughed again.

"'Tis time," Isla said. "You've been putting me off for days. You doona want me making the trek up here when it's dangerous, do you? Because you know I will."

"Blackmail?"

"Aye."

Amber sighed and scowled again. "All right. Lead on."

When Isla tugged her arm, she followed her down the hall to her old chamber, dragging her feet. A fire roared inside and a chair had been set up next to it, a bowl of water, a brush, a towel, and a blade sharpened to a razor's edge set on a table beside the open window.

"Sit," Isla said, then wrapped a towel around Amber's shoulders, wet the brush, and began to work it through her jagged curls until they were soaked. "I canna believe it's taken me so long to get you here, especially with our new laird visiting you every night."

Amber saw where this was headed and pressed her lips tightly together.

"So that's the way it's going to be, is it?" Isla asked as she put down the brush and fussed with Amber's hair, lifting it and pulling it, even playing with her part. "Not even a wee morsel of information? Niall tells me you fight with him. A lot. And he fights back."

Amber scoffed. "The two of you, like a couple of interfering old women."

"Well, maybe if you gave me some information…"

What could she tell her friend? Certainly naught about Machar Murray or being the bait to catch him. But there were other things, things she clamored to talk about, needed to talk about.

"What do you want to know?" she blurted out, her heart racing.

Isla's eyes jumped to hers, the razor in her hand forgotten. "Really?"

"Aye. Quickly, now, before I change my mind."

"Umm… Have you kissed him?"

"Aye."

"Was it a good kiss?"

"Aye!"

"Oh, Lord. Have you touched him?"

"Of course I've touched him. I just said I kissed him, didn't I?"

"No, I meant down there. Did you touch his cock?"

Her cheeks burned, and she groaned, rethinking her idea to share. "Nay."

"Did he touch you? And I doona mean kissing. Has he touched you with his hands below your neck."

Amber couldn't get the words out, so she just nodded.

"But you haven't—"

She rolled her eyes and let out an exasperated breath. "God's blood, I just told you I haven't touched his cock. Last I heard, that part of his body was an integral part of tupping."

Isla leaned down, her bonnie brown gaze intent on Amber's. "Dearling, are you still a maid? God's truth, I've been so worried for you the past few years with Machar Murray hounding you. If he touched you in any way, you have to know it's not your fault."

Amber's chest tightened, and the feeling continued up her throat and behind her eyes until she felt them tear up. She dashed them away with the back of her hand.

"He ne'er touched me. That's not to say he didn't come close a few times. Twice he came by my cottage at night when I was alone, but I managed to get out and hide before he caught me. Then that last night at the castle he locked me in his chamber, but Niall got me out in time."

She threw her arms around Isla and squeezed tight. "When I left, I ne'er thought I'd see any of you again. This terrible man, who thought he could do whate'er he wanted to me, to the rest of us, had chased me out of my home. Because he felt like he had some right to me. I was so angry. And so…sad."

Isla was crying now too, and hugged her back. "And then Lachlan MacKay appeared. Bigger and bonnier than life itself."

"He pulled me from my horse, dragged me through the scrub, and tied me up."

"So fierce. Protective and commanding. Yet…gentle."

"Were you not listening to me? He. Dragged. Me. Through. The. Scrub."

"I listened. There's listening here"—she touched her ears—"and then listening here"—she touched Amber's heart.

Amber raised a brow and tried to keep a straight face, but when she saw Isla's lips twitch, she burst out laughing—they both did. After a minute, she sighed and said almost dreamily, "He just...doesn't care."

Isla pulled back. "What do you mean he doesn't care? He's been verra helpful with everyone. Kind and generous with his time."

"Nay, I meant...he doesn't care who I am or who I'm not. If I swear, if I'm a witch, if I'm bonnie or not bonnie, if I'm elbow deep inside someone's belly, or pushing bone back into someone's leg, if I'm dirty and bloody and smell of guts and—"

"Enough!" Isla held a hand over her mouth. "He may not care, but I do."

Amber rolled her eyes. "Well, you better get used to it. What do you think's going to happen when you have bairns? I could fill your head with—" She stopped at the horrified look on Isla's face. "Aye, best you doona know. It'll be lovely. You'll push out a perfect, wee bairn, all sweet and pink, and I'll hand him or her to you wrapped in soft, white linen. Just like the baby Jesus."

Isla squeaked and made the sign of the cross over her chest. "Lord have mercy, you'll bring the devil down on both of us."

"See, now, Lachlan would have thought that was funny."

Isla gave her an assessing stare, picked up her blade, and started to shape Amber's hair. "Are you in love with him, then?" she asked after a minute, slicing and fluffing and layering the strands.

Amber found herself holding her breath. "I am in... great annoyance with him most times. And in great... infatuation with him other times. I think about him often—where he is, what he's doing, how his hands and mouth would feel on my body. Things occur to me, interesting things, mundane things, and he's the one I want to share them with." She scowled. "He makes me laugh."

Isla scowled back. "He should be hanged."

"The only man whoe'er made me laugh before was Niall."

"And you certainly doona want to tup Niall."

"I ne'er said I wanted to tup Lachlan either. I said I want his hands and his mouth on my body, but I have no interest in tupping."

"But if you were married—"

"I ne'er said I wanted to marry him, either. And I'm certain he doesn't want to marry me."

"Why doona you want to marry him?"

"Well…why should I?"

"To have bairns."

"I doona know if I want bairns."

"Aye, you do. To have intercourse, then."

"I doona want to have intercourse."

Isla rolled her eyes. "Aye, Amber, you do. You willna be able to get enough of it." She put down her blade and stared at her, fluffing and tugging strands into place. Finally, she said, "To have a man to call your own, who claims you as his own, who you can tell everything to and he'll understand what you mean even if you tell him naught."

"Sounds like witchcraft to me."

"Nay, 'tis something divine, something sacred between the two of you, not profane or mundane, and when you have it, you'll know. Do you want that, Amber?"

"I… I… Aye, maybe I do."

"Well, is Lachlan the man who can give you that?"

"I doona know."

Isla carefully took off the towel and shook it out the window. "I wish we had a mirror, so you could see how bonnie you look. If we were at court, you would start a trend for all the ladies to have short hair. Your eyes were beautiful before, but now they're dazzling. And your lips and cheeks… Amber, you look like an angel."

Amber raised her fingers to her hair. The ends fell evenly about halfway down her neck, with shorter pieces on top and others framing her face.

Isla kissed her cheek. "Niall has asked Alban and me to be there this evening, but I'm not feeling well enough. I'll leave it up to you whether you tell Niall. Maybe you'll want to be alone with Lachlan tonight."

Eleven

AMBER RACED ACROSS THE BAILEY, HER HEART IN HER mouth and Isla's words echoing in her head—*alone with Lachlan tonight*. She couldn't catch her breath, and she couldn't stop moving. Nervous, excited energy coursed through her, mixed with moments of dread.

And it never once occurred to her to tell Niall.

How had she reached the age of almost twenty-two and not experienced this tumultuousness of emotions before? She was as daft as a bat. Addled as a sun-drenched walrus.

Perhaps because she'd never met Lachlan MacKay before and she'd spent the last five years protecting herself and everyone she loved from Machar Murray—not to mention his three dogs and Father Odhran.

Speaking of which, she heard a strange sound—like the bleating of a goat, but not a real goat—and looked toward the chapel. Father Odhran had been backed against the stone wall, surrounded by three men—two MacPhersons and one MacKay. The priest had a strange look on his face: part defiance, part fear, part abhorrence.

Amber slowed to a stop as she watched them, an

uneasy feeling forming in the pit of her stomach. The priest saw her, and his face turned thunderous. He spat on the ground. She hardened her heart, reminding herself of what he'd done, what he'd said to her, and she moved on. But she couldn't help looking back. The aggressors had stepped even closer, and now the look on the priest's face was outright fear.

She ran back toward them, saw Earc, Tavis, and the stable master, Osgar—all dear, protective men, if a wee bit annoying at times, pressing in on Father Odhran.

"Tavis! Stop, please," she said.

He turned to her, his face a livid red color. "Amber, you shouldnae be here. You doona know what the priest has been saying. What he's been doing." He grabbed Father Odhran's robes and yanked at the fabric. A tearing sound filled the air, and the garment hung from his shoulder.

She pushed herself between the men and stood in front of the priest, facing his accusers. She could hear his jagged gasps behind her, feel his breath on her exposed neck. She was sure the men's aggression had something to do with Father Odhran's destruction of her gardens. Then she remembered the bleating sound.

"Is this about my goats?" she asked.

The men looked uncomfortable. "'Tis not for your ears," Earc said. He reached around Amber and ripped again at Father Odhran's robe. The priest let out a frightened squeak.

She placed her hands on her hips, trying to make herself as big as possible, and scowled. "I know what he said—he accused me of it directly. And you're right, 'tis not for anyone's ears. I found it as disgusting and infuriating as you did, all of you, but we canna stoop to his level."

"What about his plans for poor Belle?" Tavis asked, his voice enraged. For such a big man, he had a very soft heart.

"Aye. Next it will be the other animals in my stable." Osgar shuddered. "'Tis an abomination!"

Amber frowned. Animals were butchered for food all the time. Sheep, pigs, cows, chickens. It wasn't like Osgar to get so upset about that.

"I'm sure he wouldnae have killed any of your animals, Osgar, only mine. He accused Belle and Beele of being…well…"

"They're demons, and she's their witch whore!" the priest yelled.

Earc roared in fury and lunged forward. A familiar hand snaked through the men and dragged her out of the brewing fight. Lachlan pushed her behind him, his face carved in stone, and wrapped both arms around Earc, his biceps bulging as he tried to bring the bigger man under control.

"Stand down! All of you!" he commanded.

Tavis and Osgar hesitated, then stepped back.

"You didn't hear what he said," Earc yelled, still struggling to break free.

"Aye, I did. And I know what you think he planned to do to that goat, but you canna condemn a man on speculation, else you'd be as bad as him." Lachlan pinned the other two men with his stare, his face flushed with the effort to restrain Earc. "Get to the barracks, Tavis, and the stables, Osgar. And stay there until tomorrow." When they hesitated, he bellowed, "Now!"

Amber had never seen either man move so fast.

She stepped toward Earc, thinking to help Lachlan restrain him, but Lachlan gave her such a searing look she stopped in her tracks—and proceeded to fill with heat and wanting. God's blood, was she excited by the violence? She'd been around many such fights before and never once experienced the tightening of her breasts, the pooling of heat in her groin that she felt now. Her bones had loosened, and she felt like she might melt to the ground.

So 'twas Lachlan, then. His command of the situation. Or maybe the sight of his bulging biceps and chest, all sweaty and tanned, his shirt forgotten somewhere. Aye, she liked that he was strong enough to control a bear of a man like Earc and send the others running to do his bidding. She could only imagine how commanding he'd be in other areas too, making her lie back as he touched and licked her everywhere.

A small sound released from her lips, and he shifted his gaze to hers, his eyes widening as he looked at her.

He turned slowly back to the priest and cleared his throat before speaking. "If you know what's good for you, Father, I suggest you go into the chapel and bar the door. And do not come out until either Laird MacLean or I come to see you. 'Tis not safe for you here anymore."

Father Odhran scurried up the stairs to the wooden door. As he shut it, he looked at Amber, venom in his eyes, and made the sign of the cross.

Earc finally broke free of Lachlan, who'd loosened his hold, and growled. Lachlan bent forward, hands on his knees, sides heaving. His plaid, which was looped over one shoulder, slipped down. Amber couldn't stop her gaze from poring over him, taking in every indent of his ribs, the banding of the muscles that attached to his spine.

"Amber, stop it," he said. "I can barely walk as it is."

She jumped guiltily and turned her head. "Surely, I doona know what you mean."

Lachlan grunted. "I can feel your eyes all o'er me."

Earc looked over his shoulder at them, gaze shifting from one to the other. Then he nodded, as if accepting something, and marched up the steps to bang on the chapel door. "Goat tupper!" he yelled before stomping away.

Amber's jaw dropped. "Goat tupper? Is that what they meant by his plans for Belle?" Her stomach dropped, and she suddenly felt like she might be sick. "Is it true? Please, say it's not true!"

Lachlan straightened and squeezed her hand, pulling her into his side. "Nay, Amber. I doona think so. He believes they're demons, aye? He might have killed them, but not the other. You stopped him before he did serious harm."

Amber rested her head on his chest and let out a relieved sigh, the tension draining from her body. The chapel was located at the far end of the bailey, opposite the barracks, and was relatively secluded, but it wouldn't have mattered who was there. Who might see them. Right now, all she wanted was to lean on this man, to absorb him.

A drop of sweat trickled between the planes of his pectorals, and she traced it with her finger.

"Lachlan."

"Aye." His voice sounded strangled, and she smiled.

"Where's your shirt?"

"In my solar. It was too hot, and I'd just taken it off when I saw Earc and the others following Father Odhran across the bailey. I arrived as fast as I could only to find you'd stepped up to protect him. After everything he'd done to you."

Amber snorted and traced another trickle of sweat down his chest. "Not that he appreciated it."

"Nay."

"He may not be a goat tupper, but he has the brains of one."

A puff of air ruffled her part as Lachlan laughed quietly. "Aye, he does."

She lowered her voice. "Do you think he can hear us?"

"'Tis likely," he said softly.

"Then he should probably hear this."

"What's that?"

She cleared her throat, tried to quell the excitement and nervousness that was sure to come out in her voice. At the same time, she tried to speak loudly and clearly enough that Father Odhran could hear them and pass the message to Murray. "Niall asked Isla and Alban to be our chaperones at the cottage tonight. But Isla told me she doesn't feel well enough to come." Her hand flattened on his skin. "Lachlan, we're going to be alone tonight."

~

Lachlan yanked on Saint's reins for the tenth time, and

the stallion, who'd been tossing his head and veering off the trail that led to Amber's cottage, stamped his feet and huffed. It wasn't Saint's fault; it was Lachlan's fault. The horse simply picked up on Lachlan's nervous energy.

Nay, *nervous* was the wrong word.

Excited? Distracted? Full of anticipation? Aye, all of those...and nervous too.

A rueful smile creased his cheeks. He hadn't been nervous about visiting a woman since he was a lad and hoping to engage in carnal relations for the first time. Which was exactly what he wanted with Amber, but it wasn't just about that. Even if they didn't touch, he couldn't wait to be alone with her. Locked away where nobody could see or hear them. They might fight the whole time they were together, but even that excited him.

He puffed air through his lips, sounding like his horse, and heard Callum laugh softly beside him, riding his much more relaxed mount. It was past dusk, so he couldn't clearly see his foster brother, who was playing one of Lachlan's guards tonight. Tension was high with anticipation of an attack, and everyone was on alert.

"Just stay the course. Doona make her so mad she kicks you out. We need you in there," Callum whispered.

"I'm not an idiot," he whispered back, but he heard Callum's disbelieving snort, and he had to agree. "Aye, maybe I am. But I willna put her in danger."

"And doona lose your head either if she...agrees. You need to stay focused."

Lachlan knew what Callum meant. His horse tossed its head again and sidestepped, a sure sign that Lachlan's tension had just risen another notch. Callum laughed for a second time.

Lachlan wanted to elbow him in his teeth. Instead, he took a deep breath and rolled his head on his neck, loosened his shoulders. Then he patted the bag that hung off his horse's flank. If everything went to hell in there, as it was wont to do when he and Amber were together, he could always give her this. His gifts of flowers hadn't gone over well, but the last few times he'd visited, he'd brought her birdseed, a new hoe for her garden, some rope to replace the one she'd had to cut off Belle, and some medicinal mushrooms he'd picked himself.

Tonight's gift was a wee departure from the others, but he hoped she'd like it as well.

As they neared the cottage, an owl called out, the same one he'd heard every night he approached this spot, and he knew all was well with his men. Callum veered off to take his post at the back of the cottage near the door that led to Amber's garden, and the other guard remained with him until they reached the front entrance.

Lachlan dismounted, and the guard led his horse away.

He raised his hand to knock and noticed it trembled slightly. Caused by his fight with Earc, no doubt. The big man had pushed Lachlan's strength to the limit, and his muscles were weary. What else could it be?

Releasing another breath, he rapped loudly on the wood. Too loudly. He'd probably scared Amber. The door opened quickly, as if she had been waiting on the other side, and he looked down at her. His heart stuttered, then raced to catch up. Had her eyes always been that bright? Her lips that full when she smiled?

"What have you done to your hair?" he asked.

She raised a self-conscious hand to the tips of it and scowled at him. "I cut it. What do you think I've done to it?"

"Your eyes look wider, and your cheeks...they're so high."

She rolled said eyes. "Maybe it's witchcraft." She turned on her heel and stomped into her cottage.

Lachlan pushed through the door, feeling like an idiot. He hoped Callum hadn't heard him or he'd never hear the end of it. And where was his kiss? She was supposed to kiss him in the light from the door, so Murray would see if he watched them.

The cottage was warm and clean, and a fire burned in the hearth. Her crow, Lucy, sat on the back of one of the kitchen chairs, eyeing him. Amber moved into the sitting room and reached toward a kettle that hung over the flames.

"Tea?" she asked.

"Aye, please." He shut the door, barred it, then walked farther into the cottage as she lifted the kettle off the hook with a towel. It bothered him to think she might burn her fingers, and he stretched out his hand for it. "Here, let me."

She raised her brow and held the kettle away from him. "I'm not a lass of three, Lachlan. I'm perfectly capable of lifting a kettle from the fire." She stepped past him, then hesitated and said, "But thank you for your consideration."

He couldn't help smiling at how awkward she sounded. "'Twasn't so hard, was it?"

"Hard?"

"Being gracious."

She gave him a sweet smile, but her eyes turned frosty. "Why doona you sit down and settle in. At this rate, it may be a long night."

He suspected that was Amber's way of telling him he'd ruined his chances.

After making himself comfortable in the biggest chair in front of the fire, he sighed and closed his eyes. He tried to figure out where he'd gone wrong. She'd been smiling at him, albeit hesitantly, when he'd opened the door. She'd seemed almost...hopeful.

So he'd made a muck of it after that.

"'Twas the hair comment, wasn't it?" he asked. "The first thing out of my mouth."

She glanced at him over her shoulder, busy putting herbs in cups and pouring the hot water over them. "Verily, I doona know what you're talking about."

"Aye, you do." He stretched his legs out in front of him and crossed his ankles, hands resting on his belly. "I should have said your hair is lovely, and you look like an angel. Which you do, by the way. To which you would have replied...'tch'!" He made a dismissive, scoffing sound through his lips. "Maybe even rolled your eyes." Which is what he did. Repeatedly, so she was sure to see him.

A wee smile quirked her lips. "You may be right."

She brought the tea over, and after passing him his cup, she sat in her chair, the table between them. He lifted the cup to his nose and smelled honey and chamomile. 'Twas hot, so he blew on it before taking a sip.

And the moment suddenly seemed right. Nay, not just right. Perfect.

"Tastes good," he said.

"Aye, the honey is fresh. Finola gave it to me."

He nodded, and they sat quietly together for a few minutes, drinking their tea. He tried to think of how to ask her to sleep with him tonight, but everything sounded too formal or trite. Besides, she'd probably been asked in every way possible by the horde of men chasing her.

"So...what do we do now?" Her voice caught at the end, like she was a wee bit nervous too.

"Well, you could *try* to tempt me to your bed." Maybe humor would do it.

She half snorted, half laughed, and her hand flew up to cover her face.

"What? You doona think 'tis possible?" he asked. "Aye, most likely. But you could at least try."

"Oh, I think 'tis possible. I think many things are possible tonight. Like darning socks or whittling stakes for the new pen that was broken."

"I've darned socks before."

"You have?"

"Aye. Gregor made us learn how to do all sorts of things. He said we should know how to repair torn clothing, especially socks, for when we were out on long trips. Best not to leave your toe sticking out and exposed to the elements when all it takes is a needle, some yarn, and a wee bit of know-how to prevent an injury."

"I think I'd like your Gregor. When do I get to meet him?"

"Soon. I sent letters out to him and the rest of the lads, asking them to come."

"And they'll just drop everything?"

"Aye, as I would for them." A log popped and shifted in the hearth, sending out sparks. "He'll like you. A great deal. If he was twenty years younger and not still in love with his dead wife, he'd try to convince you to marry him, I'm sure."

"Marry him?"

"Aye, that ceremony the priest performs in front of all your friends and family and ties you to another person for life." By the love of God, what was he doing bringing up marriage?

"God's blood, what are you doing talking about marriage?"

He almost laughed at their dual thoughts. "I doona know. 'Twas almost as big a blunder as what I said about your hair."

"You're as daft as a bat tonight."

"But sweet too. Aye?"

She raised a brow, neither confirming nor denying, and continued to sip her tea. "What happens after Machar Murray is caught?"

"If we take him alive, he'll be hanged for his crimes—against my brother and me, against you and the rest of your clan, against all the other people he's hurt."

"Our clan."

"Sorry?"

"You are now the MacPherson laird, so it's your

clan too. Not just mine. These people care for you. They trust you to do what's best for them."

"I'm doing that, Amber."

"But for how long? Do you intend to leave afterward?"

He rubbed his knuckles along his jaw, suspecting this wasn't just about the clan. She was asking if he planned to leave her. "I willna be gone forever, love. And I'll leave someone here to make sure everyone is safe and things are progressing as they should. You'll be taken care of."

It was the wrong thing to say...again. He knew it the instant her shoulders tightened under her arisaid.

"Nay, thank you. I'm quite capable of taking care of myself."

She clicked her nails on her cup and looked into the fire. He missed the intensity of her gaze on him.

"So you'll stay until just before the first snowfall, then?" she asked.

"Most likely."

"Sounds like you wouldnae want to be trapped here o'er winter."

"I doona know, Amber. At this point, I just want to catch Murray." He leaned forward in his chair so his fingers touched her knees. "And I want to be with you."

"Until winter," she insisted.

"I have to get back. I canna leave my own clan for too long."

She nodded. Then picked up her cup and walked in a stilted fashion back to the kitchen.

"Amber—"

"When you leave, I willna be able to tell you things."

He rose and stared at her back, the tension thrumming in his veins. "Nay, but you can write to me."

"Then I will have told you everything. What about the things you are to understand even though I tell you naught?"

He frowned in confusion. "That doesn't make sense. How can I understand something if you doona tell me? Are you worried someone may find the letters?"

"Nay. I'm worried I'll lose something far more important."

He raised his hands, palms up. "Lose what? Amber, what do you mean?"

"Isla said a man could understand the things I say even if I doona use words. I said it sounded like witchcraft, but all I have to do is look at her and Alban to know it's possible."

"That he can read minds?"

"That something sacred can be formed between a man and a woman. Something divine."

He crossed the room and placed his hands on her shoulders, drawing her back against him.

"I can show you divine, Amber."

She turned her head to the side, resting her cheek on his chest, and inhaled. "I'm sure you can. I keep imagining your hands and mouth on me…"

"As do I, believe me—"

"…but I doona think it would be enough."

His fingers squeezed tight, and he forced himself to ease up. But it was hard to let go—he felt her slipping away, possibly further away than she'd been since they met.

"So you want me to marry you, then?" he asked. "Because I doona e'er plan to marry. Be verra clear on that. And I doona want bairns, either."

"I'm not asking for that."

"Then what are you asking?"

"I doona know. Divine possibility."

He released her and turned around, shoving his hands through his hair.

"I thought you were different."

"Why? Because I curse? Or I'm not afraid to get my hands bloody? I know lots of lasses who do those things."

"Nay, because you ne'er seem to care what people think of you."

"'Tis not about what other people think of me. 'Tis what I think about myself."

He walked to the hearth and leaned on it. "So is that it, then? Have you decided against me?"

"I doona know, Lachlan. I think… I think I care about you, which complicates things."

He turned to look at her, the blood thudding slowly in his ears. "Are you saying you love me?"

"Nay. I doona know you well enough to love you, do I? But…you make me laugh, and while you annoy me, 'tis not in the same way the other men annoy me. Understand?"

"Not in the least. Should I be pleased that my level of annoyance is different from the other men that dog your heels?"

"You should be whate'er you like. 'Tis not my job to placate you."

"I didn't ask you to placate me. Bloody, aggravating woman!"

"Nay, you just asked me for everything else and expect to give naught in return!"

He pinched the bridge of his nose with his thumb and forefinger. Why was this so difficult? He'd ne'er had such trouble with a woman before.

"Maybe you're right," he said. "You're young. You'll want things I canna give you."

She tossed her head, her arms crossed over her body. "I doona want anything from you that I canna have from another man. You think this is about marriage and bairns? 'Tis not. I could walk to the castle and be married within the hour if that was what I wanted."

"Then what do you want?"

She pressed her lips together, her jaw tight, those beautiful eyes bright.

He threw his hands in the air. "If you doona tell me, Amber, I canna know."

"I want balance."

His brow crinkled. "What does that even mean?"

"When you leave, will you forget me? Will you pine for me? Will you be with other women after me? If we've been intimate, that changes things for me. I doona want to pine. 'Tis not in my nature." She pushed her hair back with both hands, but the shorter stands fell forward and framed her face. "Maybe I need to be with someone else first. If I weren't a virgin—"

"What? That makes even less sense."

"Well, you can treat it as tupping and naught else because you've been with other lasses. 'Tis not so with me. So maybe if I have carnal pleasure with someone else first, someone I like who doesn't belong to my clan, I willna feel this tie to you. You said your foster brothers were arriving, aye?"

A wave of black fury crashed within him, and he stalked forward. "You are not tupping one of my brothers!"

"Who would you suggest, then?"

"No one!"

"Ever? You need to be practical about this, Lachlan. I will be alone all winter. I may meet someo—"

"Are you deliberately trying to rile me? Because it's working. These are the kind of things my mother would say."

Her eyes widened in shock. "To you?"

"Not those exact words. I meant she would try to manipulate people and their emotions. I will not be manipulated, Amber."

"What part of me telling the truth is manipulation? You want to tup me, Lachlan, and then you want to leave. Do you expect me to be chaste until you return? Will you be chaste for me?"

He opened his mouth then closed it, and did so again before saying, "I could be."

"So you want to commit to me? And for me to commit to you? Some might call that marriage."

He ground his teeth, the two conflicting emotions fighting for dominance within him: possession and freedom. "Nay. Not. Marriage."

She nodded and blew out a breath. "I agree. Maybe the next time you're here it will be different. But for now, I think we need to find some socks to darn."

She moved toward a basket full of clothes by the fire. Her hair fell forward as she leaned over, and she tucked it behind her ears. As she rummaged for a sock, a curl fell forward again, and he sighed.

At least he could help her with that.

He strode to the exit, their argument riding him hard. From the corner of his eye, he saw her straighten, watch him go. The cool air from outside was a refreshing blast across his face when he opened the door.

She made an inarticulate sound just before he left, but he didn't dare look back.

He didn't dare do a lot of things he wanted to do.

Twelve

AMBER STARED AT THE CLOSED DOOR, IN SHOCK THAT he'd left but also feeling like her heart had broken into a hundred pieces. The sock she held in her hand fell to the floor as she moved forward slowly. Were his men still here? Had he given up on her and their plan to catch Murray?

Maybe there had never been a plan. Maybe he'd enlisted Callum into getting her into a compromising position just so he could tup her, and now that it was proving difficult, he'd decided to end the ruse. But that would make both him and Callum dishonorable, and she would bet her life, had bet her life, on the opposite.

She heard a sound behind her, a soft thump, and relief washed through her. Lachlan must have walked around the cottage and come in the back door, maybe to talk to the guard out back. She thought she'd slid the bar across, but she must have forgotten.

When she turned and saw the man standing by the alcove that held her second bed—now leaning on its side against the wall, a black gap where the mattress had been—she froze in disbelief. She was almost unable to comprehend what she was seeing—a much thinner, haggard, and dirty-looking Machar Murray, his arrow notched and bow drawn, pointed at her.

He's here, she thought before terror surged through her and she opened her mouth to scream.

"Not one word, witch, or I'll shoot you through the heart and then shoot Lachlan MacKay when he runs through the door."

Her teeth snapped together—so hard she thought she might have broken them. Panic engulfed her, more for Lachlan than for herself, and her breath came in short bursts through her nose. Desperate tears pricked her eyes and she prayed Lachlan had left for good.

"I'd hoped to snare the two of you together," he said. "Catch him when he was tupping you. Maybe I'd tie up the both of you and then let him watch me swive you too."

"That's not called swiving. It's called rape," she whispered hoarsely.

He shrugged, not bothered by her words.

"He and the other one think they're so smart, surrounding the cottage, waiting for me, but they ne'er counted on your wee bolt-hole, did they?"

She moaned, part fear, part regret, and clamped her hand over her mouth to stop herself from bursting into tears. She didn't dare put Lachlan in any more danger than she already had.

How had Murray known about her escape route? No one but her knew it existed. Dug out by her grandfather when he'd built the cottage, the tunnel started behind the low, built-in cupboards that made up the base of the smaller bed and ran all the way to the goats' shed. A lever allowed her to release the lock that kept the bed and mattress in place. Once she was in the tunnel, she could reposition the trap door and lock it behind her.

She'd agonized over telling Lachlan, but her father and grandmother had sworn her to secrecy, saying someday the tunnel would save her life. And it had. Twice. Both times when Machar Murray had come looking for her in the dead of night.

Now it stood open, the mattress shoved to the side, the cold air from below pouring into the cottage. How long had he been waiting in there? And what had he heard?

"How did you know?" she croaked.

"That you had a way out?"

"Aye."

"You'd escaped me twice. The second time I searched for a hiding place. I didn't see the lever at first, but the cupboards under the bed weren't as deep as the mattress was wide. Did your grandfather build it?"

On her nod, he said, "I heard he was a smart man, as was your da. Too smart. I had to kill him sooner than I wanted, before I got rid of the old laird."

Her breath caught, and a sob squeaked out. She knew Murray had killed her father, but to hear him freely admit it released all the hurt and grief she'd pushed down—and the rage. If she had the chance, she would kill him this time. Exactly as Adaira had said. She could incapacitate him long enough to stab a knife in his heart.

She might die in the process, but no way was this monster getting away.

Lucy hopped from the back of one chair to another, moving closer to Murray. He smiled and pointed the arrow at her bird. "Should I kill your crow before we leave?"

She shook her head. She didn't want her pet to die, but she would sacrifice him, the goats too, to prevent Murray from getting away and hurting Lachlan or anyone else. He'd made a mistake coming after her when she was alone. He had no leverage over her other than her death, and she didn't think he would kill her until after he raped her. Probably several times.

She would take him down when he tried to force her into the tunnel. "I'm not going anywhere with you."

"Aye, you are, or—"

The front door pushed open behind her. Amber knew it was Lachlan, not by anything she heard or saw, just because she *knew*. Jumping on instinct and screaming, she slammed the door closed on him before he could get in. Murray loosed his arrow.

Pain exploded in her shoulder as she was pinned to the door, and she shrieked in agony.

"Amber!" Lachlan yelled, his voice frantic. "MacKays! Attack! He's in the cottage."

Murray loosed two more arrows at him as he tried to push inside. One scraped her cheek, causing splinters to fly into her face, and the other landed just above her head.

The guards banged at the back door and shuttered windows of her cottage, trying to break in, but the wood was solid and the cottage well built. Murray nocked another arrow, eyes filled with hatred. He had just pointed it at her when Lucy cawed in outrage and flew at his face.

With a startled yell, Murray lifted his arms to protect his eyes, loosing the arrow into the ceiling. He swung at the bird, hitting it with a sickening thud, and her heart broke all over again as Lucy dropped to the floor, dead.

"Amber!" Lachlan cried again. He pushed past her into the room and rolled behind the wooden table. Flipping it on its side, he dragged it in front of her. Two more arrows hit the table just as Callum broke through the back door.

Murray cursed and ran to the escape route, Callum and several others in pursuit.

Crouching beside her, Lachlan yanked the arrows out of the wood around her face and picked out the splinters. She felt a wet trickle down her cheek and could see blood on his fingertips—she was lucky the wood hadn't landed in her eye.

"Amber, sweetling, look at me," Lachlan said, his voice shaking. His eyes were creased with fear for her, but his fingers stroked gently. Exhaustion washed over her, and she rested her cheek in his hand, closing her eyes.

"Look at me, Amber. Now."

She dragged her gaze back to his. "You didn't go... after him."

"Nay. Amber what do I do? Are you hurt any-where other than your shoulder?"

She shook her head, but even that movement made her head swim, and again she had to close her eyes.

He lifted her chin, his face close when she opened

them. His lips found hers, a soft, pleading kiss. "You stay awake, love. Tell me what to do."

It was hard to catch her breath, the world spinning. She managed to force the words past her lips, suddenly dry. "Get Mary from the village... Tell her...it's a similar wound to Gillis."

"Someone get Mary!" Lachlan yelled over his shoulder. "Two men!" Seconds later, she heard horses galloping away.

"You're losing a lot of blood. Should I take out the arrow?" He ripped off pieces of his plaid and used it to staunch the bleeding.

She sucked back a gasp as he pressed on her wound and could barely think past the pain. "Nay. Wait until...Mary's here."

"Can I break off the arrow so we can move you?"

The last thing she wanted was for the shaft to be jolted; breathing was bad enough. Still, she nodded.

"Malcolm!" he called out, and the young MacKay warrior who'd refused her entry into the castle that first night appeared. "Press your fingers here," Lachlan said. The warrior did so, and Lachlan withdrew his hand. "Doona let up," he ordered, then looked behind the door.

"Hello, Malcolm," she said to the warrior, remembering how they'd first met. "Come to claim...your kiss?" Her words were low and starting to slur.

"Maybe. If you doona faint on me. You did promise."

"No kissing," Lachlan said as he moved close again, grasped her rib cage on both sides, and pulled her forward along the arrow a few inches.

She screamed as the movement tore at her wound, causing what felt like fire to lick through her body. Lachlan added more bandages to the wound around the arrow. Malcolm held the shaft tight in one hand and laid the other against her back so she leaned into him.

She moaned, knowing what was coming. "Ten kisses...if you stop him."

She screamed a second time when Lachlan slid his sword between her and the door and cut off the arrow pinning her in place with a sharp, hard slice. She sagged forward.

"You did well, sweetling," Lachlan said, running his hand over her hair.

"I'd wager Malcolm...disagrees. His hearing will ne'er be...the same."

"Aye, 'tis ringing like a bell," Malcolm said. "But we all knew you had strong lungs on you."

Lachlan smiled—more a twisting of his lips—and he pressed a bandage to the wound at the back. The arrow went through close to her collarbone, but she didn't think it was broken.

"Do you have a stretcher we can use to move you?" he asked.

Her vision had blurred—whether from tears or pain she didn't know—but she didn't think she could stay conscious much longer. "Near the back door."

"I'll get it," Malcolm said, and she was grateful to be transferred to the safe haven of Lachlan's arms, her head resting on his broad shoulder, breathing in his familiar scent.

He pressed his lips to her hair. "You threw yourself against the door. Stopped me from coming in."

"Of course... I didn't want...you killed."

"So you would kill yourself instead?"

"I'm still alive." She was growing more and more sleepy and fought to stay with him. "Why didn't you... go after...Murray? You finally had...your chance."

"Because you needed me. I'll always come for you, Amber." He brushed her hair back from her face, then reached for a torn parcel on the floor.

He pulled out a beautiful, shiny blue ribbon. "For your hair," he said as he looped it behind her neck and around her head to hold back her hair.

"You left to get...me...a present?"

"Aye. So we'd stop fighting."

She smiled weakly, wanting to laugh at the absurdity of it even as a tear trickled from the corner of her eye. "Maybe if you'd given me the ribbons first...we wouldnae...have fought."

He smiled back, but she could still see the fear in his gaze. "Maybe."

She laid her hand over his and closed her eyes. "Next time."

⌒∾

Lachlan sat in the big chair beside Amber's bed, holding her limp hand and staring at her wan, sleeping face. He'd pulled out the arrow a few hours earlier after Mary had arrived and still had an ache in his gut from how much he'd hurt her and how afraid he'd been when the blood had poured out. Especially as Mary had panicked and started to cry. Lachlan had been the one to calm her down before she could start the surgery, Amber talking her through it, which meant she'd refused a high dose of herbs for the pain.

He knew just how Gregor had felt when Kellie died.

Terrified. Helpless. Unable to breathe.

The thought startled him, and he raked his other hand through his hair. He couldn't compare Amber to Kellie or him to Gregor. Kellie had been Gregor's wife. She'd died birthing their bairns—triplet girls who had also died.

And Amber had lived. Would live.

He rubbed his hand across his chest, massaging over his heart with his palm. Still, for a while there he'd thought she wouldn't survive, and the pain and panic had been unbearable. He'd never forget the sight of her pinned to the door, one arrow scraping her cheek, the other touching the crown of her head.

He shuddered, and she squeezed his fingers, still taking care of him even though she slept.

A hand fell on his shoulder. "Lachlan."

He turned his head to see Callum standing behind him, looking dirty and bruised. His face filled with regret.

"You didn't catch him," Lachlan said.

"Nay. We came close several times, but he'd just disappear. We'll track him in the morning. I suspect he has several bolt-holes where he goes to ground. When we find his hiding places, we may be able to predict where he'll go next."

"We need the dogs."

"Aye. Gregor and the lads should be here in a week or so. I've seen Hati and Skoll track someone even after the rain."

Lachlan nodded. He rubbed his thumb over the back of Amber's hand, and she curled her fingers into his. "She'll ne'er be safe until Murray is dead."

"We'll get him, Lachlan. We'll cast a net so he canna escape, and work inward once everyone's here. We'll protect her. As we would Caitlin or Isobel. Or Maggie, if I e'er make her my wife."

"We'll protect her even if she's not your wife."

"Aye."

He blew out a breath and leaned forward to touch the bandage on her cheek. "She saved me, Callum. He must have come in after I went to get the ribbons. I'd left them in my pack, and we'd been fighting. It was a peace offering."

"He came up the tunnel?"

"Must have. 'Twas the only way in."

"Why didn't she tell us it was there?"

"I doona know. A family secret?"

"Do you think she was aware that Murray knew? Was their relationship different than we first thought?"

He jumped up, rounding on Callum. "Nay! She said he'd come after her before. She must have used the tunnel to escape."

Callum put his hand back on Lachlan's shoulder, and pressed gently. "You're right. I'm just thinking through all the possibilities. If she'd disappeared under his nose, Murray would have searched until he found the tunnel."

Lachlan shuddered again as he thought of Amber alone in her cottage and Murray coming after her. Not only tonight, but other times as well. He sank back into the chair and lifted her hand to his face. "He'd been ready to shoot me when I came in, and she threw herself against the door so I couldnae get through— into the path of the arrows. God's blood, if you'd seen them, Callum. Three of them. Any one of them could have killed her if they'd been even one inch closer."

Callum crouched beside him. "She's a strong woman, Lachlan. You're fortunate to have her."

Lachlan laughed humorlessly. "I doona have her. The fight we had…it was searing. She saved me because that's what she does—saves people."

"Aye, but that doesn't mean she doesn't care about you."

He shrugged, but he felt a cramping in his chest. "I doona think either of us knows what we want, or what to do with the other."

"You could marry her," Callum suggested. "That's a good place to start."

He shook his head. "She no more wants to marry than I do."

"Things change, Lachlan."

Callum moved to the side of the bed by Amber's head and sat down, running a hand over her hair, now darkened with sweat and tangled from the way she'd thrashed her head in pain when Mary had stitched her up. A bandage covered her cheek where one of the slivers had cut deeper than the others.

"You should come back to the castle and get some sleep. I'll stay with her," Callum said.

"I canna leave."

"Then use the other bed. Or this bed. None will think twice about it."

"Maybe later. I'm…afraid to let her out of my sight,

even to close my eyes." He lifted her hand again, laced their fingers. "We have to catch him, Callum. I need her to be safe."

"Aye. Things will be clearer in the morning."

The door squeaked open behind him, and he recognized Niall's shuffling steps.

"Laird MacKay, Laird MacLean," the old man whispered in greeting.

Callum rose. "Sit here, Niall. She'd want you close."

"Thank you." He sat in Callum's spot and brushed his knuckles down Amber's temple. "She's all right?"

"I hope so," Lachlan said. "She talked Mary through the surgery and praised her for doing a good job."

"That sounds like her."

"Aye."

The steward's cheeks were moist with tears. Callum rested a hand on his back, and Niall wiped away the wetness with his sleeve. "She's so still. Amber is rarely still."

"Mary gave her a draught for the pain," Lachlan said. "It made her sleepy."

"But not too much. She wouldnae want to be out of it for long."

"Nay."

Niall sighed. "I heard 'twas Machar Murray?"

"Aye."

"And you knew he was coming? Both of you? You'd planned it?"

Lachlan nodded once, guilt writhing through him like a viper.

"Did she know?"

"Aye," Callum said. "She knew none were safe with Murray still alive. And we were sure he would come after her. You told us yourself he was obsessed."

Niall's shoulders slumped. "So you weren't courting her, Laird MacKay."

Lachlan's jaw ground together, his mind refusing to disavow the notion.

His silence caught the steward's attention. "Ah, I see in your eyes you doona know how to answer. Both you and Amber, unwilling to see what is right in front of you."

"She wouldnae have me even if I asked," he said.

"Then you see even less than I do, and I'm half-blind." He frowned at Lachlan. "She needs to be married. To be happy and loved. She needs to be protected by a strong man. If not by you, then someone else. I doona think she'll have anyone here, though, and I heard Laird MacLean is already betrothed. Maybe one of your other brothers?"

The same fury he'd felt earlier roared through him. Callum stepped quickly in front of him, facing Niall, so Lachlan couldn't rise.

"Doona e'er suggest such a thing," Callum said. "None of my foster brothers would look on Amber in that way, and 'tis not for you to decide what is best for her. 'Tis her choice only." 'Twas a firm reprimand, but Niall only looked more determined.

"I'm an old man. I can scheme all I like if I think 'twill do some good for those I love."

Lachlan made a sound of disbelief—short and hard through his teeth—and sat back in his chair, still simmering with anger at Niall's suggestion. It brought back all the feelings he'd had during his fight with Amber when she'd raised the possibility of laying with one of his foster brothers—but without the benefit of marriage.

He didn't know which was worse.

"She canna be left alone here anymore," Niall continued. "'Tis not safe. You can claim her or not, but she still needs to be protected."

Lachlan shook his head. The old man didn't understand. No one did. "Niall, I canna claim Amber, even if I wanted to. *She* has to claim *me*."

Thirteen

"I FEEL A SPELL COMING ON. YOU WILL SOON BE VOM-iting frogs, and your cock will fall off if you doona let me up." Amber tried to sound wicked but her chest and shoulder hurt like a sinner in hell, and she couldn't inhale enough air to put the requisite menace into her voice.

Lachlan just smiled at her, his arms on either side of her body on the bed, his torso leaning over hers. "Such sweet talk."

She tried to pinch him, but he laced their fingers together and put their clasped hands on the pillow over her head. She had no more strength than a bairn.

"Where is Mary?" she asked.

"She went home to help her mother. Against my wishes, you told her she could leave last night. Doona you remember?"

Vaguely, now that he mentioned it. "Lachlan, I want up."

"As soon as you drink the pain draught she left for you. Amber, you were moaning in your sleep last night. The wound obviously hurts you."

"Maybe I was dreaming of tupping some courtly Frenchman."

"Have you e'er met a Frenchman?"

"Nay, just in my dreams."

"I have, and you wouldnae want to tup them—in your dreams or elsewhere."

He lovingly brushed her hair back from her face and put a cold compress on her forehead. She scowled. She'd been putting up with this for three days, and she'd had enough. "I doona need a man taking care of me!"

"I'm not a man. My cock just fell off, remember?"

She laughed, she couldn't help herself, then scowled again, but it was a halfhearted effort. "Lachlan MacKay, let me up. I want to have a bath—a real one—not just Mary helping me with a cloth."

His eyes lit with interest. "I can help you with a real one."

She met his gaze, losing herself for a moment in the sea of deep blue. The color had become so familiar to her these past few weeks, like she'd known him all her life.

Images from the last time he caught her coming out of the tub played in her mind, and her body warmed and tingled in all her secret places. Her dreams—day and night—haunted her. She'd been thinking of his hands, his mouth on her for so long now.

Yet just three nights ago, she'd decided against being intimate with him. Now she couldn't remember why. Oh, aye, she didn't want to pine for him when he left. Well, she was likely to pine for him anyway.

So maybe she should just allow herself this one

pleasure. She'd almost died three days ago, and Murray was still out there. Would she want to die not knowing what it was like to be stroked by Lachlan?

He would be sure to restrain himself because of her injury. Would there ever be a better chance?

"All right," she said quickly. "But no tupping."

His eyes widened, and a flush crept up his cheeks, putting her back in control. Aye, she liked that.

He tried to speak, but all that came out was a strangled groan. Finally, he said, "God's blood, you mean it, doona you?"

"Aye."

He blew out a breath and dragged his hand over his face. "You're injured. I canna, canna..."

"Touch me? Lick me? Watch me?"

His gaze jumped to hers. "All of those things. 'Tis not right. I canna take advantage of you in such a state."

She stared at him, then slowly caressed her palm down the middle of her chest and underneath her shift. Excitement and desire pulsed through her like a living thing at what she was doing...starting. He watched her hand disappear, his breath rasping between his teeth, then she lifted her breast free of the linen—the puckered, pink tip and rounded flesh an offering.

The air left Lachlan's lungs on a loud "whoosh."

"The other one," he croaked as he gripped the sheets beside her. "I want to see them together."

She'd just reached under her shift to bring out her other breast, for the first time being proud of their shape and size—wanting him to see them, to be aroused by them—by her—when a banging sounded, and Ian yelled through the door, "Amber, let me in!"

Lachlan met her eyes and shook his head. "He can wait."

She gasped when he cupped her breast, reached under her shift, and brought out the other one too. They fit perfectly in his big palms, his fingers and thumbs gently kneading and squeezing her flesh. "Lord have mercy," he murmured before he lowered his head and drew a nipple into his mouth—and groaned.

The vibration made her whimper, and she arched upward, offering more of herself to him. The heat scalded her, the softness of his tongue undid her, and she released her breath on a small "Oh."

Wrapping her arms around his head, she held on tight. He was her anchor in a storm of emotions and feelings that erupted in her body—desire and need, but trust and communion too.

His tongue laved her skin and sent pulses straight to her core, readied the sensitive flesh. She couldn't help splaying her knees, raising her hips, wishing his hands would travel to the very center of her womanhood.

He lifted his head, his lips red and glistening, his eyes hooded, almost feral. "I have ne'er tasted anything as good as you." He moved to her other nipple, his tongue sucking and stroking the bud, his thumb strumming the wet one he'd left behind. She was filled with a mindless urgency to rub against him, to be engulfed by him, and her body undulated beneath his hands, unable to keep still.

Her legs lifted with the need to wrap around his body, and he grunted with satisfaction.

She couldn't think, just bathed in sensation, her

skin hot, her heart feeling too tight in her chest. "God in heaven, that feels so good, Lachlan. Doona stop." Blood pounded so hard in her ears she couldn't hear anything and had no idea if he answered her or not—or if Ian was still banging on the door.

Lachlan dragged his hand down her body and under the covers. She squeaked, the anticipation of being touched down there by someone other than herself—by Lachlan—more than she could bear. Surely she would release on the first stroke.

He smoothed his palm down the outside of her hip, his fingers trembling against her skin, before he grasped her shift's hem and pulled it up. She was panting now and lifted her hips to help him bunch it at her waist. Cool air hit her heated flesh, and she groaned, knowing she was exposed to him and liking it.

He answered her groan with his own and said thickly, "So beautiful, lass. You are a gift."

She opened heavy lids and saw him staring down at her most private area but not in a predatory way, almost reverently.

She wanted him to look on her like this—feeling hot and wet and swollen—wanted him to slide his tongue through the folds.

She wanted him to gorge on her.

He sighed and returned to nuzzle at her breasts, like a man unsated. His fingers slid into the curls at the apex of her thighs, tugging on the strands so she squealed again, feeling desperate and greedy, wanting all of him right now.

Then he split his fingers and pressed downward on the outside lips before hesitating at the bottom, his fingers barely there, letting the anticipation build to excruciating heights.

"Touch me," she finally begged, mindless with need.

He huffed out a laugh on her breast then stroked up her slick middle with heavy, sure fingers.

"Oh, dear God," she moaned. Her flesh was so engorged she felt like she might burst any second. Like a ripened berry.

More pounding on the door. "Amber!"

"Nay, doona stop," she cried, her nails biting into his shoulders to hold him there. Wanting his weight, his touch. Wanting all of him.

"Ne'er again. I will take what you offer."

His thumb found her nub beneath the folds, and when he circled it, she let out a strangled squeal of pleasure, the sensations causing streaks of white light to explode behind her eyelids.

Her hips jutted up to meet his strokes, the pressure building until he pressed one finger gently inside her, and she caught her breath, feeling like it wasn't enough, it wasn't *him*.

"Stay with me, Amber," he said, lifting his head from the valley between her breasts. "Trust me," then he bit down on the under slope below her nipple— and she shuddered.

He pumped his hand, pressing upward on the inside wall of her channel as his thumb stroked the outside, hitting and circling that wee nub. She stopped thinking, her mind blanking to everything but his fingers on her flesh, his mouth on her skin, and she moaned— long and low.

He lifted his head, watched her as she neared the

edge. She turned her chin, ready to scream around her fist, but he cupped her nape and held her in place so he could capture her mouth. Devour her.

And finally, she felt a part of him.

Waves of release crested inside her, and she screamed against his tongue, her hips bucking, her body shuddering. And still he didn't let up.

When the frenzy finally passed and she'd slumped back onto the bed, she opened her eyes slowly. They were so close, they shared breath. His blue gaze was a little wild as he watched her intently, possessively, making her feel like she was everything he'd ever wanted, ever needed.

And she liked it.

She tried to speak but couldn't. Couldn't do anything but lie there and stare up at him.

The pain of her shoulder slowly seeped back in and she looked down to see a wee bit of blood soaking through the bandages.

He followed her gaze, and his body stiffened. "God in heaven! You're bleeding."

"'Tis naught. Doona worry."

"Of course I'll worry. How could I have lost control like that?"

"The same way I did. Verily, Lachlan, 'tis so much better being stroked by someone else."

His eyes darted up to hers, concerned. "Someone else? This isna the first time…?"

She snorted as she lowered her legs, which were pulled up to her hips. She tried straightening her shift using one hand, then just pulled up the quilt instead. "I meant someone other than me."

He leaned down and nuzzled her neck, his mouth warm, and another shudder ran though her. "Is that what you meant by watching?"

She stilled, a whole new scene between them playing out in her mind. "Maybe. It hadn't occurred to me."

The banging sounded again at her door, quieter this time, and when Ian yelled for her, it was quieter too. "Amber, if you're in there, open up now."

Suddenly a wave of worry washed over her. She didn't want to flaunt her wantonness like this for Ian to see. And what if he was in trouble? "Go out the back door and meet him at the front, pretend like you've just come back," she said. "I'll pretend like I'm sleeping and didn't hear him."

"He tried the back door too."

"I'll say the door sticks sometimes. He'll believe it."

"Aye," he rose from the bed, and her gaze fell to the front of his plaid, where it jutted out lewdly.

"And you'll have to do something about that," she said.

He shifted his sporran so it sat directly on top. "'Tis all I can do—unless you'll take me in hand?"

An awkwardness rose, and she shook her head jerkily. "I doona, I doona…"

"You doona what, Amber?"

How could she say that as much as she wanted him to stroke her body, the idea of stroking that part of him in such a way made her very uncomfortable, which made no sense, as she enjoyed a man's shape, especially Lachlan's, and medically speaking, she'd seen and touched several cocks. But…the actual act of tupping had been fraught with danger for her for so long.

"I'm sorry. I canna. At least, not now. And I doona commit to anything, Lachlan."

He stared down at her, a hard glint in his eye. But he wasn't angry, so most likely 'twas the glint of determination. "I'll accept that…for now."

He turned, and a wave of panic washed over her. "Please, doona tell anyone. Even your foster brothers and Gregor when they arrive."

'Twas obviously the wrong thing to say. He glowered at her, a muscle twitching in his jaw. "I would ne'er speak about you in such a way. What's between us is only between us. Unless you tell Isla, of course."

A guilty blush stole up her cheeks, and he planted his hands on his hips. "What did you say to her?"

"Naught. Just that I…wanted to. She willna believe we've engaged so carnally, though."

"And why not? I've been at your cottage for three days. Alone with you all last night and today."

"I'll just tell her you would ne'er touch me in such a way when I was injured. She'll believe it. The entire clan wouldnae doubt your honor."

Now *he* looked guilty. She wanted to laugh, but she knew he took his honor seriously and would be offended. At least his plaid was no longer so distracting.

He cursed and walked out the back door.

❧

Lachlan quietly closed the door behind him and leaned back against it, trying to get his careening emotions under control. The sight, sounds, taste, and smell of Amber finding her release in his arms filled every inch of him. 'Twas a moment he'd ne'er forget. A moment he'd cherish forever.

Even if she gave him naught else, he had that.

But she would give him more, and often. She was a confusing mix of boldness and fear. He'd have to tempt her to him, convince her to give to him rather than take from her in any way. He would have Amber beneath him, on top of him, and any other position she wanted before the end of summer.

He pushed away from the door with a sigh and walked around the side of the cottage, stopping by the rain barrel to rinse his hands and face. He still had men hidden in the trees and shrubbery watching the cottage, and while he didn't think Murray would attack here again, especially not so soon, he wouldn't take chances on Amber's life again.

A shudder ran through him as the image of her pinned to the door, two more arrows in the wood around her head, burst into his mind. The sight would never leave him, waking him every night drenched in sweat, his heart racing.

When he rounded the corner, he came to an abrupt halt. 'Twas not just Ian standing at Amber's front door, looking worried, Niall was there too, as well as ten other clan members, men and women. And many more were in the field streaming this way—several young men running to catch up.

What was going on? Had Niall cooked this up? Surely it wasn't an angry mob come to drag Amber from her sickbed for being alone with him? Or worse yet, for being a witch—the other nightmare he'd had.

"Laird MacKay!" Ian yelled, running toward him.

The group at the door looked at him, and he strode forward to get between Amber and the rest of the clan.

"I've been knocking for Amber, but she ne'er answered," Ian said when he caught up to Lachlan.

"She's sleeping," he said, loud enough for everyone else to hear. "Or she was. Mary left a pain draught for her. Did you try the back door? It was open."

"I did, and it was locked."

"Nay, I just checked it. The door sticks sometimes." He reached the group and pinned Niall with his stare. "What's going on?"

"Naught to concern you, Laird. We just want to have a wee talk with Amber."

He raised his brow, arms crossing his chest. "A wee talk? You've gathered at least thirty people. And of course I'm concerned. I'm her laird." His gaze swept the growing crowd and out to the field where more people were coming. He could also see Callum riding toward the cottage on his horse.

"Aye, all are MacPhersons who love Amber and want to see the best for her."

So this wasn't an angry mob, but one of Niall's schemes. He could ask the steward, but he doubted he'd get a straight answer. Maybe Callum would know.

"She's not well, Niall. You know that. She can barely sit up. How do you expect her to come out to greet you?"

"I doona, we'll go in."

"All thirty of you in her cottage? When she's been pierced with an arrow and barely survived? Has barely survived the last five years?"

"Which is why we'll go in. We should have made sure she was safe long ago."

Unease trickled up his spine. Had Niall arranged protection for Amber?

The old man banged on her door. "Amber, lass, we need to see you."

"And how do you think she'll—"

He heard the bar slide across just before the door opened, and Ian stood there. The wee troublemaker had gone around. Lachlan was about to block the entrance and exert his will as their laird, when Callum caught his attention at the back of the growing crowd. His foster brother sat atop his horse and motioned him over with a jerk of his head.

He hesitated, knowing Callum would not counsel him to get out of the way unless he had good reason. Finally, he stepped aside, giving Niall a stern look. "Doona rile her. She's tired enough as it is." He was besieged with guilt at how he'd touched her earlier—an invalid. Aye, if she wasn't tired before, she would be now for sure.

"You're not the only one who cares for the lass, Laird MacKay."

As he made his way toward Callum, he couldn't help but notice how many young, eager men were in the crowd. Mostly MacPhersons, but a few of his men and Callum's too.

"What's going on?" he asked when he reached his foster brother's side. He looked back to see people crowding into the cottage and the shutters being pushed open from the inside.

"Niall intends to see Amber married—for her own protection."

He whipped his head around. "What? We have to stop him!"

"Nay, Lachlan, wait." Callum dismounted from his horse and grabbed his arm. "Trust me, 'tis for the best."

Anger mixed with panic pounded at his temples, and he jerked his arm from Callum's hold. "'Tis not for the best, and you would not be so accommodating if it were Maggie in there."

"I would be if I thought she might choose me."

Confusion creased his brow. "What are you talking about?"

"You said the other night that *she* had to claim *you*. Well, I didn't think 'twas a good idea earlier, when I heard Niall rousing everyone up about her safety and the need to see her wed—and neither did everyone else. In fact, some are wagering Amber will hand Niall his puny, wrinkled arse, as Tavis put it—but now... well...maybe she *will* claim you when she has no other choice. Come on." Callum led Lachlan around the cottage. "We want a good vantage point."

"For what?" Lachlan couldn't stop his voice from rising, his hands from fisting. "Is he planning to take a priest in there? Marry her on her sickbed? Tell me now, Callum, or I swear your nose will end up in the back of your head."

His foster brother stopped to tie his horse. "Niall's a crafty old bugger. He intends to trot the eligible men out in front of Amber and make her pick a groom. And my guess is that he's thinking she'll pick you. 'Tis what you want, aye? Deep down?"

Lachlan's eyes widened, and that panic he'd felt

earlier for Amber turned inward. "Me? But she knows
I doona want to marry."

"Aye. So you've said. But that was before you met
Amber. Now you have to decide whether 'tis worse to
stand out here and let Amber choose someone else, or
to step inside, knowing she might choose you."

❧

Amber's mouth dropped open as it looked like half
her clan streamed into her cottage. She still lay on
her back, and she struggled to push herself upward,
but it hurt too much, so she flopped back down with
a groan. The excitement and energy she'd felt from
Lachlan's earlier attentions had drained from her body.

Isla rushed to her side. "Here, let me help you."
She lifted Amber, propped pillows behind her, and
straightened her shift and quilt so she was covered.
Then Isla smoothed back her hair.

"What's happening?" Amber asked.

Before Isla could answer, Niall came over and said,
"Are you sure your herbs are working, Amber? You're
flushed yet wan at the same time. You doona look
well."

"Most astute, Niall. Verily, I doona feel well.
Maybe 'tis because I've been stalked by a madman
who put an arrow through my chest and is still out
there, wanting to do it again. Then I had surgery without any pain draught. Now you're all in here, taking
over my home, when I just want to sleep."

The clan had hushed to listen to her, and many of
them nodded gravely. Others grinned widely at her
tone. And was that goods she saw exchanging hands?

Lachlan and Callum stepped into the back doorway, but when she tried to catch Lachlan's eye, he rubbed a hand over the back of his neck and looked down. His body language was a mess, his chest puffed up belligerently, yet at the same time, he'd dropped his head. She couldn't read the look on his face.

Callum stood beside him with one brow raised.

"You can sleep as soon as everything is settled," Niall said.

"After what's settled?"

"You, of course. Amber, you canna stay here alone anymore. 'Tis too dangerous. And even if you move into the castle, it causes too many disruptions. You must choose."

"Have you lost your mind, Niall? What am I supposed to be choosing?"

"A husband."

Deafening silence fell, all eyes trained on her, and Amber stared around in shock. They'd force her to marry? And all these people—young and old, male and female—felt that she was a disruption? These people whom she'd helped for so long, for whom she'd put her life at risk, blamed her for the acts of idiotic men?

She looked at Lachlan, his eyes still downcast, his jaw a hard line with a muscle beating in it. She looked at Callum, who caught her eye and jerked his head toward Lachlan.

What did that mean? He wanted her to choose Lachlan?

"You've all gone 'round the bend," she said. "Your brains are addled."

Some of the folks nodded in agreement. So not

everyone thought as Niall did. But it looked like most
of them did.

"Nay," Niall said. "As your clan and protectors,
we feel you need a strong man to keep you safe from
intruders. You could be hurt by someone else next
time. Your cottage is too isolated, and now everyone
knows about your tunnel. If you're attacked again,
you'll have no escape."

"And my Robbie willna choose another lass until
you're spoken for, Amber," Finola said. "'Tis not fair
to the mothers or the other lasses."

Brow lifted and eyes wide in shock, she looked at
the faces of the other women in the clan. She'd ne'er
before sensed any dissatisfaction in them, especially
directed toward her. "Isla," she asked her friend, "is
this true?"

Isla's shoulders drooped. "I was one of the lucky
ones, Amber. My Alban has loved me since we were
twelve years old. But 'tis not so for the other lasses.
Even though you doona encourage it, the lads all hope
you'll look their way. I know 'twas too dangerous
to choose when Murray was our laird, but now you
should consider taking that step."

Isla also caught Amber's gaze and jerked her head
toward Lachlan. She looked over. His eyes were fixed
on a point out the window, his nostrils flaring as if he
was breathing deeply to steady himself.

Unlike Callum, Isla didn't know that Lachlan ne'er
intended to marry, and she rolled her eyes.

"If it helps, I will have a terrible scar on my face
from when Murray tried to kill me. Surely that will
dissuade the whole lot of you." 'Twas a lie, the wound

would heal cleanly with little scarring, but she was mad enough to exaggerate right now.

One of the young lads from Callum's clan stepped forward. She couldn't even remember his name. "'Tis a badge of honor, lass. The imperfection only serves to highlight your beauty. I love you more than life itself."

Lachlan made a derisive sound in the back of his throat just as she yelled, "Love isn't about beauty! It's about being with someone for forty years and finding they can still make you laugh. Having someone whom you'd die for because their happiness comes before your own, who understands what you're saying without having to say anything at all. Being in love is about giving everything and not worrying about getting anything back because you've already got it."

Her gaze fell on Lachlan again, and it jolted her to see him staring at her this time—an odd expression on his face. But then he dropped his eyes. Shuffled his feet.

She scowled and peered around the room until she found her tormentor. "You want me to choose? All right. I choose you, Niall."

"You canna. Only eligible lads are allowed. Everyone one else must step out." He waved his arms. "If you stand within Amber's cottage, that means you are willing to take her as wife."

People shifted around, the hopeful men moving to the front while everyone else hovered at the window and the door. All except Lachlan, who still stood on the doorsill. She noticed Callum had taken a wee step back.

Eighteen men, not including Lachlan, stood before her. Eighteen men she didn't love, some she barely knew. The youngest was just seventeen years old. She'd saved his life four years ago, when he'd fallen into the river and nearly drowned. He was still a young, sweet lad, not a man she would take to her bed. None of them were.

Her eyes fell again on Lachlan, still undecided on the doorsill, still fascinated with something out the window.

"You canna do this," she said to Niall, tears of betrayal pricking her eyes. After everything she'd done for these people.

"Aye, I can."

"And if I doona choose?"

"We shall put it to a vote."

"You'll choose for me?"

"Nay. We'll ask you to leave the clan. We canna be responsible for you any longer Amber. 'Tis too painful."

A tear fell even though she heard a murmur of dissent in the crowd. She dashed it away angrily. "I shall ne'er forgive you, Niall."

"I am an old man. I shall die satisfied knowing you are safe and married."

"But not happy?"

"The two needn't be exclusive, Amber."

Several clan members nodded, men and women who'd been friends with her grandmother and her father. They felt this way too?

"My father would rip you to shreds for doing this. And my grandmother, she would make you rue the day you thought up this plan."

"I think she'd understand," Niall said.

"She'd ne'er understand. You treat me like cattle. Why doona you bring a halter for my neck and lead me to pasture? Or better yet, lead me to whate'er stud you've chosen for me."

She looked at Lachlan, who watched her now. "Are you in or out?"

He stepped farther into the room and cleared his throat. "This has gone far enough. Amber you doona have to—"

"Nay, the clan wants me to choose. I'll choose, but I'll set a few rules first. If the groom dies, I doona have to marry again. No matter how soon after the wedding, even if it's just hours or minutes after, maybe even during the first wedding toast."

She let that sink in and saw a few eyes dart furtively to her cupboard full of herbs, many of which, given at the wrong dose, would kill someone instantly. Two mothers rushed forward and nabbed their sons, dragging them out of the cottage.

"And I willna sleep with my new husband until after he makes me laugh. And I canna be laughing *at* him, it must be a happy laugh because he's said something amusing. I willna have dreary bairns."

One of her clansmen she'd known most of her life and was almost twice her age slumped his shoulders. He was a decent man but as dull as mud. He quietly shuffled out.

She was now down to fifteen idiots plus Lachlan, who'd moved to the very front and stood with his hands on his hips, frowning at her. Which was funny, seeing as he had even less desire to marry than she did.

Which gave her an idea.

"My last rule is this. If I choose and my prospective bridegroom says 'no,' I doona have to choose again. Ever."

Lachlan's brow raised, and she knew that he understood her plan. A flush rushed up his skin, and he dropped his gaze again.

"Agreed," Niall practically shouted beside her. She looked at him, and her smug smile turned a wee uncertain. A sparkle had entered his eyes even though he tried to look stoic. "Who is it then, Amber?"

Quiet descended.

She cast her eyes over the men, thinking to draw the moment out, to build it up, but suddenly her heart beat wildly and her throat tightened. Uncertainty caused a squeezing in her chest, and she just wanted to pull the blanket over her head and hide.

"Amber." Lachlan's voice soothed her, and she turned to find him watching her again, his stance wide and steady, his shoulders back and chin level.

So, he would help her after all. "I choose you," she said, and for some reason she found herself blinking back tears.

An excited babble of voices mixed with groans and cheers erupted. But it was like she and Lachlan were in their own little world. Neither one looked away from the other or moved a muscle. Callum walked up behind him and clamped a hand on his shoulder, his smile the biggest Amber had seen on his face since he'd arrived.

"Congratulations, Brother," he said, then he moved to Amber and kissed her cheek. "And to you, Sister. 'Tis a happy day to see two such fine people betrothed. I couldnae be happier for you both."

Betrothed?

"Wait!" she called out. Lachlan still hadn't moved; his eyes still held her own.

"What is it, lass?" Niall asked, looking like he wanted to do a jig.

"Laird MacKay hasn't answered yet. He may say nay."

Everyone stopped talking, and this time all eyes turned to Lachlan. Tension built as he did naught for a second, then his lips quirked, and he walked to the side of her bed, sat down, and took her hand.

"I say, 'aye.'"

Fourteen

"AMBER! AMBER!"

Amber darted into the pitch-black storage room and leaned up against the closed door, trying to soften her breathing. She heard Niall and Finola shuffle past outside, still calling her name, and after a minute she heaved a sigh of relief. The cool air was most welcome after the hot sun outside, and the quiet a blessing after all the wedding nonsense her clan were reveling in.

The door pushed open behind her, and she stumbled forward with a shriek. Strong hands she recognized immediately caught her before she fell. Lachlan drew her back against his chest as he shut the door again.

"Traitor," she whispered, but it ended on a moan as his hands found her breasts and squeezed. The hard length of him pressed into her bottom, and even that felt good and exciting, despite her refusal to go anywhere near his cock.

He'd been trapping her like this for days—as soon as she got out of bed the day after her "betrothal." Of course, she'd been hiding in closets for just as many days to escape Niall and Finola, who simply refused to acknowledge she wasn't talking to them. For one, because they wanted to talk about the wedding dress, the feast, and the ceremony. For two, because they both—Niall in particular—had forced her into this farce with Lachlan. Which is what it had to be, because there was no way that Lachlan MacKay was marrying her.

Except he said he was.

"Traitor," she said again and let out a strangled groan as he palmed between her legs through her dress. The other hand had slipped inside her arisaid to cup her breast, and he kissed and licked the side of her neck.

Her breath came in sharp gasps, and she widened her stance on instinct, wanting him to keep going despite calling him names.

"Good lass," he whispered, then tugged her earlobe into his mouth and sucked.

She just resisted bucking her hips against his hand. That gave her some much-needed strength, and she stumbled away from him.

She turned to him in the dark, unable to see a thing. And while her breath rasped heavily through her teeth, she could hear naught of him.

"Lachlan, where are you?"

"Here," he said from behind her just before he kissed her in that soft, sensitive spot where her shoulder met her neck, sending shivers through her body.

She spun toward him, reaching out her hands, but he was gone again. Next, he trailed his fingers from the nape of her neck down her spine—played her like a harp, and her sigh was the wind through the strings.

When she turned to him, he caught her head in those big hands of his and kissed her.

Just a brush of lips at first, so soft, gentle, then that hot, moist sweep of his tongue across her bottom lip. She opened her mouth to catch it, and he pressed his lips to hers.

She was enveloped by him in the darkness, her loss of sight enhancing her other senses. He tasted sweet like wild strawberries and smelled of the outdoors— leather, pine, wood smoke, and horses. His heart pounded so hard she could hear it, as well as the wee growls and moans in his throat. She dragged her fingertips across his chest to curl and tug on the coarse, springy hair that grew there.

He pulled her closer, and her arms circled his neck. Those big hands of his slid down her back, clamping to her bottom, and the resulting surge of fire had her rubbing against him like a cat in heat—wet, wanting. If she hadn't been so needy, she would have given herself a firm talking to.

The pressure of his hands brought back all those memories of the first time they'd met, his palm pushing her arse down as she crawled, bound and gagged, across the field with him. He'd been rougher then, and he hadn't kneaded her flesh like he did now. Or sucked on her earlobe until she panted in his ear. Still, she found it exciting to think about.

God's blood, what was the matter with her? He'd dragged her from her horse and across a field! She'd had bruises on her knees and twigs in her hair!

"I doona know what you think you're doing, but I willna marry you," she said breathlessly.

"I didn't ask you to marry me. You asked me—and I accepted. 'Tis a betrothal, a legal contract, and you canna take it back."

"'Tis no such thing."

"'Twas a formal agreement in front of witnesses. You even added conditions that had to be met."

He bit the tip of Amber's chin and nibbled leisurely down her throat, lavishing extra attention to the hollow at the base of her throat and making her knees buckle.

She still had a wee bandage on her face and a large one on her chest beside her collarbone, but she'd untied her sling yesterday and was tentatively increasing her range of motion. Raising her arm around Lachlan's neck pulled a bit on the torn muscle, but it didn't hurt.

Nothing hurt—not when she was lost in this sensual haze of temptation.

"Amber?" His voice had roughened, and his fingers dug into her flesh.

It took her a moment to drag herself back from oblivion. "Aye?"

"Do you want me to kiss you—down there?"

She caught her breath as everything inside her stilled. Then a flood of heat scorched between her thighs, and she squeezed them together in an attempt to relieve the ache. "You canna. 'Tis not... 'Tis not... We doona have a bed."

"Trust me, sweetling. Lean against the door, and I'll kneel before you. We'll put your legs o'er my shoulders, and I'll support your bottom with my hands."

What he suggested was so...so...wanton...so delicious—and now she wouldn't be able to think of anything else. Is this what it would be like to be married to him?

"Lachlan," she wailed.

"Is that a yes?" he asked.

"This…you…we…"

"Spit it out, Amber."

"We have to stop!"

"Nay, we doona. Well, up to a certain point we have to, but tasting you down there, in the dark, is definitely allowed. I will be your husband when I look on you fully, but 'tis dark in here and—"

"You canna marry me!"

"Why?"

She sputtered, unable to make her brain work when he was still touching and squeezing her backside. "You doona want to marry. You were verra clear on that."

"I changed my mind. I listened to what you said about being with someone for forty years, and I decided you were right. You make me laugh, I would put my life before yours, and I understand what you're saying even if you say elsewise. Like right now." He walked forward three steps with her, and her back hit the smooth, cool wood of the door. "You willna say it, but you want my mouth on you."

She groaned, and her stomach contracted as he kneeled before her. 'Twas a good thing she leaned on the door or she would have fallen down.

"Besides, I couldnae have you choosing someone else now, could I?"

He'd just grasped her hem, sending her heart rate to the moon and forcing the air from her lungs, when the door pushed open from behind her for the second time.

She flew forward with a screech, bumping into Lachlan, who'd sprung up just in time to catch her. But her weight sent him staggering backward, still holding her, until he tripped over a box on the floor and sprawled on a stack of bagged oats about waist high.

The light from outside streamed into the room and partially blinded her. She looked over her shoulder and squinted her eyes.

Callum stood in the doorway with Finola and Niall behind him, peering into the room. "Well, that was amusing," he said.

"Your timing couldnae be better," Lachlan griped, his hold on her still tight despite Finola's disapproving clucks.

Callum grinned. "I'm always willing to help, Brother."

Lachlan hurled an apple at his head—so fast Amber didn't even see him pick it up. Callum caught it just as fast, and the next one too, with his other hand.

"Thanks," he said with a laugh, stuffing one apple in his pocket and taking a bite out of the other. When he finished chewing and swallowing, he said, "Word arrived from Gregor and the lads earlier. They'll be arriving tomorrow, along with the priest. Just in time from the looks of it. You can stop doing…whate'er… you've been doing in the closet and treat your wife to a proper night between soft quilts and silk sheets."

"I'm no one's wife," she said indignantly, struggling to get out of Lachlan's hold.

"Aye, you will be after that display." Niall waved at the disarray of her arisaid, the ties undone where Lachlan's hands had slipped inside to play with her breasts.

Heat scorched her cheeks, and she hastily straightened her clothes. "'Tis none of your concern, old man. Laird MacKay understands I doona wish to marry him."

"Aye, you will. 'Tis contracted, remember?" Lachlan said as he pushed past her. "If you didn't want to marry me, you shouldnae have asked."

He left the room, Callum winking at her before turning to follow Lachlan. Amber picked up a third apple and threw it at his back, but he reached a hand behind his head with a laugh and caught that one too.

Niall and Finola crowded in, trapping her against the bag of oats.

"Amber, dear," Finola said, "do you want quail or pheasant for the fowl served at the feast? And Magda has some violet ribbon to go in your hair that will look beautiful with your eyes, but Rhona says the violet will clash with the blues and greens of the dress she's making. I thought she could add some ribbon to the dress so it matches the one in your hair, but she is most adamant you willna like any adornments."

Niall squinted down at her. "And I think 'tis best if you marry in the bailey, seeing as Father Odhran is still locked in the church. But if you like, I can send some men in there to flush him out. 'Tis beautiful weather to celebrate outside, but we need to start decorating and maybe build a trellis, especially as we know that Gregor MacLeod and the others will be here tomorrow." He clapped his hands to his head. "Tomorrow!"

He sat down beside her on the stack of oat sacks to catch his breath. "Maybe Laird MacLeod will walk you down the aisle, since your da canna be here. Imagine that, *the* MacLeod walking you down the aisle. And your bairns will be his foster grandbairns!"

Amber's throat tightened. Verily, 'twas happening. In the next few days, she would marry Lachlan MacKay, and he would take her to his bedchamber on their wedding night and expect her to cross that final barrier with him…and like it.

And why not? She liked everything else so far. Well, anything that had naught to do with his cock.

She blew out a breath, and her hair fluttered away from her face. She'd ne'er thought she'd ever marry, but especially not Lachlan. He was so adamantly against marriage and bairns, but now both were on the horizon. Her stomach tightened, and she rubbed a hand over her belly to soothe it. She couldn't think of anything more horrifying than a man pushing his cock inside her, no matter what Isla said.

Aye, she liked to be touched, loved Lachlan's hands and mouth on her, but the other frightened the devil out of her. She'd spent five years trying to avoid being raped—not that she thought Lachlan would rape her—but if she didn't want to engage fully, and he did, what would happen? Especially as she was now his wife, and the intimate act sealed their marriage vows in the eyes of man and God.

She groaned and dropped her head in her hands. "I doona think I can go through with it."

"Of course you can," Niall said. "I've seen you with him, Amber. Your life will ne'er be the same without him."

"You doona understand."

Finola wrapped an arm around her. "Are you worried about the wedding night, lass?"

Heat washed up her skin, scorched her, and she knew her fair skin had turned as red as a beet.

Finola patted her back. "Doona worry, Amber. 'Tis the same for every lass. I took a broomstick to bed with me on my wedding night. It stayed there between us for four months. That's how long it took Gareth to finally climb over it. Not everyone is intimate on their first night. I'm sure our laird will wait. And if not, you have some sharp knives in your satchel."

Amber snorted in amusement, she couldn't help herself. She heard Niall titter, and she fell backward onto the sacks of oats and laughed. Finola laughed too, and when Niall saw a broomstick in the corner and handed it to her, they started all over again.

Finally, the amusement abated and Amber sighed. She reached out her hands and folded them around Niall's and Finola's forearms.

"You're a conniving, interfering old badger, Niall MacPherson, but I doona want Gregor MacLeod to walk me down the aisle. I want you to do it. Naught would make me happier. And as always, Finola, your advice is perfect. Why hadn't I thought of that? I'll just take my knives to bed—lay them out down the middle to keep Lachlan on his side."

❧

"How many does this make now?" Lachlan asked Callum, crouching beside him on the forest floor. An innocuous-looking moss-covered stump was turned on its side to conceal one of Machar Murray's bolt-holes. Lachlan picked up a broken branch that lay among the shrubs and poked it. 'Twas obvious the dirt around the stump had been dug down to secure it.

"Four. The first tunnel was near Amber's cottage around where we lost him the night he attacked her, the second closer to the castle, and a third was found yesterday outside the village. One of the men fell into it by accident."

They'd been heading out to meet Gregor and their foster brothers at the falls when word came that another tunnel had been found, a long one that had obviously been recently used. Food scraps were found inside, along with human shite.

It gave Lachlan hope. His biggest fear had been that Murray had left the area, but knowing he was still here meant they could close the net and hopefully catch him. Warriors from seven different clans were getting into position, and on Lachlan's order, they'd move inward toward the castle, hoping to flush out the rat. But it would be slow going now they knew about the tunnels—all of the forest floor would have to be checked.

When Darach arrived with the dogs, they would track Murray, but he was smart, and several of his holes were near water. It would take the dogs time to pick up his trail again if he used the rivers frequently.

God forbid Murray slipped though the net and got to Amber. He would kill her this time, for sure. A surge of rage and fear crashed through Lachlan at the thought, and he shoved the stick into the stump, cracking it open.

Callum placed his hand on Lachlan's arm just as an arrow flew from their left and landed at their feet. Lachlan recognized the fletching on the arrow immediately and looked up to see Gregor and Lachlan's foster brother Darach MacKenzie, laird of Clan MacKenzie, on their horses about eighty paces away.

"Doona move," Gregor yelled at them, dismounting. His foster father, a big, redheaded Scot with grey streaks in his hair and beard, pointed upward, but Lachlan couldn't see anything unusual from his vantage point.

Darach, as tall as Gregor and looking almost as fierce, with a scar running though one eyebrow, also dismounted. His chestnut-colored hair was tied back with a leather strip.

"'Tis something wrong with the tree," Gregor said, still yelling.

"Aye. Looks like it's been tampered with," Darach added.

"God's blood," he muttered, imagining a tree hurtling down and taking off his head. "If I die now before I've tupped Amber, I'm going to come back from heaven and drag Murray down to hell myself."

"What makes you think you're going to heaven?" Callum asked.

"Because an angel asked me to marry her."

Callum snorted. "Amber's many wonderful things, but I doona think angel is one of them."

"Aye, she is. A warrior angel."

Gregor approached with Darach, who looked about as relaxed and content as Lachlan had ever seen him. Caitlin's doing, no doubt. Both men were peering up and discussing something as they turned in a circle and assessed the other trees. Darach pointed upward, and Gregor nodded.

"Do you think they've actually seen something? Or are they pretending to make us look like idiots?" Callum asked.

"They're not pretending. You already are an idiot."

"Says the laird who canna stay out of closets in his own keep."

Lachlan couldn't help smiling—idiotically. He remembered how close he'd come to tasting Amber before Callum had interrupted them yesterday, and he scowled. "Your timing leaves much to be desired."

Callum grinned, but a serious light had entered his eyes. "Doona diminish her place in the clan by tupping her in a closet, Lachlan. She'll be your wife soon. Do her the honor of waiting."

Lachlan wanted to minimize Callum's words with a joke, but he had a sick feeling his foster brother was right. He nodded. Once.

After clearing his throat, he yelled out to Gregor, "What's going on? What do you see?"

"A brilliant and deadly mind at work. Which will be Murray's undoing. He'll have to stay close to see his plan bear fruit. I'd say he was here watching until just a few minutes ago."

Lachlan whipped his head around. "Where?"

"Near the river, most likely. We'll search in that direction for another hiding place."

"We should go right now!"

"Nay, Lachlan, doona move. He's gone, and he's too smart and prepared for us to catch him that way.

The best we can do now is put pressure on him and wait for his next move."

"That's not good enough. He'll kill Amber this time."

Both Darach and Gregor looked over, their eyes piercing him with their intensity. They must have heard something in his voice.

"Who. Is. Amber?" Gregor asked.

Lachlan smiled, sure it was the same idiotic smile he'd given Callum earlier. "She's the MacPherson healer and the most aggravating woman I've e'er met. I'm going to marry her." Then he drew his arrow, said "duck," to Callum, and shot into a tied knot he recognized high up in the trees. He and Callum fell to the forest floor and crawled away just as a branch swept over their heads and a hail of thorns rained down.

Gregor approached and picked one up, grimacing as he smelled the tip. "Poison. 'Tis good to see you both alive."

Fifteen

"How did this happen?" Darach asked Lachlan later that night as all the foster brothers and Gregor sat around the campfire roasting freshly caught rabbits and frying oatcakes on the griddle. An owl hooted in the distance, and stars shone brightly in the black sky. "You were the last one of us I thought would marry."

Lachlan pulled his spit toward him and tore a leg off his rabbit, cursing as the hot flesh burned his fingertips. "How can you even ask me that after you married Caitlin?"

"Caitlin is an exception. I had to marry her." Darach looked at him like he was addled.

"Spoken like a man in love. Well, my Amber is exceptional too."

"Verily? Is she sweet and kind like Caitlin?"

Callum laughed and bit into his apple. "I wouldnae call her sweet, exactly."

"She's better than sweet, she's conniving," Lachlan said.

"Conniving?" Gavin MacKinnon, laird of Clan MacKinnon, sat up from where he'd been lounging against a fallen tree. He was as tall and fair as his Norse ancestors, with white-blond hair he'd recently cut even shorter than Callum's. It looked worse than Amber's hatchet job on her hair, even scraping his scalp in places, a far cry from the long locks he'd worn most of his life. Gavin had always been the bonniest of them all, with a fun, joyous spirit, but life, death, and the disappearance of his son had drained that spark away.

It hurt Lachlan to see the grim-faced man seated across from him.

"Cristel was conniving too, Brother," Gavin continued. "Are you sure you want that trait in a wife? If I'd known who Cristel was behind her bonnie hair and eyes, I would ne'er have married her."

"Aye, you would have," Gregor said, flipping some oatcakes on the griddle, "or you wouldnae have had Ewan. Even if it was only for a short time."

Gavin leaned back against the tree and closed his eyes. "You're right. The last five years will all be worth it when I find him."

"Any new leads?" Callum asked. They all thought Ewan must have died when his mother did at last year's summer festival, but for Gavin's sake, they supported him in his search.

"Nay. But something will turn up. If Ewan had died, we would have found his body. None had been burned by the time I arrived. Someone took him—maybe before the illness hit. Cristel wouldnae have noticed nor cared that he was missing." Rage burned in his eyes, and his jaw had clenched tight.

Laird Kerr MacAlister, the oldest and possibly deadliest of the brothers, his hair and eyes as dark as Gavin's were fair, and even bigger than Gregor, squeezed Gavin's shoulder. "If Ewan is out there, Brother, we'll find him."

He leaned forward and grabbed an oatcake off the griddle with his fingers. After tossing it on a plate, he handed it to Gavin, then got one for himself. "Isobel is conniving too, Lachlan. She's constantly coming up with ways to thwart and annoy me. The last thing she said before we left was that she planned to cut her hair as short as Gavin's in solidarity with her brother. I told her I'd marry her anyway and make her wear a straw wig."

The men all laughed, even Gavin, who said, "Good luck. I wouldnae be surprised if she marries someone else by the time we get home, just to spite you."

Kerr's eyes darkened. "Then I shall be committing murder." He said it quietly, and Lachlan knew he meant it. No one would come between him and Isobel, not even Isobel's mother, who had made a death-bed request of Gavin that Isobel be allowed to choose her own husband.

"'Tis her choice, Brother," Gavin said with a shrug. Kerr just grunted.

"Amber's hair is short too," Lachlan said. "As short as mine. I like it. 'Tis easier to kiss her neck. And often it's sticking out in places because she's been pushing bloody hands through it—and she curses like a warrior too. Especially when she's working and it's a difficult procedure. You should have heard her curse my cock. She said it would fall off if I didn't let her up from her sickbed."

"God's blood! Doona introduce her to Isobel," Kerr said, looking horrified.

"She sounds…lovely," Darach added.

Lachlan grinned. "She is. Although when I first met her, I thought she was a lad. She'd just hacked off her hair, and her face was covered in mud. And she wore a plaid, of course."

"Good lord, what happened?" Gregor asked.

Lachlan told them the story, relishing their responses, and he was so proud of Amber—her determination, compassion, and bravery—he thought he might burst.

Silence reigned for a moment when he finished, then Callum said, "And he's been obsessed with her e'er since, just like Murray and all the other men in her clan."

Lachlan felt heat steal up his neck. "Except she's marrying *me*." He tossed the bone from the rabbit into the fire and looked at Kerr. "And I didn't do it by wooing her, Brother. You need a plan."

Callum snorted. "A lot of good your plan did. You caught her because of Niall."

"Well, either way, she's mine now. Or she will be as soon as Father Lundie gets here." He looked at Darach, "When will that be?"

"He's coming with the wagons. A few days at least." Darach leaned closer. "You're flushed," he said, amazement in his voice. "Are you in love with her, then?"

The wee hairs on Lachlan's body stood up as his breathing stuttered. All the men had stopped what they were doing and stared at him. He rubbed his palm across the back of his neck. "Nay, I'm not in love with her…whate'er that means. I'm happy because I'm marrying a woman who willna simper or scold, and whom I'll still like and respect in forty years."

Callum lifted his brow. "Are we talking about the

same woman? Amber lives to give orders. She'll scold you to hell and back."

Lachlan smiled. Aye, she did like to give orders. He was looking forward to her giving some in their bedchamber. "We'll sort that out. She can give orders to do with the healing, and I can give orders on everything else."

Callum put his head down and laughed.

Gregor joined him. Then he sighed. "My Kellie liked to give orders too. Right up to the verra end. She said, 'You doona waste your life grieving me, Gregor MacLeod. I'll be waiting for you in heaven with our wee lasses when you die, and I expect to hear you've done everything you can to make the Highlands a safer place.'" His voice had thickened, and he had to clear it before he carried on. "I hope I've succeeded and they'll be proud of me when I see them again."

Gregor's words and the emotion in his voice hit Lachlan hard. It hit them all hard. Gavin too, even though he didn't intend to e'er marry again. The rest knew their wives, or wives-to-be, could be so easily taken from them—as Kellie had been taken from Gregor.

And Amber could be taken from him.

He found himself rubbing his palm over his body again, but this time over his heart. "She is proud of you, Gregor. We all are. And grateful too. I can only hope to make Amber half as proud."

⤳

"If I close my arms over you from behind, like this, what's your next move?" Amber stood with Adaira in the middle of the girl's bedchamber and tightened her in her embrace. They'd progressed with their training as soon as Amber was up and Adaira was well enough for physical fighting. "And doona hurt me this time; just show me slowly and tell me."

Amber resisted the urge to block her face or pull back her feet from Adaira's striking heels. The girl had a remarkable talent for hand-to-hand combat, and she was fast.

"I can smash your nose again with my head."

"Good, what else?"

"I can drill my heel into the top of your foot."

"Aye, what else?"

Adaira braced in Amber's arms, thinking. Amber could feel that she wanted to struggle, but she resisted the impulse. Amber tightened her arms for good measure. "Your attacker is stronger than you, but he or she has weak spots. What's another vulnerable spot they've placed in front of your body?"

"Fingers!" Adaira yelled excitedly as she reached for Amber's hands.

"Gently," Amber warned, trying not to pull away. "What can you do to them?"

"I can pull them apart."

Adaira wrenched Amber's fingers in opposite directions. Most likely she thought she was being gentle, but it still hurt, and Amber let her go.

"And then once they've released you, what do you do?"

"I grab my knife and stab you." The lass snatched up a spoon from the bedside table and jabbed it at Amber, who easily knocked the utensil away, spun the girl around, and grabbed her from behind again.

"Nay! You do not fight. You run."

"But I'm a good fighter!"

"Not against big, strong men who've been practicing for years longer than you have. Not even against me. Now you're trapped again. Tell me one more thing you can do."

Adaira stomped her foot. Not to get away this time, but in frustration. "I doona know."

"Aye, you do. Use your last weapon against me, Adaira."

"But I doona have any more weapons."

"You do. One more. How can you make me work harder?"

Adaira stilled, then suddenly she dropped to the ground. "My weight, You said my weight was a weapon!"

"Aye, good for you, lass!"

Amber didn't tell her that she barely weighed a thing, and dropping to the ground probably wouldn't slow down a strong man. But if she trained her muscles and was ever attacked in the future when she was a grown woman, her dead weight would be much harder for an attacker to handle.

After slowly letting go so Adaira didn't bang herself on the floor, Amber moved to the bed and sat down, holding her sore arm close to her body. "Maybe next time we can get Lachlan to help us. Then you can see just how strong a man can be and why it's important to run when you have the chance. If he catches you, he may hurt you and…"

Adaira flopped beside her on the bed, also looking worn out. "And what?"

Amber closed her mouth. She'd been about to say "rape you," but the thought of Adaira being hurt in that way was too awful to consider. And the lass didn't need to know yet that such atrocities existed.

"'Tis naught, lass. 'Hurt you' covers everything, wouldnae you say?"

"I suppose. Although you could say stab you, or gut you, or drag you behind your horse."

Amber flopped back beside her on the bed and crossed her forearm over her eyes, trying not to laugh. The girl was downright grisly. It would serve Lachlan right if she taught Adaira some of her bloodiest curses.

A sharp knock at the door was all the warning they received before Niall pushed into the room. He looked harassed, and his eyes darted toward her a wee bit wildly.

"Our laird has asked for you. He's here with the others and Gregor MacLeod." Niall said "Gregor MacLeod" like he had just mentioned one of the saints, and Amber had the urge to cross herself.

"What does he want?" she asked.

Angry color flushed up Niall's neck, and he stomped toward her. "It doesn't matter what he wants. He is our laird and about to be your husband."

Amber yawned and pulled the quilt from the bed over her body.

Adaira giggled and jumped up. "I'll go see. Gregor always brings me a treat, and Kerr lets me stand on his shoulders. I'm as tall as a giant!" she yelled as she ran from the room.

Amber closed her eyes. She really was tired and sore, and she didn't feel like pretending to be someone she wasn't in order to impress Lachlan's family.

She wanted to be herself. Whoever that was right now.

She sensed Niall standing over her and sighed. "Tell him I'm not feeling well, and I'll come down when I'm ready."

Niall pulled the quilt away. "Nay, you'll come now. Amber, this is important to him. He wants you to meet his family. He's proud of you."

"Proud of me?"

"Aye."

"But…"

"But what?"

"Well, I'm not exactly a prize, now am I?"

Niall's eyebrows rose. "How can you say that? Nineteen men, including Laird MacKay, stood in your cottage last week wanting to marry you."

She waved her hand. "Silly lads who only love me for my bonnie eyes and hair—which was not my doing, but God's."

Niall sat down with a sigh, and Amber rolled toward him.

"Och, lass. Doona you know anything? Our laird wants you for more than just your eyes and hair. He's enamored with your bosom too."

She laughed, and Niall joined in. When their amusement faded, he took her hand in his. "Just be yourself, lass. They seem like fine men, and they love Lachlan like a brother and son. They'll be happy as long as he's happy."

"Is he happy, Niall?"

"Aye, he is. Are you?"

She rolled onto her back again and pulled the quilt

over her head. She wasn't unhappy. She was more befuddled than anything else. None of it seemed real, and she still might end up running away at the last minute. "I doona know."

He patted her through the quilt. "You're the bravest lass I know, Amber, but you're also a wee bit daft and a lot stubborn. Trust me when I say Lachlan MacKay is the right choice for you. Go out there and meet his family and be yourself. Our laird wouldnae want you any other way."

Be herself.

Amber pushed the cover back and sat up. Her hair was sticking out in different directions, and she ran her hands through it. When she couldn't find her ribbon, the third one she'd lost from the packet Lachlan had given her, she tucked the strands behind her ears and stood up.

After shaking out her skirts she smoothed and straightened her dress. "All right. I'll go be myself. Really, how hard can it be?"

⁓

Amber stopped at the top of the stairs and looked down into the great hall. A nervous flutter like a swarm of butterflies had taken up residence in her belly. The men—all big, strong, braw-looking warriors, including Gregor, whose hair and beard were streaked with grey—sat in front of the hearth drinking ale.

All except a huge, dark-haired man who must be Kerr. He walked back and forth in the hall, his hands wrapped around Adaira's legs. She stood on his shoulders, swinging her arms wildly and pretending to be a giant.

"Amber!" Adaira cried out when she saw her.

The men all looked up in her direction, smiles on their faces. Gregor actually rubbed his hands together while Lachlan rose and pulled up another chair beside him. "Come join us," he said.

"Is it safe?" she asked as she walked down the stairs that rose against the wall. She kept away from the edge out of habit, as there wasn't a railing. "I doona want to be eaten."

"Go get her," Adaira told Kerr, then said, "I'm hungry!" in her best giant voice. Kerr stomped as directed toward Amber. "Human woman tastes good!"

Amber couldn't help it and lifted her gaze to Lachlan, who'd also wanted a taste of her a few days ago… His cocky grin told her he'd thought the same thing.

"Shall I come save you?" he asked.

"Nay, Amber can save herself," Adaira said. "She's been teaching me how to fight. But not with a sword, with my hands and feet."

"And head," Amber added.

"Aye, my head is really hard. She said I almost broke her nose."

Amber stopped about halfway down and pressed her fingers gently to the cartilage. It was still tender.

"Are you all right, lass?" Lachlan asked.

"I'm fine. What's a wee bit of blood when you're teaching self-defense?"

"Too much," Kerr said, then grasped Adaira's waist and lifted her to the ground. He tweaked the girl's nose. "You doona need to know how to fight, lass. Either of you. That's what we're here for. Lachlan and the rest of us will keep you and Amber safe."

Adaira scrunched up her face at him, looking

mulish. Amber suspected her own expression was much the same. She clenched her jaw in annoyance, and drummed her fingers against her leg.

Idiot man.

She caught Lachlan's eye again and saw that his smile had widened. Callum's too. Aye, maybe her betrothed did want her to be herself.

"Come here, giant," she said to Kerr, pointing to where she wanted him to stand. He came forward as she continued her descent until he stood beside the staircase, the top of his head reaching her shoulder. She stopped and flicked him hard with her finger in the middle of his forehead.

He slapped a palm to his forehead and stepped back. "Och, that hurt!"

The men watching burst out laughing.

"It was supposed to. Ne'er tell a woman she shouldnae know how to protect herself. An attack could come from anywhere at any time, and you might not be there to protect her."

He stared at her belligerently, and she stared back. "We would punish the transgressors."

"Good for you. You can do that after I escape."

"What do you think you could do to a man my size?" he asked. Not in a menacing way, just disbelief. "My father was a cruel bastard, and I saw him hurt many people, including women. It took a man as big as me to put him down for good. That's how I became laird, lass. And then I put down a few cruel cousins and uncles too."

"I didn't say I would put him down for good. Just long enough so I could escape."

"And how will you do that? Smash a knee in my groin? That's the first move I'd expect from you."

"That's what she did to Earc," Adaira said eagerly. "He didn't get up for at least five minutes after she got away."

"Then Earc wasn't paying close enough attention."

"Aye, he was. He listened with his eyes closed as she whispered something in his ear."

The men laughed again, and Amber narrowed her eyes, hands on her hips as she looked at them. They enjoyed the show but none of them, including Lachlan, believed she could take Kerr down. Aye, it would be hard, especially as he was waiting for her to try something. But if she could get close enough, she might be able to do it. She hadn't been able to escape Lachlan when they'd first met, but he'd surprised her.

Could she surprise Kerr?

"I see I've made you mad, lass," he said. "Your cheeks are flushed, your eyes sparkling, and God's truth you are a vision—almost as lovely as my Isobel— but attacking someone you canna beat will only anger them, and they may kill you for it."

"So a woman should do naught? Let a man do whate'er he wants to her?"

"Amber, you will be protected. Trust me. Lachlan will ne'er let anything happen to you or Adaira. We protect our loved ones."

"Aye, sweetling. I'll keep you safe," Lachlan said, coming toward them.

She reached out her hand to him as she stepped down, but then her foot caught in her skirt. With a wee yelp, she tumbled sideways off the stairs. Lachlan ran to catch her, but Kerr got there first, and she fell safely into his arms.

She didn't want to draw blood or do permanent damage, so she went for his nerves first, digging her thumbs in just above his elbow as hard as she could. His arms fell away from her, and she crashed with him to the ground, then caught him hard through his plaid, her nails digging in.

"Amber!" Lachlan yelled, running to her. The others followed. She gave Lachlan a hard glare, and he stopped a few paces back. "Kerr, doona hurt her," he ordered.

"Me, hurt her?" Kerr groaned, flat on his back, his face scrunched up in pain as she kneeled over him. "Christ Almighty, she's got my stones."

"Doona move, Laird MacAlister," she warned him. "If you e'er want your lovely Isobel to birth your bairns, you'll hold absolutely still."

He huffed out a pained breath, almost a laugh. "Doona call me laird, Amber. You are to marry my brother. Welcome to the family, Sister."

There was silence for a beat, then the men fell into hysterics. Callum bent over at the waist, hands on his knees, sucking back great gulps of air. Gregor and Darach leaned on each other, unable to stand on their own, and Gavin stood wide-eyed, his grim face cracking a smile.

All except Lachlan, who waited tensely by her side. "Amber, take your hands off his cock before I have to kill him."

The men burst out laughing again. Callum fell to his knees while Gregor and Darach hit the clean rushes on the floor with their arses. Gavin actually laughed.

"By the love of God, she's perfect, Lachlan!" Gregor said.

"And she can lance that boil on your arse too!" Darach said.

"She'll not be looking anywhere near your arse," Lachlan growled.

"Well, maybe someday," Amber said. "But for now, I have an assistant. She's fourteen. She lances all the boils."

She held back a laugh as Gregor's glee faded. Releasing Kerr, she stepped back. He rolled onto his side and groaned.

Lachlan pulled her against his chest and wrapped his arm around her waist from behind.

"Whate'er you do," Kerr said to Lachlan, "doona introduce her to Isobel. At least not until we're married."

Amber wanted to stamp her foot like Adaira had done earlier. "Your loved ones deserve to know how to defend themselves, Kerr—male or female. You do them a disservice by not teaching them. If my father hadn't taught me, I canna say what would have happened. Once he died, I had no one to protect me but myself."

Callum stood up. "My Maggie can throw knives, and she's better than anyone with an arrow, but I doona think she knows how to fight in close quarters."

"Then you should teach her."

Callum shrugged, his resistance obvious in the set of his shoulders and the downward tilt of his mouth. Amber rolled her eyes.

"She's right," Gregor said. "I taught Kellie some moves. Lucky thing I did, as she was attacked in our own keep by one of our guests."

"My father?" Kerr grunted as he rolled to his knees.

"Nay, your uncle. I killed him that night. Which was the start of the feud with your father."

"I'm sorry."

Gregor gave Kerr a hand and helped him up. "Doona be. You're not responsible for the acts of evil men."

He turned to Amber and pulled her into a tight hug, actually lifting her off the ground. "Welcome to the family, Amber. I couldnae be happier."

"Didn't I tell you he would love you?" Lachlan said, wrapping his other arm around her waist and kissing the side of her neck.

She shivered and closed her eyes. When she opened them, all the men were smiling at her like sappy old women. "God's Blood, you look like a bunch of fourteen-year-old lasses, listening to some romantic ballad."

"I love romance," Gregor sighed.

Amber laughed, feeling a joyous bubbling in her veins. "Seems I'm joining the family just in time, then. I can spice things up with a wee wickedness."

Adaira bounded up to her. "Teach me how to do that move!"

"Not yet, lass. You're a long way from learning anything so difficult. Keep practicing your head butts and heel stomps."

The girl darted at Kerr, head lowered, and he quickly flipped her up over his shoulder. She shrieked in delight. But Amber had seen Kerr's wince and knew he was hurting. Regret washed through her. What if she had squeezed too hard and damaged his stones permanently?

She pulled out of Lachlan's embrace and hurried to the big, dark-haired warrior. "I have a salve we can apply to the skin that should help. It'll take down the swelling. Come to my room and I'll take a look."

"Nay!" both Kerr and Lachlan yelled at once.

The others burst out laughing again as they crowded around Amber and Lachlan with good wishes for a happy future.

Sixteen

"AMBER," SOMEONE WHISPERED BESIDE HER.

Amber squeezed her eyes tight. She didn't want to leave the warm nest of her quilts. For the last week— e'er since she could rise from her sickbed and make the journey to the castle—she'd been staying at the keep. Verily, 'twas much cooler here in the mornings than in her cottage.

She'd resisted the move, of course, but Lachlan had said she either moved to the keep and her own bedchamber until the wedding, or he would move in with her at the cottage. And into her bed.

Niall also had an opinion. 'Twas her duty, he said. She was to be lady at Castle MacPherson, and the clan expected to see her there.

Sighing, she opened her eyes. The light coming from the cracks around the shutters was thin, making it just past daybreak. Ian hovered near the side of her bed.

This was her duty too. She pushed up on her elbow. "Is someone sick?"

Ian had a funny look on his face, and she frowned,

fully awake now. She sat up and swung her legs over the edge. "Ian, what is it? Is it Breanna?"

"Nay, it's Father Odhran."

Her brows rose. No one had seen Father Odhran since he'd locked himself in the chapel the day Murray shot his arrow into her.

"What does he want?" she asked, praying he wasn't sick. She'd have to tend him, and he would resist. She didn't want Gregor or Lachlan's foster brothers to hear the names he'd call her.

"I didn't speak to him. I was up early helping Osgar with the birth of the foal."

"Oh, has it arrived already?"

"Nay, not yet. Osgar thinks maybe in a few more hours. But I was getting water from the well, so we'd have lots on hand if we needed it, and I saw Father Odhran in the bailey. 'Twas still dark."

"Well, maybe he was tending someone?" He was still the MacPherson's priest, even though the clan had turned their backs on him.

"I doona think so. Amber, he had someone with him."

A chill ran down her spine. "Did you see who it was?"

"Nay, I stayed hidden, but I could see he carried a bow."

Amber rose slowly from the bed, her heart pounding. Lots of men carried bows.

When Ian squawked and turned away from her, she remembered she wore only her shift. "Och, sorry," she said, grabbing the blanket from her bed and wrapping it around herself.

"We should tell the laird." He peeked over his shoulder to make sure she was covered.

"Aye. They're planning to start the sweep today with all the clans, looking for Machar Murray. They may already be up."

She slipped on shoes before crossing to her door. When she pushed through into the candle-lit hall, she walked straight into Lachlan and Gregor. Lachlan steadied her and pulled her close. Amber couldn't help closing her eyes and breathing him in. He smelled fresh, with a hint of the lavender that was pressed into the soap.

"I thought I heard voices. What's the matter?" he asked, his warmth seeping into her. She liked being wrapped tight in his embrace. It was too easy to let herself lean on him.

"It may be naught," she said, "but Ian was up early to help with the mare, and he saw Father Odhran. Lachlan, he wasn't alone. I doona know anyone who would spend time with the priest after what he did, let alone in the middle of the night."

"Would he have been called out to give last rites?" Gregor asked, wrapping a second blanket around Ian's shivering shoulders.

"Possibly. But if someone was sick or hurt, why wouldnae they have woken me? The clan knows I'm available anytime."

"How long ago was this?" Lachlan asked.

"Maybe an hour," Ian said. "I would have come sooner, but Osgar needed my help with the mare."

"Did you see who it was?"

Ian shifted his feet. "Nay, it was dark and...for

some reason I hid behind the well. Something was wrong. All I know is it was a man with a bow, and he seemed to be in charge."

Lachlan tensed against her. "In what way?"

"Well, the father looked hesitant, like he was nervous, and the other man didn't. The father had to run several times to catch up."

"What direction were they headed?"

"Toward the chapel. I didn't see them go inside, but I heard the door shut."

Lachlan squeezed the boy's shoulder. "You did well, lad. Thank you for telling us. You can go back to the stables now, but make sure the door is barred just in case, aye?"

"Aye." He returned the blanket to Gregor before leaving.

Amber watched Ian go, then turned to Lachlan. "I'm coming with you."

"Nay. 'Tis safer in here."

"How do you know? You thought the castle was safe too. If that was Machar Murray, it means he's been hiding next to us this entire time. He could have come into the keep whene'er he wanted."

"I have men at the entrance to the keep and in the great hall at night. I doona take your protection lightly."

Her eyes widened. "Do you have them outside my door too?"

"Nay, but that's a good idea."

She pulled out of his embrace and scowled at him. "I'm coming with you. If someone gets hurt, I should be there."

"Be where?" Callum asked, walking toward them down the passageway.

Darach, Kerr, and Gavin came through the stone archway at the end of the hall that led to the stairs going up to the next level.

So, it would be her versus all six of them. She balled her hands into fists and set them on her hips, ready to do battle.

"Ian spotted Father Odhran with someone who carried a bow," Lachlan said. "'Twas still dark, but he thinks they went into the chapel."

"You blocked the tunnel from there, aye?" Darach asked.

"Aye, but maybe Murray dug more than one. He's tricky and thorough. He had two tunnels running from the barracks."

"If they're inside already, we canna get to him easily. They willna let us in," Callum added.

"They'll let me in," Amber said.

"Nay!" Lachlan wrapped a tight arm around her waist.

She pushed against his chest. "You canna tell me what to do, Lachlan."

"Aye, I can. I'm your laird and about to be your husband."

"You told me not to call you laird, and I can still change my mind about being your wife."

He shoved a hand through his hair. "Amber, I'm not putting you in danger again. I canna. He almost killed you last time. You didn't see how close the arrows were to your head." He gently touched the bandage she still wore beneath her shift and blanket. "Or this one to your lungs and heart."

"You need me."

"Aye, I do." He cupped her cheek. "I need you alive."

"Get Father Lundie," Gregor said. "Say that he wants to talk to Father Odhran—priest to priest. He should be there to witness what happens, so he can send a first-hand account back to Rome. We doona want the Church siding with Odhran against Amber. Father Lundie must see that he's addled."

"I'll go in with Father Lundie," she said, then quickly added, "we all will. Father Odhran willna be able to resist telling Father Lundie, telling all of you, how foul I am."

"Amber, I'll not put you in—"

"You'd rather leave me here?" she asked Lachlan, stepping back from him. "Who knows what other secret tunnels into the keep we've missed? At least if I'm with you, you can keep me safe."

"She sounds like Isobel," Kerr said with a sigh and shake of his head.

Gavin put his hand on Lachlan's shoulder. "Aye, she does. But what she said makes sense, Brother."

Amber lifted her chin and met Lachlan's frosty blue eyes. "You can wait for me to dress, or I'll come in my shift. It's up to you."

His nostrils flared, and he stared at her, his face grim. "Go get dressed."

⤜⤛

Lachlan walked quickly through the bailey, which had been slowly and quietly emptied on his orders. Warriors had taken the villagers' places, and the dogs were standing by. He held Amber's hand in a tight grip and scanned their surroundings. Without needing to be asked, his foster brothers and Gregor, all armed with their weapons and shields, had formed a protective circle around them. Father Lundie lagged behind the group, struggling to keep up.

They'd discussed the plan in the great hall before Father Lundie arrived. While he was integral to their success, they didn't want him to be in conflict over what might happen. His job was to assess Father Odhran, and get him talking—which meant having to hear all the horrible things he'd say about Amber—and get them inside the chapel without a fight.

They would take it from there.

They slowed as they neared the chapel, and Father Lundie caught up. Lachlan felt a twinge of remorse as the older man huffed and puffed. Amber slipped a supportive arm around his back and clucked with concern.

"Doona worry yourself, lass," Father Lundie said. "'Tis good for me to get my heart pumping once in a while. I spend too much time sitting on my backside nowadays."

"Aye, 'tis important you take regular walks, Father, twice a day, if you can. And you should make a habit of reaching up to the sky and then touching your toes several times too. 'Twill keep your muscles and joints limber."

He patted her cheek. "You're a lovely lass and a good match for Laird MacKay. I couldnae be happier for you both."

"Och, you haven't heard me curse yet or rebuke

someone for being careless. I'm afraid I can be quite ill-tempered."

"God judges the heart, lass, and I can see you have a good one."

Amber's lip trembled slightly before she firmed it up with a deprecating smile, and Lachlan's heart broke a wee bit at seeing this strong woman vulnerable.

"Father Odhran doesn't think so," she said. "He hates me for aiding the lasses—especially when they're giving birth. I'm afraid he'll say terrible things about me."

"'Tis important I hear him out, Amber, and try to help him. It doesn't mean I condone what he's saying or find an ounce of truth in his words, aye? Hold fast to what you hold dear and believe in Lachlan and the other lairds. They're good men, and they believe in you too."

Lachlan pulled her beneath his shoulder and whispered in her ear, "Aye, we do believe in you, no matter what that foul priest says or does. Doona forget that, even if we say otherwise in order to get inside the chapel."

She nodded, and Lachlan released her but stayed close.

Father Lundie walked through the group, up the stairs to the chapel's door, and banged on it. The men stepped away from Amber as if they distrusted her— they wanted to encourage Odhran's rant by showing a divide among them. Gregor had crossed his arms over his chest in disapproval, and Kerr held his fingers by his side in a sign to ward off the devil.

"Father Odhran," Father Lundie called, his voice kind and concerned. "'Tis Father Lundie from Clan

MacKenzie. We met a few years ago at the summer festival in Inverness. May I speak with you?"

They listened for any sound. Naught. Father Lundie tried the door, but it was locked. He knocked again. "Father Odhran?"

"Go away!" the priest yelled from inside, desperation and madness reverberating in his tone. Father Lundie looked at the lairds with alarm. Gregor twirled his hand in a circular motion, encouraging the priest to continue.

"I've travelled a long way to see you," he said through the door. "Gregor MacLeod asked me to come. Everyone's worried about your well-being... and your concerns about the MacPherson healer. I'd like to speak to you about her."

The priest spoke truthfully, even though he knew the lairds had their own agenda.

"She's a witch!" Odhran yelled.

"Aye, 'tis what Gregor and the others told me you'd say. 'Tis a serious accusation. It deserves to be discussed face-to-face, doona you think? The lairds would like to bring Amber before you—before us—prior to her marriage to Laird MacKay. You can understand their concern, aye?"

More silence. Lachlan ground his teeth at the delay. It wasn't working. The longer they stood here, the farther away Murray could be running—or setting up the perfect shot to kill Amber. His eyes scanned the top of the buildings again.

He was about to draw his sword and use the heavy steel to hack open the door, when he heard the hinges creak. His gaze dropped, and Father Odhran, looking haggard and unwashed, poked his head out.

He hissed when he saw Amber. "Get it away from me!"

Lachlan stepped forward, his fists like hammers. Rage burned hot at the insult to Amber and overrode his careful planning.

The monster had done enough damage to Lachlan's adopted clan. Now he harbored Machar Murray too? He needed to be put down.

Gregor grabbed Lachlan's arm in a tight grip. "Calm down, Son. Father Odhran's concern is justified. Let him have his say, and we'll make our decision. If it's true, you canna marry her, no matter how much you want to. Right, Father?" He directed the last at Father Lundie.

Father Lundie sputtered, his brow furrowed. "If it's true, aye, but 'tis a grave accusation he makes. You canna claim someone is a witch just because they're a healer. We need women like Amber to help us when we're sick."

"Not if it subverts God's will," Gregor said. "She alleviates the pain of childbirth."

Lachlan's eyebrows rose, and he stared at his foster father. How difficult had that been for him to say? Gregor would have given his life for Kellie's on the birthing bed. He must want to gut the priest as much as Lachlan did.

Gregor squeezed his arm tighter, and Lachlan realized the contact was no longer about restraint but about helping Gregor get through what he had to say next. "Ask her how many women she's saved who should have died for Eve's sin? 'Tis their cross to bear for tempting Adam." The words must feel like the worst betrayal to Kellie.

"I'm not convinced," Lachlan said. "The priest is addled as Amber said. 'Tis rumored he tups with goats."

Odhran pushed the door wide and waved his arms. A stench came with him. "I ne'er did such a thing in my life! Look at her! She has Lucifer all over her! She was made to tempt a man. She'll tear away your soul, Laird MacKay, and feed it to the devil himself." He stepped forward but still held the handle. "Strip off her clothes, you'll find his marks. The places he sucks on her. I saw her fornicating with her goats. Both of them at once."

Amber puffed out a shocked laugh. "God's blood, you've lost your mind. Your brains are naught more than stewed oats."

The priest released the door, his hands out like claws, and ran toward her. He'd barely taken two steps before an arrow struck him from behind and protruded through his chest.

He fell toward Amber.

Lachlan barreled into her an instant later. They flew sideways to the ground and kept rolling, his big body shielding her as more arrows flew through the space where she'd been standing.

Controlled chaos erupted as the other lairds and their men stormed the chapel. Lachlan heard the thud of arrows hitting shields and the clang as the portcullis dropped, but he knew it was useless. Murray would never have revealed himself if he didn't have an escape route from the chapel—most likely one that exited into the woods, or they would have seen him crossing the empty field by now.

"Amber, are you hurt?" he asked as he frantically pulled her behind a barrel. He turned her over, looking for blood.

"Nay, Lachlan. I'm all right."

"Your shoulder, then." He propped her up against the barrel and pulled her top aside to see the bandage. "God's blood, it's bleeding again."

"Not much. Verily, it was worse yesterday after training with Adaira."

"What?" He knew Adaira had hurt Amber's nose, but he had no idea she'd hurt her shoulder as well. He closed his eyes and took a moment to breathe. "When this is over, I'll train her."

Amber opened her mouth to protest, but he waylaid her. "Just until you're healed," he said. "You doona want a permanent injury. You know that."

Her shoulders sagged. "Aye."

"Laird MacKay," Hamish yelled, running over.

Lachlan signaled to him to give them a minute, then helped Amber up. "This is the last time, lass, I swear. You are not a warrior. I doona want you in the line of fire e'er again. If you died, it would devastate me and the clan. I'll do what I'm trained to do—fight. You stay back and do what you're trained to do—heal. Are we agreed?"

She nodded. Lachlan wrapped his hands around the side of her head and lifted her up for a kiss. Her mouth opened under his, soft, warm, and she melted into him. When he pulled back, her eyes swam with tears.

"We'll bring the wounded to the keep, same as last time. Murray will have a way out, and he's probably rigged the tunnel. Send stretchers to the chapel."

"Aye." Her hands clenched his arms. "Lachlan, stay safe."

"I will. Murray is not going to ruin my wedding."

She laughed, then sobered. "Nay, I'll be the one

doing that, I'm sure. You're addlebrained to want to marry me."

"No one else, Amber." He kissed her again and walked her to Hamish, placing his body between her and possible arrows from the chapel.

To his second-in-command, he said, "Keep everyone in the great hall, and station warriors both inside and out. If they have to leave, provide an escort. 'Tis obvious we missed a tunnel here. We may have missed one in the keep as well. And I want men guarding the stables while the foal is being birthed. Keep an eye on Ian and Adaira in particular. Or anyone else Murray may use to blackmail us."

"What about the villagers?" Amber asked. "I need Mary here, and I want Ian's sister, Breanna, to be found."

"Aye, good idea." He turned to Hamish. "Have the men go door-to-door to make sure everyone's all right. Tell them to stay locked inside until they hear from us that it's safe to come out."

"Lachlan!"

Looking up, he saw Darach on the steps with his hounds, Hati and Skoll. The others were already inside.

He gave Amber one last hug, inhaling deeply. Her warmth, her softness, the way she smelled of fresh air and lavender, imprinted on his senses. Then he released her and strode away—and didn't dare look back.

Taking the stairs two at a time, he drew his sword, even though he knew the area would already be secured.

The chapel was an open room with carved columns about every ten paces, depicting angels, demons, saints, and sinners. They supported the arched, stone roof and framed the sanctuary. A large crucifix hung on the wall behind the altar, and a statue of Mary holding the Christ child was off to the side.

Benches had been shoved haphazardly against doors and shuttered windows, which had been wrenched open by the warriors to let in the light. The sanctuary had also been blocked off, with benches piled on top of one another near to the ceiling.

Archers faced the sanctuary for protection as men dismantled the makeshift wall. Other men cleared any side rooms and alcoves. Father Lundie stood with his hands on his head, moaning in agitation at what he would consider a desecration, although at least the altar and Holy Book on top of it appeared to be untouched.

Lachlan approached the others as they discussed their options. Darach held a nightshirt that had belonged to Machar Murray in his hand, and the dogs, who sat beside them, already had his scent.

Callum pointed to a position behind the wall of benches where a desk stood. "That's the best sightline to the door, and it would allow for his escape."

Lachlan looked back toward the chapel entrance, imagining Murray standing or kneeling on the desk with his bow drawn and pointed at Father Odhran's back. Once Odhran had opened the door wide and stepped outside, he was a dead man.

"One shot to the back," Gavin said. "Then when the priest was down, he had a direct line to where Amber and Lachlan stood."

Darach squeezed Lachlan's shoulder. "Glad you're still with us."

"Amber too," Kerr said, his biceps bulging as he crossed his arms over his huge chest. "I still have to prove to her I'm not a weak, mewling lad with my stones caught in her grip."

"Sorry, lad, we doona have all year," Gregor said.

The others laughed as Lachlan paced back and forth, too worried and anxious to find humor in anything right now. He knew his foster brothers and Gregor weren't relaxed, even though they might look and sound it. They were assessing the situation for any traps Murray had left behind, same as he was.

Lachlan had spotted one already and eagerly stepped over the last few benches as the wall came down.

"Please, doona desecrate the sanctuary," Father Lundie begged.

"We'll do our best, Father, but you have to stand back. The dogs need to track him. And he's probably rigged some traps along the way," Lachlan said.

"Let me retrieve the Holy Eucharist first, then, aye? If there's any blessed bread or wine, it needs to be protected."

Lachlan nodded, eyes sharp as he watched Father Lundie approach the altar and pull out a basket of bread, a vial of holy water, and the bible.

When he'd retreated, Lachlan turned back to Callum and pointed out a trip wire across the ground. "I doona think it's the main one."

Callum crouched beside it. "Nay, me neither."

"Let's find out." Gregor used his great strength to lift one of the benches and shove it against the wire. A column came smashing down from their left, knocking into the altar and almost hitting Gavin, who jumped back just in time.

Dust rose, and they pulled their plaids over their faces.

Father Lundie moaned at the destruction of the sanctuary, while Darach's dogs erupted into ferocious barking.

"Hati, Skoll, hush," Darach commanded, and they quieted down.

"Christ Almighty, I wasn't expecting that," Gavin said, brushing the dust from his short hair.

"Nay, certainly not for the first trap," Kerr agreed.

"Och, 'tis the altar," Father Lundie said, approaching the sanctuary again.

They all looked at him. "What do you mean?" Lachlan asked.

"I've seen a few churches that have a hiding space below the altar—built for the priest in case trouble arises. 'Tis possible Father Odhran showed it to Laird Murray, and Murray used it as a starting point for the tunnel you think he built."

Lachlan approached slowly. "So the column was rigged to fall on top of it."

"Maybe. Let's think like him," Gregor said. "He wants to delay us getting into the tunnel."

"And stop us from finding it in the first place," Callum added.

Kerr carefully stepped over the column. "If I didn't know about the hiding spot, I might crawl o'er the debris and look for him in the back rooms."

"Aye, and we know he likes to build traps up high—traps within traps—and use poison," Darach said.

Gregor knotted his plaid over his nose. "Keep your faces covered and doona let anything touch your skin."

Lachlan covered his face as well. "Divide into teams. Gavin and Kerr, take the priest's solar. Gregor and Darach, take the bedchamber. Callum and I will remove the debris and see if there's a tunnel beneath the altar."

As the other four men disappeared into the rooms behind the sanctuary, Callum and Lachlan slowly stepped over the broken stone and began their examination.

"You take that side, and I'll take this side," Callum said, pulling up his plaid.

Lachlan nodded and reined in his impatience as he moved cautiously to the right, scanning for any more trip wires along the ground and looking up high for irregularities with the other columns and the arched ceiling. "'Tis likely there's naught else out here. At least not until we take the broken stone away and try to open the tunnel."

"Laird MacKay, is there anything else I can do here?" Father Lundie asked, as he hovered on the other side of the downed column.

"Nay, Father. You've been verra helpful. Why doona you return to the keep and see if Amber needs assistance?"

The priest nodded and had just left when thuds sounded from the priest's solar. After a second, Gavin yelled, "We're all right. Knives shot from the desk when we opened the door."

"Careful of the tips," Lachlan answered. "He's used poisoned thorns before. And careful of the hilts too, just in case. Make sure you doona grab them."

"Can I put them in my mouth?" Kerr asked.

Callum snorted as he leaned down to look for more trip wires.

"You can put them up your arse, for all I care."

"Och, 'tis always about the arse with you, isn't it?"

"Quit blathering and pay attention," Gregor yelled from the priest's bedchamber. Then he hollered, "Down!" just before another loud crash.

Lachlan tensed and saw Callum do the same as they waited. Then Darach yelled, "We're all right! Gregor tripped a trap by mistake. Oil and a lit arrow. Luckily, the arrow hit my shield instead of the oil that had spilled from the smashed container. I put out the fire."

"Christ Almighty, old man!" Kerr yelled. "Quit blathering and focus on the task at hand before you get us all killed."

"Shove it, you overgrown ablach!" Gregor yelled back.

Lachlan wiped his brow on his sleeve. It was hot under his drawn-up plaid, and sweat had formed on his forehead. He moved to the back of the sanctuary to examine the large, wooden crucifix. When he looked behind it, he saw scratch marks on the stone wall. "Callum."

Callum heard the urgency in his voice and came over, taking care with each step.

Lachlan showed him the marks. "They're fresh," he said.

"Aye." Callum wiggled the cross. "And it's looser than it should be."

Crouching on his haunches, Lachlan looked for a connecting stud or wire in the stone. "It's not attached at the bottom."

"If it fell over, it's tall enough to land on the altar, and heavy enough to kill." Callum cupped his hands and leaned over. "Take a look up top. I'll give you a lift."

Lachlan put his foot on Callum's hands and balanced himself against the wall as his foster brother raised him up. He could see the mortar had been chipped away from around the rock. "It looks like a stone has been loosened where the cross is attached to it." He pulled on the wood and the large block slid toward him. "Aye, it's coming out," he said.

Callum lowered him. "So something pushes on the stone from behind. But what? And what triggers it?"

"Most likely to do with the altar. The release of pressure when we take the broken column off maybe? Let's take the crucifix out just to be safe."

He moved to the other side and wrapped his arms around it. Callum did the same from his side, and they slowly pulled the heavy cross from the wall and laid it on the floor.

Lachlan examined the stone at the back. "It's wrapped in some kind of greased material."

"To make it easier to move?"

"Aye. Or perhaps 'tis similar to the trap that Gregor set off. Fire on top of the altar would deter anyone from going in."

A door banged shut, and Gavin reentered the sanctuary from the priest's solar. Kerr was at his heels, carrying a sack that rattled—most likely filled with the knives that had tried to carve them to pieces. He tossed the bag to one of his men. "Take this to Amber. Tell her the blades may be poisoned, and that I caught every one of them with my teeth."

Lachlan let out a humorless laugh at the jest. It was either that or scream with frustration that Murray was slipping through his fingers—again—while they slowly undid his clever machinations.

"What did you find?" Gavin asked.

"The crucifix's been rigged to fall on the altar. And possibly to cause a fire."

"We found a passageway," Gregor yelled, his voice coming from the other side of the wall. A moment later, light shone through the hole. "It's rigged back here. Do you want us to spring the trap?"

"Go ahead," Lachlan said, looking up to see a heavy battering ram swing through the hole.

"Ingenious," Kerr said.

"He's masterful at killing, torturing, and raping people," Lachlan replied, his anger getting the better of him.

"A genius at destroying lives," Gregor added. "Think what he could have done if he'd wanted to help people instead."

"Laird MacKay, this is the last, heaviest piece. Should we lift it off now?" Malcolm asked.

"Aye, but let's use some ropes and keep our distance, just in case."

They slipped ropes around the broken column, then dragged it off the stone slab behind the altar. "Clear," he shouted.

He heard a thud and looked up to the hole in the wall.

"That was it," Darach said a moment later. "The release of pressure triggered the battering ram—or tried to—but we'd already dismantled it."

"Good work," Lachlan said. He kneeled at the slab and wrenched it up, as eager to continue as Darach's hounds were to sniff Murray out. He had a half-hour lead on them.

Lachlan ground his teeth as fear chewed at him from the inside. How could he protect Amber if Murray got away again?

"Let the dogs go first," Darach said as he called Hati and Skoll over.

"Nay, there may be other traps, and if he makes it out of the tunnel and escapes the net, we'll need Hati and Skoll to track him. It's my wife he's going to come after; I'll go first."

Lachlan reached for the torch Gavin carried, but Gregor took it instead. "I'll go first. My Kellie's already gone. If I die, I'll be going to meet her and my three wee girls at long last. You canna begrudge me that. You all still have families to create." He sat on the edge of the hole, legs dangling down. "I made my family when I brought the five of you to live with me. You're grown men now. Let me do this for you—for all of you when the time comes."

Quiet descended. Lachlan wanted to grab back the torch, wanted to race after Murray and take him out for all the harm he'd done to Amber and to Donald—not to mention the rest of the clans. But Gregor was right. He might die, and Lachlan had Amber to consider now.

"I doona know why you're even thinking about it; it's not like you have a choice," Gregor said, dropping the torch down the hole. "I'm bloody well going first." He grabbed his shield, shoved off the ledge, and landed in a crouch on the tunnel floor.

"'Tis not as if anything could pierce that thick *elephaunt* hide of his anyway," Darach said.

Then the sound of arrows being released reached their ears, and Gregor groaned like he'd been hit.

God's blood!

Lachlan dropped into the hole, his shield out, and rolled to the wall. His brothers dropped in behind him, covering Gregor, who lay prone on the dirt floor. More arrows hit their shields.

Lachlan peered up the torch-lit tunnel, more a lengthy, open room that looked like it had been built and reinforced many years ago—long before Machar Murray arrived—and saw a man jump out from behind a rock, bow in hand, and take off in the opposite direction.

"Murray!" he roared, racing after him, forcing his legs faster, determined to catch the demon of a man who was such a threat to Amber, who had killed his brother and tried to kill him.

"Lachlan, no!" Callum yelled from behind him.

A part of his brain screamed at him to be cautious, to go slow, but that other part, the part that was so afraid to lose Murray again and put Amber in further danger, drove him forward, feet pounding on the dirt, cool air rushing through his teeth.

"Stay to the side!" Callum yelled again, chasing after him. "Step only where he steps!"

Lachlan looked down, his self-preservation finally coming into play, and jumped over another wire just in time—right where he'd seen Murray jump.

"Wire," he yelled over his shoulder for Callum, his eyes scanning now as he ran, instead of being glued to Murray's back.

Murray raised his bow arm, and Lachlan brought up

his shield just before an arrow struck the wood, then another. Callum loosed one from behind him toward Murray, and Lachlan started running again.

He was close enough to Murray now to see his face—gaunt and dirty—but underneath he could see the remnants of the bonnie-looking man he used to be, which surprised Lachlan, as he'd always imagined a misshapen devil.

The devil smiled at him and leapt forward into a small, dark tunnel, dug out where the room ended, before turning back to Lachlan, his body almost blending with the blackness.

"You canna save her, MacKay. Just like you could-nae save your brother. Amber is dead."

Then he pulled a lever, and a pile of rocks dropped down from above onto Lachlan.

Seventeen

AMBER PACED BACK AND FORTH IN THE GREAT HALL, her hands clenched with worry by her side and her eyes burning with unshed tears. The rushes crunched beneath her feet, and the air was heavy with the smell of herbs, blood, and unwashed bodies.

She'd had five patients in the last thirty hours and had slept little. The first had been Father Lundie, his hands and inner wrists burned from a concentrated powder of dried monkshood, which had been sprinkled on the cover of the Bible he'd recovered from the chapel. The skin had reddened and blistered, and he'd become nauseated. Luckily, he'd rinsed them right away, and his symptoms weren't as bad as they could have been.

He'd been very concerned about the holy book, the holy water, and the consecrated bread. Amber had wanted to burn them, as the poison was deadly if ingested, but the priest had refused and instead wiped down the book and wrapped up everything tight—until he could get guidance on what to do from his superiors.

Her next patient had been Gregor MacLeod, who'd been sliced open by an arrow along his right cheek in the exact same spot she'd been injured, which had pleased the idiot man. Except the arrow that struck Gregor had been poisoned too, and he'd also fallen ill.

Amber had taken a chance that the arrow was tainted with the same substance that had been on the Bible and had treated the wound accordingly. It worked, and Gregor had left his sickbed against her orders to rejoin the other lairds a few hours later. She hadn't heard anything from him or Lachlan since.

She'd had other patients, unfortunately, including one of Kerr's men, who'd been crushed by a pile of rocks in Machar Murray's tunnel and was still in critical condition. Amber had treated several breaks in his limbs, a crushed hand, and tried her best to stitch a puncture in his bowel. There had also been further damage to his ribs and lungs that even she hadn't been able to touch. She had little hope for his recovery. Her greatest worry for him was infection, especially in the belly wound.

The fourth patient had been gored by a wild boar that had been startled in the woods during the sweep. The warrior, one of Gavin's men, had been lucky. The boar's tusk had struck him to one side of the big artery in his groin, and Amber had been able to sew it up.

The last patient from just a few hours ago had been Adaira. Who had jumped off the stairs out of sheer boredom and fallen to the ground. Not only had she bashed her forehead and nose, but a twig from the floor had poked her in the eye. At least the injury and the pain draught had put the lass to sleep for a while.

Now, other than checking on patients, Amber had naught to do but pace anxiously. Being restricted to the great hall, she hadn't been able to do more than change out of her bloody clothes. So again, she was a mess—dried blood in her hair and most likely on her face.

She glanced down at her hands, vaguely noting the crusty red in the creases, but all she could think about was Lachlan and Machar Murray. Had they caught him yet? Was Lachlan all right? Was he still sure he wanted to go through with the marriage? Especially if they caught Murray, and Amber was no longer in danger.

That question had been circling in her mind like a vulture over a kill for the last three hours.

Of course, she hadn't slept and—

"Amber."

Gasping, she spun around. Lachlan stood there, dark circles under his eyes, his face and hands scratched and bruised, his plaid dirty and ripped. She took three running steps toward him and threw herself into his arms. He squeezed her tight, head in the crook of her neck, breath heavy on her skin.

"You smell good," he said.

She huffed out a laugh. "I smell of blood and other unspeakable things."

"Nay, you smell like Amber."

She pulled back and looked at him, loving the smile on his braw face, even though his words made as much sense as one of Father Odhran's hateful rants.

"I doona know whether to be insulted or charmed," she said.

"Be charmed. I meant it in a good way."

"Then that's how I'll take it."

She didn't need to ask if they'd captured Murray; she could see the answer in Lachlan's eyes and the grim line of his jaw. "Any sign of him?"

"Aye, the dogs tracked him several times, but they always lost him at the loch or the river. He's smart, crafty, well-prepared. Hati and Skoll hadn't picked up a fresh trail in the last eight hours. We came back to rest and rethink our approach."

"So I'm still in danger?"

He sighed. "Aye."

"And you'll still marry me, then?"

His eyebrows jumped up. "Of course I'll still marry you. Whether the blackheart is found or not. How could you ask such a thing?"

She shrugged, feeling vulnerable and weepy and not liking it at all. Maybe because she'd been so worried the past thirty hours, or because she was tired. Beyond tired.

Looking down, she rubbed her hands together. "I think Kerr's man will die. I've done what I can, but 'tis likely infection will set in—more than I can fight with my herbs."

He took her hand, laced his fingers through hers. "I'm sorry."

"Aye, so am I. He's barely twenty. Machar Murray as good as killed him yesterday, along with Father Odhran—not that I mourn the priest. 'Tis just...Murray seems unbeatable. With all of your,

Gregor's, and your foster brothers' men, we still canna catch him."

Lachlan pulled her close again. "Nay, Amber. Doona think like that."

"'Tis hard not to. He's always one step ahead of us. A demon of a man if e'er there was one."

"He's well prepared. He spent five years planning for just this eventuality. But the good news is we've taken away many of his escape routes and hiding places—too many to count. And we know what to look for now, so we're finding them more quickly, more easily. He's under pressure, and he's bound to make a mistake."

"So he'll act soon?"

"Nay, not too soon. I think, like us, he'll need to rest and reassess. He's a planner, and so far, we've thwarted those plans. He'll be enraged by that, and Callum says his overwhelming need at this point will be to beat us."

"He's not used to losing."

"Nay. I probably handed him his first defeat when I foiled his plans to take over my clan."

"And now he canna seem to win."

"Every moment he's alive he's winning, as far as I'm concerned."

"Aye."

He squeezed her hand and walked with her to sit in the chairs in front of the hearth. "How's it been here otherwise?"

"Crowded, anxious, people stepping on one another's toes. I had a few serious surgeries. One warrior will survive, the other is in God's hands now. And Adaira hurt herself."

His head shot up. "How?"

"She jumped off the stairs. Banged her face and got a twig in her eye. She's had a pain draught and is sleeping."

"Well, thank God for small mercies."

She smiled and ran her fingers along his face, pressed gently against the bruise on his temple. "What happened here?"

"Falling rocks. One of Murray's traps, but I crouched against the tunnel wall with my shield o'er my head. The lads dug me out. No harm done other than losing Murray again."

"That's how Kerr's man was hurt too."

"Aye, but farther on, near the opposite end of the tunnel Murray had dug out."

She leaned forward and pressed her forehead to his, closed her eyes. "I'm glad you're all right. I was worried."

"Doona lose faith, Amber. Good will triumphant o'er evil."

The outer door banged shut, and she heard the other lairds enter the great hall. Kerr and Gavin went directly to their wounded men, while Callum, Darach, and Gregor headed toward the hearth with the dogs—who flopped over immediately on the floor. Amber moved closer to one of them—Hati, she thought—so she could slip off her shoes and rub behind his ears with her toes. The dog thumped his tail weakly before he sighed and fell asleep.

"They're verra well trained. Is that your doing?" she asked Darach.

"Nay," both Darach and Lachlan said at once, then smiled, too tired and worried to do aught else.

"My wife, Caitlin, trained them. Beyond all my

expectations. The dogs would listen to me but to no one else until Caitlin took them in hand. Everyone called them my demon dogs."

"She sounds like a miracle worker," Amber said.

Darach's eyes filled with love. "She is."

"She trained Darach too," Lachlan added. "Had him doing her bidding just like his dogs. 'Twas a sight to behold, watching him fall in love."

A funny feeling bloomed in Amber's chest, and she dropped her eyes.

'Twas good to know Darach loved his wife. 'Twas the way it should be, of course, and she was glad for Caitlin, but she couldn't help feeling a wee bit envious. She wondered what it would be like to have a man like Lachlan MacKay fall in love with her?

She wished they were alone so she could ask him if that was possible. And if not, why did he want to marry her? And why on earth would she agree to marry him? Although as Lachlan would say, she hadn't agreed, he'd agreed.

So perhaps the question was whether or not she could fall in love with him.

Or had she already?

The feeling in her chest spread, and it felt like her heart might burst from her ribs. She pressed her fingers to her forehead and let her hair fall forward to hide her face. She felt ravaged by emotion, and not the good kind—fear, uncertainty, pain...love?

Is this what love felt like? Like she was being torn apart?

"Amber, dearling, are you all right?" Lachlan leaned forward and wrapped an arm around her shoulder.

She sniffed and put a smile on her face. "Aye. I'm sorry, I'm just tired. And overwhelmed."

"Worried about Murray, no doubt," Gregor said.

"Aye, that's part of it."

Kerr came over looking crestfallen.

Amber caught his eye. "I'll do what I can for your man, Kerr. Make him comfortable and help his body as much as possible to fight the infection. If the lung keeps collapsing, though, there's little else I can do."

Kerr nodded and sat down. "You've done more than can be expected. Thank you."

Gavin was right behind him and stopped to squeeze her shoulder. "Aye, and thank you for my man's life. 'Tis an injury I've seen before that I thought terminal, but Father Lundie said you saved him."

"'Tis a dangerous spot to be cut, for sure, but luckily the artery wasn't severed."

Gavin sat down too, and quiet descended on them, full of frustration and heartache. Verily, 'twas a bleak moment.

She just stopped herself from giving in to hopelessness.

"We canna do more than we're doing at this point," Gregor said. "For the wounded or for catching Murray. We willna find him, I'm afraid, until he makes his next move. 'Tis out of our control."

The other lairds nodded, and Amber sighed. Aye, 'twas a waiting game. The wounded would heal or die, and Machar Murray would kill or be caught.

"So, we'll celebrate life while we can, aye? Do our duty as lairds and try to catch the bastard, but also do our duty as family and put on the best wedding this clan has e'er seen. We need something to cheer us up."

Amber's eyes widened, and her heart began to race. "Doona you think we should wait?"

"Nay, naught good e'er came of waiting. I will see my son and his betrothed married tomorrow!"

❦

Amber stood in the middle of her room filled with sprigs of heather and pine, and pressed her hands to her stomach, trying to quell the storm inside. She was excited, aye, but anxiety had also twined its way into her guts and filled her with worry—and it wasn't just from the uncertainty of marrying Lachlan and their upcoming wedding night, but also from the notion that Machar Murray might strike today and hurt someone else she loved.

Earlier, she'd bathed in lavender-scented water before the women had descended upon her—four of them in all, including Finola and Isla—to dress her in her wedding finery and twist bonnie ribbons in her hair. She hadn't liked all of the attention, and she certainly didn't need someone to help her dress, but Finola had shot her a stare that had quieted all of her grumblings.

And truly she had naught to complain about. Her arisaid was the most beautiful dress she'd ever seen, and it fit her perfectly. Made of the softest wool, the material had been changed at the last minute to a dark blue, the same tone as Magda's ribbon, which matched Amber's eyes.

When they were done, the women had looked at

her and sighed. "You're a vision, lass," Finola said, wiping away a tear.

"Aye, our laird willna be able to keep his hands off you," Isla added with a wink. "You'll be lucky to make it through the first Highland Reel before he carries you upstairs." She saw the look that crossed Amber's face and rolled her eyes. "You'll love everything he does to you, Amber, I promise. Besides, it's not like he's ne'er touched you before. You'll be as big as me before you know it."

The others laughed, all except Finola, who gripped her hands. "Doona listen to her, Amber. You make our laird wait if that's what's best for you." Then she whispered in her ear, "And remember to take your knives."

When they left, Amber stood in the middle of the room, trying not to panic. Why had she ever agreed to this? Nay, she hadn't agreed, Lachlan had agreed. But he knew she'd expected him to say "no."

So, truly was his fault. And if not his fault, Niall's for sure.

But none of that mattered now anyway. She could hear the villagers gathered in the bailey below, laughing and singing, and could smell the baking bread and roast goose for the wedding feast. 'Twas too late to back out now. And Gregor MacLeod was right.

Her clan needed this.

She put her hands to her head and gently felt the big curls the women had helped along with a hot iron. The ribbon wove through them and tied the front back from her face, and the color was a perfect foil to her orangey-gold hair.

When she lifted her skirt, she saw supple leather shoes and new silk stockings with the same ribbon tying them up at her knee. She could put a knife in there, for sure. Two knives, if she wanted.

She hesitated before hurrying to her medical bag and drawing out her knives. They were especially sharp and small, made to cut through a person's skin. They had been her grandmother's, and someday Amber would pass them on too—but to her own bairns or someone else's?

Her eyes fell on a powder in a vial. She'd taken some yesterday and this morning. She did not consider it subverting God's will, since God had created the plant the substance had come from in the first place. It would permit her to stay barren if she chose—and that's if she allowed her husband to have intimate congress.

She looked at the knives again but then shut the bag. If Lachlan really wanted to take her in that way, she wouldn't be able to stop him. And if she truly thought him capable of that, why was she marrying him?

Because he wasn't that kind of man, and God's truth, she wasn't the kind of woman who could be coerced into things, especially when it came to a life decision like getting married. So she obviously wanted to marry Lachlan MacKay.

He made her feel something she'd never felt before. He made her laugh and made her sigh. He made her sharper and wittier, but at the same time, he made her addled. She wanted to rub herself all over him and sink into his skin.

He made her want him.

But she still didn't know if she wanted bairns, and

she definitely didn't want him to force his way inside her body, and no matter what Isla said, she couldn't ever imagine welcoming him in.

She sighed, feeling muddled and uncertain, and moved to the window to look out. 'Twas a beautiful summer day—the temperature ideal and the sky blue, with a few white clouds drifting past—marred only by the number of warriors manning the castle wall.

While Finola and the other women had prepared Amber for her nuptials, Lachlan and the other lairds had prepared for an attack. Machar Murray would be pleased to disrupt her wedding by turning it into a funeral.

The anxiety in her stomach tightened its grip.

In the bailey, a man played a rousing tune on the bagpipes, and her eyes drifted downward from the sight of the warriors on the wall to the sight of her clan bursting into an impromptu dance. Lads and lasses shouted, played, and ran about while their mothers chased after them. Everyone wore their best, and the excitement was palpable—she could feel it even up here in her bedchamber.

Aye, this was exactly what her clan needed. Maybe what she needed too.

A knock sounded at the door, and Amber spun toward it, her heart suddenly racing. She crossed hurriedly and leaned against the wood. "Niall?"

"Aye, it's me, lass. Open the door."

She placed her hand on the bar to lift it, then stopped, her stomach still turning and her head spinning with doubts.

After a few seconds, he said, "Amber?"

"I'm thinking," she said, drumming the pads of her fingers on the door.

"About what?"

"About…marriage."

"In general? Or your marriage in particular?"

"Both."

"And?"

She scrunched up her brow. "Well, marriage is about property, and I have no real property to give Laird MacKay."

"You gave him Clan MacPherson and all of our lands."

"Oh, aye… Well, marriage is also about bairns, and…I may be barren."

"Are you?"

She bit down on her nail. "I am right now."

"Ah, well that's probably wise. I'm sure Laird MacKay would appreciate having you all to himself in the beginning of your marriage. 'Tis many men I've known who doona get to enjoy their wives for long before their bairns arrive."

"I doona know if I'll e'er want bairns."

"You may not. I ne'er did."

"But you ne'er married."

"True."

She sighed and leaned back against the door. "You're no help."

Silence ensued, and then he said, "Marriage is about more than property and bairns, Amber. A good marriage is also about love. Tell me. Do you think you can give Lachlan that?"

Her throat tightened, and she pressed her fingers to

her mouth, closing her eyes to hold back those traitorous tears. How had she been reduced to this? "Aye, I think I can." She blew out a breath from between her lips.

"As I suspected. Amber?"

"Aye?"

"Open the door, lass. It's time to marry the man you love."

Her eyes dropped to the bar, and she placed hesitant fingers on it. Then she lifted it quickly, opened the door, and stared at Niall, looking quite dapper in his clean and pressed plaid and cap.

He beamed at her. "As lovely as your mother and your grandmother put together, you truly are the pride of Clan MacPherson."

The sound of footfalls startled her, and she looked toward the stairs. Lachlan walked down the hall, so handsome and braw in what must be a new plaid and shirt and jacket, that he took her breath away.

"The pride of Clan MacKay too," he said, his eyes devouring her, almost a physical presence on her body.

Niall hurried ahead of them as Lachlan took her hand in a sure grip and led her back to the stairs. She followed him without thinking, her eyes on his face, her breath moving quickly through her lungs.

About halfway down, she came to a halt. "Lachlan, wait. Doona you think—"

He wrapped one hand around her nape, his thumb caressing below her ear, and captured her lips with his—slow, soft, with just a slight sweep of his tongue.

She shivered, and he pulled away, continuing with her to the bottom of the stairs. In a daze, she followed him, then stopped again about halfway through the great hall. It had been cleared of any sign of her hospital, the two wounded men having been moved upstairs into their own rooms, and Kerr's warrior still holding on to life.

"You canna just kiss me, this is a lifetime commitment," she said, voice rising. "Shouldnae we talk—"

He wrapped both hands around her head this time, his fingers kneading the base of her skull. "Aye, I can just kiss you, and nay, we shouldnae talk. Because there's naught to talk about but this." He kissed her again, nibbling across her cheek and down the side of her neck to bite at the juncture of her shoulder and neck.

She moaned and dropped her head to the side. Lachlan wrapped his arm around her shoulders and walked her to the door. Bright sunlight poured in when he opened it, and she blinked. When her eyes adjusted to the light, she saw the bailey filled with her clan, their happy, excited faces beaming up at her.

Niall stood one step down from the top with his arm crooked, waiting for her. Gregor and Lachlan's foster brothers stood on the first five steps from the bottom, all in their best clothes, waiting for him. Father Lundie stood in the bailey beneath a raised trellis—decorated with ivy and white roses—dressed in a pristine white robe, a purple stole around his neck, and the holy book in his hands, waiting for both of them.

Quiet descended over the crowd as Lachlan took her hand, his eyes now looking a little wild. He dropped to one knee in front of her for all her clan and his family to see. "I ne'er asked you before. Please, Amber, will you do me the honor of becoming my wife?"

She stared down at him, forgetting about all her worries, about all the people who waited breathless for her reply. All she saw, all she heard was him. All she felt was that bond that had somehow been forged between them.

She nodded, feeling like she'd forgotten how to breathe.

"Say aye, sweetling. Please, tell me you agree," he said.

She pulled on his hand, and he rose to stand before her. Then she slid her palm up his chest and laid it over his racing heart. Finally, she smiled. "Aye. Lachlan, I'll marry you."

Eighteen

LACHLAN SAT AT THE LONG TABLE THAT FACED THE great hall, sipping ale from a finely carved wooden cup, and watched his old and new clans: his wife, his foster father, and some of his brothers dancing to the exuberant reels that sounded from the bagpipes in the corner. He was careful not to drink too much. He wanted to be fully present when he took his bride to their marriage bed for the first time—every time.

He was a lucky man and shuddered at how close he'd come to walking away from Amber. And why? Because he'd despised everything about his mother? Well, Amber was the antithesis of Mùirne MacKay. She was honest to the point of being rude, she was loyal to the point of putting herself in danger, she was funny to the point of being outrageous, and she was so damn clever, she made every other person in her vicinity look addlepated.

And he loved it.

Not to mention her beauty put the angels to shame, even when she was covered in someone else's blood and guts. Nay, that wasn't true. *Especially* when she was covered in someone else's blood and guts.

She also craved his hands on her. He couldn't wait for her to touch him too.

But as he watched her dancing with his foster father, he knew something was bothering her. He could see it in the set of her shoulders and the smile that seemed pinned in place. He tried to catch her eye, but she wouldn't look his way.

Most likely she was bothered by whatever it was she'd wanted to talk to him about earlier: maybe their upcoming marriage, maybe Murray.

He scanned the great hall, making sure every well-trained warrior from his foster brothers' and Gregor's clans were still in position at each entrance, the stairs, and on the balcony that ringed the hall. More men were stationed throughout the keep—in the bailey, at every building, on the castle wall, and in the fields beyond.

He may have gone overboard with protecting the castle, but he would not allow Machar Murray to ruin this day—or night—for Amber.

Nay, Lachlan wouldn't have their night together messed up for anything...although by the look of his wife, still avoiding his gaze, he may have done so already. He'd pushed her to the altar, knowing the more time she had to stew, the less likely she was to go through with the wedding, and now here they were, married, forever...yet he'd swear his wife was avoiding him.

The Highland Reel ended, and he tried to wave her back to him, but she took someone else's hand for the next dance, getting farther and farther away from him.

Gregor plopped down beside him, his cheeks

ruddy, his eyes sparkling, and smacked him on the back. "How are you lasting, Son? When I married Kellie, I was like a caged bear, impatient for the festivities to be over so I could take my wife to bed. You look about as relaxed as I was."

Lachlan grunted. He really didn't feel like being sociable.

Gregor laughed. "Aye, a bear."

"Any news on Murray?" he asked, unable to let it go even though it was his wedding.

"Nay, all is quiet and as it should be. I doona think he'll strike tonight. 'Tis too soon. He'll need more than a day to rest and come up with a new plan."

He nodded and turned his gaze back to the crowd of revelers, seeking his wife. "How was Amber when she danced with you?" he asked, his brow furrowing. "I think she's avoiding me. She wouldnae be nervous about the wedding night, would she?"

"Nay, I doona think so. Not Amber. She's as tough as Kerr's head. Like a bloody rock."

"I heard that!" Kerr yelled from the other end of the table where he sat having a drink with Gavin and Darach.

Callum plopped down on Lachlan's other side. "I wager she'll make a break for it."

The men stopped what they were doing and stared at Callum like he was mad. But all of them also knew—he was almost always right.

"But she agreed," Darach said. "She went all soft and dewy when Lachlan got down on one knee before the wedding."

Callum shrugged and threw a gold coin on the table. "Do you want to wager on it?"

Lachlan drummed his fingers on the table and continued to watch his wife on the dance floor, trying to ignore his brothers and their argument.

Amber didn't look soft and dewy now. She looked just like Callum said—like she was going to run. Aye, she'd moved steadily closer to the door, and she still wouldn't look at him.

His heart started to race, and he rose sharply from the bench and walked quickly in the opposite direction toward the kitchens.

"Lachlan, lad, where're you going?" Gregor called out.

"He's just realized I'm right, and he's running to intercept Amber before she makes it out of the castle," Callum said.

"She willna run. She loves him," Gavin said. "Didn't you see her eyes? Your mind is addled."

Gregor scoffed. "I'll meet your wager. She's definitely in love."

"It doesn't mean she willna run," Callum said.

Lachlan rounded the corner and sprinted for the kitchen exit, but not before he heard betting coins landing on the table behind him.

He stepped outside and made his way around the keep to the main entrance, his gaze searching every dark corner for signs of Murray, even though Gregor had assured him the devil wouldn't come tonight.

The stairs were empty but for one guard at the top, and he increased his pace. He would catch Amber at the door, lead her back into the keep, and finally have his dance. Then he'd take her upstairs where they could talk. After he'd made her his wife in every way.

But when he put his foot on the first step, the door squeaked open, and light fell onto the bailey. Amber stepped outside, lifted her skirts, and ran past the guard and down the stairs, eyes on her feet.

He braced himself, and when she finally looked up with a squeal, she tumbled and fell right into his arms.

"Lachlan? What are you doing out here?"

"Nay. The question is, what are you doing out here?"

It was too dark to see her face, but he could feel the tremors that shivered though her body. Her hands clutched at his fine linen shirt, squeezing tight in the fabric, but at the same time she pushed him back.

"I'm… I'm…running away," she finally said, and he could hear the panic in her voice.

"But why? You agreed to marry me, Amber. In front of everyone."

"That was hours ago. Now I'm running. I'm going to my cottage and locking myself in—alone—and you canna stop me."

He stiffened, surprised to feel hurt rising alongside his anger. "You. Are. My. Wife. We willna spend our wedding night separately."

"Aye, we will, Lachlan, and if you think—"

"Nay, I doona think. I know you'll sleep beside me tonight. And every night after that. This is forever, Amber. You agreed to forever."

His pulse beat at him angrily, his jaw tight, his muscles rigid. She would leave him on their wedding night. God's blood, she'd planned to run from him without even a goodbye. "What did you think would have happened when you disappeared, Amber? What do you think I would have thought?"

Guilt transformed her face, but it did little to mollify him. If anything, it made him angrier.

"That's right. I would have thought you'd been taken by Murray. Or worse, you might have indeed been taken by him as you wandered outside on your own."

"I'm sorry," she whispered.

"Not good enough, Wife." He leaned over, wrapped his arms around her thighs, and lifted her over his shoulder—just so damn angry that she cared so little.

She let out an alarmed shriek as he marched up the stairs she'd just come down, yanked open the door, continued through the dancers and up the second set of stairs. His clans began to cheer as they noticed and crowded toward them. The drink they'd consumed was addling their brains if they thought Lachlan would allow them to accompany him to their bedchamber—no matter what tradition dictated. No one but he would see his wife naked.

A sharp whistle got his brothers' attention. They intercepted the crowd and blocked off the stairs so no one could follow the newly wed couple.

When he turned the corner with Amber toward their bedchamber, she finally began to struggle.

"Lachlan, put me down right now!"

"I will put you down, Amber. Beneath me on our bed. This is how we'll be going forward in our marriage. Together. Not separately."

She stiffened, and he thought he heard a sob break from her lips, but it was still loud in the passageway. He pushed into their bedchamber, the fire burning brightly, a beautiful blue quilt and fluffy pillows on the bed. Lit candles burned on either side. A washstand stood in the corner, and on the table beside the bed, a jug of mead sat with two cups.

He shut the door behind them, and using one hand, slid the bar across, locking them in. Amber twisted her body and slipped off his shoulder, taking several steps backward, staring at him. Her breath sawed through her lungs, her fists clenched, her eyes filled with...fright?

He stopped, his anger and hurt slowly replaced by concern. He raised a hand toward her, and she took another step backward. "God in heaven. Amber, sweetling, are you scared of me?"

Her jaw set in denial, but her eyes scanned the room as if looking for a way out, and it felt like someone gutted him.

"I would ne'er hurt you. What's going on? Amber, talk to me."

She opened her mouth, then shut it, and he saw her chin tremble for a moment before she cleared her throat and tried again. "We shouldnae have married."

"Why?"

"Because I doona want...this." She waved her hand at the bed.

He looked to where she'd waved, his brow furrowing in confusion. "Beds? Quilts? Pillows? What exactly is *this*? Are you talking about living at the castle? Do you want us to stay at your cottage?"

Her cheeks turned scarlet. "Nay. It's not that. I doona want...carnal relations with you." She crossed her arms over her chest, and her teeth clamped together so tightly he could see the tension in her jaw.

His brow rose. "But...you love being touched

by me. You begged me not to stop." He took a step toward her. When she didn't back off, he took another. "When I put my hands on your body, you melt. I feel the same way."

The rigid lines of her face and body softened, and she looked so vulnerable, so scared and miserable, his heart nearly broke. He lifted his hand to caress his fingers down her cheek. "Tell me what's going on? Why are you so upset?"

Tears wet her lashes, and they glistened, brightening her violet eyes to an unbelievable color. Her lips and cheeks had flushed, and her hair, that gorgeous orange-gold hair, was twisted so intricately with ribbons that matched her eyes, she looked like a Celtic queen.

Like his wife.

"I shouldnae have married you, Lachlan. I shouldnae be married to anyone. I like being touched, aye, but everything else is…horrifying to me. I know that sounds terrible, and I'm sorry, but that's the way I feel. Isla tells me I'll love having you inside my body, but…"

He slowly lifted his other hand, moved a wee bit closer to her, and gently cupped her face, his thumbs rubbing away the tears that had trickled down her cheeks. "But you've spent the last five years thinking a man penetrating your body is an act of violence. A forced invasion."

She nodded, her lips trembling, the tears falling faster. "Rape," she whispered.

He drew her head toward him to rest on his chest. "Ne'er, Amber. I would ne'er rape you."

"But I'll ne'er consent. So it must be rape."

"Amber, I willna rape you."

"So you doona care about your own release? You're willing to do as we did before and touch me, kiss me as you once asked to do, but not reach your own pinnacle?"

"I doona need to be inside you to release, sweetling. 'Tis no different for me than it is for you when you touch yourself. Or when you touch me."

She pulled away again, and he let her go. "Nay, I doona want to touch you, either. I doona want my hand anywhere near a cock—at least, not for the purpose of carnal pleasure."

His eyes widened, and he stared at her, his mind whirling. Sweet Jesus, how frightened she must have been all these years and ne'er showed it to anyone.

But he was her husband. 'Twas his job to take on her burdens and make her feel safe. How could he get through to her?

"I see you thinking," she said, "trying to decide what to do, how to convince me. Well, I also doona want bairns, so you should just turn around now and have our marriage annulled."

He couldn't help it, he laughed. It was brief, and he didn't feel at all amused by her words, but the irony was strong. "You doona have to worry about bairns if you willna touch my cock, sweetling."

"I doona have to worry about it anyway, I've taken precautions. An herb that stops conception." She said it defiantly, her hands closing into fists again and her chin rising. She expected him to be angry with her.

"'Tis a good decision. We have a long way to go before we bring bairns into our marriage—if we do."

"How can you not want bairns? You're a laird. You have to pass down the title."

"I ne'er thought I'd be laird and had decided not to marry. I thought I'd pass it to another clan member. Or let the clan vote. Being married doesn't stop that."

He walked past her to the window, rubbing the back of his neck. He saw her eyeing the door. "Please doona leave, Amber. Like it or not, we're married now, and I meant what I said. We will sleep together every night. Naked."

"But I—"

"I said sleep, Amber. The other is up to you." He crossed back to her, gently took her hand. "We need to build trust and ties between us. If touching you is all you'll allow, then that's what I'll take."

"I'll not sleep naked."

"Aye, you will. Skin to skin. That's how we connect. You doona want me to claim my husbandly rights—"

"Rape is not a right—married or not."

"Aye, I agree. But I'd like you to agree too." He released her hand and ran his fingertips all the way from her knuckles, up the backs of her wrists and arms, across her shoulders. She shivered when he trailed them down her back to her waist and pulled her closer. "Agree to sleep naked with me Amber. Feel my heat, my touch. Wake with my fingers and mouth on your breasts. My palms on your thighs, stroking them, pushing them apart for my kiss." As he spoke, his hands moved lower over her backside and squeezed. She buried her head in his chest and groaned.

He turned her in his arms, hands never leaving her body, so her back was pressed to his chest. "Think of it, Amber. Waking up like this." He stroked upward this time and cupped both breasts. "If you were naked, my thumbs could strum your nipples. Or slide down and touch you here."

She let out a sob and grasped his arm for support as he lowered one palm down her body to cup between her thighs. "I would kiss you and lick you and suck you and rub you all over, all through the night. I would spread your thighs and bend your knees and position you for my tongue or my hands or my fingers. I would bite, I would knead, I would devour you."

He turned her again so she faced him, her body lax, her lips plump, red, and wet, just like her other ones down below, he was sure. Her eyes were heavy-lidded, her cheeks flushed. "You and I, Amber, in our bedchamber, under our quilts, hot skin against hot skin. Night after night. I willna push you for more unless you ask me to."

She licked her lips. "I willna ask."

"Nay, you'll take. There will come a time, sweetling, when *you* will take *me*."

❧

Amber didn't speak. Just let the silence, the warmth and crackle from the fire, the stirring of her hair from his breath deepen the connection between them. Build those ties and bonds.

The need to see him naked grew inside her until her fingers twitched. Aye, she wanted to be under the covers with him, skin to skin.

Finally, she raised her hands, slid them to the belt around his waist and pulled it free—his sword and sporran too. His breath left his lungs in a shudder as his plaid fell open and she tugged it off his body.

He stood in a fine, white linen shirt, long-sleeved, tied loosely at the neck and hanging halfway down his thighs. Her eyes caressed him—broad shoulders, strong hands, arms, and chest. And down below, the bulge at the front where his cock twitched and jutted toward her. She forced her eyes to stay on it. To think of it as a part of Lachlan, her husband, no different than his hand or his arm rather than an object of hurt and destruction.

Isla said she received pleasure from Alban's cock. She didn't find it aggressive or intrusive. Nay, she accepted Alban into her body. Invited him in.

Could Amber ever invite Lachlan in?

Aye, she already had. She'd opened for his fingers and soon would feel his tongue inside her too. A surge of desire swept over her and pooled in her loins. She felt soft and wet and welcoming.

"Please...take the ribbons out of my hair," she whispered.

His fingers trembled as he loosed her curls. He carefully undid and unwound four ribbons. He placed them in her palm as he worked on the next one, then the next one. When they were all out, he gently pushed his fingers into her hair, combing the curls and kinks into place. Then he cupped her cheek, brushed his thumb over her lips.

She wanted to capture it in her teeth. Instead, she walked to the table beside the bed and placed the ribbons by the pitcher of mead. Lifting her hands to her breast, she unpinned her silver brooch and let her dress fall away too, laying it across the end of the bed. Her shift was longer than Lachlan's—to her knees—but it was also long-sleeved and made of fine white linen. Hesitating for only a second, she slipped off her shoes, lifted her skirt, and loosed the ribbons at her calves so her stockings fell down.

She heard feet treading softly on the wool rug as Lachlan moved behind her. She peered over her shoulder and saw him place his shoes and socks by the chair in front of the fire, his eyes never leaving her, caressing every inch—from her bare toes, over her shift, to her orangey-gold curls. It excited her. Aye, she liked knowing he watched her as she undressed. Liked that only a thin piece of linen hid her body from his sight.

She wanted him to see the fullness of her breasts, how they swayed when she moved, the hardened nubs on top so red and sensitive for his tongue. Wanted him to see the tight gold curls, wet now, at the apex of her thighs, and the cleft between the globes of her backside from behind.

Her heart battered against her rib cage, and her belly clenched at the thought. After a brief hesitation, she pulled on the tie that held her shift closed, and slipped it off, slowly over one shoulder, then another, baring herself to him as it fell to her waist and to the rug on the floor.

The breath whooshed from his lungs on a loud exhale, and she glanced at him. Skin flushed, eyes bright, he looked almost feral, his lips red, his cock standing tall and broad against his shirt.

"Turn," he said, sounding strangled.

She did, slowly. Toward him first, then in a circle. Heat and pressure pulsed at her core, a heavy, full feeling between her legs, knowing that he watched her. She had the urge to spread her thighs, to open and stay open for him.

When she faced the bed, which reached the tops of her thighs, she leaned over to pull back the covers, and he groaned, which caused a spasm of need to clench low in her body, to flood her sheath. She closed her eyes and stayed there, trembling, the quilt clutched in her hand. Then she lifted her knee, finally spreading her legs how she wanted, and crawled onto the bed, moving across to the far side as he watched.

She wanted to stop in the middle and lay her head down on the quilts. Exposing herself to him, at his mercy, anticipating what he would do to her. That thought raced through her head, built in her mind's eye until she panted.

Reaching her side, she lay on her back and pulled up the quilts. He'd moved as she'd crawled across the bed, and now stood perfectly still and rigid—other than the quick rise and fall of his chest—a few feet back from where she'd crawled on.

Her eyes met his, and they stared at each other for a long moment before he loosed the tie at his neck and yanked the shirt over his head.

She closed her eyes, suddenly afraid to see him naked, knowing there was no going back. Whom was she kidding? There'd been no going back the moment she'd crawled over the bed, drawing it out, excited that he watched her.

"Amber, open your eyes."

She shook her head.

"Aye, lass. Now."

He said it with such command that a shiver of need raced through her body—the same as when he'd controlled Earc and the other men from attacking Father Odhran in front of the chapel.

She'd married a warrior lord, and she loved his strength as much as his gentleness.

Lifting her eyelids slowly, she stared at her husband's body, forgetting to breathe at the impact of seeing him naked. His muscles were heavily roped—his shoulders and arms bulging, his chest wide, hard, and scattered with a light dusting of hair. His waist and hips barely narrowed, his torso rippled long and lean to his pelvis.

She skipped past the part of him she didn't want to acknowledge, and instead focused on his massive thighs and calves, before dropping to the ground. Unsurprisingly, his feet were big too. Not ugly, but not bonnie, either.

"Amber."

She knew what he wanted, but she wasn't ready for it…yet. "Aye."

"*Look* at me."

She shook her head, still staring at his feet.

"You have to acknowledge what you're frightened of before you can e'er hope to beat it."

She pursed her lips mulishly and slowly raised her eyes up the middle of his body. Her heart rate rose again, but this time not in a good way, and she had to resist looking away.

He was long and wide and jutted up toward his belly from a nest of dark hair. His sac hung heavily below. The head mushroomed over the top, and a drop of seed pooled at the tip.

"'Tis not the first cock I've seen," she said, a wee bit defiantly. "I've treated three of them over the years. Pus and pincers abounded." She said the last just to make him wince. He laughed instead, his eyes dancing, and she couldn't help but smile back.

Taking a deep breath to calm her fear, she looked again at his cock and found herself noting how smooth and muscular it looked. Nay, not 'it.' His cock wasn't separate from Lachlan. *He* looked smooth and muscular. The perfect shape for her own soft sheath.

Aye, God had made men and women to fit together. She couldn't imagine their joining would hurt, at least not after the first time and not with Lachlan. His fingers inside her had felt amazing, but she'd still felt…unfilled.

"'Tis a nice cock, as cocks go," she said, suddenly feeling awkward just sitting there staring at it. "Maybe someday…"

His grin returned. "Aye, maybe."

As he stepped toward the candle in a sconce on the wall and blew it out, her eyes were drawn downward again. His cock bobbed when he walked. She found herself swallowing, wondering how it would feel on her palm…in her mouth.

He proceeded around the foot of the bed to her side and blew out the other candle.

The room had darkened considerably, lit only by the fire in the hearth. The light glinted warmly on his body, dancing over the ripple of his muscle and smooth skin. She stared at his curved backside, long, strong thighs, and equally long, strong back, and thought that as much as she loved his front view, the back view might be her favorite. The sight of his manly arse made her want to do something addled— like bite it.

When he turned, she found herself staring at his cock again, and this time, when her pulse accelerated, she knew it wasn't out of fear. The broad head glowed in the firelight, and she had the urge to open her mouth and let him slide in, to tup her mouth.

He walked to her side of the bed. She looked up almost reluctantly. "Did you want to sleep on this side?"

"Nay. I sleep between you and the door. Always. And 'tis not to keep you in, but to keep you safe lest anyone comes in."

And just like that, she was back to teary-eyed. For so long, she'd had no one to defend her—through horrible circumstances. Now she no longer had to sleep listening for her goats to bleat, alerting her someone was outside her cottage.

"Thank you," she said.

"'Tis no need to thank me, Amber. I wouldnae have it any other way." He put his hand on the edge of the quilt. "May I come in?"

Her breathing stopped for a moment before she nodded.

He pulled back the down-filled quilts, his eyes on her body, especially her breasts, as he climbed over her, slid beneath the quilts, and pulled the covers up to their shoulders. He faced her, his head on his pillow, and after a brief hesitation, she rolled to her side so she faced him too.

His fingers found hers against the pillow and laced them together, their hands palm to palm. Warmth spread from the point of contact, and she took a deep breath, feeling like her chest might burst.

"What do we do now?" she asked, the words whispered as if she were afraid to say them aloud. Afraid the feeling between them might shatter.

He raised her hand, kissed the back of it, then tucked it against his heart. "Now we sleep."

Nineteen

THE HEAT WAS ALL-ENCOMPASSING. FROM HER TOES, which pressed back against Lachlan's shin, his top leg thrown over hers, her backside firmly in his lap, his arm around her waist, and his chest glued to her spine, to his breath that warmed the curls on the top of her head.

He surrounded her, enveloped her.

She tried to lift her eyelids, sensing the light had changed, but after an exhausting night of little sleep, her body wouldn't cooperate. They'd touched all through the dark hours, but not in a carnal way. Nay, they'd lain together, skin to skin, soaking each other in, and in Amber's case, fantasizing about and wishing for his hands to move. She'd been overwhelmingly aware of him, too wound up to sleep, and if the stiff rod nestled along her arse was any indication, he'd been overly aware of her too.

They'd slept, or not slept, in tandem. When she shifted, he did too. When he rolled over, she did too—their bodies aligning to stay together no matter what position they chose.

She sighed sleepily when he dropped his head to

nuzzle in the crook of her neck. Then his heat, lips, hands, and soft skin retreated, and she felt him slip out of his side of the bed. She automatically turned toward him, nestled into the warm spot he'd left behind, and pressed her face into his pillow.

She inhaled…and smelled her husband.

The sound of splashing water penetrated her sleepiness, and she dragged open her eyes to a feast of maleness. Lachlan stood on a linen in front of a washbasin in all his muscular glory, cock still standing up in front of his belly, cleansing himself. Pressing her fist to her mouth so she wouldn't make a sound, she watched him, aroused to the point of needing to touch herself under the covers.

She squeezed her breasts with her hands, and pulled up her knees and pressed her fingers into her damp center. An inarticulate sound escaped her throat, half growl, half moan, and he looked over at her.

What was she doing? He was her husband, and she needed him.

He hadn't attacked her in the night, despite the pressures of his body—he'd suffered as much as she had, and never once after he'd climbed into bed with her had she felt unsafe. Tears sprang to her eyes as she felt a physical letting go in her body. And she sighed.

She could trust him.

She sat up and let the covers fall away, eyes saying everything she couldn't put into words. His gaze dropped to her breasts, to the hand still clutched between her thighs.

"Amber?"

Pushing up onto her knees, she raised her hand to

him. He dropped the cloth he'd been holding and reached the side of their bed in two long strides. He wasted no time, kneeling on the mattress in front of her and wrapping those big hands around the sides of her head.

"You're certain?" he asked.

"Aye."

She barely got the word out before he kissed her, their lips melding together, tongues stroking and sucking, invading and retreating into each other's mouths. She melted into him. Her eyes closed, arms snaking around his neck. Her need for him was palpable. A living thing that squirmed within her.

His hands slid down her spine to her backside and kneaded her flesh, pressing her closer. She rocked against him, moaning, aching to feel his mouth and hands everywhere. Wanting to be as close as she possibly could.

"Lift your legs and wrap them around my waist," he commanded.

She did, her ankles linking in the small of his back, shuddering as her wet center pressed against the hard ridge of his cock and rubbed.

He groaned and held her hips tight so she couldn't move.

"Lachlan," she whimpered, and bit his chin in protest.

"You canna move on me like that, love. Not yet. I need better control. I'll either lose my seed or I'll enter you by accident."

"But I need…"

"Aye, you *need*. I'll take care of you, Amber."

He laid her back on the bed, his hips pushing her thighs apart, heavy between her legs. Kissing her again, one hand stroked the sensitive skin of her neck while the other found her breast. She moaned into his mouth and arched her spine for more contact, feeling like the world was spinning away and Lachlan was her anchor.

He squeezed the rounded flesh and lifted his head to feast his gaze on her. "I have ne'er seen anything as beautiful as you. I could stare at your breasts all day."

She laughed, a puff of air on his cheek. "Isna that what you've been doing the last several weeks? I've felt your eyes all o'er me."

"Aye, you like me to watch."

He sounded so satisfied, so pleased with himself and her, that she groaned, knowing it was true and it wouldn't be long before they did that too.

He shifted down her body, his taut stomach sliding along her core, and she suddenly found it hard to breathe, her muscles clenching in response. The air whooshed from her lungs as her hips rocked.

Taking the tip of her breast in his mouth, he sucked hard before laving the nipple with his tongue. She sank her fingers into his hair and held him in place, her body undulating against him.

But then he moved again, and that hard, exact pressure was gone from the apex of her thighs.

She wanted it back. *Needed* it back.

She tugged on his hair, but instead of moving upward to her mouth again, he kissed down her belly, finding every dip and soft swell, licking and nibbling and breathing her in. He half rumbled, half sighed, a happy, contented sound, and she suddenly felt like her heart might burst. Throat tight, she pressed a hand to her mouth to hold back a sob.

Of happiness. He made her so happy.

He bit her hip bone, and she squeaked in a sharp breath. The anticipation of where he was headed and what he'd do next was more than she could bear, and she found herself panting.

"Lachlan," she cried out.

"Almost there, love."

He slipped his arm under her leg and positioned it over his elbow, then put his big palm on the inside of her other leg and pressed it wide. She whimpered, excited to be spread before him, at his mercy. Her hips jerked upward, seeking him.

"Aye, that's it." Then he blew on her hot, wet flesh before biting her thigh.

She mewed, that was the only word for it—like a kitten—wanting his mouth on her. Instead, he rested on his elbows and stared at her mound, mouth parted, chest heaving, like he'd run to her cottage and back. She bit her lip and tried to stop her hips moving, but she felt feverish, delirious with longing, and her body wouldn't listen.

God's blood, she needed him now!

He pushed his fingers up through her curls and down into her slick folds, finally touching her. She groaned, beyond any control now as her belly clenched, and she almost came off the bed.

Their eyes met as he continued to stroke her. Up and down. Up and down. He looked half-wild, his skin flushed, his lips swollen and dark red, his eyes hooded. He inhaled deeply, as if taking in her scent—the air thick now with the heady musk of their arousal—and his nostrils flared.

"My wife," he said, almost a growl. Then he closed his lips over her core and devoured her. His tongue, broad and heavy, swept the length of her, dragging across wet, swollen skin, the rhythmic pressure driving her toward release faster than she'd ever gone before.

When she felt like she might burst, she pressed her arm over her mouth and bit down on the soft skin to muffle her cries. Her other hand gripped the quilts, needing something to hold on to, feeling like she might break apart.

Then he stopped. The tip of his tongue at her entrance. His top lip over her sensitive nub—and he sucked. Hard.

She cried out. Frantic. Feeling like she was coming apart. Her hips bucked, but he held her still.

The pressure built. At the last second, he shifted a hand beneath her bottom and lifted her for a better angle, slid his tongue all the way inside. At the same time, he pushed his thumb on her engorged nub and circled it.

She arched her neck. A mass of sensations tore through her. They coalesced in her core as he speared her with his tongue. Using her heels, she pushed her hips higher. High as she could. Seeking deeper penetration. More pressure. She jerked against him. He matched his thrusts to the roll of her hips. Again. Again. Until her whole body clenched. At the pinnacle of arousal, she released in great, long spasms that contracted down her thighs and up her belly into her breasts. She flooded with silky, wet heat and screamed around her arm.

He kept going, slowing down, almost soothing her, then pushing harder to take her over the edge again. When she neared climax a third time, he withdrew his tongue and crawled up her body between her legs, laying on top of her, just where she wanted him, one of her legs still hooked over his elbow, so her hips stayed tilted and her thighs wide.

"Lachlan?" she asked, too wound up to resist if he chose to push inside her and break his promise—as his position suggested he might. And she realized with shock that part of her—a big part—wanted him to do it. Was desperate for him to do it.

"Trust me," he said just before he captured her mouth.

The hard ridge of his cock lay over her swollen flesh and nub, and when he rocked his hips forward, the broad head pushed upward on her belly. He groaned, his big body shuddering, and she wrapped her arms around his torso, trying to anchor him the same way he'd anchored her.

He stopped, dropped his head into the crook of her neck and panted.

"I want us to release together this last time, but I may not last. I willna push inside you, I promise, but I'll have to hold you still lest you jerk too hard and end up taking me inside, do you understand? I'll stay higher so I spend on your belly."

"You've done this before?" she asked, then squeezed her eyes shut in embarrassment. Of course he'd done it before. He'd done all of it before.

He raised his head and cupped her cheeks, the weight and pressure of him between her legs and on her body feeling just right—despite all her insistence yesterday that she had no desire to be close to him in this way.

"Amber, look at me."

She raised her eyes, feeing vulnerable and needy, but also jealous that this experience wasn't special to him.

When their gazes locked, he said, "I have ne'er in my life felt for anyone what I feel for you. I have ne'er worried that I might spend my seed before I wanted to, like a lad again, because I canna control my body. I have ne'er worked so hard to give someone else pleasure, solely because I craved your taste and the feel of you pulsing against my tongue. You do this to me. Only you."

"And you're happy finding your release this way?" she asked. "You'll find pleasure in it?"

"More pleasure than I've e'er had. Amber, just the sight of you, the sounds of your arousal, give me pleasure enough to lose my seed."

Her throat tightened and tears pricked her eyes, trickling out the corners and into her hair. He leaned down and kissed them, lapping them up with his tongue before capturing her mouth again and beginning a gentle roll and thrust over her sensitive flesh and nub. She pushed her fingers into his hair with a groan and wrapped her free leg around his thigh so the sole of her foot rested on his calf. It felt good, so good— the weight of him on top of her, his arms around her, his mouth devouring her.

His grip on her hip wasn't tight at first, but as the pressure built inside her again, she pulled him closer. Her breasts squashed against his chest, her pelvis thrusting upward, trying to capture him, and he held her in place.

His own thrusts increased, became jerky as his breathing fractured, and she felt a nudging at her entrance that became a thumping, then a slamming that she could hardly wait for, the heavy, warm blows sending vibrations up inside her. She tried to arch, to get even closer, but he was relentless in holding her still, his glides along her core longer and harder and faster. The pounding on her opening had her clenching and releasing her muscles, trying to catch whatever was there. Her sheath longed to be filled, to be stretched open. Longed to grip and milk her husband of his seed.

God's truth, she wanted to be tupped by this man. She wanted to hold him inside her and pump him of every last drop.

He broke the kiss, his face tortured, his breath heavy on her cheek. And still the thumps at her entrance continued, driving her wild.

"More," she cried. "More."

He responded with a groan and put even more muscle and weight behind his thrusts, and she realized the pounding was his swinging sac, his stones inside making her empty flesh beg to be filled.

She opened her mouth to tell him to tup her, but he invaded her mouth again, carnal grunts coming from him now. When he grabbed her hand and dragged it between their bodies and over his cock, the feel of his broad, slippery head thrusting against her palm sent her right over the edge. She screamed into his mouth, her leg wrapping around his waist, her toes curling, her hand fisting around his cock.

He followed seconds later as his body stiffened over

her. He pumped into her fist, releasing his seed into her hand before he collapsed on top of her.

They lay together, spent, the breath sawing from their lungs, her body feeling boneless. Except where she clenched his cock—fist tight, muscles strong. She hadn't released him, and she didn't want to.

She was fascinated by the feel of him—now that she'd finally touched him—how soft his skin had been over the iron rod beneath. How the bulbous head had powered through her fingers.

He pushed his weight off her, but she stopped him from going far by gripping her hand tighter and pressing down with her leg over his waist.

Their eyes met. He looked sated but guilty. "You didn't want to touch it. I'm sorry."

She answered by sliding her fist down his length then up again, her thumb pressing along the underside and over the slit at the top. "'Tis not an 'it.' 'Tis you. And I've changed my mind."

The shaft had softened, become more pliable, but he was still hard enough to be interesting. "How long?" she asked.

His eyes widened, understanding her meaning, then he shut them and groaned as she stroked him again. "If you keep doing that, not long at all."

He'd rested his body on his elbows, and in the space between them, she could see the head of his cock and her hand squeezing over it, then down again. She was fascinated with the feel of him, the look of him. A deep red color, the broad head flared at the top and glistened with clear liquid. The shaft was hard underneath, her hand unable to circle all of it, but the skin covering it was soft and moved over the shaft with her hand.

More than anything, she loved the strength in his cock. The muscles and engorged flesh excited her, and she squeezed harder, pumped faster, making him groan and rock into her hands. She remembered how it had felt to have his stones thumping against her entrance as he thrust on her belly, and she turned her hand so her fingers slid below the base of the shaft to the heavy sac. He shifted his weight and spread his knees somewhat so she'd have better access, which spread her thighs wider, the cooler air stimulating her, making her sheath clench.

"'Tis rough down here, not smooth like above."

She thought he said, "aye," but the word was strangled, making her smile.

The tips of her fingers lightly traced the rough hair covering his sac, fascinated to feel the pouch tighten, the loose skin hardening and wrinkling. She slipped her fingers underneath and gently squeezed, feeling the stones inside. She circled and massaged one stone slowly, then the other, before looking up and seeing his face red, his mouth open, his eyes glazed. Aye, he liked that. She'd liked it when he'd tugged on her hair down below, maybe he'd like that too.

She grasped the short hairs in her fist and tugged. He groaned hard, his neck arching back, the tendons tight and his jaw clenched. She tugged again, this time pulling them in a spiral. His cock twitched, and he quickly pulled her hand back up to his chest. She was amazed at the strain on his face.

"Sorry, love, but I'll spend soon. I doona want you surprised or…repulsed by it."

She weaved her fingers through his hair and brought his forehead down to hers. "I'm not repulsed or frightened anymore, Lachlan. Nay, I love your cock." She let out a happy laugh and kissed him. "Isla was right. I want to be filled by you." She pulled his hips down with her legs and rubbed her pelvis against him. "Truly, I want to ride you and tup you in every way possible." Joy cascaded through her, making her laugh again, and she squeezed as tightly as possible around his neck and hips, squirming as if trying to wriggle under his skin.

Eyes hopeful, he enveloped her too, then rolled so she lay on top of him, her legs resting on the outside of his legs, her arms still around his neck, the broad head of his shaft pulsing at her entrance. Her breath caught and she stared at him. Her heart beat faster now, and she knew he was giving her the choice.

She closed her eyes, pressed down, and felt the heat and hardness of him spreading her soft, wet flesh. It felt so good, and she groaned, rocking around the tip, pushing him farther inside.

But this time it pinched, and she stopped, the pleasure and desire still there but mixed with pain now.

"It hurts a bit," she said.

His eyes clouded over. "If you doona want—"

"Nay, I do want. 'Tis just…what do I do?" she asked, her eyes back to his.

"Pull your knees higher, by my hips, and sit up. Let your weight take me inside you, if that's what you want."

"Stop with the 'if you wants.' I'm not a woman to do something I doona want to do."

He grinned, grasped her face in his hands again, leaned up, and kissed her. "Aye, 'tis what I love about you."

Her breath stopped, and their eyes met again. "Do you?" she whispered.

He brushed the hair back from her face. "Do I love you?"

She nodded. Once.

"I've ne'er loved before, so I have naught to compare it to, but I know that you are my everything, Amber. I want to see you safe, I want to see you happy, I want to touch you every minute of the day, even if it's just to hold your hand—although this, making love to you, being inside you, is more than I could have e'er hoped for."

Her throat tightened, and her chest felt like it might burst. Then those annoying tears started again. She sniffled and wiped them away. "Well, I wouldnae want to make a liar of you so…"

Pulling up her knees, she used her hands on his chest to push herself upward and slowly slid down Lachlan's shaft until she'd taken him all the way into her body. It hurt, but she breathed through the pinching sensation until it subsided.

She blew out a breath. "Now you're inside me." The feeling of being filled by him was like naught else she'd ever experienced. She was afraid to move, yet she also felt the urge to grind down, to rub herself against him. "'Tis most…compelling."

"Compelling?"

"Aye."

He grunted and raised his knees behind her, then sat up, so she was enveloped by him again. Her breath came in short bursts.

"I'll show you compelling."

He kissed her, gently at first, hands brushing her cheeks and into her hair. Then he nuzzled along her jaw to suck on her earlobe. She groaned and rocked her hips as a flood of wet heat saturated them, and he groaned too.

He lowered his knees a bit and pushed her back along them so she lay open to him, his cock still inside, pressing against her front wall. Then he played her—sucking and licking and rubbing her body, the peaks and valleys, the wet plains and hard nubs.

When she put her hand down to feel his shaft pumping into her, he grunted with approval and moved her fingers over her center. "Show me," he said.

Her eyes widened and her belly contracted in anticipation. He wanted to watch her touch herself. She didn't hesitate in dragging her fingers up her swollen center to the hard nub up top, which he'd primed so well. She circled her fingers over it. When his hand gripped her hips and raised and lowered her over his shaft in time with her rhythm, she almost exploded right there.

"Oh, dear heavens," she said, her eyes closing, "doona stop."

"You like it right there."

She laughed then moaned, "I like it everywhere, Husband."

"Aye, Wife. You will." He clamped his arm around her hips and pushed into a kneeling position on the bed. "Hands on your breasts, I want to see you work your nipples. And hook your ankles around my back."

She was slow to respond, not wanting to drag her fingers away when she was so close.

"Now, Amber," he barked. "I canna last much longer."

She did as he demanded, secretly liking it when he commanded her, and glided her hand upward to cup and squeeze her breasts. He shifted position, so his thrusts hit that spot inside—directly on it—over and over as he pressed down firmly on her nub.

"Ahhh," she screamed, head and eyes rolling back, body boneless and at his mercy, fingers digging into her breasts. Then he closed his mouth over her nipple, hot, wet, and sucked.

She came apart—and he followed along right behind her.

Twenty

Amber walked sedately down the stairs to the great hall, which was filled with warriors eating their noonday meal, several lasses moving amongst the tables with platters of meat and jugs of ale, and other servants who worked under Finola or Niall. She held her chin high and placed her arms regally across her waist, reminding herself she was lady of this castle. Even if she had spent the last two and a half days locked in her bedchamber with her husband, being tupped every which way and doing things she'd ne'er imagined she'd do.

Who knew she could be so wanton and love every second of it?

But she didn't want anyone else to know that—other than her husband, of course—and she just dared any of her clan to say anything about it.

Lachlan sat with Gregor and his foster brothers over by the hearth, leaning over what looked like a map spread out on a low table—no doubt discussing the latest sightings of Machar Murray and their plan to catch him.

Her heart squeezed upon seeing Lachlan, as it did every time. He faced the stairs, and she knew he'd done so in order to see her come down. He lifted his head and smiled when he saw her, raising his hand in acknowledgment. She smiled and raised hers back to him, wondering for a moment if he would follow her if she turned around and went back up again.

He had come down earlier than her to give her some time alone before she faced everyone, and to make sure all the ribbing he'd receive from his brothers and Gregor happened before she appeared. And to talk about Murray, of course.

Lachlan hadn't said that, but it turns out wives could understand all the things their husbands didn't say too.

She was just like Isla now, with that special connection to a husband who loved her—he'd said so.

And she loved him too. She hadn't told him yet, but she would. The next time they were alone, she'd sit him down, tell him to stop touching her breasts, with which he was definitely obsessed, and just say it. She'd had ample opportunity before to tell him, but for being a woman who spoke her mind, she'd suddenly found herself unable to form the words.

"Well, well, look who finally got off her back," Isla said from down below, one eyebrow raised, smirking up at her like a round, wee weasel.

Amber darted a look around the great hall to make sure no one was within earshot, then said, "I was hardly e'er on my back. You need to teach Alban some new tricks if that's all he's doing to you. Lachlan is most inventive."

Isla's mouth dropped open, then she laughed. "Aye, I knew you'd love it. How long did you last? I saw Lachlan carrying you up the stairs like he meant business after you ran out of here."

She hurried the last few steps toward her friend, all thoughts of living up to her title evaporating. They hugged, and Amber found herself getting teary-eyed again. God's blood, she was turning into a wee lass, crying at everything.

"Not long. We slept through the first night and then in the morning…" She gave Isla a look.

Isla gave her a look back and tugged her in the opposite direction from the hearth, where they sat on a bench in a secluded corner. Amber had to help her friend down, and she wondered if she would ever change her mind about having bairns and end up as round as Isla.

"Not much longer now," she said, slipping into healer mode and palpating her friend's belly. "Are you all ready?"

"Aye, I've been ready for weeks. I canna wait to be done."

"Send a message when your pains start, no matter what time of day. It doesn't matter if Machar Murray is sitting at the gates, I will come. I may be lady here, but I'm your friend and healer first, aye?"

"Aye, no one doubts you're still our healer, Amber, and you've always been our lady, whether you were married to the laird or not."

Amber pulled her into a tight hug, those annoying tears filling behind her eyelids again. When they parted, Isla said, "Now…tell me everything."

She blushed, and again found herself tongue-tied. "I canna tell you *everything*."

"Aye, you can. Have you told him you love him yet? You do love him, right?"

She felt herself melting, softening, and she looked across the great hall to where Lachlan sat in front of the hearth with his foster father and brothers.

Isla took her hands and melted too. "Aye, you love him, I can see it in your eyes. What did he say? Has he told you too?"

"He told me I was his everything."

Isla also got teary, as pregnant women were wont to do, and she wiped them away. "What did you say?"

Amber pursed her lips, and Isla's eyes widened in dismay. "Och, you didn't say you loved him back?"

She shifted uncomfortably. "Not yet, but I will."

"Aye, you will." She pinched Amber on her backside and pushed her up. "Right now. Imagine how you would feel if you told Lachlan he was your everything, and he said naught in return."

"I didn't say naught in return. I... I...well, I took him inside my body for the first time, and he knew exactly what I was telling him. You're the one who told me that husbands should be able to know things without their wives saying it."

Isla rolled her eyes and pinched her backside again to get her moving. "He needs the words. Same as you. Go tell him. And I want every detail, so come back as soon as you can."

Amber stepped toward the hearth and looked up to see Lachlan watched her. She wasn't close enough to see his expression clearly, but she knew by his posture he'd seen her coming and was pleased by it. She smiled and hurried toward him, excited to sit beside him and whisper in his ear that she loved him. And maybe something else too. Something carnal—while his step-father sat on his other side.

Aye, she could have great fun with that. How long would it take him to scoop her up in his arms and carry her back to their bedchamber?

When she was about halfway to the hearth, the outside door slammed. She glanced over, still smiling, and saw Ian. His face was wan, dark smudges circled his eyes, and he looked like he might burst into tears at any moment.

He took a step toward her, swaying, then took another and broke into a run. Amber's smile dropped, and she grabbed his arms to steady him when he reached her. Several of her clan had noticed and looked toward them, concerned.

"Ian. What's wrong?"

Oh God, please let Breanna be all right.

He leaned heavily on her shoulder, shaking, and whispered into her ear, "I was supposed to tell you yesterday, but you didn't come down. And I wasn't allowed to tell anyone but you."

"Tell what? What's happened?" Fear twisted her stomach. Her heart raced.

"Machar Murray—he took Adaira. He said he will only trade her for you."

࿔

Lachlan swallowed his irritation. Amber stood in the middle of the great hall, hugging Ian.

First Isla, now Ian. Who would waylay her next? Niall?

Lachlan wanted his wife beside him now. In fact, if he could just tie her to him, he would be happy. Which, of course, made him think on last night when he'd tied her to the bed and had his way with her. Slowly.

She'd promised—nay, threatened—to bind him next. Maybe if they went back upstairs, she would do that right now?

"Shall we take bets on how long he'll stay down here?" Callum asked Gregor and the other brothers.

"Not long, by the look of him," Kerr said.

Lachlan shot them a dark look and shifted his sporran over his body. He returned to watching Amber, seeing that she'd turned her back on him and held Ian's shoulders in a tight grip, as if she talked to him seriously.

He sat forward, a feeling of disquiet seeping through him.

Still, he threw an aside to Callum. "Quit thinking about what I do with my wife in our marriage bed and get your own. Wife, that is. Maggie's waited long enough."

The brothers all laughed or "ooohed" at Lachlan's comment.

Callum sat back and scrubbed his hands through his short hair. "Aye, she has. Maybe I'll ride back with Gavin and stop at Maggie's clan on the way home. Both Caitlin and Amber said I was an idiot for waiting."

Lachlan knew that what Callum had said was important, and he wanted to pay attention, to lend his support like his other brothers were doing, but something wasn't right. He could see it in the angle of Amber's head, the rigidity of her back.

"Where's Adaira?" he asked suddenly.

The lairds fell silent, hearing Lachlan's tone and going on alert.

"I haven't seen her since the morning after the wedding," Gregor said.

"I saw her in the stables with Ian later that same day, but not since then," Darach added.

"You think something's happened to her?" Gavin asked, his expression turning grave. Aye, a missing child would indeed concern Gavin.

"I doona know, but something's wrong," he said as he shot from his chair and strode toward Amber. His brothers and Gregor followed.

"Amber," he called.

She turned to him, her face stricken. "Murray has Adaira," she blurted out.

He broke into a run, his heart pounding. "When? How?"

"Ian was in the woods this morning, and Murray accosted him. He gave Ian a message for you. He has Adaira at the falls. He wants you and the rest of the lairds to come get her. He said he'll only trade her for you."

"It's a trap," Callum said.

"Aye. We'll have to spring it like we did all the rest." Lachlan looked at Ian and noticed Amber still had a firm grip on his arm. "Did you see Adaira? Did Murray have any proof he has her or that she was still alive?"

Ian raised his gaze, his eyes filled with guilt. "She was with me. We were tracking an injured doe when

Murray grabbed her. I tried to stop him taking her, but I couldnae."

A scratch and bruise marred his face, about a day old, and Lachlan noted he held his hand close to his body. Something didn't add up. "You're hurt, lad. Did you fight him this morning?"

Amber's hand clenched Ian's arm again just before she answered. "Nay, those are from yesterday. He tripped in the stables. Just avoided landing on the new foal."

He switched his attention to his wife, and she gazed back at him. Her lip trembled, and she burrowed into his arms. "Please, Lachlan. Find her. She thinks she knows enough about fighting to defeat him, but she doesn't. I'm afraid she'll anger him more than he already is, and he'll kill her before I…before you get there. Go to the falls, but be careful. He may have a way out."

Lachlan wrapped his arms around her. He could feel her trembling, and he pulled her tighter. All his instincts to soothe her and keep her safe roared to the forefront, blocking out everything else. "We'll find her, Amber, and we'll catch Murray. He must be at his wits' end to even consider this. 'Tis not a well-thought-out plan. We've already searched the caves thoroughly, and they doona lead anywhere."

Amber nodded, squeezed even closer, as if she thought she'd ne'er see him again. Then she stood on her tiptoes, wrapped her arms around his neck and whispered in his ear, "I love you, Lachlan MacKay. You are my everything too. Always remember that."

❧

Amber stood on the castle wall with Ian, watching the lairds and half their men ride out toward the woods. The other half Lachlan had left guarding her and the castle. He still thought abducting Adaira was only the first step in Murray's plan, and he'd assigned her bodyguards, including Earc, Malcolm, and Hamish, whom he trusted with his life.

And he was right. It *was* only the first step in Murray's plan. The rest of it was Amber's plan. Get Lachlan and the lairds away from the castle, evade her guards, find the last remaining escape route Murray had told Ian about, and sneak back to her cottage undetected—as Murray had instructed.

Amber knew Murray's promise to trade Adaira for her was a lie, so she'd have to free Adaira herself. And that meant Murray would probably kill her—but she wouldn't go down without a fight. She had knives stashed in her cottage under both mattresses and in the kitchen. She had an iron poker against the hearth, and she had a vat of pickling juice that would sting if splashed in his eyes.

She also knew poisons, as did he. She would go through her bag here, and once she was in her cottage, she'd try to access her supply of herbs there too. She'd do her best to slow him down that way. Just long enough for her to pierce his heart.

And this time she would do it. He'd put the people she loved at risk for the last time.

"You canna go, Amber," Ian said, his voice low and shaking.

"Aye, Ian. I can and I will. Otherwise, he'll kill Adaira and still come after us. He'll go through everyone

I care about, including Breanna, everyone Lachlan cares about, until there's no one left. 'Tis not in my nature to sit back and let someone else fight my battles."

"You said he'll kill Adaira. Well, he'll kill you too."

"Maybe, but he'll die in the process."

Ian groaned and shoved his hands in his hair. Amber heard him sob and wrapped her arms around him, pulling the lad in close. "I want you to stay back from the cottage until you see Adaira come out. Then get her to the castle. Only after you're both safe do you tell everyone the truth. Otherwise, Murray will capture you and use you against me just as he's using Adaira. And doona tell anyone before then or they'll storm the cottage, and Murray will kill Adaira and me." She squeezed Ian tighter, pressing her face to his dark, shaggy hair. "'Tis the best plan we have, Ian. Please, tell me you'll help."

He nodded, straightened, and wiped his face. She saw him age before her eyes, going from a lad of fourteen to a man. It broke her heart that she had to force such a decision on him. Nay, Murray had done that. He'd done all of it.

And now it was time for Amber to kill him.

"Go get something to eat, lad, and take something to give Adaira later too. We doona know if Murray has fed her. Then go to Murray's old bedroom and wait for me."

He left, and a few minutes later she went to her bedroom. The covers on the bed had been straightened, the jug of mead refilled, and her evening meal placed on a tray as she'd requested.

She had about two hours before dusk and considered

saying goodbye to Niall, but knew she'd break down, and he'd suspect something, the old badger. Instead, she wrote a letter to him, to Isla, and then one to Lachlan. The ink ran in several places as she wasn't always fast enough to wipe away her wayward tears before they hit the page.

When she was done, she put them on the table with the mead and wrote their names on the front before laying the contents of her bag on her bed, knowing she had limited resources and little time left.

She started with her knives, hiding them in her socks, her dress, and even in the braid she plaited at the back of her hair. Then she went through her medicines, deciding how she could use each vial. By the end of it, she decided it was useless—unless she could hold Murray down and pour the entire contents into his mouth and down his gullet. And she was afraid to dip the knives in the poison lest they nick her skin.

When the gloaming came, she squared her shoulders and left her room. Earc and Hamish waited outside. Malcolm was at the top of the stairs leading to the great hall.

"I'm going upstairs," she said. "I want to go through Murray's belongings in his room. Maybe Niall missed something when he looked through. He's getting a wee bit senile."

Earc and Hamish looked at each other, and she could read in their eyes they thought it was a useless task, but that it would keep her occupied until Lachlan came back with Adaira.

"Aye, lass," Hamish said. "We'll take you up."

She tried not to show any impatience as she

mounted the stairs with them to the fourth floor. It hadn't occurred to her they would check the room, but with all the secret tunnels they'd unearthed, they would do so, for sure. She panicked a moment before saying, "Ian's inside. I asked him to help. Doona spook him. He's verra upset about Adaira."

"Aye, lass," Earc said this time, his voice thick with worry. "We all are."

Amber squeezed his arm. "We'll get her back, Earc. I promise."

Hamish knocked, and the door opened a second later from the inside. Amber peeked around her guard and saw Ian looking scared. "Come here, love," she said. "Let Hamish have a look, so they know Murray's not hiding under the bed."

He scurried to her side, and she squeezed his arm to calm him. Hamish reappeared a moment later. "All clear. We'll let you know when we've heard anything from the lairds."

"Thank you, both of you. I appreciate all you've done."

She entered the room with Ian and closed the door. The quilts were mussed up, like he'd been lying on them. She hoped he'd gotten some sleep. By the look of him earlier, he hadn't slept at all the night before, worried sick about Adaira and not being able to reach Amber.

"Did he say what we should look for?" she asked softly.

"Aye. Under the mattress."

"But they would have looked there for any tunnels."

"Nay, not a tunnel. A rope."

Her jaw dropped open. "But...but... Are we to go out the window?"

"I expect so." He flipped the mattress onto the floor, and she saw a strong, thick rope tied to the bed's heavy, wooden frame.

Her stomach turned, and she felt like she might throw up. They were four stories up. She'd fallen and hurt herself just going over the edge of the castle wall on a rope. She would kill herself if she fell this time.

It made sense now that Murray had chosen this room as his sanctuary. Not only was the bar for the door extra thick and the bolts and brackets extra strong, but this side of the keep was flush to the curtain wall, so Murray would be able to climb all the way down to the outside of the castle.

She sat on the hearth and dropped her head in her hands. "I canna do it. I doona have the strength."

"It's not that hard, Amber, once you know how." He sat on the edge of the bed frame, unspooled the heavy rope, then placed it beside his leg. "Look, you loop the rope under one foot and over the other foot to stand on it. The tighter your feet are together, the slower you'll go down. To go faster, push your legs apart." He widened his legs to show her, the rope still looped around his feet.

"Who told you that? That's crazy."

He smiled, the first one she'd seen from him today. "Your laird and husband. And he showed me how too. He's incredible at it. Verily, as fast as a rabbit, and he can climb up the rope too." He stood and motioned her forward. "Here, sit down." She did, and he looped the rope under her left foot, then over her right foot.

"Feet in to stand on it. Feet out to slide down." He hefted the rope over to the window. "Look, I'll go first, then I'll try to catch you if you fall."

"Nay, you'll stay back," she said, alarmed. "I doona want to crush you."

He scrunched up his face, thinking, and she looked at the door. Whom could she get to help them? Earc, maybe. He loved Adaira and would want to see her safe. But how could she let him in and get him to listen without alerting Hamish?

Closing her eyes, she shook her head. She couldn't. Instead, she moved to the door and very quietly, so as not to alert her guards, slid the bar across. Now they were locked in.

"I'll go first," she said, moving to the window and staring out into the black night. The moon was a tiny sliver, and she couldn't see the ground. "You can hold on to me at the top until I get my feet right."

Ian had fed the rope through, and she realized she needed to go out feetfirst on her belly. "Help me up."

He did, awkwardly, and by the time her legs were dangling out the other side, her skirts had pushed to her ears, and her bare arse was waving to the wind. She would have laughed at the absurdity of it, but she might possibly be seconds away from her death. And if she did make it down, then she would probably die by Murray's hand within the hour.

She looked at Ian, for the first time not begrudging the tears that flooded her eyes and ran down her cheeks. "If I doona make it, tell Lachlan how much I love him, and how happy he's made me these last few weeks."

"You willna die, Amber. I've got you. Just loop your feet how I showed you—under the left, over the right—and find your footing."

She did, and discovered she had some stability when she tested it. Ian let her out the window a wee bit more, and she had to hold back a frightened wail.

"I have an idea," he said, and let go with one hand as she gripped the rope. A moment later, he pushed her skirts out the window, so her arse was covered, his cheeks heating in embarrassment, then slipped his long length of plaid behind her back, under her arms, and tied it. "All right, I'll have you from up here for at least halfway. Now just widen your feet a wee bit and lower yourself down. 'Tis not that long a fall after that."

"Long enough to break my neck." But she felt better knowing Ian held her from the top, and she carefully lowered herself over the edge…and kept going. The hardest part was holding on to the rope with her hands. Halfway down, Ian's plaid fell away, and she knew she was on her own. Well, if her husband could do it, so could she. She widened her legs a wee bit farther, then yelped as she flew down.

In a terrifying moment, she lost her grip and fell backward into the black abyss. Only to land a half second later on her backside on the ground. Ian landed moments after her.

"'Twas not so bad, was it?" he asked.

"Nay, not at all," she said weakly. "Let's go get Adaira."

Twenty-one

THE ROAR OF THE FALLS DEAFENED LACHLAN. HE stood apart from his brothers and Gregor, staring into the darkness. His stomach roiled, and a feeling of foreboding plagued him. They'd arrived at the falls just as dusk fell and hadn't seen any sign of Adaira or Murray. They'd called out to let him know they were here, of course, but received no response—not even a poisoned arrow or a falling tree from one of his traps.

He squinted in the darkness, trying to see more of the lay of the land, bringing it up in his mind's eye. Why would Murray choose this place? It was familiar land to them, and if Murray was behind the falls with Adaira, he had to know Lachlan and his men would storm the caves—which didn't lead anywhere. He'd had several men, who were trained in caving, search every inch. There was no safe way out.

So why? Murray was smarter than that. Way smarter. And he'd have to know Lachlan wouldn't leave Amber and the castle unprotected. He wouldn't be able to sneak in and abduct her when Lachlan was gone. But maybe he thought someone might be able to get her out?

Did he have a traitor in his clan?

He thought back to Ian and his odd behavior in the great hall earlier. Those wounds on his face and arm were definitely defensive, and at least a day old. If Adaira had been taken this morning, and Ian had fought to protect her, the wounds would still be fresh.

And now that he thought about it, Amber had been acting strangely too.

God's blood, nothing sat right with him. No matter what may happen here, he had to return to his wife.

He strode back to the other lairds, feeling like he was running out of time. "Something's wrong," he shouted, trying to be heard over the rushing water. "I'm going back."

Callum followed him through the dark toward the horses. "I'll go with you. I feel the same."

"He wants Amber. Not Adaira," Lachlan said, barely able to get the words out past his clenched jaw.

"Agreed."

"So abducting Adaira was just a way to get to Amber. But how? He knows I wouldnae leave her unprotected. I left my best men with her. I trust them with my life."

"Aye. So assuming all the tunnels into the castle have been plugged, and he canna get in, he needs to get her out. An escape route."

Lachlan broke into a jog despite the uneven terrain and dark skies, his heart racing and his breathing shallow. Aye, that would work. "Amber's not stupid. She would ne'er follow anyone she…" He stopped as that nagging feeling in his chest unknotted and the pieces fell into place. Ian hadn't delivered the message,

Amber had. "...she would go herself." Lachlan cursed and raced toward his horse.

Callum ran after him. "You think she sent us away so she could escape and go to Murray?"

"She ne'er put up a fight to come with us. Not one word. When have you e'er known Amber not to fight? She wanted us gone from the castle so she could get out. Ian's message was for her, not us. She's going to trade herself to Murray for Adaira."

Callum whistled and signaled the other lairds as he ran. They were already in pursuit. "He must have sent Ian to tell Amber to come to him or he'd kill Adaira."

"Aye." Lachlan stumbled and caught himself against a tree. For a moment, fear for her safety overwhelmed him. "Oh, sweet Jesus, he's going to kill her, Callum. Where would he take her?"

"Somewhere significant and within walking distance of the castle."

"Her cottage."

Callum nodded, and Lachlan sprinted for his horse, calculating how long ago Amber would have escaped the guards, how long it would take her to get to the cottage, and how long it would take Lachlan to ride to her rescue.

Too long.

He mounted Saint and urged him into a dangerous gallop. Lachlan might die if the stallion stepped wrong and threw him, but if he didn't get there in time, Amber would die for sure.

And his heart would die with her.

❧

Amber stood in front of her cottage, which Lachlan's men had repaired weeks ago, trembling with fear. She expected to die, maybe painfully, and sorrow for herself, for Lachlan, squeezed her throat shut. They'd had such little time together, and she knew her passing would hurt him terribly.

But she was Adaira's only hope, and just maybe God would be on her side and help her take the devil down. She wasn't defenseless. She had her knives, she knew how to fight, and this time she was determined to kill.

And she had surprise on her side too. He wouldn't expect her skilled attack.

The cottage was quiet. The windows shuttered with no light peeking through the cracks and no sparks or smoke coming from the chimney. Still, she knew he was inside, and she prayed he had Adaira with him.

She'd left Ian in the shelter of the trees with instructions to run with Adaira and alert the warriors as soon as the girl came out. If Ian and Adaira ran into a patrol, maybe they would get to her in time. But Murray wasn't an idiot. He would have planned for every outcome and would either take Amber with him or kill her in the cottage and run.

And if he did kill her, she wanted the MacKay warriors to find her instead of Lachlan.

Lifting her hand before she lost her nerve, she knocked on the wood, hard and abrupt. Something sharp and pointed touched the back of her neck, and she froze.

"Open the door and step inside," Murray said from behind her.

She did as he asked, her heart beating like it was making a break from her chest. She stumbled as she went over the sill, quickly righted herself, and scanned the room. Adaira lay before the hearth, bound and tightly gagged.

"Adaira!"

Amber ran to her as Murray checked outside one last time, closed the door, slid the bar across, and locked them in.

Amber quickly pulled a knife from her sock and cut the bonds around Adaira's feet before Murray could stop her. She needed the lass to be able to run.

"I'm going to get you out of here," she whispered. "Remember what I told you. Run when I say. I'll be right behind you."

The knife was smacked out of Amber's hand before she could finish cutting Adaira's wrists free. The blade flew into the ashes in the hearth below the low-burning fire and disappeared.

Adaira screamed and lunged at him, but Murray kicked her into the corner.

Amber threw herself between them. "Stop! I'm here. You said you would let her go if I came to you. Trade me for her." She knew he wouldn't honor his word, but she wanted to stall for as long as she could, try to figure out a plan. And she wanted him to think she was in a weakened position. One he controlled.

"Foolish woman," he said, his bow lowered, his other hand fisted, ready to strike. "Now I have two people he cares about. I'll hurt you both, then kill him from a distance." He lifted his eyes, looking for the knife she'd used. "Where is it?"

She hesitated. He would search her if she denied knowing where the knife was—God's truth, he would search her anyway—and find her other knife in her sock. Maybe he would think that was her only weapon and stop looking. Then she'd have two hidden knives, one in the ashes, and one in her hair.

"I doona know," she said.

He punched her in the jaw and she fell facedown onto the hard-packed dirt floor. She almost blacked out, seeing stars. He landed on top of her and pinned her in place, her hands behind her head, her face pressed into the dirt so she could barely breathe.

"Let's look, shall we?" He ripped up her skirts and shift, exposing her to her waist, and spread her legs. Then he tore off her shoes and socks—and found the knife. "Here it is. Just a wee one, but sharp. It could do a lot of damage. You lied to me, Amber. What should I do to a lass who lies?"

He lifted the knife to her left buttock and sliced down, cutting though the fleshy skin. She screamed, the pain more than she would have imagined for such a soft spot on her body, and squirmed to get away, but he'd trapped her. Then he sliced her other buttock too. Not as deep this time, as she managed to move at the last minute.

Adaira was pressed back in the corner, screaming around her gag. She'd dug her hands into the dirt floor, scraped it up with her nails.

"You doona want me to cut your arse with your knife?" he asked her. "I can tup you with it instead. But a bigger knife, aye? Like the one your husband has." He pushed her knife in his boot and pulled out a large, wicked-looking dagger with a honed edge.

Amber sobbed when he turned her head and waved it in front of her face. "Please, Laird Murray," she begged. "Have mercy. I'll do anything you ask, I promise." But she could see it in his eyes—he wanted to hurt her in this way—and she knew she was about to die. She would ne'er recover from these injuries. And even if she did, her life as Lachlan's wife would be over, his eager lover replaced by a woman irreparably damaged.

And Murray wouldn't stop there. If she didn't bleed to death immediately, he would torture her in some other way.

He leaned down and placed his lips by her ear, the hand on her head gentling, his words soft and lover-like as he trailed the blade slowly up the back of her thigh. "I'm not such a monster, Amber. I do want to please you. Is this how you like it, dearling? Soft and sweet?"

She almost cried in relief at his tender hands and stupidity. "Nay, I like it rough. Like this." Twisting her head and lunging up, she bit his cheek as hard as she could, tearing through skin and underlying tissue and chomping down. He yelled and pulled back, but she managed to get one hand free and jab a finger in his eye. He stumbled back, roaring with rage, a bloody, gaping hole in his cheek, his hand over his eye.

She scrambled back toward the hearth, spitting out the offending tissue in her mouth before she choked on it. "Run, Adaira!" She reached for the iron poker with one hand and the knife buried in the ash with her other. Murray charged her. She swung the poker. He caught it and yanked her toward him. She struck with her other hand, the small knife stabbing into his shoulder.

"God's blood, I'm going to kill you, ye wee cunt."

From the corner of her eye, she saw Adaira run past. Murray grabbed her by the hair at the last minute and pulled her back, but Adaira still had the dirt in her hands from the floor and threw it in his face. He let go as it hit his eyes, and she kept going. Amber tried to get by him too, but he dived for her, grabbed her ankle and pulled her down.

She looked up and saw Adaira pulling the door open. "Run, Adaira. Doona stop!"

                         ∝

Lachlan heard his wife yelling, heard the terror and determination in her voice a second before he saw Adaira race out of the cottage. Exultation burst through him, knowing Amber was still alive and fighting to stay that way, but at the same time he was terrified—he was so close, yet it took only seconds to kill someone.

He heard Callum's horse veer off toward Adaira and urged his own ride faster toward the cottage. At the last minute, he jumped off, sword in hand, blood pumping through his body. The door was open, and as he charged over the sill, he saw Amber lying face-down on the floor with Murray on top of her, pulling her head back with one hand and raising a dagger in his other. Lachlan's eyes met Amber's for an instant before he hurled his sword at Murray. It clipped his knife on the downward sweep toward Amber's neck and knocked Murray back. Lachlan grabbed Amber, dragged her out from under Murray in one giant heave, and shoved her behind him. Then he landed on Murray, who was covered in blood. His face was torn apart, one eye swollen shut, a knife sticking out of his shoulder and another one in his side. Lachlan pinned him to the ground.

"I've got her," he heard Callum yell.

"Let me go!" she screamed.

"Nay, Amber. Let Lachlan do his job."

He heard her sob. Then Callum said softly, "Watch him, Amber. See him avenge Adaira and his brother. See him avenge you. See him keep his people safe."

Lachlan stared at Murray, felt the monster's strength fade, his mind fogged with shock, pain, and loss of blood. A man who could have done so much good in the Highlands, could have helped so many people with his drive, intelligence, and skill. Instead, he'd been bent on destruction.

He leaned closer to Murray, saw a beaten man. "My family did this to you. My wife, my cousin—a woman, a young lass. They took your sight, ravaged your face. My wife's knives are in your body. She caught you, and now I'll kill you."

Murray tried to speak, but too much blood poured from the wound in his face and down his throat. Possibly into his lungs, drowning him. 'Twas best that way. Naught more needed to be said.

Lachlan leaned both knees on Murray's arms and picked up his sword, laid it across Murray's throat till the blade cut in.

"Machar Murray, I sentence you to death for the murder of my brother, Donald MacKay, his wife, Rose MacKay, Father Odhran Scott, Laird Sòlas MacPherson of Clan MacPherson, and his second-in-command and father of my wife, Ivar MacPherson.

I sentence you to death for the attempted murder and abduction of my wife, Amber MacKay, the attempted murder of myself, Lachlan MacKay, and the abduction of my cousin, Adaira MacKay. And for crimes unspoken." He shifted his plaid over the blade of his sword in order to protect his hands, and said, "Today is a good day to see peace and justice reign in the Highlands."

A chorus of "ayes" resounded behind him, his brothers and Gregor agreeing to the judgment. Lachlan pushed down on the edge of his sword, through skin, muscle, and cartilage, the warm blood pouring over his hands. Murray's eyes widened and his legs kicked before Lachlan hit bone.

He felt no joy at Murray's death, just relief that the threat to Amber had passed. No sense of achievement and fulfillment after a five-year hunt, just a heart full of gratitude that his wife was safe.

Rising and turning, he saw his brothers and Gregor. They stood side by side in an arc behind Amber, who was supported by Callum, looking bloodied, scratched, and bruised.

And alive.

He strode toward her. Callum released her, and she hobbled toward him. He rushed to scoop her up. Her arms squeezed his neck, her sobs shook her body as he pulled her close. In the background, his brothers and Gregor filed out of the cottage.

"You're hurt," he said.

"'Tis naught. We're alive. That's all that matters."

"And Murray is dead."

"Aye, justice prevailed."

"Nay, Amber. Love prevailed. Your love for everyone through it all."

She cupped her hands on his cheeks. "Most importantly, my love for you, Lachlan MacKay. I know I said it before, but I want you to hear it again. You are everything to me. You have given me a bright future filled with so much love, when I thought I had no future at all."

"As you have done for me. I love you forever, sweetling. But can we agree you'll ne'er get hurt again? Ne'er have evil men plot against you or shoot arrows at you? Ne'er escape castles through dangerous tunnels in order to survive?"

"Ne'er dress like a boy and cut my hair again?"

"Nay, I love your hair. Please cut it as often as you wish."

"And if I wish to grow it long?"

"Then I'll wrap my hand around it and tilt your head to the side so I can do this." He lowered his head and nuzzled the side of her neck, kissing toward her nape.

She sighed. "'Tis a good thing I only have flesh wounds."

He quickly lifted his head. "Where?"

"Well…on my face obviously. He punched me."

She was obfuscating, and he frowned. "Where else?" He squeezed his hand over the back of her skirt, and she tried not to wince. "Your arisaid is wet."

"He sliced my arse with one of my knives. 'Tis not as bad as you think. And I may have a scratch on my thigh as well. He was searching me for weapons, Lachlan. Naught else."

He wanted to kill Murray all over again. Instead, he squeezed her close and shuddered. "Thank God your father had the sense to teach you how to fight."

"Aye 'tis something we shall teach our own lasses." When he lifted his head, slowly this time, she blushed. "If I decide—we decide—we want bairns, that is. And if we have lads, we'll teach them to treat women as they would themselves."

He half laughed, half groaned. "Trust me, you doona want our lads treating our lasses the way my brothers and I treated one another."

"Our lads?"

'Twas his turn to blush, but he did it with a grin as he spun them in a circle. "Aye. If *we* decide. And right now I'm just happy to have you to myself."

"Me too."

He kissed her again, capturing her lips this time, gentle but still demanding. She opened beneath him and sighed happily into his mouth. Then he kissed each eye and the tip of her nose before pulling back. "Let's go back to the castle and have Mary take a look at you. It'll give us a reason to have three more days in bed. Four if your injuries need it."

"Aye, definitely four. Maybe a week. But I warn you now, you'll have to be inventive—you canna put me on my back, and you canna bang against me from behind."

"Och, I'm not such an amateur, Wife. And I doona 'bang' against you. 'Inventive' willna be a problem—as long as it doesn't involve you figuring out ways to escape a castle."

"Well, that's another thing we'll teach our daughters, although they'll have to wear pants.

'Twas most unnerving knowing my bare arse hung out the window."

He stopped, the blood pounding again in his veins and his temperature rising. "You went through the window? On a ladder?" He couldn't imagine any ladder being tall enough to reach their bedroom window. And how would she have escaped the bailey undetected after that?

"Nay, not a ladder, are you addled? Ian and I went down a rope from Murray's old bedroom. Once my skirts fell back into place, and I was safe on the ground, 'twas most exhilarating."

He stared at her, jaw clenched as he imagined her falling.

She reached up, kissed the twitch in his jaw, and whispered in his ear, "We're alive, Lachlan, Murray is dead, and we have days ahead, loving one another. Life couldnae be better, Husband."

He sighed, releasing his fear, and hugged her back. "Aye, Wife. Life couldnae be better."

Here's a sneak peek at

HIGHLAND BETRAYAL

BOOK #3 IN THE SONS OF GREGOR MACLEOD SERIES
by Alyson McLayne

MacDonnell Castle, The Highlands, Scotland, 1452

MAGGIE MACDONNELL CROUCHED IN THE DARK, cramped tunnel—her candle by her side—and slowly, silently, slid aside the stone above her head until a sliver of light seeped under the edge.

She peered into the laird's solar, through the legs of a chair she'd carefully positioned over the tunnel entrance weeks ago, and tried to figure out who was in the chamber. Someone sat in the chair—a pair of men's feet, shod in dirty shoes, rested on the floor in front of her—and from across the room she heard the sound of a quill scratching on parchment at the desk.

That would be Irvin, of course—no one else would be so bold as to sit at her brother's desk.

Wedging a stick between the ledge and the stone so it would stay open wide enough for her to eavesdrop, she picked up her own quill and parchment—ready to write down whatever was said. Although why she had to resort to spying when she was the laird's sister and her cousin was the scheming blackheart attempting to steal her clan and castle, was beyond her.

The sound of sand being scattered on parchment reached her ears, followed by an expelled breath as Irvin blew the excess ink and sand away.

"He's at Clan MacPherson."

Aye, that was her cousin's nasal tone, and she scowled. After dipping her pen in ink, she wrote "Clan MacPherson" on the parchment.

"Lachlan MacKay killed the laird there and then married a MacPherson lass. I hear the rest of the lairds, including Gregor MacLeod, came for the wedding but are leaving soon. I doona know how long MacLean will stay, but if he heads home when the others do, you should be able to intercept him along the way."

Maggie stopped writing and barely held back a gasp. Was Irvin talking about Callum MacLean? Were they somehow working together?

Betrayal and hurt raged through her at the thought, and she clenched her hands into fists, smearing the ink

"Aye, Laird," the man sitting in the chair responded, and she knew it was Irvin's man, Blàr. "And if I miss him?"

"Then carry on to Clan MacLean. Deliver the letter and speak to our friend inside about the other matter we discussed."

Maggie had learned a lot about Irvin's plans since she'd started spying on him, but she had a hard time piecing the information together. It wasn't in her nature to plot or deceive—she tended to be as direct and sharp as her daggers—and she couldn't always figure out which scheme he was talking about and how the different threads weaved together.

Unfortunately, she had few people she could turn to for help—his treachery ran deep in the clan—and no one remained who could bring Irvin to justice. She'd tried speaking to Ross about him, but nothing she said got through the haze of grief and drink that had muddled his brain and slowed his wits, and John had been out of touch ever since he'd left the clan four years ago—the day after Ross's wedding to Eleanor.

Maggie often wondered if John even knew Eleanor and her bairn were dead.

She pressed her hand to her mouth and closed her eyes as unexpected emotion welled within. The once proud and happy MacDonnell family had been reduced to her—a disagreeable, dagger-throwing spinster crouched in a dark, dank tunnel trying to thwart her cousin's next move.

"And Ross. What do ye want me to do about him, Laird?"

Maggie's eyes slowly opened as she listened. Normally she would have been irate at Blàr calling Irvin *laird*, but this time she ignored it.

What did they intend for her brother Ross—their real laird?

"Naught. He's doing it to himself," Irvin said. "He's near dead already with the drink. I give him less than a year. 'Tis the other two we have to plan for."

"So you'll kill Maggie, then?" Blàr asked from right above her.

"Nay, I willna kill her. She has value. I'll take her bairn instead."

Her brow creased in confusion. *Her bairn? Was he addled?* Then a growing horror bloomed as she realized his meaning.

Blàr's feet danced in front of her. "She's with child? The wee besom."

Irvin sighed. "You havenae any imagination, Blàr. *I'll* get Maggie with child—or someone else will. She'll marry me and stay with me to protect the first bairn and the rest after that till I'm done with her. The clan will be happy to have Donnan's beloved daughter as their lady, and 'twill seal my lairdship with rightful heirs."

Blàr's ankles sagged dejectedly. "Well, what about the other brother, John? Can we kill him?"

"Aye. But first we have to find him."

Maggie dropped her hand and fingered her daggers hanging from her belt. Four of them, all perfectly balanced and as sharp as the day they were forged. She considered striking out right then, slicing first through the tendons above Blàr's heels, and then coming through the passageway. But then what? Kill her cousin in cold blood? The man was a weasel. He'd never fight back.

She'd have to put a dagger in his back as he ran.

She released a silent sigh. Nay, she couldn't do it, even though she might soon find herself locked up and tied to a bed for her cousin's—or someone else's—use.

'Twas a grim imagining, and she shuddered.

A chair scraped back at the desk.

Blàr quickly stood and stepped forward. "Shall I take the letter with me, then?"

"Nay. Pick it up at first light. Less chance of it falling into the wrong hands. Maggie's been curious of late—asking about my goings-on—and she's been trying to interfere with Ross's drinking. We canna have that."

"Nay, Laird. But I doona think anyone could pull Ross from his cups. He loved your sister verra much."

Irvin laughed. "Aye, he did. John too, the wee ablach. And my sweet, dull-witted sister loved them back. 'Tis a shame she had to choose just one."

Irvin made grunting sounds followed by high squeals, simulating sex, and they laughed in a lewd manner. Maggie could imagine him gyrating his hips, and she swallowed back the bile that rose in her throat. That he should speak so about any woman, let alone his dead sister, sickened her.

"It worked out well for ye, though," Blàr said as they walked toward the door. "I always wondered if ye shoved things in the direction ye wanted them to go."

Aye, Maggie had wondered that too. She heard what sounded like a hand clapping a shoulder then Irvin said smugly, "I doona e'er shove, Blàr. I nudge."

The solar door opened and their footsteps faded before the door closed and was locked from the outside. Maggie pressed her palm to her forehead and breathed deeply to calm her anger. She had to proceed with a clear head. If they caught her snooping, she'd be locked up for sure—or worse.

Lifting the stone, she pushed it to the side so it lay on the solar floor before moving the chair out of the way. When she stood, the floor came to her waist and she climbed out, taking her candle and parchment with her.

The room was dimly lit by a dying fire, but Maggie knew the room's layout by heart, having played in here with her brothers when her father was laird.

Crossing the room, she placed her candle on the desk and searched until she found the letter that had recently been sealed, the wax with the imprint of her brother's ring still warm. She carefully peeled off the seal and placed it to the side.

She paused then, dread that Callum may be in league with her cousin filling her stomach. She didn't know why it would hurt so much. Callum had betrayed her long before now—three years ago in the spring, to be exact, and every spring after that when he'd failed to keep his promise.

So why was she so affected?

With a scowl, she opened the folded parchment and read her cousin's small, perfect script. It barely filled the page. She clenched her teeth to contain herself as relief weakened her knees.

Callum was innocent…in this at least.

Not that it mattered. Nothing about him was of interest to her anymore. Although she wanted to be the one to tell Callum that. Not her lying, scheming cousin.

She read the words again—informing Callum that the marriage contract between him and Maggie was broken. Since no goods or land had been exchanged, and both of their fathers, who had arranged the marriage, were dead, the contract had been withdrawn.

Maggie stood there for several minutes, emotions she thought long dead cascading through her—anger at Irvin for presuming to end her betrothal, but also anger and hurt that Callum had never returned for her.

At one point, she'd had high hopes for their future. She'd respected him—*liked* him—and he'd made her laugh, which her father had always said was important in a marriage. And when Callum had kissed her, she'd more than liked him. Aye, those feelings had stayed with her for a long while, haunted her dreams long after his betrayal.

A betrayal she would never forgive.

She huffed out an exasperated breath. Should she write a note to Callum explaining the situation at Clan MacDonnell, and ask for his help? She was sure Irvin had blocked the other letters she'd tried to send—to her brother John, to her father's best friend, who had the ear of the King, and to her mother's family. It would please her to finally get a message out, tucked inside Irvin's own sealed letter.

Or should she simply let the letter stand, let their betrothal officially end? It had already been over in her mind for years.

For all she knew, Callum would be happy to receive the news. Maybe his whispered words of affection three years ago had all been a lie—the same as his pledge to come back for her.

And if he did come to fight for her hand, insist the contract was still valid, what would happen? He'd have no idea of the danger he'd ride into. Irvin mentioned having a man inside Clan MacLean, so he would know Callum was coming, and she had no doubt he'd plan something.

Aye, Irvin would not let Laird MacLean upset his plans.

Her chest tightened as she imagined a dagger or

arrow piercing Callum's heart, and she dismissed the idea of asking for help. 'Twould be best if he carried on with his life not knowing of her plight. She was a strong Highland lass. She didn't need saving.

Lifting her hand to the intricately designed silver brooch on her breast that held her arisaid together, she played with the clasp. The brooch had been a wedding present from her father to her mother on their wedding day—passed down to her upon her mother's death thirteen years ago. She'd sobbed in her father's arms when she'd received it. He had too.

Maggie had worn the brooch every day since to keep her mother close, and to remind herself how fast things could change.

She unpinned it. Her arisaid sagged and she looped it under her arm, then wedged her nail into an almost invisible crease in the silver and pulled off the top of the brooch. Maggie fished inside the small hollow and snagged a piece of parchment with her fingernail. She pulled it out and slowly unrolled it.

She'd almost forgotten the parchment was in there. She'd pushed it to the back of her mind, almost as if she hadn't wanted to rid herself of this final piece of Callum.

Two holes pierced the center of the dirty, ragged parchment—dagger holes—and a third hole pierced the top where the parchment had been pinned to a tree. Under the two holes, Callum had scribbled a *C* and an *M*.

She remembered the look in his eyes when he'd pulled out their thrown daggers, a contest to see who had better aim, and written their initials on it before giving it to her. For a lass like Maggie, who preferred daggers to flowers, it was the sweetest love note she could have received. She'd carefully rolled it up and fit it into her brooch, so it would always rest next to her heart.

Now she would include it in the letter to Callum, and he would know she was done with him.

Before changing her mind, she placed the parchment within Irvin's letter and re-sealed it.

She set the letter back in place, ignoring the melancholy feeling that rose within her. Callum MacLean was better off without her. And she was certainly better off without him.

What were the chances he would come back for her now?

❧

Callum MacLean leaned against a tree, legs stretched out on the ground in front of him, eyes closed. He'd tucked the letter from Maggie and her brother Ross into his sporran a few days ago, after receiving it from a shifty-looking man named Blàr, who wore a MacDonnell plaid and claimed to be sent by Laird MacDonnell, but obviously wasn't a MacDonnell. Obvious to Callum, at least. The man's speech indicated he came from farther south.

When he first received the sealed letter with the dagger-torn parchment inside, he'd read it several times before passing it without a word to his foster brother Gavin MacKinnon, laird of Clan MacKinnon, who was travelling home with him from Lachlan and Amber's wedding.

Gavin scanned it and looked up. "We'll go see her, then?"

Callum had said nothing, unable to get even one word past the mess of emotions jamming his throat. Mounting his stallion, Aristotle, he'd spurred the horse forward. Gavin quickly caught up to him on his stallion. The rest of their men, six strong MacLean and MacKinnon warriors, fell into formation around them along the forest trail. Following farther behind with the supply wagon and three more of Callum's men, was Father Lundie.

"Is that what you'd do?" Callum asked, reaching out to take back the letter and the parchment from Maggie—which he had no doubt came from her.

"Nay, I'll ne'er chase a woman again—unless she's got my son. But that's what you should do."

"Why?"

"Because everything inside you wants to go to her no matter what the letter says."

He grunted and said nothing more on the matter that day. Or the next.

When they finally reached the juncture in the trail, one path heading north toward MacDonnell land, the other heading south, he reined in his mount. Gavin took one look at his face, and told the men to make camp.

As always, when it came to Maggie, Callum's heart and head were not aligned.

He'd slumped against the tree and closed his eyes while Gavin and some of the men scouted the area after seeing wolf tracks. When he heard the riders return to camp, he wasn't any closer to a decision.

"Laird MacKinnon," he heard Father Lundie whisper to Gavin from nearby. "Laird MacLean is still sleeping."

Callum cracked an eyelid to see his foster brother bearing down on him, the priest hovering by his side.

"I doona know what *you* see, Father Lundie," Gavin said, "but *I* see a man stuck—like a wee lad forced to choose between sweets."

"Nay, Laird," Father Lundie said. "He hasn't moved since you left. I think he must be ill. 'Tis unlike him to sit so still."

"'Tis exactly like him to sit still when he's trying to solve a puzzle. But this isna a puzzle. He just needs to get his head out of his arse, so he can see clearly."

Callum kicked out his feet just as Gavin came within striking distance. Gavin jumped up just in time, expecting it, of course, but when he landed, Callum scissored his legs and knocked him to the ground.

"You wee shite," Gavin said as he pushed up onto his elbows.

"Oh, were you there? I didnae see you."

Father Lundie stared down at them, looking startled, before he hurried away.

Gavin crawled up beside Callum and leaned with him against the tree. "Give me the letter and the other parchment. We'll talk it through."

With a sigh, Callum fished the messages from his sporran, then handed them over. "I've already assessed them from every angle."

"No doubt."

"The first is from Ross, or so it says. But 'tis not Ross's script nor manner of speaking."

"So someone else wrote it for him. His steward perhaps? 'Tis not uncommon."

"But what would compel Ross to cause such a

breach? The marriage is a good alliance for Clan
MacDonnell, and it has only gotten better since the
original contract was agreed upon. My allies are his
allies. If he was upset I havenae returned for Maggie,
it makes sense he would demand the marriage take
place, not terminate the contract. And from what I've
heard, Ross has not been himself since he lost his wife
and bairn. I was at the wedding. I saw how much he
loved Eleanor."

"You think it's someone else's doing then? Someone
pulling the strings?"

"Aye."

"Maggie?"

"Nay. Maggie wouldnae pull strings. She'd throw
daggers."

Gavin lifted the second parchment. "Isn't that what
this is?"

Callum ground his teeth and nodded. "I doona
doubt Maggie sent that. And the message is clear. She's
ending our betrothal—and making a point. The day I
wrote our initials on that parchment was the first day
we connected as a man and a woman—rather than
as a lad and lass. 'Twas the first day I knew she was
mine. We were competing, tossing daggers. We tied
on every round. I kissed her for the first time after I
gave her that parchment."

"So she kept it, and now she's throwing it back at
you."

"Aye."

"She's hurt."

"Aye."

"And angry."

"Aye."

"Well, 'tis obvious you have to go and win her back. And find out what's going on with Ross."

When he didn't answer, Gavin looked at him.

Callum sighed. "If I go there and sort everything out, win Maggie back, which willna be easy, what do I do then? Marry her? There's a reason I havenae gone back for her."

"Your father's murder."

"Aye. I canna in good conscience bring her back to Clan MacLean and put her in danger."

"Well…marry her and then she can come home with me until you find the murderer. Although Isobel will want to learn Maggie's skill with the dagger, and that will cause trouble."

The corner of Callum's mouth twitched despite the fact that he hadn't smiled in days. "I'd like to see that. Kerr will have a fit."

"What about me? I'm her brother. She'll be tossing knives at me every time I suggest it might be time for her to marry him."

Callum shook his head. Gavin and their other foster brother Kerr, had been trying to convince Isobel to marry Kerr since she'd turned eighteen. She was dead set against it even though Callum suspected she'd be devastated if he married someone else. "The two of you have it backward. Isobel likes being defiant. She canna be persuaded otherwise. She'll stay unmarried to spite you both."

'Twas Gavin's turn to grunt. "So what do you want to do about Maggie, then? We canna stay here forever."

He drummed his fingers on the ground. "She wouldnae have included the parchment if she wanted me to come, so she knows the letter was sent, but the circumstances surrounding the letter are troubling."

"If she's no longer your betrothed, then maybe 'tis not your problem. You can ride away with an easy conscience."

'Twas a logical argument, but Callum knew his brother had only said it to push him into action, because no matter what Maggie might want him to do, he couldn't ride away knowing something wasn't right at Clan MacDonnell.

What if she needed help?

She didn't want him to come. But he couldn't stay away—not until he knew for sure she was safe.

He sighed. "We'll head north to Clan MacDonnell."

Gavin grinned and rose to his feet, then reached down to help Callum. "'Tis a good thing I'm here to get you moving, otherwise Father Lundie would have ended up performing Last Rites on your prone body."

Callum took the offered hand and was brushing the dirt from his plaid when a wolf howled in the distance, followed by several others. He straightened slowly, the hair on the back of his neck prickling, as he and the other men listened intently.

The pack was hunting.

Better a stag than one of his men. But then a horse screeched far off, and he heard a woman scream.

"God's blood," he said, and he and Gavin ran for their horses. "MacLeans! Mount up!" he shouted as Gavin rallied his own warriors.

His second-in-command, Drustan, a lean, hardened

warrior, wheeled his mount toward him. "Should we light the torches?"

"Aye. And leave two men with Father Lundie. Have them build a fire and stay near the trees. Tell them to hoist the priest into a tree at any sign of trouble."

Drustan nodded and rode away.

It wasn't the first time Callum had faced off against wolves, and God knew it wouldn't be the last. Each time it was terrifying, knowing the wolves had no malice toward you, they were just hungry…and you were prey. 'Twas far worse than coming up against another man.

Callum would do what he could to help the woman—pray he and his men weren't too late—but he had to prepare himself for the worst.

Another scream sounded.

Callum's man, Gill, tested the wind, then pointed his arm to the northeast. "She's over there. Maybe a half mile?" Callum didn't doubt he was right. Gill was the best sniper he had. "Should we follow the trail north and then veer east? Or go as the crow flies?"

"I'm afraid we'll miss her if we follow the trail."

"Agreed. Through the bush then," Gill said.

They spread out in a line, distanced far enough apart to cover as much ground as possible, but close enough to be safe, although the wolves were unlikely to attack them with their lit torches.

When they heard another yell, they honed in, invigorated to know the woman was still alive. After what seemed like hours, but was more likely just minutes, they entered a clearing, riding hard.

They reined in at the sight of dead and injured wolves on the ground, cut and bleeding, and a woman's skirt torn to pieces. One of the wolves had a dirk sticking out of its ribs.

Callum's heart pounded as he looked at the dagger, and he slowly raised his eyes to follow the trail left behind—more blood, another dead wolf, crushed grass and flowers. And bits of plaid in the blues and greens favored by the weavers at clan MacDonnell.

Someone had run across the glen, the wolves at their heels.

His gaze reached the base of a lone tree where three more wolves lay dead—all with daggers in them. The pine tree didn't look sturdy enough to sustain someone's weight, much less the weight of wolves clawing at it, but the bark was scored high up in places, indicating the wolves had been jumping and reaching for their prey.

The trunk was bare of branches most of the way up and would have been difficult to climb, but he caught a glimpse of bare feet and legs tucked up on the lowest bough. The rest of the woman's body was hidden from sight by the pine needles…but he knew.

He urged Aristotle forward, the others fanning out behind him, and tried to quell his rising panic. *God, let her be all right.*

When he stopped beneath the branches of the tree and stared up at a woman barely holding onto a bough that dipped beneath her weight, relief so intense washed through him that he nearly fell from his horse. At the same time he felt jaw-dropping disbelief, for the lass glaring down at him—her auburn hair as wild as ever, her hazel eyes just as bright as he remembered— was none other than Maggie MacDonnell.

His Maggie MacDonnell—no matter what she might think.

"For the love of God, lass," he roared, his temper spiraling out of control, sparked by his fear for her—for what might have happened. "What are you doing up there?"

"I would think that was obvious, Callum MacLean. I am attempting to stay alive."

He ground his teeth, trying to rein in the storm of emotions barreling though him. "Are you hurt?" he asked, his words clipped and harsher than they should have been.

If anyone other than Maggie had clung to that tree, her dress torn to pieces, her legs bare and skin cut, he would have spoken in gentle, soothing tones. As it was, he could barely stop himself from pulling her down and galloping all the way to his castle.

Where she'd what…be safe?

Her chin trembled, and she thrust it out belligerently "What do you care?" she asked, flipping that long, glorious hair behind her shoulder. "'Tis not like we've spoken in years."

Guilt stabbed at him and he rubbed a hand over the back of his neck.

Beside him, Gavin gasped in recognition. "Is that Maggie? Your Maggie?"

"Nay, not *his* Maggie," she said, directing her attention to Gavin. "Just Maggie."

"Aye, it's her," Callum answered, barely able to get the words past his clenched teeth. He heard a murmur pass through the men, and his tension rose another notch. She may insist she wasn't his, but as he looked at her, noted everything from the freckles across her cheeks and nose to the dark sweep of her lashes, remembered what it felt like to be in her presence—the heightening of his senses, the quickening of his mind and body, the anticipation of touching her—he knew he would do everything possible to win her back.

He glanced over his shoulder and tried to catch Drustan's eye, but he was staring up at Maggie with a strange look on his face. "We'll stay here tonight," Callum said, and Drustan, his skin pale and lips tight, finally looked at him. "Set fires at regular intervals in case the pack returns, then go back for the others."

"Aye, Laird." Drustan nodded, his voice hoarse. He signaled to the men, and they retreated.

Callum shot Gavin a look, but his foster brother ignored him, as he was wont to do. Was it too much to ask for a private moment with Maggie, especially as she looked half dead and ready to kill him?

Gavin rode forward and smiled up at her. "Hello, lass. It's been a long time. Do you remember me?"

She switched her gaze to Gavin, and her eyes widened. "Is that you, Gavin MacKinnon? What have you done to your bonny, blond hair? 'Tis even shorter than Callum's. 'Twas the envy of every lass in the Highlands."

Gavin raised a hand to his bristly, ravaged scalp and sighed. "I know. 'Tis how I feel now. When I find my son, I'll grow it back."

The hardness left her eyes. "Aye, I heard about your loss. I'm sorry."

"Thank you," he said, then smiled. "And you,

Maggie, other than being up a tree and chased down by wolves, are you well?"

A small laugh puffed from her lips. "Well, I'm not dead, am I?"

Callum urged Aristotle past Gavin and stopped directly beneath Maggie. "Nay, and let's keep it that way." He stood on his stallion's back and reached his arms up to her. "Come down, Maggie. I'll catch you."

"I doona need you to catch me."

"Aye, you do."

Her eyes flashed, and she reached for one of her daggers only to find her belt empty. Her mouth set mulishly. "You said you'd be back in the spring…four springs ago."

"Three."

"Well, that makes it all right, then."

He wanted to blurt out his reasons for staying away—the dangers in his clan, the threat to her life if she married him—but now was not the time.

"Please, come down. I'll tend to your wounds before they fester, and then I'll see you back home."

Her spine stiffened, causing the bough to sway, and she slid a little closer to the edge. "You can give me a horse, naught more."

He tried his most conciliatory tone. "Maggie—"

She jerked her arms in displeasure and pine needles showered down on him. "You are a lying scoundrel, Callum MacLean, and I doona need you or anyone else."

He brushed the needles from his hair, "And that's why you're stuck in a tree, half naked, with no horse and a wolf pack on your heels. How many were there,

Maggie? I'm assuming they've run down your horse by now."

Her bottom lip quivered before she firmed it, and regret washed through him. He dropped his arms. "Och, lass. I'm sorry. For everything. I meant it when I said I'd be back in the spring. Things…changed. It grieves me to see you up there knowing what you went through, that you almost died. Please, come down, so I can help you."

Maggie stared at him, a gamut of emotions running across her face. He used to love watching her— whether she was dancing or laughing or scowling at him. Wild Maggie MacDonnell, who'd just as soon take your eye out with one of her daggers than try to catch your eye with pretty curls or a swishing walk.

They'd been betrothed since childhood and he knew without a doubt she was meant for him. He felt it with a certainty in his bones, the same way he knew his father had been murdered despite what everyone said. The same way Gavin knew his son was alive.

Unfortunately, she no longer had the same feeling for him.

Well, he'd just have to convince her otherwise— he'd done it before, he could do it again. Of course, she'd been seventeen then, but still set against him. Against marrying anyone, really, and too used to doing whatever she pleased since her mother's death, whether it was tossing daggers or jumping off cliffs.

"Maggie," he said again, his tone firmer this time. He had to get her out of the tree so he could see the damage the wolves had done.

She raised a brow, and he knew he'd made a mistake.

"You want me to come down?" she asked.

"Aye." A wariness tinged his words, and beside him he heard Gavin snort.

Maggie shrugged and moved closer to the edge of the bough, saying, "Catch." Then she jumped from the branch and kicked out with her feet, hitting him squarely in the chest. He fell from his horse and landed hard on the grass.

He heard Gavin hoot with laughter, and looked up to see Maggie straddling Aristotle, her legs bare from mid-thigh to her toes, her skin scratched and bloodied. In one motion, she wheeled the stallion around and leaned to the side to pull her knives from the wolves— three of them. Then urged Aristotle into a gallop.

Callum jumped up and whistled, loud and shrill, and his horse came to a jarring halt, almost knocking *her* off this time. She rounded to stare at him, a sight to behold with her flushed cheeks and flashing eyes, her tangled hair cascading over her shoulders. Then she pulled a dagger and hurled it at him. It landed in the tree trunk just above his head. Exactly where she'd intended.

'Twas a start. And Callum smiled.

Maggie MacDonnell did not want him dead.

COMING AUGUST 2018

Acknowledgments

Writing this book was the first time I truly became a working mom. I wasn't working my writing around my kids anymore, I was just *working*. I had a contract, I was writing to deadline, people were depending on me to hand in my work on time, and I'd *cashed* the check! My kids and I both had to learn what *Mommy's working* means. They didn't always like it, but we got through it with some great babysitters, late nights on my part, my husband stepping in to fill the void whenever possible, and friends helping out when they could. And now kindergarten has started—a.k.a. the heavens have opened up—and I feel like we've made it through the past year with everyone still feeling loved and cared for. So a big shout-out to Maddie and Cooper for being such troopers, and to everyone else who took such good care of them when I couldn't, especially my husband. Words cannot express how much I love you guys.

And to all the working moms out there—you work HARD. Don't ever let anyone tell you chocolate and wine is bad for you—so is stress and information overload. Close your eyes for a minute, breathe, and have your treat. You deserve it.

About the Author

Alyson McLayne is a mom of twins and an award-winning writer of contemporary, historical, and paranormal romance. She's also a dog lover and cat servant with a serious stash of dark chocolate. After getting her degree in theater at the University of Alberta, she promptly moved to the west coast of Canada where she worked in film for several years and met her prop master husband.

Alyson has been nominated for several Romance Writers of America contests, including The Golden Heart, The Golden Pen, The Orange Rose, Great Expectations, The Molly's, and The Winter Rose.

Her self-published works in short contemporary romance include her Santa Barbara Billionaire Bachelors series: *How to Catch a Bride*, *How to Claim an Heiress*, and *How to Outplay a Player*. *How to Catch a Bride* (formerly *The Fabrizio Bride*) was recently nominated for a RONE Award.

Alyson and her family reside in Vancouver with their sweet but troublesome chocolate Lab puppy named Jasper.

Please visit her at alysonmclayne.com and look her

up on Facebook (facebook.com/AlysonMcLayne) or Twitter (@AlysonMcLayne). She loves chatting with her fans!